COLD
PASTORAL

MARGARET DULEY

COLD PASTORAL

BREAKWATER
MAINSTAY
SINCE 1973

UPHOLDING THE LEGACY OF GREAT NEWFOUNDLAND LITERATURE

P.O. BOX 2188, ST. JOHN'S, NL, CANADA, A1C 6E6
WWW.BREAKWATERBOOKS.COM

COPYRIGHT © 2014 Margot Duley
LIBRARY AND ARCHIVES CANADA CATALOGUING IN PUBLICATION
Duley, Margaret, 1894-1968, author
Cold pastoral / Margaret Duley.
Originally published: London : Hutchinson, 1939.
ISBN 978-1-55081-479-8 (PBK.)
I. Title.
PS8507.U45C6 2014   C813'.52   C2014-900563-6

We acknowledge the support of the Canada Council for the Arts which last year
invested $24.3 million in writing and publishing throughout Canada. We
acknowledge the Government of Canada through the Canada Book Fund and the
Government of Newfoundland and Labrador through the Department of
Tourism, Culture and Recreation for our publishing activities.

PRINTED AND BOUND IN CANADA.

 Canada Council
for the Arts
Conseil des Arts
du Canada
 Canada
 Newfoundland
Labrador

Breakwater Books is committed to choosing papers and materials for our
books that help to protect our environment. To this end, this book is printed on a
recycled paper that is certified by the Forest Stewardship Council®.

RECYCLED
Paper made from
recycled material
FSC® C103567

To my brother
CYRIL DULEY

...maidens overwrought,
with forest branches and the trodden weed;
...Cold pastoral!

— JOHN KEATS, ODE ON A GRECIAN URN

INTRODUCTION
BY JOAN CLARK

Margaret Duley was the first Newfoundland writer to gain an international reputation, having been published and favorably reviewed in Britain, the United States, Sweden, and Canada. Newfoundland was still a separate country when *Cold Pastoral*, Duley's second novel, was published in Britain in 1939. Both her first novels were written and published in the aftermath of the First World War and prior to the Second, and like many Newfoundlanders, the Duley family was deeply affected by World War I during which the island lost a generation of young men. Margaret's younger brother Lionel was killed at Ypres less than two weeks before the armistice, and her older brother Cyril severely injured at Les Boeufs, the Somme, in 1916. Duley's decision, then, to write a romantic, coming-of-age story about peace and beauty can be seen as an attempt to mitigate the horrors and ugliness of war.

Decades after the publication of *Cold Pastoral*, Canadian novelist Margaret Laurence famously advised aspiring fiction writers to write about what they knew, and Margaret Duley wrote about what she knew, both from her own family's experience of war-time tragedy and from situations and stories she had heard from across the island. No doubt she would have known the story of Lucy Harris, the girl from New Melbourne, Trinity Bay, who survived after being lost in the winter woods for eleven days. Duley's romantic heroine, Mary Immaculate, was lost in the winter woods for three days, but unlike Harris, Mary benefitted from the ministrations of Philip Fitz Henry, a young St. John's doctor, and her frostbitten legs were spared amputation. Mary was also spared returning to the cove where she existed almost as a stranger to her father and brothers, and after being discharged from the hospital, Philip Fitz Henry brought Mary home to live with his family. Mary never returned to the Cove, and her mother, Josephine Keilly—arguably the novel's most impressive character—agreed that her daughter be adopted by the Fitz Henrys, who provided Mary with all the advantages a genteel, townie life.

Today's readers might find it incredulous that Josephine handed over her daughter to people she barely knew, but such arrangements were not uncommon in Newfoundland at the time. And Duley had a *true* story close to hand. Margaret's mother, Tryphena Chancey Soper, one of seven children born to a fishing family in Carbonear, Conception Bay, was adopted by an aunt and uncle as a girl and lived with them in St. John's until her marriage to James Duley. Although she cultivated a prosperous townie life, Tryphena took her children to Carbonear for summer holidays, and as Margaret Duley's biographer, Alison Feder, observed, "Townies, though they were, they [the Duleys] learned a lot about out port life and the fishing industry." It was this firsthand knowledge of the hardships of outport life that Margaret effectively made use of in *Cold Pastoral*.

Margaret also incorporated the Duley family's strong ties to Britain. When she was seven, Margaret's British-born father took Margaret and her older sister Gladys to England to attend the wedding of their aunt. As a girl, Margaret was to return to England twice more, and later, as a young woman, she attended the London Academy of Music and Dramatic Art, which provided her with skills useful to an incubating writer with a voracious appetite for poetry and fiction, which she often read in school at her desk, the open book in her lap.

As valuable as her experience of living in Britain was, readers should not underestimate the value of growing up in an often overlooked British colony. Duley's biographer put it more succinctly: "Margaret Duley wrote truthfully and poetically about a little known region that she loved more than she hated."

Feder goes on to say that beneath Margaret's grand manner and play-acting, lay the spontaneity of a child. She loved to dance and often spun around the room for pure joy. Margaret was also an accomplished mimic. This description of the author explains, in part, Duley's strength as fiction writer. It explains her fresh, exuberant prose, her ability to create characters that leap off the page. It also explains her gift for writing dialogue, her ability to create conversation that remains fresh and immediate.

The main character of *Cold Pastoral* is the impressionable and imaginative Mary Immaculate, a fisherman's daughter who, though born in a skiff, goes out of her way to avoid the water and the fish-rooms where her father and brothers gut and salt their daily catch. Mary prefers the forest:

> the secret groves where the sun shone through in golden chinks, and ponds covered with heart shaped lily pads where she could make the fairies hop from pad to pad…and send them to sleep on the gleaming lilies.

The fairy-tale landscape of Mary Immaculate's imagination is reminiscent of the lake of shining waters that so delighted Anne Shirley, the imaginative heroine of *Anne of Green Gables*, who was rescued from an orphanage and flourished on Prince Edward Island.

The name Duley chose for her protagonist is highly symbolic, suggesting as it does the existence of an imaginative and innocent child born and reared in an outport focused on faith and subsistence and relatively protected from the cultural aftermath of the war. It is precisely the qualities of imagination and innocence that first disarm the grieving Fitz Henrys when Mary becomes the adopted daughter of the family.

Through much of the novel, Mary's outport upbringing and her new life in St. John's stand at odds, and she is divided between these two allegiances. But after she finishes her schooling, Mary travels to London, and she is shocked by what she witnesses. An innocent who has lived a sheltered life, Mary interprets London's decadence and free-wheeling sex as a loss of beauty and faith, and she returns to Newfoundland a changed and more realistic young woman. Her newfound maturity involves a merger of the urban and the rural, a merger of Philip Fitz Henry's "directive thinking" and Josephine's strong, unbreakable faith. So in Mary's eventual coming of age, Duley suggests that to avoid the cultural decline at the empire's centre, Newfoundlanders should learn to amalgamate the values inherent in both the outport and the town. In some sense, Duley proposes that, like Mary, we can't know where we're going without knowing where we've been.

And this is why it's nice to have *Cold Pastoral* in print again after so many years. We can perhaps look back and find some sense of ourselves in Margaret Duley's message from the past.

"WHAT AILED THEE THEN TO BE BORN?"

The fisherfolk knew what they knew! There was no gain saying that the Little People lived on their shore. The sea was different from the land! There romance ended and realism began. Where cliffs dropped in sheer descent, challenge roared at their granite base. From the flat meadows above, an occasional sheep dropped to death, remaining impaled on jagged rocks until the sea sucked it strongly to itself. On still days venturesome children lay on their stomachs, staring down with ghoulish eyes. The green waves playing over the woolly heap held them with a strange attraction. They couldn't know it was there and not look! One memorable day a cow dropped over. It was heavy and gave the sea stronger work. Green and blue, grey-green with seaweed brown, colour changing, fading, leadening, it all washed over the red and white cow. Through the windswept days of a whole summer it supplied a fearful thrill. When the children went to peer at the cow the only little girl who played in the valley was Mary Immaculate. Deserting her, they left with shrill derision. Their scorn was for her squeamishness. She had never been known to seek the beach or slit open the belly of a cod. She liked to run through the woods or rest by the waterfall and watch the white clouds sailing by—things the other children never saw. Their choice was on the beach, in the fish-rooms, on the stage-heads, catching the cod tossed up from the boats.

Sometimes Mary Immaculate tried to show them other things: the blue shadows of the evening, the round orange of the sun, and once she took them in a body to see an autumn tree. Branches, from a silver trunk, retained a fall of gold leaves. Wispy and frail, like tissue-paper gold, they drooped over the children.

"Look," said Mary Immaculate in a muted voice.

"Birch! Wood for the stove!" her brother Dalmatius shouted, running home for his axe and his saw. Chop, chop, while wedge-shaped bits dropped to the ground. The other children pranced, while Mary Immaculate put her fingers in her ears to stifle the sound of the fall. When the leaves were crushed on the ground the sawing began. Gold like the leaves the sawdust spilled out. "Mary Mother!" she whispered to the trunk of a spruce. "It had gold blood."

The playing age of the children was brief. They were always useful on the beach, learning to row when oars were too large for their hands and legs dangled in the skiffs. Childish hands soon acquired the callus of the sea, and skin became sprayed from salt-water. Even with the indulgence accorded to Mary Immaculate, at the age of five she was handed a knife to slice the leaves from pink turnips. Accepting her chores like the other children, she chose those on the land. It was impossible to touch the slime of cod or press spawn from the belly of a caplin. The sea was something to watch, but its offal offended her. When the waves tossed wildly demented she climbed the cliffs to look out. Loving the sea in its calmness, she grew exhilarated when she saw it in its hate. She knew it was a threat to her food. It gave and took away.

With the surety of knowledge that the Little People followed them on the land the fisherfolk knew the sea had a voice, a tongue to lick at their boats, an arm to wrap round one of their own and drag him unblessed to his grave. In their effort to lessen the toll of drowning they followed their own traditions. Wives and mothers rested in the knowledge that two breadwinners would not go in one boat. Even with the faithful observance of this rule there were many widows. Some of them kept their blinds drawn for a year and mourned inside without light of day. The windows were as awe-inspiring to the children as the spilled sheep and cows. Death was often untimely, and the sea kept it. Sometimes it gave it back. Then it was gathered to the land and anointed with belated blessing. Death was always fearful—though holding a bit of a change in a wake, with the rare treat of an orange or an apple. They could mourn, pray and eat at the same time.

The land standing high above the sea was almost unbroken in its curve of granite cliff. One gap made a concession to the needs of man. In the centre of the cove the heads dipped and broke, forming a ravine that flowed back for half a mile. A beach was the one bit of utilitarian coast which everyone shared. Even that was cut by a river flowing from a waterfall at the head of the valley. Every grey stone bore the weight of some object. Fish-rooms, landing-stages, beached dories, anchors, tar-barrels, moorings and whitened fish-bones jostled one another in vast confusion.

The land conceded man a beach! The sea bore him out to his traps and his trawls and often tried to restrain him. The wind and the waves gave him the buffeting that was his heritage. When he was feeling too secure the sea rose and spat at the land. Boiling with rage it hurled itself at puny buildings, sucking their foundations, lifting them high and battering them back to floating timber. When the sea was appeased it lay down. Then the men left their houses to look. Almost without comment they trudged to the forests to cut again.

Scattered houses clung to the sides of the ravine. Painted and square like anyhow boxes they looked small for their burst of people. With many mouths to feed, food came from the fruit of the sea. A few hens pecked round every door and wandered unchecked as far as the cod-strewn beach. The flesh of dead fowl invariably retained a fishy flavour. Mary Immaculate's mother was optimistic about it on the rare occasions when a hen lost its head on the block. "Sure!" she would say happily. "We're getting two courses in one—a bit of fish and a bit of flesh." Josephine Keilly knew what was what! She had been a cook in the city for three years before Benedict wooed her back to her Cove.

Cattle were scarce—far too scarce to lose over the heads. The people lived up to the old adage: "One more in the cradle means one less in the stable." The cradle was never defrauded. A settlement of continual pregnancy, the women took up the cycle again, as soon as Nature could assert itself. Nobody rebelled. Not to conceive was the sin of Sodom and Gomorrah!

Josephine and Benedict had the smallest family in the Cove. Eleven, twelve, or a baker's dozen made the quiverful of most couples. They were blessed with a bare seven. It was all on account of Mary Immaculate; Mrs. Keilly getting a chill in the skiff! She had been brought to bed like a Christian for Dalmatius, Ignatius, Francis Xavier, Benedict the Second, Pius and Leopold. She often wished she had a family large enough to name after all the Popes in the Vatican. She was very devout. Her first-born, Dalmatius, had roared so much that she had called him her Papal Bull. Her husband said she had gone into blasphemy when she named her daughter Mary Immaculate; but she had been mumbling to the Blessed Virgin when the midwife asked her to name the child. From drawing its first breath in the east wind it had to be baptised at once. Even then she had liked the feel of Mary Immaculate on her tongue. The change of sex or some prognostication of the unusual had made her daughter too eager for appearance. She came most informally! If Josephine hadn't gone for a jaunt it wouldn't have happened; nor if Benedict had stuck to his fish-room. He was always running up from the beach for a drop of strong tea. The same leaves did for the day. Josephine merely added boiling water and a tannic brew ran into the cup. Benedict's face was like a bit of tanned hide, with two blue stones laid on it for eyes. One morning when Benedict ran up for his mug-up, Josephine saw a hole in the flour-barrel.

"Woman," he said, "I'll borrow the skiff and go to the store."

"I'll go with you, then. 'Tis a grand day, and I'll be off my legs."

Benedict muttered a warning about the sharpness of the land against the sky, foretelling a squall—but the skiff was solid and true to the sea. A competent motor-boat, it belonged to six men.

The day was still as death, the sea tranquil as sleep. It stretched away in shining level.

"Sure, 'tis a grand rest," sighed Josephine, as they left the stage-head and the spit of the engine settled to a steady phut phut. She had not been in the skiff for a long time, and its vibrations shivered her heavy body. Inert and comatose she sagged in the stern, watching the gulls wheeling overhead. Then she thought of the shop, and her mind fastened on a few remnants of material. Something told her her child would be a girl. Benedict saw no danger for his wife in the outing. The thought that she should stay at home would not cross his mind. Women worked up to the last moment of childbirth and rose again very quickly. Sunk in her unaccustomed rest he had to haul her out of the skiff when they reached the next settlement.

Inside the shop she shook off her heaviness. That one room could hold so much! Its whole ceiling was hidden with clusters of hanging kettles, enamel mugs, earthenware tea-pots, pipers, skillets, pots and pans. Josephine stared, wishing for money to buy herself a skillet; but ready cash was scarce, so she lowered her eyes to the remnants. Bolts of blue and pink flannelette were hidden by bits of motley material overflowing from another shelf. Benedict had retreated to pass the time of day with the shopkeeper and discuss the price of fish. They were surrounded with salt-encrusted barrels of pork, while athwart their lids lay harsh-looking hooks. The food side of the shop was piled with boxes and bottles holding every necessity of life. On a narrow counter stood a large cheese, gleaming golden through a veiling of cheese-cloth. The draping and the spotless white of the covering reminded her of the day of Corpus Christi. Thinking of herself veiled for first Communion a pain tore through her body. Startled, she leaned against the bolts of flannelette until it was over. Fingering the woolly fabric she wondered if her hope of a daughter would be realised. She wanted one to dress up in pink and blue. When she had waited long enough to verify her fears she called to her husband. "Ben, I'm going back to sit in the skiff. Don't be long, now."

Had Benedict not been arranging for the transportation of the flour he would have known she was saving herself by the shortening of his name. Josephine always gave full value to every syllable. When she was back in the skiff the level of the sea had become ripples. As she waited the ripples grew to crests and the sea slapped against the sides of the boat. When Benedict appeared with the barrel the waves were white horses. When they were out to sea she told him. His blue eyes were fixed on the tumbling sea.

"Nonsense, woman! You can't go dropping your child in a skiff. Tell your beads. That'll stop you a bit."

"Children choose their own time, Benedict Keilly," she said tartly.

"You'll have to wait until we get home, then," he answered inexorably.

Benedict was occupied with the skiff. She belonged to five others, and the sea was giving her a drubbing. He was a steady husband, but a skiff was harder come by than a woman. His wife was facing elemental pain in elemental surroundings and claimed his attention.

"Ben, I'm dying!"

"Stop it!" he roared. "You'll put a haunt on the skiff."

"Skiff or no skiff, I'm dying." There was an uncontrolled screech. "Jesus, Mary and Joseph, have mercy on me!"

Above the sound of the rising sea he shouted to her. "Pull yourself together, woman. You can't go dying with no Priest to bless you."

At the end of a pain she gasped with spirit. "Don't fash yourself, Benedict Keilly. Those that pass in childbirth walk straight into Heaven."

"You'll never have a better chance, then. The likes of this won't happen again."

Josephine didn't die! Between wild agonies she lay under her husband's coat and a tarpaulin, beseeching the Saints in Heaven. With the sea and the wind in her ears she gave birth! As mysterious agencies were accepted in the Cove, legend grew that Mary Immaculate was delivered by the Blessed Mother herself. How she was born in the skiff became the premier tale of the village, taking precedence over those that had been held: the sailor who had seen the phantom ship; the story of Molly Conway; and the man who was murdered on the Ridge. It was told again and again, over black kitchen stoves holding a bombardment of spruce-logs. It held an honourable place in their lore until Mary Immaculate's twelfth year. What happened then became an unbelievable super-story, satisfying a lifetime of yearning for romance.

At first they thought she must die—until something reminded her of her heritage. People born to the assault of the wind and the slap of the sea had a "Y" quantity of endurance. It was impossible to be defeated by the accident of birth in a skiff. Although infant lungs, violated by the air of the North Atlantic, showed signs of not being able to contain it, they became soothed by the glow from her mother's stove. She thrived, not in size, but in quality. Josephine was soon up and about, and during very cold nights slept on the kitchen settle, getting up to feed the stove with spruce-logs. It was a luxury unheard of in the Cove, but the manner of Mary Immaculate's birth and the change of sex in her issue made Josephine superstitious about tending the breath of life. By day her daughter slept in a wooden cradle, was taken up and fed, put down to sleep again until she grew to some waking moments. Then long eyes in a minute face followed her mother's figure round the kitchen. Often while Josephine was stirring a cauldron of food the spoon would slow as she stared at her child. "Glory be to God, Mary Immaculate, by the looks of you I had no hand in your makin', nor your Pop, neither. Did the fairies come out to the skiff to leave me a changeling? If they did, you're a powerful change to Molly Conway! By the sweet face of you I'd say the angels were ticklin' your feet."

After the loutishness of her sons Josephine loved to wash the tiny baby and hold it naked in her lap. Like a skinful of milk it looked, in contrast to the blackleaded surface of the stove. A small, narrow baby, long for its age! And how it strained towards the few spots of colour in the kitchen! The bright red in the robe of the Sacred Heart, the blue of the Virgin's hood and the gold of the lustre jug! Even the glow from the bars of the kitchen stove was an attraction! She didn't like anything dark. On her first Ash Wednesday she roared when Josephine bathed her with a smut on her brow: but when her brothers returned from Mass on Palm Sunday she grabbed the bright green boughs.

Benedict would gaze at his daughter from far-seeing blue eyes, as if trying to focus something out of his vision. With a cup of stewed tea in his hand he would declare, "Woman, she's powerful light from stem to stern."

"That she is, Benedict! And a fair treat to wash after them with a stern like a western craft."

Benedict could doubt the advantage of such lightness.

"This is no life for canoes. She's like nothing yet!"

Such comments were balm to Josephine. "That she's not! She's the dead spit of the angels in Heaven."

Unprepared to call up the imagery of the angels in Heaven, Benedict would clod-hopper back to the beach. Once he wiped his mouth with the back of his hand and stooped to lift the baby from Josephine's lap. At that moment he saw his hands for the first time in his life. The sight of them against a delicate skin gave him an acute shock, and he jerked them back to the pockets of his overalls. His hands were his maintenance and knew a multiplicity of crafts, having built his house, his fish-room, his stage-head, his boat and his oars. Calloused, cracked, blunted at the finger-tips, scarred with lines and twines and splitting-knives, their ugliness hurt him against his child's skin. In his world of work and wrest and food eaten from hand to mouth he had no knowledge of any other kind of life. In that brief second he saw his daughter amongst different people, with work that gave them smooth hands. After that he was afraid to touch her, and he came to regard her like the sun or the horizon—something visible to his eyes but out of reach of his hands. It was necessary to dismiss something he could not handle. As she grew she became her mother's child.

To her brothers she was a toy. They poked at her with fishy fingers and hung over her cradle with loud claps of laughter. Then her white brow would contract, as if she found their size and violence oppressive. But she was staunch and took a great deal of poking before she gave way to tears. When her lip went down in protest Josephine raised her voice. "Leave off, now, you great loons! You haven't got the sense to see she's not a great heifer like yourselves. I've a mind to raise my hand to the lot of you." A few impartial cuffs would disperse them, and if any of them howled she placated them with slices of bread and molasses. There was no rancour in Josephine. She blew through her day like a high wind without edges.

In Benedict's world a woman could make or break a man. Had he been bound to a slattern the toil of his hands would have been for naught. Josephine made him! By encouraging him to a clean cure of his fish and being unsparing of her own energy they always made both ends meet. Benedict and his elder sons worked at the fish, while Josephine managed the house and the sloping square of garden. Decent she was and kept herself apart from the shiftless! In many improvident houses where six crowded under one set of bedclothes Josephine represented gentility. Her family slept two in a bed! Moreover, every person under her roof had two of everything. Others that liked the clean thing had to content themselves with turning a garment inside out. Nor was Josephine sombre in the meagre centre of her house. She could slave from morning till night and speak a civil word at the end of the day. Many dragged through their work with dejected bodies and joyless faces. They had inherited from their ancestry the dim twilight fear of the Celts, and the wind worried them when it filled the valley.

When Mary Immaculate was big enough Dalmatius was allowed to carry her down to the sea. In sight of the beach her nostrils expanded and contracted with the smell of fish and offal. There was a definite expression of disdain on her face. When the wind lifted her hair she crowded into her brother's shoulder. Carrying her inland she lifted her head and nearly danced out of his arms, straining towards the new green of the junipers and the white pear-blossom drifting uphill.

Soon she began to waver round the kitchen in a blue dress of her mother's fashioning. Josephine satisfied her yearning for colour by knitting wool the colour of the Virgin's robe. Ready to pick up at odd moments, garments were always on the needles. Since the birth of her daughter the coarse garments for her husband and sons did not increase as quickly as the white shirts and pale blue dresses.

Talking, she became Mary Mac'yate to herself, while developing decided tastes. The sea was full of soap, and the beach very "pooh-pooh." The wind hindered her by lifting her drift of pale gold hair and diminishing the sight between her eyelashes. Dull days were passed in the kitchen, round her mother's skirts, while sunny days found her playing on the granite slab at the back door, circling round the stacked-up wood-pile, round and round the wood-horse, or jumping backwards and forwards over the chopping-block. Her companions were her two youngest brothers and a few speckled hens, but both of their preferences lay on the beach. Leo and Pius trotted after their elder brothers, while the hens pecked their way down the valley, heading towards the sea. Growing more venturesome she would turn her face towards the land and wander down the slope, drawn to the waterfall at the head of the valley. Scarcely on her way her mother would screech: "Mary Immaculate, Mary Immaculate, come right back, now." When she would not heed, her mother would swoop and catty her back to the kitchen. And always that strange ceremony would take place! Mary Immaculate could perform it instantly, as soon as her mother made her face the door.

She grew tall and slender like the delicate scent-bottles growing at the edge of the forests. At a very early age her minute hands would bless herself before touching the simple fare of the village. There was always fish, dried and fresh, and vegetables from Josephine's garden. In the winter the stomach was frequently filled with the bulk of pea-soup floating with fat white bang-bellies. All of the meals were supplemented with bread and tea. There was a period when it was drunk black—until Josephine became reconciled to the acquisition of a goat. It was very much of a poor man's cow after her pale gentle Jersey. Mary Immaculate had a strong memory of it before it died of milk fever. Running into the stable one morning she had become fascinated by the strange emergence of a nose, lying on two tiny hoofs. She was thinking it was a very pretty little nose when her mother descended and dragged her away.

When she was able to peel potatoes and turnips she was sent down the valley to the one-roomed schoolhouse. After her first day she returned chanting, c-a-t—cat, r-a-t—rat, m-a-t—mat. As she grew her questions became a trial to her mother. She accepted nothing without a why or a what, and Josephine accepted everything as the will of God.

What was the sky made of? Was it solid enough to hold the feet of God and his holy angels? If it wasn't, why didn't they fall down in the valley? Did God lie on his stomach and look down? Were the stars peep-holes? Was the devil rich enough to buy coal for hell fire, or did he stack up a woodpile like themselves? How much kindling would it take to burn a lost soul?

When Josephine was defeated she replied vigorously: "Hold your tongue, Mary Immaculate. You'll talk me deaf, dumb, blind and silly. Get on with your lessons. Your Pop pays for you to learn out of books."

A great many questions were answered by the devout formula: "It's the will of God, that's what it is." That was the most unsatisfactory answer of all. Sometimes Benedict silenced her when she directed her questions to the sea. Why did it freeze white when it was such a lovely blue on sunny days? Benedict merely replied: "Have sense, maid;" but when she asked with quite definite hope in her voice: "Pop, couldn't I walk on the water when it looks so flat and blue?" he was angry. "Mind yourself now. There's only One could do that." Occasionally he was more satisfactory and less convinced of her sense-lessness. When she stood in the valley questioning why the junipers bent to the east when the wind blew the other way he gave her a look of approbation. "It's the poor man's compass, that's what it is." That was the sort of answer she liked! It made her pleased with God that he gave her father a compass he couldn't buy.

Her mother took her to Mass, and she became very devout, praying with the face of an angel. Taking advantage of her piety, Josephine had her prepared for first Communion. It took longer than most Catholic children, as Father Melchior had three settlements under his charge. Josephine helped by teaching her daughter the Catechism. Convinced that her child was a rare and precious jewel she was shaken by occasional incident. One day she was showing her off to the Priest on an honoured day when he was drinking tea in her kitchen.

"Sure, she knows her Catechism fine, Father. Mary, tell the good Father who made you."

"Pop," replied her daughter with cold finality.

Josephine was dismayed. "Beg pardon, Father, that child has as many changes as the sea. There's no counting on what she'll say next." But the Priest was tolerant, giving a reassuring laugh.

"Josephine, you're rearing the belle of the village. It won't be long before the lads will be round."

Josephine sniffed, although a sniff was out of place in such company.

"Indeed, Father, I hope she won't go to the likes of them. Drawin' water would break her in two, and she's no love of the fish-room."

"Indeed," he said, putting his cup down on Josephine's table. "It won't do, Mary? Don't you like the sea at all?" Mary Immaculate was standing in front of him, by order of her mother.

"Yes, Father," she said politely. "I like the sea very much, but I hate the smell of the beach."

Father Melchior looked reproachful. "It's bad to despise your bread and butter, my child."

She said nothing, waiting to go. It was a beautiful September day and she wanted to pick whorts. She knew a place where they grew, big and purple, with a dry clean bloom. Then there was the little plant that was a white star in spring and four red berries in autumn. They were holding her worse than the Little People. All at once the Priest made her forget the whorts and the cracker-berries.

"*You* should like the sea and its fruits better than anyone, Mary."

"Why?" she asked with immediate interest.

He smiled indulgently as if enjoying the intensified glow of her yellow eyes.

"Because you were like Venus, born from the sea."

"Who's she, Father?" she said eagerly.

"Venus, my dear, was…"

Josephine listened, watching the interest in her child's face. Mary Immaculate's mind was like a bit of ground. Sprinkle any seed on it and it would grow. *What* was the good Father telling her? Had he lost his senses? She was hard enough to quell without giving her ideas about the state of her birth. Foam of the sea indeed! It wasn't the way she remembered the skiff! Pity he didn't tell her about the lives of the Saints and teach her to be reverent to those above. Torn between respect for the infallibility of the Church and her dislike of the tale she grabbed a bit of knitting and continued a rib of two plain two purl. Her cracked hands worried the needles as doubts increased. Goddess of love! What talk! Perfect knitter though she was, she nearly dropped a stitch. Incense on her altar! What blasphemy! The sacrifice of a white goat. That was better. A good enough end for the poor man's cow! Venus, Venus? Her mind stirred to the stimulus of the name. Like a flash she went back to the house in the City. There had been a great picture at the bend of the stairs, with three women posturing in front of a man seated on a bit of a platform. Three naked women! Quickly Josephine mumbled an Aspiration, for fear of impure thoughts. The Judgment of Paris! That was it, though for a long time she had thought the picture had something to do with the capital of France. The housemaid had told her differently. Paris was a man, setting himself up to decide which woman was the most beautiful. Venus was one of the hussies!

With a red face Josephine went on with her knitting.

"And the Greeks called her Aphrodite because she was born of the foam of the sea. She fell in love with Adonis, a very beautiful youth, and because of that she had to leave Olympus—"

"Where's that?"

"Olympus was a high mountain with a peak that touched the Heavens. After Venus came down to earth Adonis was killed by a wild boar, and because she loved him so much she changed him into a flower—"

"A cracker-berry?"

"No," he said smiling, "not a cracker-berry."

"A scent-bottle?"

"Wait till you're told," commanded her mother.

"No, Mary, neither of those flowers. It was an anemone, sometimes called a wind-flower."

"Oh!" she said breathlessly. "A wind-flower! They should grow in the woods, where we've all kinds of wind."

"But they don't, my child. They're a little too fragile for these parts. Now, Mary, I told you that story because I want you to remember that Venus became a patron of commerce, and commerce in your life means your father's fish. For that reason you must try and get in tune with your life, because by and by you'll marry a fisherman, and you wouldn't be any help to him—"

Josephine sighed with relief. The moral at last, though Father Melchior had been a long time getting to it. It seemed to her that he might have got to Benedict's fish without winding his way through a crowd of naked women.

"Can I go?" asked Mary Immaculate, looking at her mother.

"Stay where you are," her mother commanded.

"No, Josephine, let her go. I know she wants to go berrypicking."

"And fearful I am for her, Father, when she goes flyin' off. I'd feel safer if she stayed near the beach."

The Priest knew his people! In his long sojourn he had never been able to eradicate the Celtic folk-lore they mixed so strangely with religion.

"Nonsense, Josephine," he said perseveringly. "You must not encourage superstition."

"Superstition, Father!" she said, dropping her knitting in her lap. "Sure, Benedict was held when he went in for a few birds and, beggin' your pardon, Father, there's the living example of Molly Conway."

The Priest shook his head. "Just a poor village simple, Josephine, stricken at birth by the will of God."

"It's not what we say," muttered her mother, unwilling to argue with such authority. "Bless my child, Father, against them that get held."

The Priest looked at the white-skinned child. With elfish rudeness he saw her dart away, out the door, over the granite slab, over the wood-horse and over the hills to climb Olympus.

Mary Immaculate did not want to be blessed against the fairies! They were her companions, along with the sun, the wind and the sea. Some day when courage was high and her blood ran with exciting daring she was going to defy the ceremony at the door. Then she might have a real adventure!

TWO

Those that get held.

The annals of Celtic folk-lore had dwindled to a fear of the Little People. A life on the fringe of the sea had released them from any identification with fairy dells, forts or grots. Nor were they sure whether fairies were little men with beards or flitting figures in spangled dresses.

Mary Immaculate devised her own lore! Like a person doing research she gathered the stories of the village, making a world around them. Over the hills and away from the sound of the sea the fairies seemed friendly and real. There were many places for them! Secret little groves where the sun shone through in golden chinks, wayward marshes threatening to the feet, and many ponds blowing with sedge and purple weeds. Others were completely covered with heart-shaped lily-pads and white and yellow flowers dreaming in the sun. She could make the fairies hop from pad to pad, tire them out with leap-frog and send them to sleep in the gleaming lilies. There was much to hold her in her strong and vivid world. The sea dominated the life of her people, and the land reflected its mood. It was a bold world with many faces.

Mary Immaculate did not spare the Little People. Her own light body took the variations of weather, and in turn she gave them to the sun, the wind and the sea. Sometimes she saw them with bedraggled dresses, other times frozen and held themselves, in crystal frost. It amused her to think of the fairies being held. Many times she felt cruel towards them and called them out of the trees and flowers. It was exciting to defy them, knowing they could not get her when she was protected by the ceremony at the door. Her knowledge of them as evil agencies had filtered into her mind from conversation with older children. That they might be a threat came as a revelation from a big girl when they were in the woods looking for berries. Running ahead, Mary Immaculate had kicked over a fairy-cap. Large and flat, like the crust of new bread, it lay spilled from its stalk.

"Glory be to God, Mary," whispered the girl. "What have you done? 'Tis their home you've kicked over. They'll come and get you to-night."

"Get me?" she questioned with wide yellow eyes.

"Get you," I said. Say your prayers for sure! They'll come to your bed and spirit you away."

"When?" she asked, half in terror and desire.

"To-night, and no mistake. There's no savin' you, nohow."

Mary Immaculate tossed her head and flitted through the woods. Just as well to be killed for a sheep as a lamb! Every fairy-cap and puff-ball she saw she kicked over, daring her goggling companion.

In the night she did not feel so brave. Cowering in bed she pulled the quilt up under her chin. Quietly she lay, with her eyes wide open in the darkened room. Through the uncurtained window the white moon watched her, casting a pool of light on the statue of the Sacred Heart. Back to the outside world it guarded the room from invasion. Only the sound of the sea was let in to speak in its changing voice. For the moment she forgot her danger to hear what the sea had to say. Quiet tonight but longing, crying for something it had not got, sighing against the heads and easing up the beach with a mumble of loose stones. It had to suck most of the time and feel something on its tongue. Green eye, greedy, that was the sea! It held her listening until she remembered she was waiting for the fairies to spirit her away. Would they? Some of the courage of daring days made her wish she could get out of bed and remove the statue of the Sacred Heart. All of Josephine's windows had statues! They were there as a rebuke to lightning and a deflection of every evil. Trusting the Sacred Heart she opened her windows to the night. Having lived in the City, she knew air was the thing for her child. Many times Benedict grumbled against her draughts. "What ails you, woman? Am I cuttin' wood to warm the out-doors?" He could endure the most Arctic blasts when he was on the sea, but inside he liked to be stuffy and fill his lungs with bad air.

The fairies did not get Mary Immaculate that night, though she waited until her eyes stung. She was inclined to praise and blame the Sacred Heart and the Holy Picture on her wall. The pool of moonlight moved from the statue and illuminated the Lord in a long robe, with a crook in his hand and a lamb round his neck. His hands and feet had the marks of nails, and a stray little tree grew close to the hem of his gown. It was pointed like a baby spruce! The picture was named in three languages: "The Good Shepherd"; "*LeBon Patron*"; and "*Der Gute Hirt.*" It was all too much for the Little People! Like a breakwater to the sea Josephine had built up a blessed barricade. Half regretting the fairies' non-appearance, Mary Immaculate knew she must tempt them again. She slept, and her dream was full of spangles and cobwebs, and the tinkle of tiny bells.

Those that were held! There were many tales, and they came to her one by one. Uncle Rich's story was the most interesting because it had happened to him when he was a little boy. It was hard to think of Uncle Rich as a little boy! He seemed older than God, with a white beard that hid the dickey he wore to Mass on Sundays. Held in a wood for a whole day, he couldn't get out until he sat down and remembered the way to freedom. He was held! By making the sign of the Cross and turning his coat inside out he ran home without interference.

Many had known the same experience. Benedict was taken when he was shooting partridge in October. In sight of his camp fire he walked all night without advancing a step. He was slow to remember the sign of the Cross, and knew a growing irritation for the loss of his wood-craft. When he performed the releasing ceremony he walked to his camp in three minutes. That was early in his married life, before he capitulated to Josephine's protecting ceremony at the door. Since then it had become a matter of routine before he left his house.

Molly Conway! She was a stranger tale! Nobody seemed to be sure of her age, even her own people who harboured her in a pink house. She was a deaf mute, strange to look at, with flat feet, a lumpy body and a strange hair-line that left the back of her neck very naked. In summer she wandered unhappily through the valley and in and out of the lanes on the slopes of the ravine. Her appearance was a signal for a wild flight of the children. Mary Immaculate became ashamed of the treatment meted out to her by the village. Even the adults never threw her a kindly word. They had a double dread of her appearance and the thing she represented. A changeling, a substitution, something accomplished by the Little People! For a long time Mary Immaculate was part of the herd, experiencing a real terror as she sped away. One day as she was flying like a hunted deer, her mind spoke to her feet: "Why are you running? I thought you liked the Little People. Stop and see what they did." She slowed and stopped until she found herself alone in the lane, with Molly Conway coming on. As she approached there came before her the strange wordless sounds that always told her she was near. Feeling her heart rising in her throat, Mary Immaculate knew it was too late to get away. Molly Conway was almost opposite! There she was in a black dress that looked green in the sun, a white apron, shoes like derelict scows and a dusty hat revealing the awful expanse of bare scalp. It was worse than the baldness of old men! That could be smooth and shiny! This was pink and pitted and wrinkled like a prune. Her hands were the same, clasped over her breast. Making low noises in her throat she stopped by the terrified child and the two stared in the strangest regard. Mary Immaculate's fear began to leave her, and in its recession she was conscious of pity and a desire to treat the old woman gently. What could she do? She heard the wordless voice and knew it wasn't hostile! It had the sound of the sea in wistful moods, sad and whimpering at the foot of the heads. She saw the old woman's eyes and knew they were as clean and blue as the wild iris growing on the fringe of the river. Why didn't people know Molly wouldn't hurt a fly? Father Melchior was right. "Hello," she said, smiling.

The vibrations of a gentle tone brought the changeling's hands in the air like a mute blessing. They ventured as far as the fair head, while her blue eyes explored the effect of her daring. Mary Immaculate stood quite still, waiting for the hands to fall. If they did she knew she could bear it. There were a lot of other things she could like less, such as carrying home a fish from the beach, or separating the skull of a cod's head from its tongue and its jowls. Molly Conway barely touched her! More than that would have been incredible daring for a mute who had walked alone all her life. She seemed in an agony of gratitude.

"Poor thing," said the child out loud. "Nobody has ever been kind to you. 'Tis a shame." She smiled, withholding none of her radiant youth.

The returning sounds were full of inarticulate eagerness.

"Wait a minute," she said eagerly, running up the lane and slipping through a gap to a meadow. Standing by the fence so as not to trample the hay, she reached for a few buttercups, bachelor-buttons and pale magenta clover. Speeding back she offered the small bouquet.

"There," she said regretfully. "I wish I was in the woods. Do you know about the wild roses there, and the scent-bottles and the maiden's tresses? And there's lots of others I don't know the names of."

Molly Conway was holding the bouquet as if it were precious ointment.

Mary Immaculate was running through the lanes, waving and looking back.

"Good-bye," she shrilled, "good-bye."

As she leaped over the granite slab of her mother's back door she was planning to make her treatment of Molly Conway her first Confession.

"Mom," she demanded, "tell me about Molly Conway. Everything you know."

Josephine jumped. "Glory be to God, Mary Immaculate, has she been after you?"

Mary Immaculate was impatient. "No, Mom! I just want to know about her. She's nice."

"Nice!" screeched Josephine incredulously. She was bleaching flour-sacks and prodding in a saucepan with a bit of stick. Her daughter sat down on the kitchen settle and told her mother about her encounter with the changeling. She had no hesitancy about finding the right words for her feelings.

"Mom, I felt good, as if I'd been blessed. Like it must be when you're absolved. Her eyes are like the blue iris and as gentle as the pictures of the Saints in Heaven."

"That right?" questioned Josephine, unwilling to warn her daughter against anyone who could make her feel like that.

"Yes, Mom, the Cove doesn't treat her right. Tell me what it really means to be a changeling."

"It's an elf-child," said her mother, answering one question.

Mary Immaculate laughed on a wild young note.

"Have sense, Mom," she said in Benedict's manner. "An elf-child! That would be sure to be pretty. Poor Molly is like a great clod-hopper."

"And *why* is she so queer-looking? For the very reason that we think. And I don't think the fairies are so pretty, neither! That's just your nonsense. 'Tis not superstition, in spite of Father Melchior."

"Well, what is it then, Mom? Tell me, I'll keep on till you do."

"That you will," said Josephine resignedly. "Did you ever give me any peace when you wanted to know anything."

"No," she said agreeably. "But how can I know without asking?"

Josephine hooked up a bit of the sacking to see if the coloured letters were fading out. Seeing a blur of blue she poked it back in the saucepan.

"This is the story they tell, Mary Immaculate. Molly's mother had been out of the Cove and had notions."

"Like you, Mom? You were out of the Cove for three years."

"And I'm back without notions."

"Mrs. Houlihan says you've got them about me, Mom. Every time I pass her door she says something about being raised above myself."

"Does she indeed?"

Josephine's tone was tart, and she was frowning into the saucepan.

"Yes, Mom? What way was Molly raised above herself? Never mind Mrs. Houlihan. I hate her mouth. You'd think she was trying to eat it herself. It's so far inside."

Josephine took the bit of wet stick out of the water and shook it at

her daughter. "Haven't I told you to speak no ill of your neighbour?"
"Yes, Mom," said her daughter blandly. "I'm speaking good of
Molly Conway."

"Well now, Molly Conway's mother always had her children
wheeled through the lanes in a bit of a pram! The like of that, now,
when she could have given the baby a rock as she went on with her
work. A sort of cousin of hers used to push the children round
the lanes and into the woods, knowing as well as we all do that the
Little People take quickest to children. She…"

Josephine lifted the sacking and had another look at its colour. "Fast
colours they put in, and no mistake."

"Go on, Mom! She was wheeled through the woods…"

"Her mother knew what was needed to protect her children, if she
had to have them wheeled. She had that much sense! Every day before
setting out she used to put a slice of bread under the baby's feet, in
case the fairies made off with the child."

"Spirit it away?"

"Spirit it away, and no mistake, or take the soul and leave the body.
But neither could happen with the slice of bread. That always placated
the fairies. But one day the cousin girl got careless like and set off with
Molly with never a crumb under her feet. She left the house with a
fine bonny child and came back with what you saw this morning."

Josephine believed it! Her tone implied conviction. Mary Immaculate gave her high childish laugh.

"I don't believe it, Mom."

"You don't believe in the fairies! Well now, that's something new."

"I didn't say that," said Mary Immaculate.

She looked at a long shaft of sunlight slanting through the window,
whirling specks and faint flying dust. The light became a luminous
hill for the fairies to climb. Spangles, wands, wings and tiny silver
bells! Whatever the fairies took they would be sure to make beautiful!

THREE

"FORTUNE'S ICE."

"Sure, tis a dream of a day!"

From her back door, Mrs. Keilly stepped out in the snow and looked down the ravine. Mary Immaculate ran after her and brought up on one foot, gazing, gazing, with her hands mutely clasped. The whole world was held!

It had rained in the night, frozen lightly in the morning, leaving a magical silver thaw. Enchanted, dazzling, glittering, the village stood covered in a cellophane coating of ice. Glazed ground swept down the valley, up the other side, sparkling with luminous dots. A rich deluge had poured the stardust of Heaven down on the snow. Masquerading as fairy forests, spruce and fir rose in tiers of glass. Where the rain had started to drip it had congealed in light blobs and icicles. The darkly captive evergreens had become Christmas trees with pendent silver ribbons. The junipers fell towards the sun, taken in homage like stricken vessels.

The sea was level, soothed and subdued at the feet of the land.

Mary Immaculate found her tongue, lost in thrall to the delicate day.

"Mom," she pleaded. "I can't go to school. We're only doing review."

"You're always reviewin' when you want a holiday."

"But we really are reviewing, Mom. Please let me stay home."
With the sun on her head Josephine felt benign. After the long drag
of winter the day was like a miracle.

"You're right, child! I don't blame you for wantin' a holiday. I'd
be saddle-sore myself in a desk to-day. Run after your Pop, now, and
ask him if you can stay home. He grudges the money for your
schoolin' if you don't use it."

Mary Immaculate shaded her eyes and turned her face towards the
sea. Far out on the slope Benedict and his train of sons made a dark
moving line.

"They're too far, Mom. They're all setting to on the lines and the
twines, and then they're going to take the sled to the woods. Pop said
the spruce was getting low."

"And a grand day for haulin' indeed. I don't know about
stayin'—"

"Let me stay, let me stay, let me stay! Just this once, Mom. I wish
I had an icicle dress and icicle hair to match the day."

Mary Immaculate danced up and down like a slim streak straining
towards the sky. Her feet returned to the ground with the easy balance
of children born to walk on ice.

"Powerful cold you'd be then," said Josephine, practically. Her
voice rose to a cheerful screech. "Good morning, Mrs. Houlihan."

Across from them and a little above, a woman had emerged from
a house. Bending to the weight of a bucket, she splashed its contents
out on the snow. Clean glimmer became befouled with a grey jagged
stain. Mary Immaculate felt a breath of hate for the woman with her
dirty water.

"Mornin', Mrs. Keilly. Ain't it frozen now?"

The woman put her bucket on the ground and rested her arms on
the glazed pickets of a fence.

"Fair beautiful it is, Mrs. Houlihan. This child is tryin' to stay
home from school."

"You spoil her, Mrs. Keilly, and set her above your boys. And what
would she be doin' home from school? Not working, I'll be bound!"

Entranced with a promise of a holiday Mary Immaculate held her
tongue. She knew she had a better chance now, since Mrs. Houlihan

had criticised her mother. She was right. Josephine answered with a tart edge to her voice.

"And why shouldn't she, Mrs. Houlihan? 'Tis little enough childhood we get in these parts. The Lord never sent this day to give to long division. As it is she romps through her lessons. Do her good to take a spell after the winter."

"This won't last," said the woman gloomily. "After the rain 'twill be pullin' and haulin' by night. You'd better run back, Mary, when you see the sky come over."

The child looked at the woman with a pity as cold and clear as the ice-stroke of the world. Mrs. Houlihan was the ugliness of the beach destroying the beauty of the land and the sea. Her skin was as grey and mottled as the belly of a cod, and her eyes had the same wet look. Her lips were so intimately withdrawn that she seemed to be sucking them herself. Her arms on the picket fence were as flat as two thin boards. Her bones were immodest, poking through the thinnest coating of skin. Mary Immaculate's eyes deserted her ugliness, while Josephine answered with the lightheartedness of the day.

"Land sakes, Mrs. Houlihan, she wouldn't know the weather till it fell on her."

Mrs. Houlihan puckered her toothless mouth and searched her mind for another hindrance. Finding it she shook her head.

"Those that walk in the woods today will be up to no good. 'Tis a grand day for *them* to come out."

Mary Immaculate scarcely breathed.

For once Josephine was not dismayed. The day itself was like a Benediction, and she felt as responsive as her daughter. She anwered her neighbour from the sanctuary of her faith.

"And what do you think I've had my doors and windows blessed for, Mrs. Houlihan? Those that leave my house rightly come home again. I see to that."

Her mother saw to that!

Mary Immaculate stepped stealthily ahead from under her eyes.

Adventure shouted in the air. It was a hair-breadth day and she knew it. Tilting her face to the sun, she felt bathed in a golden wash. At the same time her body received the tang of the icy world. Ice, heat, diamond-dust snow, blue of the sea and the sky blended to make a wild alchemy. Every sense was accentuated to a fine awareness. Dazzled eyes saw the world as a dream, nose dilated to invigoration, flesh eased against atmosphere blent of warmth and chill, while parted lips savoured the day in a distillation of taste. A cold clack of voices came from the tops of the trees. The whimpers and the whistles of the branches had changed to a crystal summons.

Josephine stirred with a long sigh. In spite of the day work had to go on. There would be no fairy appetites returning from the fish-room. Her dishes were waiting! She spoke briskly to her daughter, but for a few more moments the briskness only went into her voice.

"Well now, Mary Immaculate, as you've got a holiday you may as well make use of it. I could idle, myself, and no mistake."

Mary Immaculate turned to run into the house to get her outdoor things. In that position she was taken with the strangest moment of her life. When she was free of it her youth and ignorance relegated it to the realm of queer feelings. When years had spun strangely away and she heard her husband talking about the sensation of arrested time her mind took an instant leap to that morning in the Cove. Like Molly Conway's eyes it could always become a projection on her mind.

A childish Lot, staring back, she was part of the silver thaw. Frozen on her ice-picket fence Mrs Houlihan's chin, nose and brow looked as if the fins of a fish had been joined to give her a face. The wood-pile was a stack of glass spruce. Glazed sawdust by the wood-horse made a pool of yellow on the ground. A bit of wire netting had become a frosted cobweb. The snow sloping up behind her mother threw her figure into hard relief. Glass trees tiered up and made an occasional clearing for a house like a coloured box. Somebody had cut the Cove out of ice and stuck it up in front of her eyes. They were all held and clamped to the ground. Even the trees had stopped the dry clack of their stiffened branches.

Captive as the Cove, Mary Immaculate saw her mother. Her hair was fair and oily round a face scorched from the kitchen stove. Her cheeks were plump and loose, sagging away from bones and muscles. Her lips were soft and open to the air, revealing even teeth needing attention. In the glare of the sun the cavities were black-edged, like the sombre line of a Mass-card. Her body was plump, unconfined in the hips and the bust. Both had the same globe-like lines straining at wool. Above the arms the skin was fine and white, but the hands and wrists that had known constant submergence in pails and dish-pans of water looked swollen and red. Mary Immaculate saw what her life had done to her mother. She was not beautiful! Only her eyes commanded attention. Big and black-lashed they looked down the ravine with the rich brown of molasses. She had been a servant! What did it mean to be a servant? A servant was a creature who did other people's work. Hewers of wood and drawers of water. Where had she heard that? From Father Melchior when he had told her of the homely honour of work. Work! That was the Cove! Fish from the traps and the trawls, fish from the hook and the line. Bait to follow the seasons! Fish thrown up on the stage-heads, fish with black backs and silver bellies, fish with goggling eyes. Fish slit with knives, and spurting blood and guts! Fish drying on the flakes, and flies buzzing in a horde. Smell wafting to the land, smell penetrating to the groves of spruce and fir!

Standing like an ice-dream the child was released by her mother's voice.

"Stir yourself now and get off, or we'll both dream the day away."

Mary Immaculate moved cautiously, feeling that her mother had not noticed a thing. What strange moment had revealed the Cove like that? When the sun and the day came back to her she cast it away. All the recklessness of youth, childish abandon and intense joy of living went into the hop, skip and a jump she made towards the granite step at the back door.

Her clothes were on a hook in the kitchen.

"Mom," she pleaded, reaching for her woollen cap. "Can I leave off my over-stockings? I'll run lighter without."

"You'll have to run heavy, then," answered her mother firmly. "It's only March. Ne'er cast a clout—"

"All right, Mom," she said agreeably, sitting down on the floor and throwing out a knitted stocking that came up to her thighs.

By the work of her mother's hands she was the best dressed child in the village. From her neck to her toes, her skin to her coat, she was clothed in wool. The wool was coarse, but the garments were fine and beautifully shaped. Josephine increased and decreased in the right places, and her child's clothes fitted smoothly. The wool she had knitted could be measured in miles.

Mary Immaculate dressed with her eye on her mother. Pulling a pair of rubbers on her feet, she looked towards the door and back to her mother again. Josephine's red arm was raising a kettle from the top of the stove. Steam ran over her face as she poured water into a basin stacked with dirty dishes.

The ceremony at the door!

Aloft on its frame rested a narrow shelf bearing a homely altar of the Sacred Heart. In front of the pottery figure stood a tiny lamp with a frosted globe. The tending of this everlasting flame was Josephine's most holy chore. The last thing at night and the first thing in the morning she creaked on a chair and brought the lamp down to her kitchen table. There it was trimmed, polished and oiled, to burn in odourless devotion. Like a florid vestal she was dedicated to its continuity. When the house rocked like a cradle and whistled in its seams and its sills it seemed as if the tiny lamp must be hurled to the floor. Josephine knew that it would not! The Sacred Heart held it up better than any law of gravity! In summer it burned in an imperceptible flame, dulled by the sun. Then Mary Immaculate searched the woods for the most delicate flowers and made an offering to the altar. Under the supporting shelf and all round the door ran a row of brass rings, fastened with an occasional nail. These were blessed! Thus at the door of her kitchen Josephine guarded her family. That they should be sure of a safe return it was necessary to make certain observances. Mary Immaculate had made them many times a day as long as she could remember. Genuflecting to the Sacred Heart, she would step out, step back and walk freely away in the knowledge of a safe return.

Mary Immaculate planned things to take her mother out of the room. Through the open door the light was golden and the snow glistened with its diamond shower. One leap and perhaps her mother wouldn't notice! That seemed impossible. Josephine set the ceremony at the door above the care of their bodies. Delay was necessary.

"Mom, give me a slice of bread in case I get hungry."

"Now, Mary Immaculate, you're not going to make a day of it. You come back and eat properly. I'm going to make a boiled pudding with lassey sauce."

"Nice," said her daughter appreciatively. "But I'd like the bread just the same."

From the steaming pan of dishes Josephine looked at her child. A denial came to her lips and died in the warmth of her love for her child's face and body. Her white skin, fair hair like a nimbus and eyes shining like agates won her the slice of bread. Stooping under the table she dragged out a tin and cut a large slice of bread, adding a smear of butter. Wrapping it in a bit of brown paper, she gave it to her daughter.

"There," she said. "That'll hold you." Adding with happy inconsequence, "don't eat it, now, till you get back, and then you'll be safer. Be off with you now. You'll enjoy yourself I'll be bound. Your face looks that bright."

Josephine went back to the table and picked up her dishcloth. Peering round the pan she searched for a piece of soap. Dropping the cloth her hands made a clatter, parting saucers and plates. Not a soapsud appeared on the disturbed water.

"I declare," she said impatiently. "This family eats soap, and it's not from washin' faces either. Them big galoots..."

Josephine had disappeared through a door. It was ordained—as irrevocable as the flame at the foot of the Sacred Heart. The soap was kept in the cold front room they never used. More storehouse than anything else, it was packed with boxes and many objects. In the winter it was as cold as the grave and the place for butter and milk and an occasional dish of cream.

With a step like an inspired spring Mary Immaculate was out the door. She was running down the slope when her mother called her.

"Mary Immaculate, did you make your bow?"

"Yes, Mom," she said with instantaneous assurance.

"Good-bye then," said her mother with a cheerful wave of her dish-cloth.

Mary Immaculate's smooth rubbers went skating down the slope. With the face of an angel she sang as she went.

"*I've* got a sin on my soul. *I've* lied as big as a dog. I'll go and burn in hell fire. The devil's got horns and a tail. The fairies have little wings. Who'll chose, who'll chose? Left hand, right hand..."

Singing her thoughts and the account of her misdeed she ran to where the river flattened the verge of the ravine. The power of the sun and the run of the undercurrent were breaking the ice on the surface. Small rivulets seeped through cracks, pressing frosty pancakes under water. On the banks, snow crested and curved like waves leaping to meet.

Mary Immaculate followed the river, running, walking, stepping from side to side and making a short distance a very long way. She idled on an uncovered stone and sat down in the snow to let the sun warm through her clothes. She had the world to herself. The men were on the beach, the women were in their kitchens and the children were in the small schoolhouse. By the grace of God she was out of doors. In an ecstasy of freedom she lay down on her stomach and licked the snow. The feel of it in her warm mouth was like the hot-cold day. Once she tried to pick up the diamond-dust, but the bright specks died under her hand. She took off her cap and raced to the waterfall and saw that the sun had freed it, giving it back to its foam. Down it rushed, boiling from its very first dip over the rocks. Above soared land to the height of the heads. She started to climb, stopping to look at the occasional emergence of a glazed rock. Under glass the iron-stains of granite had a richer gleam. Suddenly she finished her climb with no more hesitation. The sea was blue and far away, while on the land stood forests and forests of crystal trees. Running into them she sped through endless trunks. Sometimes the sun came through and made golden spots on the snow. Even the shadows were full of light, and where the junipers bent and met a slim spruce they made a glittering arch. Deeper and deeper she ran into the crystal forests.

FOUR

"TO STARVE IN ICE...AND THERE TO PINE,
IMMOVABLE, INFIXED AND FROZEN ROUND PERIODS OF
TIME, THENCE HURRIED BACK TO FIRE."

The thaw and the frost fought all day over the captive trees. Burning in the sky the sun travelled to the west, but in spite of warmth the frost watched its image like a petrified narcissus. Baffled in intensity, heat withdrew to the radiation of bright orange colour. The western sky went out, resigning the village to the moon. White and impersonal it saw the trees without desire. The wind rose for a tussle with the stiffened branches, and the sounds that resulted had a dry clack, like moans grown brittle. The sea sobbed on the beach, turning the stones and searching for something it had lost.

Wrapped in a three-cornered shawl Molly Conway emerged for the first time since winter. She kept shambling to the waterfall and back again, trying to beckon people on. Nobody noticed her. As familiar as the common day she was something to see without sight. The red murk of lanterns moved beside figures trudging up the slopes of the ravine. Reaching the height of the heads they disappeared under the trees. Men, who had not left the valley for many days, commended themselves to God and made a dutiful search for Mary Immaculate. The ghostly light of the moon and shadows glassed by ice made them uneasy. Far-sighted eyes found the forests too near for observation. The night was bewitched! Sight turned inwards, calling up ghosts of some icy purgation.

Josephine's kitchen was full to overflowing. Women with faces prematurely withered rested drudging hands. Above the oilcloth top of the kitchen table shadows lurked in hollowed eyes. In silent meditation under the homely altar Josephine knelt, impervious to her neighbours. One hand clutched her beads, while the other was closed over a Child of Mary medal. Her eyes were glazed on the door. Open, it made a cavern of darkness fading to grey and melting towards the gleam of the moonlit snow. The women let her alone. It was natural to pray at such a time.

Mrs. Houlihan was leader. Having seen the child go, she had a right to the floor. Her mouth made a home for the blackest shadow. Sibilance from indrawn lips held tones of retribution.

"I warned her! She can't say I didn't warn her! Says I: ''Tis a grand day for *them* to be out.' Did she heed when I spoke? That she didn't, neither she nor her Ma! Down she went lickety-split, like the dart of a trout, with her hair flyin' away from her face. Held, that's what she is, and they say Molly Conway has come out of her house moanin' like a loon."

"Like unto like," said Mrs. Walsh accusingly.

"The child was good to her," said Mrs. Flynn staunchly. "Perhaps she knows where she's at."

"'Tain't likely," sniffed Mrs. Walsh; "with all the sensible ones searchin', and those stayin' at home doin' their bit too. Since I heard she was held I've offered St. Anthony a settin' of eggs to find her. 'Tis a sight to offer."

Mrs. Walsh looked challengingly round for equal sacrifice. Mrs. Houlihan's voice depreciated her offering. "I'd wait, Mrs. Walsh, to see if she's carried in feet first. 'Tis freezing."

The women shivered and bent inwards. All except Mrs. Rolls who sat solid as a boulder, with her clothes shelving down from her neck. Above, her nose and chin elongated to preserve the same line. She was profound, mystic and dirty. No matter how much information was imparted she continued destroying the circle. When she was ready she scattered the whispers with a voice that seemed to return from some deep world. Her bass rumble did not disturb her immobility.

"There I sat last night watching the white clouds sailin' by, and I was reminded of them that had trod the valley before me. There they are, says I, lyin' down on their backs with their faces turned up to the same moon, and here am I, above the ground wonderin' who of us'll be next—"

"That's right, Mrs. Rolls," whispered Mrs. Flynn.

"And when I heard the child was gone—"

"Please God, not gone—"

"*And* when I heard the child was gone," continued Mrs. Rolls with mystical certainty, "I was reminded of my own childhood and the things I learnt in the Reader, and I called up the poem of Lucy Grey—"

Mrs. Houlihan's whisper was tart" I don't hold with poultry, Mrs. Rolls."

"Poetry, Mrs. Houlihan," boomed Mrs. Rolls, making the word sound like a mystery.

"Poetry, then, or whatever it is. I don't hold with lookin' for two words—"

"That's right, Mrs. Houlihan," agreed Mrs. Walsh, "plain speakin' and sayin' what—"

"I was reminded of Lucy Grey! And the sweet face of Lucy Grey—"

"I remember it, too, Mrs. Rolls,"said Mrs. Costello, rushing in with a sudden memory of the Royal Reader. "'And the sweet face of Lucy Grey nevermore was seen.'"

"Hushhhhh," reproved Mrs. Flynn with a kind look at Josephine. In her wish to show off, Mrs. Costello had recited loudly.

"When oft she crossed the moor—" boomed Mrs. Rolls.

Mrs. Houlihan's whispers gathered contempt. "'Tis not Lucy Grey they're searching for, Mrs. Rolls, and I never heard of no moor in these parts. 'Tis Mary Immaculate they're searchin' for, and no mistake."

"And a hard punishment to the mother for making so light of the name," said Mrs. Walsh, with the acceptance of justice.

"She wasn't rightly baptised by it," reminded Mrs. Flynn. "It was only Mrs. Whelan who gave her that, and not Father Melchior."

"And I should say not," said Mrs. Walsh reprovingly. "Where is he, anyway, at such a time?"

"Gone over the heads," volunteered Mrs. Houlihan quickly, for fear Mrs. Rolls should answer before her, but she had withdrawn to the world of Lucy Grey. "He got a call this morning."

"It's the fellow two coves up, with the fallin' sickness."

"The like of that now," said Mrs. Houlihan, with a suck of her lips. "The Father must be sick anointin' him."

"You can fall once too often, Mrs. Houlihan," boomed Mrs. Rolls, with the weight of a boulder crushing a pebble.

"That you can, Mrs. Rolls," agreed Mrs. Walsh. "Put a bit of wood in the fire, Mrs. Costello. You're nearest the stove."

"I'll do it," said Mrs. Houlihan, making a scrape of her kitchen chair. "I know her kitchen better than the rest of you and I'll make the tea. The men'll want a nice warm drink, and I'm the one to get it for them."

"Will they stay out the night?" asked Mrs. Walsh in a hopeful voice. The occasion was sad but rare.

"And what else would they be doin', Mrs. Walsh, with that slip of a child in the open?" Now that Mary Immaculate had gone Mrs. Houlihan approved of her more. When the stove had been fed with spruce-logs she returned to the circle at the table. Bending further in, she gathered the women's faces nearer the lamp-chimney. "If she sleeps in this weather there'll be no runnin' about for her any more." The circle echoed with whispers that lacked solidarity from Mrs. Rolls. When Mrs. Houlihan was planning a wake for Mary Immaculate, Mrs. Rolls discarded her aloofness. With a shift like the fall of an avalanche she slid to her knees and became a boulder on the floor. "Thou shalt open our lips, O Lord."

The women dropped in one descent, while the lamp was left to shadow their brows. "And our mouths shall show forth Thy praise," came in unison from their mouths.

Mrs. Rolls was leader, and she guided them through the Rosary where the women had to answer her according to her mood. Suitably it was a day for the five Sorrowful Mysteries, and her voice gave value to their contemplation. Returning from her own world of silent meditation, Josephine led the responses. The women prayed, with no hope of recess from Mrs. Rolls.

Molly Conway shambled by the waterfall whimpering for attention until a relation ran her down the valley, locking her inside her house.

The temperature rose, releasing the trees. Dripping away their masquerade they returned to spruce and fir. The junipers drooped further to the east, dragged in a deeper bow. The moon receded, paled by a morning sky. In a chill dawn snow was revealed without sparkle, trees without magic and box-like houses empty of their owners. Heavy with the burden of winter the village shivered in a nadir of rest.

At seven Benedict and his train of sons dragged up the slope. Slack and speechless they clod-hoppered in their long rubbers. Entering the kitchen, more shadows found homes in hollowed eyes. Pale, silent women rose and filed out, insensate with sleeplessness and the thought of their own tired men. Mrs. Rolls moved like a mobile mountain.

Josephine's eyes focused on her husband. "Any sign, Ben?"

"No," he said briefly. "We're going to wire to the City for the police. There's a boat gone across the Bay to the telegraph office."

Benedict and his loutish sons died to the thought of Mary Immaculate. Fully dressed they sprawled and slept in a vast indifference to the toll of sea or land. Only Josephine prayed on, until she crumbled like an animal lost in turgid sleep.

The first day of Mary Immaculate's disappearance she was village and shore news. The second she was City news. The third she was Island and World news. While the village was recovering from its first search strange skiffs and dories came in from the sea, and other men climbed the slopes of the ravine. Authority arrived, and uniforms mixed with blue overalls hitched over long rubbers. The fisherfolk lent themselves to organisation, but they did it in silence. In front of the invaders not a word was said. "A little girl was lost." Lost, was she? Let them say what they say, she was held! The Little People had taken her, and what they had begun the winter would finish. They searched, almost without looking, while three days passed without a sign of the way she went. The men were ready to give up. For three days the sea had gone on by itself. Resignation came easily, and there was always the consolation of prayer.

Josephine rose from her knees and dragged round like a lack-lustre drudge. Swollen in the eyes and mouth she continued working for her husband and sons. The romance in her life was spilled, gone with the last sight of her child dancing down the slope. Her duty was left, and she prayed on her feet. Father Melchior sat in her kitchen and tendered the consolations of religion. For once Josephine had to fight unorthodoxy. Who could think of Mary Immaculate expiating in Purgatory? If she was dead, she was flying through Heaven asking the Saints and the Blessed Virgin many questions.

Benedict was ready to give up. Already Mary Immaculate was approaching a legend. Far-sighted fishermen looked uneasily at the beach, but the police pressed them on. They wanted evidence of a hopeless search.

The weather varied but changed without venom. The frost was light, the air damp, the wind constant but moderate and the snow dry, wet and frozen in turn. Once it blew with a snow-flurry and powdered the world with a new covering. Once it drizzled and froze, and the trees were taken in another glaze. The day was grey, and the forests rattled, steely and cold. The police were ready to bring home the body of a dead child.

The fourth day the sun was in the sky and the snow under foot had the tread of coarse salt. Many men had gone back to the repairing of lines and twines for the coming fishery. Only Benedict went on, but his mind was back with the men.

Molly Conway was released by relations grown weary of restraining her. Her gaolers were back on the beach, acquiescent to let things be. Mrs. Houlihan was tired telling the same story, and Mrs. Rolls was unmystically scrubbing her floor. The village wanted to be ordinary again. The rigour of living did not permit a continuation of exaltation. The time came when Benedict climbed down by the waterfall and landed in the valley with finality.

"'Tis useless," he declared to his sons. "Go home and get a mug-up and go down to the fish-room." Wordlessly they filed down the valley.

Molly Conway stayed Benedict's progress, but he ignored her, trying to brush past. Whimpering, she touched him and ran back a few steps towards the waterfall. Her retreat gave him an unimpeded way down the valley. He was stopped again by the approach of a police-sergeant. "It seems hopeless, Mr. Keilly. We've searched every point within ten miles. No child could go further."

"No," said Benedict, looking towards the beach.

Molly Conway ran back and touched the sergeant. "Who *is* this woman, Mr. Keilly? I've been watching her all morning. She's like a dog trying to draw someone away." In sight of the sea the long range of Benedict's blue eyes refused focus to Molly Conway. "Daft," he said laconically.

"But what's troubling her?" persisted the sergeant, turning to see Molly Conway beckon him on. She looked wild and distraught, with baffled blue eyes.

"Deaf and dumb," said Benedict dismissingly. "Take no notice."

"Does she know the child is lost?"

"How could she?" asked Benedict stolidly. "Didn't I tell you she was deaf and dumb?"

"So are animals, but they've got something else. I had a dog once who acted like that, and blessed if it didn't take me to the thing I couldn't find."

"She'll find nothing but a few clouts if she keeps on."

"Did she know the child? Have any contact with her? Try and think, man. It might help."

With his face turned to the sea Benedict screwed up his eyes.

"Well, she did, now I come to think of it. I heard her mother say she used to pick her a posy, and my girl didn't mind if she touched her. That's a lot in this Cove."

"Ah," said the sergeant thoughtfully.

"What help would that be?" asked Benedict. "It's sense you want to search the woods. I'm done. I'm goin' back to the beach."

"Pity to give up, Mr. Keilly."

"I've got six sons and a woman to feed, and I'm behind for the spring. 'Tis no good. Come and have a bite with us and talk to her mother," he said civilly. Benedict was determined. Straightening his shoulders, his long rubbers slushed through the snow. He knew work, endurance, acceptance and the faculty of keeping his mind on his hands. What sorrow he felt for the loss of his daughter was dulled by the strain of his body. He had glimpsed in her something different from himself, but he was not fitted for the processes of thought, and she lasted in his mind like the memory of intensified summer. She was beyond him. Much better he understood the ways of his skiff.

As a father the sergeant dismissed him and returned to his study of Molly Conway. She had stopped another police man, climbing down by the waterfall. Whimpering, she fell back when he brushed her aside.

A few steps brought the sergeant to her side.

"Hello," he said genially.

Kind vibrations reached Molly Conway. Wheeling on her scow-like feet she examined his face. Wonderingly, the odd pair regarded each other. Both were baffled, but both wanted the same thing.

"Hello," he said again, reassured by her eyes. The police sergeant recognised her gently, as Mary Immaculate had when tendering bouquets of flowers. The changeling gibbered into formless speech. Old hands plucked at his sleeves, while her shawl sprawled away from her back.

"All right, Mother," he said receptively, "I believe you! Now, where do you want to go?"

It was Molly Conway's great day. The sergeant swooped after her shawl and gave it a comfortable hoist over her shoulders.

"There, Mother, keep yourself warm. It's not summer, you know."

One look behind told her he was following. Reaching the water-fall she made upward motions and started a scrambling climb. From a position of grotesque unbalance she was drawn back, while a pat and a smile stilled her to patience. The sergeant raised his voice and yelled down the valley.

"Here, you, run and get Mr. Keilly! Tell her mother we're going to try again. Get the party together and the first aid equipment."

A policeman gaped for a minute at Molly Conway and then slushed down the valley.

Hope that had waned to acceptance sprang back to hope. People began running, and soon Benedict was seen returning from the direction of the beach, while Josephine almost fell down the slope. Reaching the waterfall, the sergeant's quick hand saved her from sprawling on her face.

"Steady now," he said kindly.

"Glory be to God!" she sobbed. "Have you found her?"

"Not yet, ma'am, but I think we're going to. We've tried sense. Now I'm going to give this woman the lead."

"Molly Conway," moaned Josephine. "'Tis the will of God. I might have known! I should have guessed." Feverishly she blessed herself, while tears made dirty rivers on her cheeks.

Benedict clod-hoppered up and heard the new plan. "Molly Conway," he muttered. "She couldn't find the head of a pin."

"Shush, Benedict," reproved his wife. "We must have faith. 'Tis strange ways He chooses sometimes."

Benedict grunted but squared his shoulders for another tramp.

Walking like a scow lying back on its keel Molly Conway led the way. In her awkward scramble up the slope the sergeant lent a hand, but when she was on the heights he let her go. She walked like a woman certain of her way.

The snow was dull, loose as salt and heavy round the feet. All sound became condensed to crunching and slushing. Entering the forests black-green gloom closed over their heads. Through trees, thick, thin, tall, bare, evergreen and those purple with blight they moved in single file. Once somebody muttered protestingly, "We've been this way a dozen times already. Have a heart." He was silenced with a sharp, "Shut up."

In a coma of faith Josephine pressed close to Molly Conway. Her mind had left her body and whispered of Acts of Hope. The ways of men had failed and He had pointed the way. At that moment she could have endured martyrdom, her mind floated in such exaltation. She knew without doubt that they were walking towards her child. Molly Conway! Molly Conway! What she had to spare from her singing soul went into planning rewards for the village changeling. She would visit her in her affliction, and when she was dead she would have Masses said for her soul. Benedict would lay aside a few quintals of fish for the purpose.

The changeling walked on, undisturbed in her own world. Compensation for undeveloped faculties was apparent in the decision of her lead. The frequent dilation of a fleshy nose indicated she was smelling her way. When they came to a grove too thick for penetration, she walked to where the trees were better spaced. The evergreens were wearisome in their sameness. Variation lay on the ground, in a dip, a rise, or a granite rock. Several times they crossed a clearing where the snow undulated like a frozen sea. Once they had to jump a river. Its banks looked solid, but as they paused for a leap their feet sank to the pull of an icy current. Their recoil lent a sharp impetus to their springs. Molly Conway landed with the flat slap of a dory, Josephine with the inspired lightness of her mind, while the men splashed with the weight of their boots.

The walk went on until there was a discernible change in Molly Conway. Raising her head and dilating her nostrils, she had the appearance of a horse in sight of its stable. The increased speed of her walk diffused a herd quiver of excitement. Breath quickened as they stumbled towards another clearing. Breaking through, Molly Conway stood back on her heels with a cessation of motion. All followed her example, stilled to wild anticipation.

The sergeant's eyes raked the snow and then contracted in disappointment. The clearing was the same as many others. Snow, rolling away like the frozen waves of the sea. Scattered single trees stood out in black relief.

Molly Conway gave a long strange cry, the cry of a mute trying to make joy form on her lips. Dropping her immobility she crashed forward in a lop-sided run. For a moment they watched, bewildered by the inadequacy of their eyes. Josephine's dry sob beseeched Heaven for sight.

Molly Conway was stumbling, hindered by snow that sustained her on one leg and broke under the other. In her grotesque lop-sided strain every step seemed to threaten her with a fall on her face. There was no impediment in her determination or the line of her direction, leaving as she stumbled holes and footprints in the snow. As if she gave them sharper sight they saw what they had missed.

"Glory be to God!" sobbed Josephine.

"Christ!" ejaculated Benedict.

"Good woman, good woman!" exulted the sergeant, congratulating himself and Molly Conway.

The wind had drifted the snow, cresting it in waves and leaving an illusion of unbroken undulation. When they saw their mistake they sprang as one body. Molly Conway was almost there! She curved, knelt in the snow, raising her hands in habitual hovering.

Following, they found a half-dome of snow, sheltering what was left of Mary Immaculate. She lay like a child dead in a shell. The change in her shattered Josephine's exaltation, making her grovel on the ground.

"Mary Immaculate, are you dead, are you dead?"

The child's eyes unclosed from blue sockets.

"Hello," she said, like a tired bell. "You passed before, but I couldn't call."

Josephine moaned in anguish. "Oh, oh, Mary Immaculate, are you starved to death out in the snow?"

In the momentary suspension given to shocked examination her voice touched them like a snowflake.

"I wasn't alone. The Little People stayed by me. When I was hungry I ate snow. I slept when 'twas dark and woke when 'twas light."

The flare of life went out, succeeded by blue pallor.

"No, no," protested her mother. "Open your eyes, Mary Immaculate. Oh, has somebody got a drop of rum?"

The sergeant and a policeman had been unrolling a pack.

"Not a drop of spirits," said the sergeant sharply. "Step aside, now, everyone, please."

The sergeant and the policeman worked for Mary Immaculate's second survival. That she had endurance and intelligence was apparent by her efforts to preserve herself. Before she lay down to sleep she must have gathered spruce boughs to make a bed. They were scant but sufficient to break her contact with the snow. All but her feet. They stretched beyond, revealing the black heels of her rubbers frozen to the ground. Under her ankles lay the glazed white of a slice of bread.

"God Almighty!" said the sergeant. "She had a piece of bread and didn't eat it."

"Glory be to God!" cried Josephine hysterically, "that'll save her against the frostbite." In a frenzy of gratitude she threw her arm round Molly Conway and rocked her backwards and forwards.

One glance told the sergeant that the quickest way to free Mary Immaculate's feet was to cut her out of her rubbers and over-stockings.

There was no feeling in the hands and feet that were bared in the snow. Against the white surface they lay livid and black.

"Loose snow," directed the sergeant. "And take the stopper from the thermos of milk. The circulation can't be stimulated with this frostbite."

"Yes, yes, give her a hot drink," implored Josephine. "She looks like death."

"Can't be done, ma'am," he said briskly, rubbing Mary Immaculate's feet in loose snow. "The circulation must be started gradually."

They worked fast. After a thorough rubbing, the blackened limbs were wrapped in cotton wool, and a few drops of cooled milk poured between her lips. Then she was bundled in blankets.

"Now, Mr. Keilly," said the sergeant, straightening. "We've had our orders. When you called us in I was instructed to find her, and if she needed attention beyond the scope of this village to transport her to town. The quickest way would be by boat across the Bay, and then by catamaran to the railway. Your consent is necessary, but you can see for yourself the state of her hands and feet. Extreme danger from gangrene if she gets the wrong attention."

"The skiff!" said Benedict. "I'll go ahead and get her ready."

It was his only answer. What help he had went into action.

While they were stooping to lift Mary Immaculate from the ground Josephine scrunched to the bundle of blankets. "Wait a minute," she commanded.

She had stopped crying and her voice was calm. The sergeant made way for her while she parted the hood over her child's face. Knowing only its constitutional health and the warm tints of its skin she was appalled by the blue shade suggesting dissolution. Mary Immaculate was dead! Dead without need of her mother's hands to compose her last sleep! That frozen coma could not belong to childhood, nor suggest any assurance of survival. Lightness, gaiety, colour, pink and blue wool and the coming and going of a pale gold head were all gone! It was the will of God! Her daughter had been lent to her as a lovely plaything. Josephine would go on, with heavy clod-hoppering men, eating silently and sleeping the sleep of rest from the sea. This remnant of her child was not survival! Exaltation had not been justified.

"Now, ma'am,"said the sergeant. His voice was kind but firm.

"Yes, yes," said Josephine respectfully, scrunching away on her knees.

As light as a frozen ghost, Mary Immaculate was carried away. Molly Conway pulled at her shawl, following without a backward glance. Josephine was left with her torment. She had the wish to lie down in the snow and dwindle to the frozen shape of her daughter. For a few minutes she indulged herself in sobbing inertia, until she saw the procession disappearing into the trees.

"Benedict? Dalmatius? Ignatius…"

Shivering, she rose to her feet and crunched through the snow. The distance between herself and her daughter was widening, and she could not catch up. Hurrying as fast as her legs would permit she could only keep her in sight.

Mary Immaculate was going to town!

FIVE

"SAILS RIPPED, SEAMS OPENING WIDE AND COMPASS LOST."

The little girl had been found! Mary Immaculate was a story! In the throb of a day's news, she signified an unbelievable survival of folk-lore: a manifestation of its spirit. In dispatches she made colour between armaments and disasters. In longer columns her story was elaborated, and the superstitions of her Cove magnified to fantastic proportions. She was a stir to imagination and a jolt to reason. Everything about her compelled interest: her birth in a skiff; her name; the slice of bread under her feet; and the incredible fact that she could deny her hunger to placate the Little People. Over the cable it went to build up a story. The words she had used when she was found shook the most rational. "The Little People stayed by me. When I was hungry I ate snow. I slept when 'twas dark, and woke when 'twas light." The stark reduction of three days' exposure defied classification. It suggested a simplicity past comprehension, or the imperviousness of under-privileged classes. Either from exposure or terror she should have died! The press said she was in hospital, suffering from frostbite. It seemed her one link with normality. In momentary interest the thoughts of countless people were projected to her bedside.

Pity she should die!

Better she were dead!

She was tossed on the imagination and dismissed.

Some of the repercussions had far-reaching results.

A New Yark philanthropist read about her over a pile of begging letters.

Coming from print as youth, colour and adventure, he experienced a resurgence of Celtic feeling. Leprechauns and fairies, charms and talismans, roods and banners had animated the atmosphere of his youth. The little girl must have invaded a "gentle place" and been unable to run home. Convinced that she had been held he abandoned his channels of charity and started an interchange of expensive cables. At the end of a day Philip Fitz Henry found himself the custodian of two thousand dollars towards the preservation of the little lost girl.

Mary Immaculate was a trust!

Spectacular gesture died, leaving her restoration to the tenacity of her doctor and interested nurses.

In the hospital her door held a magnetic attraction. Those of authority were permitted a professional peep. None saw her without a quick regret. In her waxen immobility she was condemned to a narrower bed than the one she occupied. She seemed two-dimensional, except for the neat head and the high planes of the face starvation and exposure had reduced to bones. Nostrils looked insufficient channels for air, and eye-sockets evident through dwindled flesh. Lids were flower thin and closed with a burden of lashes. What remained of her seemed too frail a container for replenishment. Doctors and nurses departed with mute gestures of pity and regret.

In her world life was as unsubstantial as a white sea-fog.

It was light and warm, in a room without a stove. Outside she had lost the waterfall and the strong suck of the sea. Swishes and slushes entered from wheels she did not know. Several times there was a quiet voice and smells she could not recognise. The voice belonged to hands imparting a glimmer of sense. Once, in lifting her, they seemed to hold her whole body. Rescuing her from her clouded world, she returned when they let her go. She felt as light as a puff-ball until she changed to feet and hands.

The room was different then! Dark and warm, with one white moon on the floor. Outside there was a dead calm, but the restlessness of the sea had entered her body, making her roll in waves of pain. By her head she could hear an occasional crack of starch, like Uncle Rich's dicky, in Mass on Sunday mornings. Then she kept meeting the rim of a spoon.

Delirium was intermittent. She was lifted, floated, grounded, while seaweed hair streamed back from her face. Momentarily cool, it was washed by the sea. A lucid interval told her she was wrong. Somebody held her in containing hands while another wiped her face with a cloth. She could hear a quiet voice close to her ears.

"Don't bother her with the powder any more, Sister. I'm afraid it must be the needle. She's wearing herself out. The circulation is returning and there's inflammation. Try and keep the blood back by elevating the feet. Has she been delirious all evening?"

"Nearly all the time, sir. She thinks she's a wave, leaping up the beach."

The remnant of Mary Immaculate's mind resented the slur on her identity.

"I'm not a wave," she said weakly. "I'm in Purgatory, with hands and feet."

"No, you're not," said the voice close to her ears, while hands under her shoulders settled her. Something safe had come between her and that floating fog. Could she dare think she had skipped Purgatory?

"I'm in Heaven," she sighed. "In the hands of St. Joseph."

"You're neither," said the voice, as if the idea was absurd. "You're in hospital because your feet and hands are frost bitten. It's very simple and natural."

It seemed so, then. She let her head fall against somebody's arm, but tired and dispirited as she was she had to look. In a momentary glimpse she retained a memory of a high white forehead, brown eyes and a nose as carved as the edge of a shell. She would have liked to look longer, but a weight of exhaustion lay on her lids.

Once she could have been so interested. For the time being she was cured of zest. She was lying in bed because of her own leap after romance. Nothing of that silver day remained, nor could she recapture any of its beauty. There was no aftermath of diamond dust, crystal trees, or wings skimming over the snow She was conscious of consequences and the effect of her own misdeeds. Her body had trespassed on her mind, and imagination was subdued to the throb of hands and feet. The Little People had not come with her to hospital, nor did she think she could find them there. What place could they have in this clean new world where doors had no rings and windows could be opened without the protection of the Sacred Heart?

When her shoulders were released she went whirling away in the fog.

"This won't do," said the voice. Waves washed over sound and leaped over a pin she felt in her arm.

Black flakes were filling the room, down to the moon on the floor. They cooled her body, ran over her hands making a recession of pain.

Down she went!

She was running on a winter's day when the blue was weak in the sky. The valley was deserted and the houses looked empty outside. Her feet were racing by the river, straining to reach the waterfall. The current ran one way and she ran the other, and she didn't seem to get on. Behind, came the sound of hoofs, and each clippety-clop fell nearer to her ears. Looking behind she saw a black horse, with a rider low on its neck. There were two red lamps and a long streak of fire. When the horse got nearer she saw the lamps were its eyes and the fire its breath. It was almost on her, and her neck felt a wave of heat. Wildly she strained, looking at the steep ascent of land! If she could reach it she could clamber up by the waterfall and get away from the horse. Then she tripped! Her body sprawled on the ground, while the horse leaped over her, scorching her as it went. She was burning against ice! Flattened, she waited unknown destruction. The clippety-clop grounded and the heat came down from above.

"Look up," said the rider.

She looked up into lamps that were eyes and saw the coat of the horse gleaming in the sun. The rider wore a white shirt swollen with wind.

"This is the horse that gets you!"

Then she saw teeth.

"Only one thing can save you!"

Her voice had curdled in her throat and she couldn't ask, "What?"

Leaning out of the saddle the rider held out his hand.

"The horse can't get you until he brings back this ball. You can run while he finds it. Throw it as far as you can."

The ball was brown and made of iron. Leaping to her feet the rider dropped it in her hand. Her palm sagged with its weight. Laughing, she knew she was saved. The ball was so heavy it could be thrown a long way. With her eyes measuring the distance to the waterfall she swung her arm in a curve. Before she could fling, her hand went light as a feather. Opening her fist, she saw it held a puff-ball....

Struggling and screaming, she was the core of terror.

She had lost her bearings. The Cove had been cosy, a circle of sea and sky and a cleft in the heads for a valley. Its spectres were clearly defined in the toll of the sea and the lure of the Little People on the land. Now she spun in a world containing dementia.

The quiet voice was back, and hands snatched her back from unreason.

"Hush, my dear child! You've had a bad dream. Don't struggle so and I'll tell you about it. I had to give you morphia for the pain, and to make you sleep. Sometimes it gives dreams—"

"The horse," she wailed; "and the weight that was only a puff-ball. Oh, oh, oh—"

"Stop," he commanded, in a voice that was one to obey.

It was quiet but it held a fall of frost on hysteria. She stopped, shivering in his hands.

"Now," he said soothingly, "you're going to sleep, and if you dream you're to remember it's a dream. You must be patient and sensible, and very soon you'll be well again. You're very safe and protected. Do you hear me, Mary? There's nothing to be afraid of—"

"I'm not a coward," she chattered. "Dalmatius is afraid of his shadow—"

"No, of course you're not a coward. You were very brave when you were lost—"

"I was held! I was held! Was I held? Was I lost? Nobody knows, nobody knows, nobody knows—"

Her voice shrilled on a rising panic.

"Stop," he said in the frosty voice. "There, that's better. Now I'll stay with you until you go to sleep. Think of how nice it will be to see the town when you're better, and if you're good I'll take you for a ride in my car. You've never been in a car have you? It goes much faster than the train you came in on—"

"I was on a train and I never knew. Oh, oh, oh," she wailed like a person obsessed with major tragedy.

"Shushhhh, there are lots more trains if you'll go to sleep. We're going to buy you some new clothes—"

"Blue?" she asked faintly.

"Any colour you like."

"Could I have something not made of wool?"

"Yes, yes, whatever you want. Do you feel sleepy?"

"Yes," she sighed; "if you won't let me go."

"No, I won't let you go until you're asleep, and when I go there's a nice nurse to look after you. Don't talk, don't talk…"

Later, years later it seemed, the centre of her blackness was pierced by a throb. Like a pebble dropped into a pool it went widening away in painful extension. At first it beat in her mind until there was a hot report from her hands and feet. This time she did not cry out. She was sick but sane and capable of endurance. Once or twice she opened her eyes to try and identify her surroundings. Finding she was indifferent, she shut out the pool of light, the blur of the dressing-table and the dim square of the window. Where was the man with the cold quiet voice, and the women in white robes? She wished she had a drink. Where did they keep the bucket in the hospital? How silly she was! Here they had taps and deep white baths and basins. Her mother had told her about them. What was she hearing? Whispers by her door.

"…fairies. They say she's fey."

"Pure Irish, I'd say, by the sound of her. I know the Shore she comes from. I was there once, and it took me back to Grimm. Heard about the money?"

"Yes, imagine! Rags to riches, and all for a little Bay Noddy. I suppose she's as common as bog-water."

"Not a bit of it. Very appealing, with a beautiful face and a lovely little body. Her people must have been decent. Dr. Fitz Henry says there's no malnutrition beyond exposure and starvation."

"He's all burned up about her."

"And how! I've never seen him like it before. When he gave her the hypo he waited to see how it would react. Then we sat like a pair of dummies until she woke up with a dreadful screech—"

"I heard it! It woke number nine."

"He talked to her like an angel and held her in his arms until she went to sleep. I was as much use as an extra degree of fever. If she was older I'd say it was hearts and flowers for doctor."

"If it is, it's his first crush. They say he's more in love with that old barracks of his—"

"It's not his barracks. It's Lady Fitz Henry's. He gets it at her death. They passed over the eldest son. He got a wad from a maiden aunt."

"They're as poor as rats, since the war."

"Well, I wouldn't mind being as poor as they are. She got a cold hundred thousand insurance, even though the business failed."

"That's poor for the Place. They say the coal bill is a thousand a year. My father often speaks of their grand days when the gates were flung open to let her ride out. And now she walks."

"But how she walks—shush, there's the bell...."

The whispers ceased. It sounded like a Cinderella story: coaches and horses, rags to riches. Was she Cinderella? She had no ugly sisters, but she had many ugly brothers. How pleasant it would be to live with men who had voices and hands like the man of last night.

A dim white figure stooped over her bed, and a nurse found herself staring into glazed yellow eyes.

"My dear, why didn't you call?" she said kindly. "I was only at the door."

"Could I have a drink?" she whispered.

Ministrations helped her towards the morning. It seemed an infinity of time, an endlessness she'd never known before. The three days in the woods had been timeless, past weight or weariness in the light frost of her mind. Dozing fitfully, she woke to another face.

Outside the sun was shining and the world sounded very big. Once the unfamiliar noises would have wooed her to exploration, and she would have had to follow the richness of bells and blasts of whistles and horns.

"Are you awake, Mary?"

"Yes," she said unhappily, opening her eyes on a girl with waved hair under a starched cap so far on the back of her head that it seemed to rest by the will of God.

"How do you keep your cap on?" she asked with faint interest.

The nurse was young with blue eyes, brown lashes and a plump face. When she smiled Mary Immaculate felt a little better.

"With a very little pin," she whispered.

"It's very pretty."

The nurse laughed and smoothed her patient's hair. "Now I'm going to make your bed, give you a bath and feed you like a little baby."

"I was bathed yesterday," she said politely.

There was a laugh, gay but not loud. "So you were, Mary, but here we do it every day and sometimes twice."

Mary Immaculate felt shocked.

"You must be very dirty people."

The laugh was louder, but it did not hurt her with its quality or vigour.

"You're in hospital, my dear, and hospitals are very clean places."

With closed eyes she endured a hospital routine, and only opened them once to say reproachfully: "You do queer things to me." It was the dismay of a body that had always been well. The nurse was soothing.

"Don't mind, Mary. Just relax and leave everything to me."

"Where's Mom?" she asked without interest.

"At home and very glad, I expect, to think you're so well looked after. I know Dr. Fitz Henry will let her know how you are. You've got the youngest doctor in town."

"Have I?" she asked, not sure of her blessings. "Is he the man with the barracks and the mother that's a Lady instead of a woman?"

"You'll find out in time, dear. Don't talk. I want you to save your strength."

Later the room became filled with people, depleting her with their volume. First came a tall dark man, followed by two women in white and another bearing a tray stacked with packages. What were they going to do with her? Panic glazed her eyes and made her mouth dry as dust. The tall man made an easy approach to her bed and slipped his hand round one of her wrists. The four throbs in her body were centralised in her heart. Some motion sent the women away and made her own pretty nurse turn her back and gaze out of the window.

From a dark six-foot height Philip Fitz Henry smiled at his patient.

"How are you?" he asked in the voice of the previous night.

A dry tongue went over her lips.

"Sit down, please," she whispered. "You're so big."

His hair was shining and black and inclined to curl on the top of a neat head. His brow was high, white, making a shelf over thoughtful brown eyes. A chiselled nose made a classical profile, ending in nostrils arching in a decided curve. Underneath the nose, which was the feature of the face, a straight mouth defied its curves by shutting itself in a thin line. The chin held a cleft rather than a dimple.

"I know how you feel," he said, watching his patient with cool brown eyes. "Because I'm tall and well you feel smaller and weaker."

"Yes," she said, surprised. "How did you know? Do you always know how people feel inside?"

He shook his head, and she began to admire his face.

"I'm afraid not," he said, gravely. "But I understand feelings from a professional standpoint."

Habit was strong. "What's that?" she asked instantly.

"Being a doctor," he explained, "and trying to find out what makes people miserable."

"Oh," she said, losing some of her throbs. "I've never had a doctor before."

"Not even when you were born, I suppose?"

"Of course not. I was born in a boat, and those that weren't have Mrs. Whelan. She goes round with an axe and puts it under the bed to cut the pains in two."

A very long hand went across the doctor's mouth.

"I see," he said gravely. "Haven't you ever been ill yourself, Mary? I'd like to know how strong you are. Have you had measles, scarlet-fever—"

"I've had nothing," she said, frowning over her inexperience. "Once I had a bit of whooping-cough, but Pop cured me. It went, overnight."

"That was quick for whooping-cough," he smiled, as if he had all the time in the world. "What did your father do?"

The doctor knew she was calm again. She was looking at him with acute sight, and taking an interest in her story.

"Pop caught a little trout, alive, and brought him home in a bucket. Then he made me open my mouth wide, and he held the trout down my throat. That was all. Then he put the little trout back in the river, and it swam away with the whooping-cough."

Her eyes explored the effect of her story as if doubting its efficacy in this world of bottles and bandages. There was a choke from the window. Her nurse was trying not to laugh.

"Did you like that cure, Mary?" asked the doctor. "It seems mean."

"Yes," she sighed. "It wasn't my fault. I often thought of the little trout whoopin' in the river."

He leant towards her bed, and she noticed that his arched nostrils moved very slightly. He seemed to be saying some thing with his nose. Above, his eyes looked warm, as if he found her nice to look at. She wondered why she had been afraid.

"Mary…"

She was beginning to like the way he said it, and the long value of each syllable. Her name sounded nice in her own ears.

"Mary," he asked, "may I have the nurses back now? We want to dress your hands and feet."

"Oh, is that what they're for? Sure it takes a lot of them for such a little job."

He laughed, making a sign to the nurse at the window.

The crowd would be back again.

"Doctor?" she asked hurriedly.

"Just a minute, Miss New." The nurse came to rest by the door.

Mary Immaculate was frowning, looking at the lumps representing her hands. From them she looked at her doctor. Very gravely they stared into each other's eyes.

The child had listened all her life—to the wind, the sea, the waterfall and the lap of quiet ponds. By placing her ear to the ground she had heard the Little People. By easing into silence and darkness she could tell when they were friendly. By finding the mute voice of Molly Conway in her eyes she had earned a rescuer. Now she listened to the silence of Philip Fitz Henry. She could hear him—as trust, sense, protection, and a reassurance of every day.

In his turn he saw a regrettable depletion of life, a stripping of flesh revealing anatomical perfection, the dulling of hair and eyes that must shine golden in health. The child had been flung to him, like a frozen ghost, mute in her call for rehabilitation. She was the colour of a life he did not know, the beat of the natural earth and an unquenchable spirit surviving unusual ordeal. Not a word of fear had been uttered in memory of the white loneliness that must have been hers in the icy forests. Was she so much part of them that she could outstrip their hostility?

"What is it?" he asked encouragingly. "Anything I can do?..."

"Would you please write to my mother? Tell her..."

Her eyes explored him again.

"Yes?" he asked, taking a pad from his pocket and unscrewing the top of a fountain pen. "I'm to tell your mother—"

"Tell her," she said, taking the plunge, "that I didn't make the ceremony at the door, and not to blame the Sacred Heart for my foolishness. Tell her the fairies came up to my feet and danced all round. Tell her the slice of bread was fine. Not one of them could get me."

The doctor was frowning, but writing carefully.

"There were no fairies, of course, Mary. You were lightheaded from hunger." His voice was conversational, but extinguished life in the fairies.

"The slice of bread saved me," she contradicted flatly.

"Very well," agreed the doctor. "Anything else?"

"Ask her to give something to Molly Conway. That's all."

She closed her eyes, feeling as if she'd been to Confession.

"Quite enough," said the doctor. "Will you obey me, and rest now, for the whole morning?"

"Yes," she said. "I'm that tired."

The dressings were accepted with fortitude. All the time the doctor was tending her hands and feet she was wondering why anyone so nice did not believe in fairies. Something told her they might return when she felt well again.

SIX

"NO HOUSE WITHOUT MOUSE, NO THRONE WITHOUT THORN."

The square of her window was blue, underlined with yellow. Through the raised sash the wind blew, warmed with sun. Pendent in the air, spring swung like a censer burning winter away. It was a morning when the mind jumped out of bed before the body.

Mary Immaculate woke with a bounce. For the first time since leaving the Cove she felt impelled to explore the outside world. With dangling legs she was held by the thought of her doctor. His voice demanded obedience and his hands suggested restraint. Could she heed him when her ears heard a challenge of daring? What was his world like? At least she could look. There was no one to stop her. The night nurse had been dismissed, and Miss New came with a rich peal of bells ringing eight o'clock. With bandaged feet skimming the floor she craned her neck for a view of the town. She could see it was tall, with four hill-drops to the sea, but which clump of trees concealed the doctor's barracks?

Fitz Henry Place was old, in a town with hills barely parted to make an exit to the sea. It was a wooden city with little architectural beauty. Four times in a century fire had been a scourge. Newfoundland was a country where wind and fire could travel as one fury. Buildings kept rising from ashes, like a phoenix growing plainer with each revival. On the outskirts of the town the Place stood in two acres of ground, with its shabby paint screened by sprawling trees. Peering through, the outside world had its own way of ascertaining Fitz Henry fortunes. A great name in the history of the country, general prosperity could be estimated by the state of their paint.

The wealth of Newfoundland was subject to the caprice of weather and the varied richness of its waters. The wind could disperse the cod and seal and blow them together another year. Prosperity fluctuated. The sea and ice-fields could be fruitful, and fortune sure. Then the foreign markets might decline, leaving products rotting in their sheds. The country existed with its mind on the state of Spain, Greece, Portugal, the West Indies and South America.

It was 1931 when Mary Immaculate became the patient of Philip Fitz Henry. Then the paint of the Place was shabby, and Lady Fitz Henry lived inside blistered walls. Diminution of wealth was little compared to the desolation of her heart. Change had come with shattering death, and when her life was cut in half she became recluse from social life. The Place felt for her, knowing nothing but Fitz Henry joys and sorrows. It gave back the voices of its own, rich with the recollection of happier days. The trees bent over her, shadowing her sombre walk. When the wind blew its frequent melancholy she accepted it as the bite of her adopted country. Entwining herself in its roots, she lived to nurture the Place for her youngest son.

Reared to five stories in 1846, it was a tall house with a mansard roof. Discouraged by holocausts, people built without beauty. Barely completed, a fire razed all before it on its way to the Place. Dazed crowds left their ashes to see the largest sacrifice of all. Inside were the reputed treasures of wealth: mahogany imported on a sailing-vessel from England; carpets, pictures, china, crystal chandeliers: and the whole wonder of a Regency drawing-room transplanted from a London house. Flankers flew ahead to threaten all that, while heat blistered the new white paint. Destruction seemed inevitable, and the house was looted of everything light enough to carry away. When heat was scorching the young trees wind became capricious, distracting its mate over the hills. The Place stood its first assault. Later in the same year a gale tried to tear it up by its roots, but it endured with the loss of two chimneys, four windows and thirty-two trees. Years passed before its second fire-peril, coming a year after the last owner of Fitz Henry and Sons, shipowners and fish exporters, brought a bride out from England. She had been born in Quetta, of parents with Colonial experience. Accustomed to adaptation, the windswept Colony did not defeat her. In 1892 her first-born was delivered during the fourth holocaust of a century. Aloof in her bed she breathed smoke, seeing her room turn crimson. The faces of people around her were blood-red when she saw her son wriggle like a salamander in a core of heat. When the Place seemed doomed she permitted herself to be carried downstairs, preceded by her maid, making a witless exit with a pillow. With her son and her jewel-case beside her, Mrs. Fitz Henry lay as detached as an aristocrat in a tumbril, but when she passed the dining room she bade Hannah drop her pillow and fetch the tea service saved from the fire of '46. Arranging her salvage, she was carried to the farthest corner of the garden. As far as he could, her husband guarded her from intrusion, but crowds seethed round, lost to all sense of privacy. All held the spoil of snatching hands. She remembered women with washboards, men with flower-pots and one unforgettable boy holding a hen relentlessly to his side. Fitz Henry Place was looted again. Useless to protest. She lay supine while Hannah held wet clothes to her baby's nose. Once again the wind saved the Place, but it was in the imperviousness of her husband to a vanishing background that she began to understand his country better. From that day she became a one-minded woman nurturing a love fanned by fire. His interests became hers, embracing even the faint touch of flamboyance distinguishing him from any successful Englishman. During their frequent Atlantic crossings and in England she noticed his relaxation, but when they steamed in his own harbour he became taut as if bracing himself for bolder living. A great figure in the financial life of the country, he was knighted early in the new century, and his wife became Lady Fitz Henry with the ease of a woman who had always been gracious. It was inevitable she should de-velop a reputation for exclusiveness and local snobbery. Preoccupation with her family made her emerge merely for spacious events like the

Navy, Government House or eminent visitors. Four sons were born to her, David, Arthur, John and, after an interval of five years, her youngest son, Philip.

David, born on the day of the fire, did not shape towards the family traditions. He disdained business and could not understand the difference in fish-tails. Cures were a foreign language to him, and ships means of transportation to enjoy the surface of the sea. What swam under did not concern him. His father had to accept it in view of his affable repudiation of such knowledge. The fruit of the ice-fields brought the same reaction. The killing of the seals distressed him, and when one of his father's captains told him they wept real tears, he no longer went to the wharves when the laden ships came in. His brothers, Arthur and John, had no such repugnance. They could transform the nursery floor into ice-fields and dash at cushions and mats with gaffs and scalping-knives. Whooping like Indians, they would pile up pans, topping them with their father's flag. Their dearest possession was a white-coat with the tears in its eyes reduced to shining glass. They were the promise of Fitz Henry and Sons, the product of their father's line. When Philip was a little boy tumbling round the floor in awe of his magnificent brothers, it was David who always picked him up. Similar in appearance David and Philip were their mother's sons, with her pale face, black hair, prowlike nose with nostrils arched in delicate disdain.

August 1914 found David a dilettante with enough money from a maiden aunt to keep him in comfort for life. Arthur and John were assimilating the ramifications of Fitz Henry and Sons. Philip was on the Atlantic, returning from his first year of English school. He was thirteen, with a fixed determination to be a doctor. He landed to find his brothers on the eve of volunteering and his father grim with worry. Cargoes with war risks, the Mediterranean ports closing, fishermen leaving their bays and coves—it was a little more than fluctuation. As if to pursue the down-curve of his fortunes, two bad fisheries ensued, and later an appalling sealing disaster. Steaming in like a hearse garlanded with ice, one of his ships unloaded a crew of frozen men. With the memory of their stark bodies in his mind, Philip Fitz Henry heard of the toll of Beaumont Hamel. In the harvest of one day Arthur was killed instantly, John blown to pieces and David severely wounded.

Resilience was almost spent, and house and heart felt the same impoverishment. Paint dulled, grass became overgrown, dust settled on the unused rooms. The Place mourned for its gallant sons, feeling the drag of springless feet. Hannah crept round after her mistress, trying to perform three people's work. The sons had been her children!

In England Philip waited for David to be transported from France. During that period he received his last letter from his father.

My Dear Son,

Your mother and I speak of you particularly, realising your desolation from the loss of your brothers. It seems incredible that they are dead. We could be convinced of it more if they had lain for a while in the Place. I seem to require that much evidence. We are glad you did not risk coming out. Lonely as it is for you, it is a comfort to know one of us will be there when David gets to England. His report said wounds multiple, and he appears to be full of shrapnel. Much of it is innocuous, but a large piece in the knee makes him unfit for further service. I enclose his letter. It explains certain things and the fact that he is married. Your mother took it with great understanding, and we have heard from the girl's people. They seem to be solid financially if a trifle eccentric. As you know, the firm is hard hit and, with Arthur and John gone, its continuity in our name seems impossible. Neither you nor David are business men. It is useless to regret such things when there are greater losses to consider. Perhaps you are wondering why I talk so finally, when I might carry on myself. The fact is, my days are numbered. I have had two heart attacks with excessive pain in the arms and chest. I know it is angina and the word is a knell to worry and action. The first attack I kept from your mother, as it occurred in my office; but now she is aware of my condition. A magnificent woman, the sort that makes a man regret his hour has struck. This is the year of our Silver Jubilee. We intended it to be such an occasion, with all of you home. However, our tradition has trained us to accept acts of God without the waste of rebellion.

With regard to the Place. Two years ago I made it over to your mother. For her security I have always carried a hundred thousand life insurance, which will be hers entirely and yours after her death. There will be nothing from the business. Your education is assured. That sum I set aside in good years. I suggest you finish your English school and enter a Canadian University. It will keep you closer to your mother, and make your return easier should she need you. Further, a combination of that kind equips a man better for life on this side of the water. I am writing to David of this. Some of it is his own suggestion. He has acquitted himself most creditably, and we are very proud of him. With his temperament he hated war more than most men. I hope he will get invalided home and bring his wife out.

To you I commend your mother and the Place. Four generations of continuity in this country is a great deal. It is a life so many leave when fortune is made. Age makes one conscious of the long springs and the bitter winds. It is foolish of a man to wish to dispose of property beyond one generation, but in spite of that I wish the Place could stay in our name. Your mother's income cannot support it, but in time a successful practice will give you the augmentation. Your ability and our name will help towards that end. David will come and go, and I trust keep his rooms in the Place. From this moment I feel I am passing you a great responsibility, and it means the curtailment of youth and all its privileges. Your brothers were brought up more spaciously, with everything we could give them. Acts of God, my son! I try to dwell on that. We have been subject so often to the winds and the waves.

And so I leave you, your mother and the Place.

Your affectionate father,
    PHILIP FITZ HENRY

David's letter was peculiarly David.

Dear Father,

It is understanding of you to excuse me from giving details of the action. At present it is too close to see, but now that it is over I am glad I did not make a complete ass of myself. It would have been so fatally easy. War is uncomfortable, and so very inglorious and dirty. I wonder if anybody enjoys exalted moments. What remains of me is not much use for further service. I had a nice sprinkling of shrapnel and a few O.S. pieces in my chest and knee. The bits that lodged in my knee are the worst. They tell me I am going to have a decoration. I remember doing something with a machine-gun, but it seems so ridiculous. I intended to make myself as inconspicuous as possible, only I tripped over Arthur. He looked asleep on the ground. I was raging. However, there was no time to say vale *to one's brother. The rest is just noise and bewilderment and the proverbial waking up to hear someone say*

'*Drink this, please*'. *I see nothing in war to commend it, and my mind seethes with heresies.*

I cabled about my marriage which I trust will not be too great a shock. This is the day of impulsive actions. I found Felice being a Fany in Calais. Like myself she was thoroughly out of step with her world and agonising over a small kitten in undesirable surroundings. She is at her best with lame ducks, and wants a world where a cat, a dog and a bird can lie down with the lion and the lamb. Other than that she plays the piano divinely, speaks languages and runs S.P.C.A.'s in unwarlike days. Her mother went mad round fifty and Felice is haunted she may do the same thing. Her mother began by hiding under trees. In view of their preponderance round the Place I intend to take a cottage by the sea.

Just at present it's impossible to speak of the other two, but because of their going I must mention the Place. We have discussed it before, but this is final. Let's not be stupid because I am the eldest son. Everything must go to young Philip. He is the breed with roots, steadiness and a faculty to stay in grooves. Besides, he has a sense of duty which I have not. He will be steadfast, and the occasional tempers will be knocked out of him at school. I have my inheritance from Aunt Sarah. It was good of her not to marry, and to hoard up her pile for me. Dear old skinflint! I used to think she was poor. It's the first time I have ever approved of thrifty spinsters.

It may comfort Mater to know that we three were together intermittently ever since we landed in France. The rest is silence until I see her. It may be easier then.

Your affectionate,
    DAVID

While Philip Fitz Henry's special patient was craning her neck to see where he lived, Lady Fitz Henry was stepping into her emerging garden. The dirty edges of the snow looked like the dwindling of a moth-eaten blanket. Through a clot of last year's leaves green tongues poked through, showing evidence of a prodigal autumn planting.

Tall in her garden Lady Fitz Henry relaxed in the sun. Winter was taut, a season of whipcord winds, wearying to the flesh. Spring told her she was muted, but not extinguished when she could feel the pulse of the earth.

A white-skinned brunette, her sixty-four years were only apparent in skin-sag and fine lines round her eyes. Her nose was ageless, disdaining any toll the years could take. Eyes were brown, but their colour was dead. A trifle myopic, pupil and iris merged into one. Stooping to poke in the earth, she displayed the suppleness of a slender woman. It was in her hands that age was evident. Grey-white they looked bleak, and blue round the long, ridged nails.

With a quietude of content she picked her way back to the house. Inside, the hall was square with an overhead gallery of wrought-iron uprights, topped with a walnut rail. From a window at the curve of the stairs sunlight streamed in a shaft. It subtracted from walls rendered sooty by furnace-heat. It embellished the gleam of wood and the mellow paint of English landscapes. It made an ebony cap of Philip's head as he ran downstairs.

"Morning, dear. I heard you go out."

From his considerable height he barely stooped to touch his mother's cheek with his own. As the faces came together their similarity was arresting. Carved noses jutted toward each other with a unity of design.

At breakfast in a wine-red dining-room with chaste furniture, she poured tea from the Georgian tea-pot saved from the fires. Sitting upright and eating little, she gazed at a conservatory lighting one side of the room. She was enjoying the velvet bloom of a cineraria when she heard Philip's voice.

"Mater, will you do something for me this morning? It's fit for you to go out."

"Certainly, my son. It's a lovely day. It makes me long to see David."

"He'll be out in June, dear, and I'll be able to get away in July for two weeks' salmon-fishing."

"You need the rest, Philip. It's been a hard winter. I wish Dave would stay out. It would be more company for you."

"It's the winds, Mater. They pick out his wounds, and Felice doesn't like the wind in the trees."

"M'mm," said his mother dryly. Tolerant as she was, it was dislike a little beyond her. "What do you want me to do, my son?"

Philip was smiling at a pair of eggs. "See somebody who understands the wind in the trees."

"Your little girl," she said at once.

He gave her a quick look. "How did you know?"

"Easily. You pay her so many visits. It's a remarkable survival."

"Medical miracle!"

Still looking at the cineraria, Lady Fitz Henry pondered out loud. "Philip, why wasn't she afraid? It's uncanny...."

"I don't understand that side of it." Philip frowned with definite pleats in his white brow. "I'm not a neurologist, but she might be an elemental for all the experience has affected her nerves. There was so much nonsense talked about her."

"Perhaps the fairies did look after her," suggested his mother with a small smile.

The pleats in Philip's brow looked jangled. "I've been trying to diminish that idea. She's a mass of superstition, but she's lovely to look at. At least she is now. The modelling of her face is perfect, and her skin...She's something to see after some patients."

"No doubt," said his mother, regarding him with deeper interest. He was smiling to himself, and she thought his face looked younger. "Perhaps she bears out your father's theory that the best blood in this country is in the Bays. Many old families came out in the early days, and there's that odd tale of the line from the Irish Princess."

Philip laughed. "I don't know about that, Mater. Her people are simple fisherfolk, but I hope Mary will have a better chance with this endowment. I couldn't bear to think of her going back to that narrow life."

"It's the crock of gold, my son." Lady Fitz Henry's voice was ordinary, but she was regarding her son with a mother's scrutiny. "Is she quite recovered?" she asked gently.

"Almost, and I feel so pleased about her feet. I had to fight the surgeon against amputation. We had many a wrangle, and he washed his hands of it and said I could take the consequence if gangrene set in."

"You put your foot down," said his mother, smiling.

"This time it was a good foot," he said, smiling back.

"Philip, are you planning to pay yourself out of that money?"

Philip put down his knife and fork in frank surprise. "Certainly not, Mater. The little thing is poor. I'll pay the hospital, which is considerable, and the rest I'll save for education if the parents consent. They're not to touch it so the agreement runs."

His mother regarded him with smiling approval, but she touched his most vulnerable point when she said: "You'll never paint the house if you're so prodigal with visits."

He went on eating, unperturbed. "A doctor loves a fight, Mater, and I did some research on frostbite. I feel personally responsible for her...."

"M'mm, did you hear from the mother?"

"Yes, I did."

Putting his hand in his pocket he produced a letter in a cheap envelope.

"It's a curious letter, Mater. I'll read it to you."

Dear Sir,

It was a Christian act on your part to write me. I've said a prayer for your house. To think that my child is getting better, and I made up my mind she was dead. When they took her away I felt she was gone forever. It's like the dreams of the dead. Between waking, you think it's not so that they're gone, then you come to and you know that they are. Her living seems as likely as that—

"An understanding woman," interrupted his mother thoughtfully. "I dream of your father that way."

I'm glad about the money. It seems a wonderful lot, but the poor can't think past a dollar or two. I don't know all that it means, but it might lift her out of the life I don't want for her. It comforts me to think of her looked after by one of your name. Your father, and your father before you, bought the fish from our men and always treated them right. I'd be a grateful woman to hear again, and to get advice about my child. Lovely she was and she dazzled my eyes.

Respectfully yours,
    JOSEPHINE KEILLY.

Philip folded up his letter, finishing his breakfast without comment. There was a pause, during which Lady Fitz Henry gazed out unseeingly.

"Strange," she said after a while, "the mother speaks of her in the past tense."

"Yes," he agreed; "it looks that way."

Rising from the table, he bent over her, putting his arm round her shoulders. "Will you meet me at twelve-thirty, Mater? I'll be busy until then."

"Very well, my son. I'll be at the hospital."

When Philip saw his patient her bed was pulled by the window. The radiant day had gone into her face.

"Look," she said. "Miss New has fancied me up."

A hair-ribbon made a jaunty bow on her head, and her shoulders were covered in pale pink silk.

Then she saw Lady Fitz Henry.

At once the child acclaimed a quality she did not know. The lady seemed impressive, grand, with a grandeur that was not dependent upon externals. Her imaginative mind associated grandeur with velvets, trains, crowns and the ermines of a fairy-tale world. True the lady wore a silver fox. Mary Immaculate knew it at once, because the men often brought them home from Labrador. It wasn't that! She couldn't look at the doctor's mother and not know. Her clothes were as harmonious as the smoothness of a shell round a kernel. Gloves enclosed her hands without restriction, and all of the fingers were smoothed down to the tips. Instantly there came a picture of her own mother's hands in Mass on Sunday mornings. Gloves and a pair of grey stays represented Josephine's difference between Sunday and Monday. Many times, kneeling beside her, Mary Immaculate had heard the creak of the corsets and noticed the cushion of her fingers seep damply through the gloves. Beyond the wet spots, there were always points the fingers could not reach.

Contrasts were beginning to shape in her mind. As she had absorbed the quality of her doctor she absorbed the fine emanation of his mother. Lambent with inner delight she greeted her without consciousness. Her mother's world was civil but not servile.

"Oh!" she said, seeing the beautiful nose. "You're the dead spit of him. You've got his nose on your face. You're both lovely," she finished sunnily.

Philip laughed but his face expressed relief when his mother's finger tilted his patient's chin. Some transfusion of gaiety went into her answering voice.

"I'm his mother, my dear. Don't you think he might have my nose?"

"Sure," she agreed happily. "Do your nostrils do it too?"

It was a long time since Lady Fitz Henry had heard so many personal remarks.

"Perhaps," she admitted graciously. "I know David's do. He's my eldest son, and he finds his own reason for it. Many years ago we had a French ancestress who got caught up in the Revolution. David says she couldn't express her disdain in her voice, so it went into her nose."

"I expect it smelt bad," said Mary Immaculate, wrinkling up her own nose. "Did they cut off her head?"

"No," said her visitor gravely. "If they had they would have cut off our heads too. She escaped to England and founded a line of noses."

It was a story after the child's own heart. Laughing on an unrestrained note, she made her elders laugh with her.

Miss New placed a chair for Lady Fitz Henry, and as she sat down Philip laid a long, cone-shaped parcel on the bed.

"Open it, my dear," said Lady Fitz Henry, "and see what I've brought you."

"Me?" she gasped, with wild incredulity.

While she tore excitedly at the paper her visitor drew her own conclusions. Beauty was there, naturalness and an ingenuous unconcern for careless chatter. It was the attitude of a child so happy in itself that the world was bound to fit in. Mary Immaculate evinced her own quality in the way her motion was stilled over flowers.

"Oh!" she said wonderingly. "Oh!"

Surrounded by tendrils of fern, cultivated carnations lay on the bed. From the open paper fragrance rose like a march of cool cloves. Hands, still bearing a reddened reaction to frostbite, touched the heads of flawless blooms.

"What are they?" she asked. "I've never seen anything like them before."

"They're carnations, Mary. Don't you know them? Smaller varieties grow in gardens."

"No, ma'am, I don't know them," she said, holding up a flower and cupping it in her hand. "We don't have flower gardens—just potatoes and turnips. But I know a lot about the flowers growing in the woods." Bringing the flowers to her face she smelt, with eyes closed like a cat content with some rich morsel.

"How could they grow in winter, ma'am? There's still snow on the hills."

"In a hothouse, my dear; a place that's heated and made of glass. Won't you let your nurse put them in water?"

"Yes, ma'am," she said with instant obedience. "They're the nicest thing that ever happened to me. If I could hold on to them."

There was a shadow in the voice, and a sigh for the fading of beauty.

"There will be more flowers, Mary. When you're well. Philip will bring you out to see my garden."

Her son walked to the door with a buoyant step.

"Mater, I have to visit another patient. I'll be back for you later."

The child's smile followed him out and then came to rest on his mother.

"He's been like St. Joseph," she said in a full voice, conceding her visitor a knowledge of saintly qualities.

Lady Fitz Henry's response was benign, arresting the child with its emanation of large repose. At once her teeming veins flowed calmer, as if her stream of life widened to an estuary round the quiet woman. Shrillness was muted in an effort to emulate grace. Shyness did not oppress her, and response was ingenuous and friendly. Nor was she on her best behaviour as she had been when Father Melchior came to call. Lady Fitz Henry showed no inclination to point a moral or extinguish the Little People with a frosty note in her voice. The flavour of conversation was interest, inviting a stream of artless prattle. Unconsciously the child painted a strange picture of herself, climbing the heads to watch the sea, lying in the forests waiting for the Little People, or crouching, predacious, for observation of some wood-creature. Flowers gave them a bond, and the visitor could talk of her cloth of gold crocus while the child babbled of bouncing-bets and calvary flowers. It seemed a strange contact with reserves laid down in a spontaneous desire to please.

There was an element of novelty in visiting a hospital where illness was not mentioned. The child leaned forward in her bed as if frostbite, inflammation and incipient gangrene were distant ordeals. Lady Fitz Henry was more than capable of disguising vigilant scrutiny. Neither did she show the smallest sign when her ears received an indisputable imitation of her own voice. It came experimentally, grew stronger, while a secret smile hovered round the child's mouth. She looked triumphant, as if the veneer of culture could be hers for the asking. Eyes were lambent, with an animal yellow, resembling a hound starting delicately on a chase. When asked if she felt lonely without her people, the reply was forth right and spontaneous.

"No, ma'am, not much. This is an interesting place. I'm quite close to the operating-room and the nurses tell me about the groans that go past. Sometimes they go by with just a smell, but when they have little operations they wake up and nearly always cry. The men make most noise, and sometimes they curse. No, ma'am, I don't want to go home at all. Then when the operations are over the nurses read to me, and there's the doctor, he comes twice a day, and often three times."

It was so much the natural truth that there was no room for filial shock. Lady Fitz Henry seemed to understand. When her son returned she was standing by the bed, looking down at a glowing face. But she shook hands in a grave adult way.

"Would you like me to come again, Mary?"

"Would you, ma'am?" she said with flattering awe. "I knew 'twas a day for the wonderful to come. Now I can look forward to your voice and not back."

Philip laughed, touching his patient as if he couldn't help it.

"Are you sure, Mary, you were born in a skiff?"

"I mean every word," she said sunnily; "though Mom says you catch more flies with molasses than vinegar."

Her head was back and she was laughing, laughing with a face of white incandescence, sun-illumined. She looked like a wild wood-thing about to spring off a leash. Her mouth was open on even teeth and Philip's sharp eyes saw a tiny cavity. Instinct stirred in him to rush her to a dentist to preserve the white perfection of her mouth.

Lady Fitz Henry had a sudden desire to give the child a haircut and a voice to match her face and body. She had a sense of having witnessed a supreme exhibition of classlessness. On a bedside table there was a copy of *Through the Looking Glass*, and for a moment she saw inside where Humpty Dumpty was explaining the meaning of "slithy"—lithe and active. She left the hospital feeling it was a "brillig" day.

Back in her Cove Josephine was reading her second letter from Philip Fitz Henry, while her mind recorded thanks for the consideration of a mother. Surrounded by her work, her eyes travelled to a statue of St. Anthony. There was the source who would find the way for her child. As she prayed her mouth gave a half-agonised quirk. She was remembering that her daughter had turned the Saint to the wall because he failed to find her lead pencil. Josephine decided to make a Novena! Nine days' intercession would open their doors and their hearts. It was the will of God!

SEVEN

"ALL SAILS AND NO BALLAST."

D id the house welcome her? She
would know by the sound.

The sea-voices that used to enter her window in the Cove had
changed to the wind in Fitz Henry trees.

She lay in bed wide-eyed and vigilant. Between open curtains
moonlight filtered through branches bearing secret leaves. Dark and
patulous the trees bent pliant in the wind. It seemed to worry them in
the same way that the sea had worried the beach. There must be still
nights when the branches rested, like the nights in the Cove when the
sea slept against the cliffs.

She listened inside. There were cracks and creaks like the bend of
old joints, and long sighs round the window-sills. The floors and walls
settled. A tap dripped in a marble basin in her room. The sound
soothed her. Let the tap drip on! It was the symbol of her new life.

The house received her! It held but one hostility and she knew
it already. This dislike was deep and dark, mute as an ancient
rock. Hannah was old, loose in the skin and disapproving as Mrs.
Houlihan. The old woman worshipped the family and resented her
intrusion.

Her new mater was great, grand, with manners like a queen. She
was the same every day and wore no special dress on Sunday. She did

not draw attention to her mistakes until they were alone. After her
first meal in the dining-room, Philip had been dismissed.

"My dear, I think it would be wise to have Lilas back. We'll
pretend it's the meal over again. If I show you once do you think
you'll remember again? There's a small proverb I like very much:
'It's disgraceful to stumble against the same stone twice.' Do you
understand what I mean?"

Mary Immaculate did! Such word-painting was the breath of life to
her. They sat bolt upright while Lilas passed empty dishes. Aptitude
had earned praise and a promise of reward.

"Mary dear, I shall question you at the end of a week to see how
much you have retained. If I find it satisfactory Philip will take you to
the cinema."

She had something to earn!

Sleek and warm between linen sheets she slept to the tune of Fitz
Henry trees.

When her adoption was mooted Lady Fitz Henry was ready. An intangible bond had grown up between herself and the child. A spiritual
loneliness and the melancholy of winter made Mary Immaculate seem
like ardent spring. The depletion of the house helped, and possibly the
weight of Josephine's prayers. Mother and son were drab, heavy with
many memories. Philip's wish was obvious, but had she not displayed
the qualities suitable for his mother's direction he would have returned
her to the Cove. When Lady Fitz Henry visited the child of her
own volition and went again and again, the venture became easy and
gradual.

Josephine had written characteristically.

Dear Sir,

*It's not unexpected what you plan to do. I never thought to get her back.
It will be like thinking of her passed on to Heaven. It would be a poor life
for such as her in the Cove. I saw that from her birth, and perhaps
this has come in answer to prayers. I've wondered if the sea gave her a
bit of wildness, and it's not wildness that's boldness—in the manner of
speaking. I mind what you say about taking her right over, and me and*

her Pop having no claim once the papers are signed. I can't say it's not hard, as she was the light of my life; but I wouldn't stand in her way. Her father says I can do as I like, as she was always my child and he'll have nothing to say. I'll sign the papers if you send them along. The Priest will instruct me where to put my name. For that, sir, I must speak about the religion. I know you are good people, but for one I can't see what happiness there is outside the Catholic faith. I would have her remain a Catholic and observe the rules of her Church. I'm sorry you don't have the jewel of faith yourself, but there's such a thing as invincible ignorance, and to them that haven't seen the light, God will be good. My child has. If she can remain a Catholic, I will give her up. If she can't, please send her back to the Cove. I don't hold the world above her hope of Heaven. If, sir, the unlikely happens that I ever come to town, can I visit her once?

Respectfully yours,
    JOSEPHINE KEILLY

Lady Fitz Henry had frowned a little. On reflection she made an announcement.

"The woman is sincere, Philip. Mary can go to Mass. Any bias will be mitigated by other associations. It's necessary to dilute a great deal of her training. Her mind is a medley of folk-lore and religion, and she compares everything to the elements and the Saints in Heaven."

In her rootless acceptance of her adoption Philip found grounds for concern.

"Mater, is it human to shed her past like that. She doesn't even mind leaving her mother."

His mother was easy and reassuring. "Natural enough, I think. It's merely sentimental to cling to the places where there's little harmony. I'm sure she made her own world. I understand her because she's so like David. He could always pass on to something else. If Mary ever belongs, it will be a development. There's one thing I see in her—"

"What?" he asked quickly as his mother paused.

Lady Fitz Henry went on like a woman trying to say something significant in an impersonal way.

"She will always have a life of her own. At present she lives in a world she can inhabit at any moment. A strict routine may eradicate that. But early years count, and she's very self-contained. To the possessive type that may be unsatisfactory. Again like David. Can you imagine him breaking his heart because one special thing went wrong?"

Philip frowned, speaking shortly. "No, he'd translate Catullus or something. His affections are not fixed."

"Quite wrong, my son," said his mother coolly. "His affections are very fixed but they can always expand. He and Felice have never had an estrangement, and I must admit before the war I thought Felice was the last girl I could anticipate. Marriage—"

"Like politics, makes strange bedfellows," he said lightly.

"The oddest people marry," said his mother impressively, as if he must receive the information seriously.

Philip looked as if he was ready to agree. Then he frowned again. "Will Mary be like that?" he asked vaguely.

"Perhaps not, if we make her one of ourselves, but it's wise to take people as they are, Philip, and not as one wishes them to be."

Philip went, conscious of a warning. On his way to a surgery in another part of the town he reflected. There was no fault in the child except in the things dividing her from himself. He worked with greater zest since she came. She had been an extremely co-operative patient, docile in his hands and Spartan in endurance of pain. Now she was where he could give her closer direction. She could be moulded! He turned his attention to his profession, convinced that he knew Mary better than his mother.

It was his wish to show her the rooms behind closed doors, and she stayed honourably outside until he could give her his leisure.

The drawing-room was fascinating in its chill formality and ornate fixtures, but it held the air of untenanted places. Heat was maintained to preserve the furniture, and Hannah kept it swept and dusted. In spite of its care it smelt of desolation. A tall white marble mantelpiece dominated it like an iceberg wall. Combined with the icicle chandelier Mary Immaculate had the feeling of a dead winter day. It was necessary to feel something from a room, and this did not give back the voices of the other parts of the house. Tables with gallery tops, cabinets holding glass and Chelsea figures, chairs with faded damask did not inspire her sense of touch.

"Philip," she asked, standing in the extreme centre of the room, "did you use it much, even when you were rich?"

"I didn't or any of my brothers. It was principally for entertaining. When the time came for me to come home we were too poor for parties. My mother was never a halfway woman, and if she couldn't give dinners with the right wines she didn't give any. After father's death she stopped forever, and I can't induce her to ask anyone in. She doesn't seem to want it. That's one of the reasons why I'm so glad to have you with us, Mary. I like to think of her with a fresh interest. You do try and please her a great deal. Mary..."

He paused and seated himself in a slender Hepplewhite chair in which he looked long and thin.

"Mary," he said, as if he were talking to a contemporary, "have you noticed how frail Mater's hands are?"

"Yes, I have, Philip," she said, sitting down on the extreme edge of a settee. "And her nails are not as pretty as the rest of her."

"Symptoms," he said with a little shrug. "Mater has a weak heart."

"Oh!" she said in illumination. "Is that why she gets dizzy when she stoops in the garden?"

"The very reason," he said with worried brown eyes. "I didn't know it was so noticeable. It's a point of honour with her not to fuss. You can save her a great deal by running up and down stairs. Don't pretend, you know, but make it unobtrusive and kind."

"Indeed I will," she said happily. "I love to wait on her and walk past the stairs and the gallery." Then as she digested the mater's weakness she frowned at her son.

"You're a doctor, why don't you do something?"

He gave a slight shrug accepting inadequacy.

"Worn-out organs can't be repaired, my dear. They can only be nurtured. Mater's grief was too repressed, and the strain took a toll of her heart. What are you frowning about? There's no special worry."

"I'm not worrying," she said reprovingly. "I'm trying to remember. They were always doing things with herbs and roots. There was crackerberry leaves for indigestion and coltsfoot for consumption, but hearts—what did Mrs. Whelan boil up for hearts? There was a man in the Cove as blue as a whort—"

Philip smiled with contented tolerance. "Would it be foxglove?" he asked helpfully.

"Philip, you know!"she said, springing towards him. "Can't we find some foxgloves?"

Rising, he put his hands on her shoulders.

"We have lots of it, Mary," he said gently; "in bottles, called digitalis. If Mater gets really ill she'll have every remedy known to man, but hearts are uncertain things."

His tone was natural but the child felt her mater slipping away. She had seemed so solid and permanent. It was like a heresy to think of death touching her. She had seen it often. It was public in the Cove. Shrouded windows and open doors, people rocking and moaning, and men carrying a long box up the slopes of the ravine. The child shivered. Chary and economical in her touch of others, she pressed her head against Philip's coat. Tall for her age, she came up to his breast.

"Philip," she said in distress; "don't let her die. Where would I be without her now?"

"With me," he said possessively. "You're my child."

In David's room she deserted him for places he did not want her to go.

On the second flat he threw open a door.

"David," he said, as if that were sufficient explanation.

"Oh!" she said entranced. "This looks like a lot of things."

"It is," he said dryly. "The result of many hobbies. When he comes out without Felice he stays here and drops back. When she comes they have a cottage about twelve miles from town."

"Don't you like her?" she asked acutely. "The house is so big it could hold as many wives as Bluebeard's."

"Yes, we like her, but she likes to flow over with cats and dogs and birds with broken wings. Then the cats eat the birds and the dogs fight with the cats and there's confusion, which the mater hates."

"Sure, they sound cracked," she said sunnily.

Stepping to a wall with faded paper she examined a picture. "Isn't that the Place falling down?"

"Yes, though I wonder you recognise it."

"I just can," she admitted.

Philip explained. "David's painting came after his music. He thought distortion looked easy, so he drew the Place falling down."

She wanted to ask what it all meant, but there was no time. David's room had zest. A small upright piano bore a stack of music, pictures hung on the walls in wild array, bits of sculpture stood peering from bits of china, books listed on a shelf and common glass jars held whitish-looking objects floating in liquid. Squealing suddenly, she backed away.

"I don't like those dead things."

"Neither did we," he admitted. "That was the invertebrate period when he was overcome with the iridescence on the back of an earthworm."

The child giggled and went back to the bottles.

"It's a snail, Philip."

"That's what I thought," he said gravely. "He said it was Helix Hortensis."

"Daft," she said, going back to the pictures. "He must have improved when he painted those."

Philip removed some clutter from a chair and sat down.

"I must tell him that, Mary," he said chuckling. "Those happen to be prints by Cézanne, El Greco and Picasso—his models for distortion. Don't ask me who they are. You'll learn in time. Mater will tell you."

"What will he be doing this year, Philip?"

"Don't ask a doctor, my child. We're going salmon-fishing in July, and he'll wade into the pool and dream without casting."

"Will I be there, Philip? My father casts the longest line in the Cove. I can cast, myself, only I don't like it much."

"No, you won't be there," he said, joining her at the mantelpiece. "You must look after Mater. Later, Felice is coming out and they'll open the cottage. You'll love them both."

"Sure I will," she said confidently, poking round the clutter on the mantelpiece. Suddenly her hands clasped and lifted a group of slender bronze figures.

"Oh!" she said in delight. "I know just how they feel."

Three nude girls were running off a stand. Elongated, eager and elfish, they bent forward in an attitude of flight. Hand in hand they suggested intensified youth speeding full tilt into life. In touching the bronze her hands held the same long look. Replacing it on the mantelpiece, her hands stayed on it with a sensuousness of touch.

"What a pity they can't get on," she whispered. "They're held like the trees in the silver thaw. Can't bend—"

"What do you mean, held?"

Philip's voice suggested frost.

"You know, taken as they went at the very tip-top."

"I know nothing of the sort," he said firmly.

An opening had arrived for which he had waited.

"Mary, I want to speak to you about this fantasy life of yours."

She went quite still, retaining a hold on a bronze leg.

"Yes," she said politely, giving him a quick look. His nostrils were moving just a little. Always a portent of seriousness with him, she knew she had to listen. With her body restored to radiant health she had become a traitor to his idea about her adventure.

"The life you led in your own world became full of fantasy because you had nothing to absorb your overflow of energy. It was natural to emphasise the legends of folklore—"

"What is folk-lore?" she asked politely.

"Don't be evasive, Mary. You know what I mean. The belief in fairies—"

"Oh, the Little People," she said as if acclaiming friends she had been unable to identify.

"Yes, the Little People," he said patiently. "Those things are picturesque if they don't distort daily life."

"Like David's painting?" she asked blandly.

He frowned at her acuteness.

"Perhaps, like David's pictures, Mary; but his are the results of well-rounded taste and not wild undisciplined impulses that…"

He paused but she said nothing, and he found himself watching her pale head, the curve of her cheek and long brown eyelashes.

"That what, Philip?" she prompted.

"It's hard to say, Mary. I couldn't formulate your delirium in hospital, but it was a strange blend of fantastic beliefs. You were lost in the woods, Mary. You're convinced of that, surely?"

His tone demanded the answer, spoken to the three nude girls held in bronze.

"When I was in hospital I was sure I was just lost and suffering for my foolishness. If anybody had asked me then if a fairy had tried to run up on my feet—"

"They didn't," he said sharply.

"No, of course not," she agreed without rancour.

At that moment she learned of the stifling that could go with the fairest relationship. She felt defrauded, closed up with herself. Where was the person who could receive everything? She spoke to Philip with the poise of his own mother, and for a moment he heard a perfect imitation of her voice.

"Tell me more about David, please, Philip."

"Another time, Mary. I must say this to you. What I want to suggest is that you co-ordinate with a normal world. Put the energy that went into fantasy into directive thinking and your capacity will increase for all the things Mater wants you to learn."

"I want to learn them, too, Philip," she said with a quick turn of the head. Even in illness he had never looked at her without amazement at the clearness of her face. In the economical tightness of her flesh and skin she had tissues that would never sag. It was a face that could be taken so safely out of doors. Light and sun could reveal no blemish.

"Don't you believe I want to learn, Philip?" she insisted.

"Yes, I do, Mary. I was merely suggesting that you don't spend yourself recklessly."

"I won't wear out," she said with a gay laugh. "Do you think I could have those girls in my room? Let's go and look at your room now."

"It will be dull after this," he said a little stiffly.

Mary Immaculate smiled blandly.

"Never mind, Philip, it will be good for my directive thinking."

There was no insolence in her tone, nothing calling for reproof. The wood-child had evaded him, snubbing him gently in his determination not to include her old life in her new. He felt he had made a mistake and could hear an echo of a didactic voice.

He was confused. She was stirring his imagination and presenting him with the unknown. He had the scientific mind searching for a clarification of his emotions, but he was not prepared to admit that the child was mother of the woman he would find irresistible. He admitted fascination with her artless chatter and bewilderment when she assumed an expression of enigmatical emptiness. His interest never waned. He was finding her not quite so docile as the patient; he was hearing her shrill with youth—and yet one look into her face made him wonder that such attraction could be. Hitherto he had painted his own canvas. Now it was at the mercy of a greater artist. Mary Immaculate was splashing on it willynilly and crowding it rapidly with gobs of crude colour.

The house included Lilas, Hannah and a kitchenmaid the child rarely saw.

Lilas was the housemaid who crept round the table, made the beds, dusted and swept. She was thin, young, yearning and gone under her apron. Mary Immaculate thought her skin beautiful, but her mouth drooped and she looked cold. Her hair was puzzling and bright—gold beyond any hair the child had ever seen. In the house three days, she animated Lilas to their eyes. After dinner in the mater's sitting-room she was breathless with interest. Philip was reading the evening paper by the fire and the mater was knitting under a shaded lamp.

"Mater," she whispered in a voice claiming their attention. "Lilas has been jilted! She left her place to get married. She lived in a small Cove like me, and she had a white dress and a veil and a pair of white canvas shoes, and she was all ready to be joined—"

"What, Mary?" asked Philip, laying down his paper.

"Joined, Philip, that's what she said. With her marriage is not a sacrament," said the child with the jewel of the Catholic faith. "She was a Methodist waiting for her beau to come in on the train, and all that came in was a letter to say he had changed his mind and was marrying another girl."

"If you would get your book, dear—"

"Oh, but, Mater, please let me tell it. It's very interesting and sad. She was that down-hearted—"

"So down-hearted," interrupted Philip.

"So down-hearted that she raised the damper of the kitchen stove and threw her ring in the fire. It had a ruby with two pearls and cost eight dollars and seventy-five cents. Then she packed up her wedding dress and came back to look for another place, the one before this, and she moped and moped and nearly went into a decline, and when her flesh was melting off her bones she met somebody who persuaded her to join the Salvation Army. And that's what she did and, as soon as she had testified, the spoken word eased her of her burden, and it rolled off her like water off a duck's back. Now she wears the bonnet and goes to number one barracks every night. But Hannah won't let her wear the bonnet out of the Place, so she carries it in a paper bag and when she's down the avenue she hides her beret in a shrub and puts on the bonnet. Then she goes off to the barracks, and when she feels herself getting down-hearted she testifies again. After the service is over she meets a boy and walks home with him. She doesn't love him, but she says he's someone to hook up to—"

"My dear child," said the mater firmly. "I—"

"Please, Mater dear, let her finish."

"Mater stopped me, Philip, because of the idioms, but that's what Lilas said, 'hook up to.' She said anyone was better than no one, and the avenue gave her the creeps. Hannah told her David drinks every night, and she's very worried for fear she'll have to carry the wine—"

"Indeed!" said the mater coolly, but Philip was laughing with real enjoyment.

"David will have to reform, Mater. Mary, why won't Hannah let her wear her bonnet out of the Place?"

"She told Lilas this was no house for tambourines."

She did not divulge Hannah's remarks to herself, that it was useless to be strict with the maids when the heads of the house saw fit to defile it with Popery.

From the moment of her entrance in the house, Hannah denied her a place. Outward expressions of aversion were only evinced when her mistress and Philip were well out of hearing. The woman's sense of caste was outraged by the transplantation of a fisherman's child. Already the intruder had ousted her in the service of her mistress.

Hannah had a pompadour of yellow-white hair that seemed to be dressed over a pad. Having seen something coarse poking out,

Mary Immaculate was sure of the pad. Hannah's eyes were grey and surrounded with wrinkles, and her skin was loose on her cheeks and chin. Often the child imagined herself taking a tuck in Hannah's face. Her mouth was remindful of Mrs. Houlihan, under a bulbous nose as fleshy as the lobes of her ears. Of German extraction, she had come to the country with her mistress. Stolid in loyalty, she was equally stolid in hate. Mary Immaculate had lived too close to hostile winds not to know that some would always blow cold.

Only once she tried to lessen the aversion.

"Why don't you like me, Hannah?"

The old woman was polishing the Georgian tea-service in the wine-red dining-room. Sunshine poured in from the conservatory and enriched the colour of walls and carpet. Silver emerged brightly from Hannah's cloth. Without looking up she unclosed her thin lips. Her voice was deliberate, with stabs of considered dislike.

"Don't bother me! I've no time for the likes of you, but let me tell you this: when my mistress wants a stitch picked up you leave it to me. You may be able to knit. It's right that you should. People like you should be clothed from the sheep's back and stay in their places. That's my last word to you."

The child felt differently. The unwarranted dislike made her feel puckish in a desire to goad. The sun caught her yellow eyes and brought out the gold in her hair. Leaning against the sideboard, she was the picture of sleek impudence. Her voice came softly, in a singsong of careful enunciation.

"It's a lovely tea-service we have, isn't it, Hannah? Do you know it's in the classic design of the time, without the scrolls and knobs that were evident in other pieces? Not that I don't like the knobs, Hannah, and there's a bowl with a cherub's head that I fancy above those plain pieces you're polishing now. But Mater thinks I should train my mind to value lines. Do you know, Hannah, that tea-services were first introduced into England about the time of Queen Anne? She was a tea-drinker and used to sip with the Duchess of Marlborough. Now that I'm a Fitz Henry we—"

"We, we; let me hear less of the we. There's one that'll never see you beyond your own class. Your kind comes to the back door of this house. What do you know of the Place?"

"A lot, Hannah," said the child in an unaltered tone. "I know the sideboard is Adam, and he has nothing to do with Eve, either. Did you know, Hannah, that in the fire of '46 the knife-urns were stolen and the owner of the house had to search in every pawnshop until he could buy them back? If you don't know those things, Hannah, it shows how much above you I am, for having learned so quickly."

In spite of sealed lips the woman was goaded to reply.

"And why should I know things that belong to the minds of my betters? I do my duty and polish—"

"The tea-service, Hannah! Did you know it was saved from the fire—?"

"Do I know, do I know? I should say I do." The old woman stood up and flicked out a yellow cloth. "Didn't I take it from the sideboard when the trees were burning outside and put it in bed—?"

"Did you, Hannah?" she said in another tone. "Tell me about it, will you? Tell me about the day David was born—"

"David, indeed!" snorted the woman implacably. "If I had my way it would be Mr. David and Mr. Philip."

Mary Immaculate drew herself to her slender height.

"Then isn't it fortunate, Hannah, that you don't have your way?"

She left the dining-room with the tone and manner of Lady Fitz Henry. Her impersonation was so real that for a moment she felt herself tall and dignified, with black hair on her head and brown eyes for yellow. To the old woman it was insolence in the highest form. In using Lady Fitz Henry for her pattern, she prepared a rod for her own back. Hannah was slow and could bide her time.

When the child's first week was spent Lady Fitz Henry asked for her reckoning. They were in the same position as when they had heard the story of Lilas. Philip, watching, felt the child was sure of her treat. In the sleek look of her face and the secret fall of her lids she had the quietude of accomplishment. In a black dress under a shaded lamp Lady Fitz Henry was seated with her hands resting in her lap.

Mary Immaculate sat on a straight-backed chair with her eyes fixed on vacancy.

"Can I—?"

"May I?" corrected Philip.

"May I tell it in my own words, Mater?"

"Yes, you may, and leave out all that you've learned about the house. Tell me things in relation to yourself."

Mary Immaculate's voice came slowly. "I've learned," she said, "that my daily bath is more than my daily bread. To go to bed here means putting my teeth, hair, hands and face above my prayers. Mom said cleanliness was only next to godliness."

Philip stared with grave concentration at his surgeon's hands. For a moment he feared that her treat might be postponed. The way she expressed her findings suggested a question. It was like the incident of Martha and Mary. Who had chosen the better part? Josephine and his mother were unwittingly thrown on the scales. Her voice saved her from any implication. It was the tone of a person trying to condense a long adventure. In his momentary worry for her, he found he had missed some of the findings.

"...and I must not enter a room at the top of my voice or slam the doors when I go out. Modulation can be brought into all things. I mustn't talk to Lilas while we're at table or make personal remarks about the way she caves in. I know that an apple must be eaten with a knife and fork if it's at the end of a meal, but if I have it between whiles I can gnaw it with my teeth. When there's a finger-bowl I don't put in two hands at a time and have a wash. And it comes without soap! I must try and eat more green food and drink lots of water. Philip says my system has had an excess of starches."

Philip looked up from the contemplation of his hands. He had heard himself saying it as if he had voiced the opinion at that moment. He hoped she would not mimic his mother.

"I must not be slovenly in my speech or use idioms that are purely colloquial."

Now it was Lady Fitz Henry's voice.

"I must not drop my *g*'s! Above all I must not say guts or belly. If I must mention such organs I make my voice a little ashamed and say tummy."

Her white brow contracted. To Philip it was apparent that she had returned to the robustness of her own strong world. The doctor in him gave her sympathy.

"I must not compare everything I like to the elements or talk about the Saints in Heaven. Religion is not as obtrusive as I make it. I can forget about souls sizzling in torment. It is a relic of uneducated minds. I can dwell on the kindness of God rather than His awfulness. Mom says the awfulness is good to frighten the wits out of people. She says one must beat with a stick—"

"That will do, Mary. You may get your hat and coat. It is a creditable test although some of your deductions are not quite accurate."

"I go, do I?" she said, leaping out of her chair. "Oh, Mater, won't it be beautiful? I looked in the paper and picked out a drama of thundering herds and broken hearts. Wouldn't you like to come too, Mater?"

Lady Fitz Henry smiled contentedly.

"No, dear, I don't care to go. You may tell me about it when you come home. I'll be very happy with my book."

It seemed incredible denial to Mary Immaculate, but she flew off, leaving a light impetuous kiss on the mater's cheek. Attainment crowned her. As she reached her room more findings popped into her mind. It was better for them to stay there she reflected. She must not mention the Little People to Philip or talk too much of her own mother to the mater. Both frowned inside when she did.

EIGHT

"LIGHT QUIRKS OF MUSIC...MAKE THE SOUL
DANCE UPON A JIG TO HEAVEN."

F inding an economy of indulgence from her own age and
sex, school made her wary. She learned to let others speak first.
Curiosity prevailed, and a divided camp as to whether she should be
snubbed for her lowly birth or accepted for her adoption. A minority
inclined towards romanticism, influenced by adventures alien to
childish life.

The school was small, standing in a square of trees. It was a place
where daughters were sacrosanct from the rough and tumble of larger
schools. There the curriculum was enhanced by many graces. The
graces were all highly extra, embracing music, art, elocution, dancing
and deportment. Mary Immaculate was down for all the extras, with
a special arrangement for private tuition in voice and elocution. They
expected her to face everything, but they gave her a prevision of events.

The mater spoke freely.

"You may notice attitudes. Take no notice! If you maintain an
integrity of spirit yourself, little stings will not hurt you. Stay on the
edge of things as an observer until you find your own feet."

"Do you mean hold my tongue, Mater?"

"Yes. And if you're called up in class take your time and do your best. It doesn't matter if you fail, but it matters a great deal if you don't try."

"I was bright in the Cove, Mater. I got up to Elizabeth and pounds, shillings and pence."

"Maybe, my dear, and I'm sure you'll fall in line very fast; but your school was in an isolated district. You'll find girls with more knowledge than yourself, and in some respects with a great deal less. Different ways of living! Above all, do not be combative or pert. Remember, Philip and I are here to help you."

It was a thought she could dwell on if she became hard pressed.

As she was leaving the Place under Philip's escort she heard something that was a sturdy reinforcement.

"You look very nice, Mary. Your clothes are becoming."

Her uniform was satisfactory: brown tunic over a cream silk blouse, brown shoes and stockings, and a brown cloth coat, with a felt hat. Every pleat hung with precision, and seams were in their proper places. Inside she felt smooth and harmonious.

Her identification with nature had given her courage to lie on the ground in dreamlike frost. Such courage could disintegrate in different circumstances. As she endured the scrutiny of forty pairs of eyes she became conscious of her throat as an obstruction to swallowing. The adults were reassuring, but she had no knowledge of pampered little girls. For the first time in her life she wanted to be part of the furniture—something they would not notice. It was impossible. She was a target of interest. The routine of class kept everything normal until she heard her name.

"Now I think we will ask our new pupil, Mary Fitz Henry, to read the next verse."

Hands cold on the book, she rose to her feet. To herself her voice sounded like the rattle of a tin with a stone inside. The passage was difficult and she faltered uncertainly.

> "Beneath these rugged elms, that yew tree's shade,
>   Where heaves the earth in many a mould'ring heap,
> Each in his narrow cell for ever laid,
>   The rude forefathers of the hamlet sleep."

"Very well attempted, Mary."

She knew it was the kindness of an older person trying to help her out. Her ordinary facility seemed to have fled. As she sat down a cool little voice behind whispered, "baynoddy!"

It was what she needed—the slap of childish rudeness. She became herself with a light varnish of ice. Faculties returned, ready to be called forth. Daughters of kings could not upset her now. When she could peer round she met a pair of blue-fringed eyes in a face framed in dark curls. It was a very pretty face. Very detached, Mary Immaculate decided brown did not suit it.

At recess they were given an apple and turned out on the square of grass where she braced herself against the trunk of a tree. Several girls spoke tentatively and she responded with civil brevity. It surprised her to find they knew all about her.

"Are you better?"

"Your feet and hands look as if nothing had happened!"

"Fancy Lady Fitz Henry adopting you!"

"Weren't you frightened out in the woods? I've never been out after dark without my parents or a maid."

"When the policemen were searching for you they prayed for you in church. Fancy seeing someone they pray for in church! 'Tis like meeting our gracious Queen Elizabeth, Mary the Queen Mother—"

"Don't be so foolish, Phyllis, prayers can be more than words. I prayed for her, too, because Mother said she couldn't sleep, thinking of a child lying out in the snow. Mother wanted to go and see you in hospital, only the Fitz Henrys said no visitors."

"Yes," said a cool little voice; "a lot of charitable organizations wanted to send fruit and flowers."

"What a pig you are, Betty," said a nice voice; "she's prettier than you are, thank goodness, so your nose is broken at last."

The small girl tossed her black curls.

"She looks all right, but she shouldn't open her mouth. Her voice is common and her mother was a cook."

Ice-cold, Mary Immaculate leaned against the tree. What was there in this world to make her deny her own mother? Josephine with her red hands stood invisibly in front of her bidding her speak no ill of her neighbour. With eyes hard as agate she looked straight at the blue-eyed girl.

"Yes, my mother was a cook, a very good cook. Now she cooks and does all the work besides."

"Well, my mother wouldn't let me invite you to my house."

"No," said Mary Immaculate gently; "Lady Fitz Henry wouldn't let me go. She wants me to have nice things in my life."

"Ha, ha, ha, Betty, serves you right, you deserved it."

A tall, ungainly girl with horn-rimmed glasses rushed at Mary Immaculate and threw her arms round her neck. Her voice held the feel of a slobber.

"I think you're lovely. Look at her hair and eyes, girls. I'm going to walk home with her."

Are you, now? thought Mary Immaculate. The girl's hair smelt dry, like a pony's mane. Extricating herself, she replied, "Thank you very much, but for a few days my adopted brother is calling for me."

A bell put a stop to her considerable attention. She had tried to keep her voice within the bounds of courtesy, but she was savouring all the feelings the mater had warned her against. She felt she understood murder.

When she found Philip's car waiting she sped towards him on eager feet. The faint hospital smell that clung to him on operating days returned her to the breath of her adopted world. Settled in the seat beside him, she watched him steer through a congested school area. But the founts of volubility were stilled inside her. A sidelong glance at her face made him question, "What is it, Mary? Have you had a difficult morning?"

His voice invited her to ease her mind. There was no stifling like his tone to the Little People. Very slowly she told him about her experiences. She was oppressed with the criticism of herself and her mother. As if her troubles were his, Philip's nostrils responded mutely to her tale.

"Dreadful little snobberies, Mary. Don't take your standards from that wretched little girl. Think of Mater! I'm delighted you acknowledged your mother so strongly. As for your voice, it's improving every day. Keep your chin up, my dear, and if I'm no good to you, Mater will be."

The child gave a released wriggle. It was one of the moments when Philip was a god.

"So kind, Philip," she whispered.

That morning having repudiated a physical touch she rubbed her face against his arm.

Philip stopped his car and bought her a box of chocolates.

The strain lessened; she was busy following a crowded routine. School and extras over she had to return to the Place to practise five-finger exercises. Loitering on the way was strictly forbidden. From five to six she was allowed to do as she liked in the garden. Often Lady Fitz Henry joined her and they poked in the earth together.

In spite of Josephine being a cook there were invitations to tea and small maidenly parties. The mater dealt with them all. Many times Mary Immaculate heard her graciously discouraging voice on the telephone.

"Very kind of you, but at present we think it advisable…"

"She's very occupied with as much as she can manage…"

"Perhaps at a later date, if you would be kind enough to repeat the invitation…"

Spring progressed, drawing the harshness from the land. Daffodils trod down crocus, Darwin tulips waved tight secret heads, trees in new bloom veiled the faded fronts of wooden houses and, where open country flowed back from the town, meadows made jade squares in sombre green. A winding river, full from snow, rushed through a lake on its way to the sea.

Winter-born children sped to the country trailing home with hardy blooms. Several times as Mary Immaculate turned into the Place she looked wistfully at the loitering children. Invariably she could identify the flowers in their hands. Where were her own woods, blue ponds and lily-pools, and wet meadows hoarding many secrets? Where were the marsh-marigolds and pale cuckoo-flowers blooming by themselves with no one to see?

Scales, lessons, voice, dancing, elocution; and reminders of her hair, nails, manners and mien! She ached to walk with her eyes on the ground and part the alders on a quiet pond.

She forgot her scales for the river in her ears. From its sound it must have a series of short waterfalls and still stretches lazy over stones.

Neither premeditation nor disobedience made her go! It was an instinct of necessity. Heedlessly she dropped her schoolbooks in the shrub sacred to Lilas' beret and ran toward open country.

The western sun was dying in an orange dapple when she strolled up the avenue. All over her was the sleekness of some fulfilment. Her ears held the sounds of birds settling down, children shrilling the last shout of the day and woods and trees singing with sap. Her arms held a cluster of pale mauve flowers and her brown hat dangled from her hand.

Philip stood at the wide-open door looking as if he had been there a long time. His figure held no peace and his eyes fired like hot coals.

"Where have you been?"

She should have been extinguished by his voice, falling like a frost on new flowers. A long hand on her shoulders seemed to dig into her bones. For a moment she blinked at him without focus.

"Come in at once!"

The pressure of his hand urged her along. Inside she saw the mater seated quietly by the open fireplace. Furnace heat was gone, but the grate held a pile of crackling birch-billets. Bowls of spring flowers stood on tables and stands round the hall. Raising her eyes from her knitting, the mater regarded the child without anger.

"Mary dear—"

"Mater, if you please, let me attend to this."

Wonderingly the child gazed at Philip. Here was anger, cold, hard, with an undercurrent of heat. Contained on the surface, it held the undertow of the sea. In the Cove angry people shouted and bawled at the top of their voices. Philip seemed to be shouting in his nose, dilating like a disturbed animal.

"Answer me, Mary, where have you been?"

"Just in the country, Philip," she said mildly.

The simplicity of her explanation fanned his anger.

"What do you mean, just in the country? It's seven o'clock and you left school at three-thirty. Isn't it a definite rule that you come right home? Whom were you with?"

"I was alone, Philip, picking flowers and running by the river."

Her crime might have been mitigated if she had gone off with her school-friends. The pressure grew on her shoulder.

"Mary, it's most unnatural to go off on long tramps at your age. Isn't one lesson enough for you? Remember the last experience that nearly killed you. Think of—of…"

He became inarticulate with doubts he could not formulate.

Her light laugh annoyed him further.

"Sure, Philip, the Little People are afraid of the town and, if I got lost now, the woods are beautiful with spring."

It was the peak of wrong remarks.

"Be quiet!" he snapped. "I've no intention of permitting a repetition of that. You've been disobedient and Mater has been extremely worried."

The child glanced at Lady Fitz Henry. In the black and white of her tranquillity she looked as if anger could not touch her. Philip was giving the wrong reason for his anger.

Then she saw Hannah peering from the dining-room and making a great show of arranging silver on the sideboard. She was nodding her head in applause to Philip. As his voice went on the folds of her face deepened to sardonic approval.

"Mary, go to bed at once and Hannah will bring you bread and milk. Also you will remember conclusively and irrevocably that you will conform to the life we plan for you. I won't have any furtiveness or sudden impulses to run away and leave us at the mercy of fantastic thoughts."

Furtiveness! The child hated the word, although unsure of its meaning. Convinced that her happiness had been insulted she answered with smooth insolence, "'Fantastic', Philip! You told me your thoughts were directive."

"Go to bed!"

Releasing her, the energy of his voice propelled her towards the stairs. For a moment she paused and looked at her great cluster of flowers. Lady Fitz Henry rose from her chair.

"Give them to me, Mary. You must do as Philip says, but I'll attend to your flowers. They're very pretty."

"They're no good now," she said, shaking her head. With a stately back she walked upstairs, with the feel of Philip's frown boring her spine.

In a childish night-dress gathered at the neck, she lay in bed.

Arriving with bread and milk, Hannah dumped it on a bedside table.

"There," she said with genuine malice, "you've discovered that you can't be a fly-by-night in this house. If I had my way you'd get the flat of the slipper."

Mary Immaculate reached for a book and opened it upside down.

"Please leave me, Hannah," she said with great aloofness. "I have a quiet hour to myself."

From the bottom of the bed the old woman gave an outraged snort.

"The airs and graces of you! I'd like to make it my job to find out what you were doing. Picking flowers all that time? More likely running wild with some of your own kind."

For a moment the child felt soiled, but she gave no sign and the woman had to go. Hannah hated her and none of them saw. She sighed and sipped her milk. Philip was angry with her for her vagabond hour. It had been such happiness, such an escape from conformity. Philip loved her when she was amenable and swung to anger when she did something by herself. Philip who was so kind, who took her to the cinema, called for her at school, bought her chocolates even though he said it was bad for her teeth. Philip who had taken her to the dentist's that week and stayed until she got used to the sharp picks and whirring machine making a noise in her head.

How beautiful it was in her room now! Quiet and washed by the setting sun. The three bronze girls on the mantelpiece looked as if they had run lighter-footed for the mildness of the day. Putting the tray aside she reached for the book. The mater had been telling her about India and had given her a copy of the child-stories of Kipling. Settling into her pillow she luxuriated in quiet.

When Lady Fitz Henry entered two hours later she was gazing unseeingly ahead.

"Mater," she sighed, "I've just read such a lovely story, *The Drums of the Fore and Aft*. When the regiment fell back two little boys Jakin and Lew walked out in the open and piped it on with fife and drum. Then they were shot."

"I know it well, Mary," said Lady Fitz Henry, seating herself with a slight smile. "We'll talk of it when we have more time. In a moment you must go to sleep. I presume, my dear, you did your homework before you ran off. I should imagine it would be extremely uncomfortable to go to school unprepared."

Mary Immaculate fell back to cold reality and a preversion of what the next day would be. That awful Betty Wilson with her cool derisive voice! She was still in the position when she wished to remain as unobtrusive as possible. Looking into the mater's eyes she knew she was being shown the results of indulgence.

"Mater," she sighed woefully, "you say everything without saying anything."

"It's unfortunate, isn't it," she said pleasantly, "the natural results of a lack of discipline? What made you run off, Mary? I think I know, but tell me yourself."

She sighed on her pillow and a little shake of her head made the light dance through her hair.

"Mater, I'm sorry if I upset you but I just had to go. I haven't been by myself since I left the Cove. I love to be with you, but I was used to spending whole days alone and playing a sort of make-believe. Then I saw the children coming back from the hills with the flowers I used to pick and I got tired of that time-table pinned to the wall. Think of days going on in the country and days in town sliced up into squares."

Lady Fitz Henry nodded her head.

"I expect you've been much better than we imagine, dear. Now go to sleep and try to forget that Philip was cross."

The child showed no signs of having remembered.

"Yes, he was cross, Mater. Philip is always mad if I like things he doesn't like."

There was so much adult in the child; a natural maturity from her strong bleak world. In spite of her complex mind, there were moments when she was the sternest realist; the side of her that wanted to say guts and belly. Although she had conformed to all the amenities of daily life, Lady Fitz Henry occasionally discerned a cold wonder for the perpetual need of convention. She could visualise her unshocked in situations that would shake many children.

Downstairs she found her son holding a medical journal, in a library that had belonged to his father. Wall-space not packed with books was panelled in oak. She found him as she had found the child, gazing unseeingly ahead. Rising as his mother came in, he pulled forward a brown leather chair.

"Philip, I found Mary reading *The Drums of the Fore and Aft* and enjoying every second of her punishment. I was so reminded of David. If he was sent to bed it was just what he wanted, because he was very tired. If he had bread and water there was nothing like a glass of nice cold water. Mary had forgotten why she was punished."

"I haven't," he said grimly. "I thought she might be worrying because I was so angry."

"Too angry, my son. I should suggest another attitude."

Reasonably she discussed the child with him, but his ideas of Mary Immaculate had no room for wayfaring on lonely country roads.

There was no reconciliation between them. Perhaps he was glad to find her at breakfast, trying to learn out of two books.

"Oh, Philip," she said genially, "I had to find out how many pieces of paper it takes to paper a room, and I haven't papered it at all, and that awful Betty Wilson will call me a bay-noddy."

His more sombre nature could not understand her light repudiation of yesterday. He felt relief for her normality and complete lack of rancour. In spite of himself he said as he sat down: "Couldn't I do the sum for you, Mary? It wouldn't take a minute."

"Oh no, Philip, thank you just the same. It's too late to make a pen-and-ink copy in my book so I'll just have to manage somehow."

Watching her long hands over her food at lunch, he had to inquire, "How did you get on with your paper-hanging, Mary?" She looked at him quickly and gave a smile verging towards a grin.

"When they collected the books there was nothing from me, so I was invited to the desk to explain."

The smile left her face and she became serious.

"Miss Good asked me why I had failed to do my homework, and I told her the truth."

Such candour was a shock to family reticence. His voice was reproachful.

"Was that necessary, Mary? Surely we keep those things to ourselves."

"I had to explain, Philip. School-teachers want a real reason for things. I said I went for a long walk yesterday, several miles in fact, and when I got back my guardian, who is a doctor, said it was very bad for me and he made me go to bed with a glass of hot milk."

The truth, told with a wistful shading of the voice, suggested childish fraility.

"Yes," she said gently. "Miss Good was very sorry I had tired myself so completely, and she told me not to run round too much at recess. She said I looked white."

There was nothing to say. She had told the truth and the mater had warned her she must stand on her own feet. Mother and son felt some reproof should be forthcoming. In view of her bland innocence and enigmatical face it seemed impossible to find a chink through which to attack. White she certainly was, but white with the clearness of health.

The mater was out for a walk and Mary Immaculate was playing scales. The window was open and soft air ballooned the curtains. It seemed impossible to concentrate on scales and see that her thumb went under her fingers. Twice she had heard a beguiling whistle, thin like a gimlet boring a sound.

Between the mater's flowers and a disused tennis-court stood a kitchen garden surrounded by a tall privet-hedge. Like a fruitful secret, vegetables grew inside, tended by a man who came three times a week. Age and impoverishment lay at the end of the garden. It had been velvet turf when the drawing-room had been in constant use. Neglect had allowed it to revert to native coarseness, and grass was ousted by dandelions and flat-leaved plantains. Mary Immaculate loved it. It was a hide-out when she was allowed to be alone in the garden. Behind the old trees ran a high wooden fence, screening the Place from audacious eyes. When the trees were bare, houses could be seen on either side. They were dots compared to the big white house.

Mary Immaculate went out in the garden. Treading the plantains and dandelions she raised her head to look for the whistle.

Across the grass came a long, sweet note, expiring as if lips had suddenly opened. It came again, more shrill and compelling, stopping with staccato finish. Then a little jig dropped from a tree, light as a leaf, calling to her feet. Dancing over the plantains, the music left her on the tips of her toes. Silence came down, rich with the smell of earth and the soundless flight of a pair of white butterflies.

"Hello!" said a voice from a beech tree.

Mary Immaculate clasped her hands.

"Hello!" said the voice again. "I drew you out from your rotten scales."

"Who are you?" she whispered. Soft as it was, it reached the tree.

"The Pied Piper! Just wait a minute, I'm going to pipe you up in this tree."

"I'm not a rat," she said, airing recent knowledge.

"Yes, you are! You're the one, stout as Julius Caesar, who swam across and lived to carry his commentary out of the woods! I'll say you had guts to lie out there."

"Oh!" she said, very pleased with herself. "I'm not allowed to have guts any more. They're not polite. Who are you, anyway, and where do you live when you're not in a tree?"

"I'm Tim to you and I live in the next house. There's a field behind us and I make it my summer home. As soon as the trees get green enough to hide me I climb up to my armchair. I've seen you lots of times. I know what you're like because I've seen you when you didn't know I was looking."

"Oh!" she said doubtfully. "What am I like?"

"Swell," said the voice with enthusiastic brevity.

"How old are you?" she asked hopefully. "Fifteen and a bit. What are you?"

"Nearly thirteen!"

The voice became considering.

"You're so tall you make me think of reedy music. You know, 'down in the reeds by the river'. I drew you out with my music, didn't I?"

"Maybe," she admitted graciously. "I heard the whistle twice. Why do you want to have summer quarters in a field?"

The voice sounded a trifle impatient, as if making unnecessary explanation.

"To be by myself, of course, and to read the books I want to read and not those recommended by my lousy uncle."

"Oh!" she said wonderingly. Here was freedom of speech indeed and a mood she could readily understand. For a moment she held her breath, standing very still.

"You—you want to be alone sometimes?"

"Sure! I want to play in an orchestra when I grow up. I'm swell at the piano and I can get a tune out of tumblers and a knife. If I had any decent instruments I know I could play them..I'd like the blowers best, the wood-winds, you know."

"No, I don't know," she sighed, "but you can tell me."

"The wood-winds are the flutes, oboes and things, *but* they wouldn't give me one if they died for it. No, they give me manuals on mining engineering, because they've made up my mind that I'm going to be a mining engineer like my father before me. *And* when my uncle comes in to look me over I have to talk about pyrites and whatnots! Sure, when I go to church I always think the Hittites are minerals too."

This was a rich field of exploration with an undisciplined side like her own.

"Are you far up in the tree?" she asked.

"Not too far for you to climb if I give you a hoist."

"Oh!" she said virtuously. "I have to practise my scales."

The answer came in the gay little jig that had set her dancing over the dandelions and plantains. For the life of her she could not refrain from walking to the square of earth beneath the tree. Conveniently by was a trunk, sawed off to give the larger trees room for expansion. Temptation always seemed so well arranged! Looking up she saw a pair of grey flannel legs and the edge of a blue blazer.

"Is that all of you?" she giggled.

There was a chuckle from the tree.

"Wait a minute, sister, till I pocket my whistle. I've got a mouth-organ, too, and a uke. I'll hook up the uke. O.K., now, don't break, or Uncle will ask why I want a new string."

There was a quick change in the position of the legs. Leaning over a leafy branch, Tim looked down.

"Gee!" he said, blinking hooded eyelids rapidly at her upturned face. "Gee, you're pretty, close to!"

"You're not bad yourself," she admitted agreeably, stepping up on the sawed-off trunk. It brought her nearer to an outstretched hand. Instantly she noticed its length emerging from a smooth wrist too far out of a sleeve. All the nails of the hand were blunted at the tips. Her own hand seemed a perfect fit for the wiry grasp pulling her to the same branch as himself. They seemed to be in the centre of a bowl of green, with hardly any sky visible through thick foliage.

"This," he said gravely, "is the cavern that suddenly hollowed, and the Piper advanced—"

"And Mary followed! Don't speak yet, Tim, please, for a minute. Let me look at you. If it's not right I'll have to climb down again. 'Tis no good wasting my time from my scales if it's not something worth while."

"O.K.," he said, without objection to possible doubt of himself. "Look away."

His hooded blue eyes rested on her in a half-dreaming regard. Unselfconsciously he endured her scrutiny, returning interest in herself. His head was deep, rounded at the back, and covered with fair hair having a tendency to curl away from the scalp. It grew in a curve in the middle of his forehead, receding at the temples. His face was broad across the eyes, suddenly short and narrow at the chin. His nose was straight and his mouth girlish in its curves and dents at the corners. His cheeks were soft with a fair down. As he smiled at her, she noticed his teeth were hard and white, but the two centre ones were crooked, making a jut in the front of his mouth. With his lazy hooded eyes, he looked interesting and strange. She had a sudden feeling if she slid from the tree he would sigh and shrug and play another tune.

"Well," he demanded, raising his eyebrows and making a deep wrinkle in his brow. "You look the pure fruit to me."

"You're nice," she admitted; "but your eyes are funny. Nice, but funny."

With a thumb and first finger he pulled at the skin of an eyelid.

"Music," he explained briefly. "A crystal-gazer told me at a circus. She said I'd go two ways and die in a day."

"Will you be married, Tim?" she asked, unconcerned about his death.

"She said I'd be married and not married."

"Sounds silly to me."

"Me, too," he admitted, adding with a grin, "You don't look very silly, although lots of people said you were for running away to the woods."

The candour of her school-friends had revealed the same attitude. With yellow eyes fixed on his face she said blandly, "They could say the same thing about you, Tim, for climbing a tree and playing your whistle."

"Sure," he admitted, surprised and looking more interested. "Did you go off to the woods for the same reason?"

"Another reason. I know the woods. I've known them all my life and I had fun with the Little People. Do you believe in the Little People, Tim?"

Sitting side by side on the branch, she waited with some tenseness.

"I believe in anything I hear in music, and the fairies run through lots of it; little tunes in the treble, dropping off like a leaf. I make stories on the piano! When I leave the house I play the gate, the honk of horns and the rattle of a tram. Then there's confusion with no special theme, *but* suppose I see a park and go in and walk into woods—"

"Yes, yes, yes," she said breathlessly, "go on."

"Then I play the woods like a nocturne—"

"What's that?"

"Night-piece! You play it with its secrets, and that, of course, brings in the fairies."

This was companionship surpassing all others. It was youth, gaiety and kinship with herself. She sighed in a rich joy. It was not long before Tim knew a great deal about her. On her demand that she would like to play his mouth-organ he handed it over, first wiping it with a crumpled handkerchief.

"Thank you," she said gravely, putting it to her mouth. "Can you play it?" he asked.

"I don't know. Is it hard?"

"Not if you've got a sense of pitch. Have you?"

"I don't know," she said, frowning. Surely there could be nothing beyond her! Searching her mind for a tune, she realised she knew very little music.

"Go on," he commanded; "any tune will do."

"Sure, I don't know many. I'll play 'Adeste'."

"What's that?" he asked doubtfully.

Ignoring him she sang softly to herself.

"Adeste fideles
Laeti triumphantes."

"Gee!" he interrupted. "You know Latin."

"Sure," she said. "Father Melchior taught me. Mom loved it. She had two books, the Manual of Prayers and the cook-book."

"It's not classical Latin, anyway. I'm learning classical Latin. Church Latin is not right."

"Church Latin must be right Latin," she said inflexibly.

"O.K.," he said peaceably; "play it, can't you."

She couldn't. Try as she would, the notes were always wrong.

"You do it," she said, feeling sure he must fail.

Without hesitation he put the mouth-organ between his lips and played the Christmas hymn in perfect tune.

"Tim," she said, shaking her head, "I'm not a musician. Queer, isn't it, when it makes me feel so wonderful? But it's beautiful when you play it."

"Yes, it is queer," he admitted; "and your hands are so musical. Can I look at them?"

"Yes, if you want to."

Holding out her slender hands he received them on his open palms. Examining them carefully, he exclaimed in wonder, "Gee, your nails are perfect! Such long fingers! You ought to have a cantabile touch."

"Well, I haven't, whatever it is. Gracious, I must go! Give me your hand while I get down."

She was out of the fork and on a lower branch in the space of a second.

"Will you come again? I'm always here between four and six, and often between seven and eight."

Looking up into his blue eyes she knew she would come again, but she said reproachfully, "No, Tim. Things are not the same when they're arranged. When they happen it's different, and sins are not sins when they're on you before you know they're around."

"I see," he said with an understanding grin; "it's the difference between murder and manslaughter. Do you read mystery stories?"

"Yes, I read everything. Tim, I must go. It's been fun."

"Fun, more than fun. I'll be looking for you. Now I'll pipe you across the garden."

"Like *The Drums of the Fore and Aft*?"

"Do you know that? Gosh, you're swell."

A lithe slide and a jump landed her on the soft earth in the garden. Pulling down her sleeves and adjusting her dress she walked to the house with great unconcern. As she passed the corner of the privet hedge she thought she saw Hannah's white pompadour from one of the attic windows. It was no more than a shadow, gone before she was sure anything actual had touched her vision. Perhaps she had been mistaken! Surely Hannah wouldn't climb all those stairs just to see what she was doing? The top flat of the Place was never used and held two rows of dusty rooms with slanting sides from the mansard roof.

Walking, her blood danced to a little tune. Light and gay, it made her hold up her head. As she went into the house it expired on a long, dying note.

Four and six, seven and eight! They were nice hours and included a bit of her leisure!

Virtuously she sat on the piano-stool and played the scale of G major. By playing it several times very loudly, she tried to convince herself she had been practising a long time.

NINE

"DEAR FILIAL HUMBUG."

The house was being painted. Every morning she woke to slap of brushes and the creaking of scaffolding. Intimately near her window painters talked while she dressed. Except for the disused tennis court every spot was reduced to order. Inside, Hannah polished with a certain venom in her cloth, while Lilas climbed a step-ladder and dusted walls in David's room. Bending to the weight of a bucket, she seemed more concave than ever. By this time Mary Immaculate knew more about her. Restless, one moonlight night she had watched the maid's return from number one barracks. Her findings were that Lilas must have grown to love the boy she hooked up to! Seeing two figures become one and the bag that held the bonnet make a pale blur against a back, she concluded no girl could kiss like that, because someone was better than no one!

Philip was out early watching dirty wood being painted under. He was extremely busy, seeming to come and go at the imperative ring of the telephone. There were emergencies, and occasionally Mary Immaculate woke in the night to hear his muted step past the gallery in the hall. Then in the morning his hair and eyes would look blacker against his face. Watching day by day, she learned to read his symbols. So little of Philip's routine went into words that it was necessary to make her own interpretations. With the knowledge derived from the hospital, she could visualise his clinical world. When he was abstracted striding towards his car, he was anticipating a difficult day. If he returned with his nose a prow and his black curls standing away from his head, the day had held disasters. If he retired to his father's library and sat with his hands under his chin, he was thinking out a diagnosis. If he took the same position with a droop, a patient had died. Once, surprising him like that, his mute dejection made her lay her face against his hair. Confronted by professional anxieties she could not encompass, she strove to return the kindness he gave herself. Somewhat surprised, she found herself giving vent to Josephine's formula. She did not know whether Philip found it soothing to learn about the will of God, but she learned a way to his replenishment. Strain went out of him when his long arm took her in. He seemed to have little time for anticipation of David's arrival. He was attending a medical convention, with lunches and dinners, where doctors debated and lectured. With the many things on his mind he included an intense preoccupation with mastoids. Philip was going to specialise!

Everyone was busy! It left her leisure unquestioned. Tim was always near for those hours in the tree or, greatly daring, in the shade of the privet hedge. Those sessions were more thrilling for their danger. Coming to find her one evening Hannah stabbed the garden with her eyes.

"I heard you talking," she accused.

With the hairbreadth chuckle of Tim's flight in her ears Mary Immaculate ran wildly across the grass.

"Yes, I was talking, Hannah. I do that sometimes. I'm cracked, so they say in town, because I got held in the woods. I'm a changeling, something the fairies left…"

"I'll changeling you," muttered the old woman to her back.

It never crossed her mind to explain Tim, any more than she could explain the games she had played with the Little People. Their contacts were old while yet they were new. Looking back, it was difficult to picture a day that did not include something they had shared. They became to each other the something mislaid from life. Mutiny would not come again when she saw children in spring returning from the hills. Tim could direct her to richer wayfaring.

There was a whole world of him that demanded elucidation from books. She was a most obliging friend. He had only to say he was reading the lives of Schumann and Schubert to make her do the same thing. Reading about music encouraged her to bring it forth from radio and from a gramophone she found in David's rooms. In it she found the transposition of all that she knew from the earth. It held the wind and the sea, their torment and calm. It held the whimper of low sad days and the sudden ache of beauty. It held the range of all people. Surprised at the many mediums for the interpretation of life, she wanted to embrace them all. As yet she had no selection and did not know what to discard. Tim helped her. His way was more formed and he had the courage of definite tastes. As the replacement of her lost vagabondage she was his substitution for music. Without knowledge of the fact, they were more satisfactory to their elders because of each other. He called her Gretel! Colouring her own world, he could colour it more vividly. Quite solemnly he told her she had been saved by seven pairs of angels walking down the cloud stairs to guard her while she slept. What she knew from Grimm he knew from Humperdinck. Winding their way to a gingerbread house, as yet there was no witch or witches' oven to burn them.

Then she became Isolde, and the tennis court was the yard of an ancestral castle. Waiting for a ship to come in with a white or black flag, he was Tristan, under a lime tree that was a beech. The heap of David's records was culled for Isolde's love-death. She played it until it scratched, and knew a wild irritation because she couldn't sing the torment and exultation of grand heroic women. Tim told her the first lovers of the legend were buried in a common grave from which sprang a rose bush and a vine that could never be separated. When she said she'd be the rose bush he was firm and made her be the vine. Fighting without venom she capitulated. Tim seemed to think it mattered. In view of his heavy-lidded eyes asking a concession, she graciously submitted to being the vine. Drinking a fateful love-philtre of ginger ale, Tim took it very seriously.

Tim was the only son of his mother, his father having been killed three years before by a premature blast from a mine. In telling her about his home he spoke with a pucker on his brow.

"I liked him. He knew about music, only he thought it should be a hobby. Whenever he was home he used to sing in cantatas and he thought oratorio was the last word. It was so funny when he died. I wanted to see him, but they sent me to my uncle's and my aunt kept giving me Marie biscuits! She thought because Father was dead I must be hungry all day. I was just cold and not a bit hungry. They were shocked because I played Chopin's Funeral March. Then Auntie Minnie came to live with us, and Mother went back to being like her instead of Father. Now they both cook for me and make sweaters when I like machine-knit ones best. People are queer, aren't they?"

"Don't you have maids, Tim?" she asked from a world that seemed impossible without them.

"Sure," he said with a grin; "Auntie Minnie wouldn't have anything to talk about if we didn't."

Without confirmation she knew Tim loved to be with her. Conversation could be suspended while he reached for her hand or drew a finger down her cheek. Quite uncloying, his gestures were gentle, made on a sudden impulse of intensified sight. His appreciation of her was expressed in musical form. He said she had rhythm and her life was a theme for an opera. Other times he would let her talk, becoming dreamy and heavy-lidded behind a smile lingering on his lips. Puzzling over the quality of the smile, she satisfied herself with its simile. Often in the tranquillity of a summer evening she had watched their grey hen settling over her chicks. The commodious ruffle of the feathers had spoken of warmth, sleep and places where it was quiet to go. At moments like that Tim's smile seemed to take her like the hen took its chicks.

All his life Tim had wanted something for himself. From childhood he had known glimpses of melancholy, like the double-bass notes of the spirit. Some of it was inborn, encouraged by the position of an only child. The gods that presided at his birth deputed that his predispositions should increase. Disharmony helped, unshared joys and unchildish shivers over musical moods. His soul went to brinks and looked over. His compensations with vital things had been unlucky, leaving scars of self-blame. The softness of a kitten had been squeezed to death by overt raptures. His dog had died trying to follow him over a paling-fence. The dog had slipped and a paling had gone through its neck. He developed a sense of fatality in affection and grew troubled over the mortality of lovable things.

Mary Immaculate was more robust in spirit. She could grieve but she could not prolong. The knowledge that certain things were the will of God must have had an unconscious effect on her mind. If a dog shook a kitten to death she could grieve for the kitten without hating the dog. Other things called, permitting her to continue light-footed and light-hearted. Free of her body nothing was irksome. Good minds directed her, affection was less critical because it was not bound with her own blood. There was no flaw in her life after Tim's substitution for sylvan independence. Days could be eaten up, and she could sigh with fulfilment and drop into night. That rare thing, a perfectly happy person, she knew the scope of a heart when it widened to include David.

The English boat steered through the harbour in the late afternoon. The water was still, reflecting the iridescence of sun. Men stood by gang-planks and moorings as the ship eased broadside to the wharf.

Searching the rows of passengers, Mary Immaculate found David at once. The hand that was flung in the air for an impetuous wave was a hand that she knew. So was the beautiful nose, high up against the sky. The face seemed almost the same, a little fuller, with the addition of horn-rimmed glasses and a small moustache above lips that smiled unreservedly. Moving her eyes to Philip to confirm similarity, she knew he was moved by the sight of his brother. His thinner lips were uncurled in a smile, and his face looked boyish and eager. It was inevitable that his nostrils should contribute to emotion. She was sure that the brothers loved each other when they met. Despite the warm day David wore a thick overcoat. Beyond the hills lay the toss of the North Atlantic and the pinch of its winds. Passengers retained a look of mid-ocean. As David put his foot on the gang-plank, Philip found his way to its base. She sensed his expectancy in the drag on her hand. David might be eager, but he was leisured. He limped down as if no one was before or behind.

"Philip!"

"David!"

The hard clasp of hands lasted until her turn came. With a laugh of more abandon than she had ever heard from him, Philip put his hand on her shoulder.

"David, the last of us all, Mary Fitz Henry."

"Gracious," said David, taking her hands, "what a tall lovely person! I thought we had a little girl round the house. You're the baby sister I always asked for at inconvenient times."

"Yes," she said gravely. "Philip found me in the woods."

David bent and kissed her.

"I know where, Mary," he said. "Curled up under the bushes. Where's Mater, Phil?"

She had not come. She was waiting at the Place. Somehow it seemed more suitable to think of her surrounded by flowers from her garden. Some unconscious sense of good manners made Mary Immaculate drop into the background. During the fret of baggage and customs she walked very mutely, and during the drive up the tall hills she listened quietly. David's voice was a pleasure to hear. It was low and infinitely leisured, the voice of a man who had rarely gone from here to there without inclination.

In the square hall David's affectionate greeting of his mother and the reception of her arms exemplified one of the greatest contrasts between her old life and her new. The grace of touch continually sent her mind back to an examination of relationships in the Cove. There, flesh was frequently bleak and unresponsive. Try as she would, she could not recall any picture of her father kissing her mother. Benedict left often for a day and a night to another Cove, to a river for salmon, to the woods in the autumn for shooting. Mary Immaculate could recall him quite clearly walking away and returning with no visible sign that he had been farther than the beach. Clop-hoppering into the kitchen, he would pick up where he left off. Josephine's questions were answered with inarticulate grunts. Here, people came and went with gracious gestures. Such things lay warmly on her heart. The old way had made her chary of touch. Response was one of the things she had needed to learn. It came easily with the natural goodwill of her heart.

Another thing was noticeable in David's return.

Hannah!

She was behind the mater as if she had a place. While David was kissing his mother Hannah's hands were hovering with a strong reminder of Molly Conway. It was puzzling to see the tall impressive man turn and kiss the old woman's cheek.

"Why, Hannah, bless you, you don't age a day! I believe you're a dear old evergreen."

The folds of Hannah's face actually smiled, and though her voice responded in its same grumble, it was a loving grumble.

"And, Mr. David, isn't it a good thing that I am? With you in the house not a few seconds and me stooping to pick up after you. There now, don't mess up the hall. I'll take his things, Mr. Philip, and set him to rights. And there's a fire in your room, Mr. David, because you're such a frosty cat."

Mary Immaculate was allowed to honour David with a yellow dress, leaving her arms bare under a collar encroaching to the shoulders. Looking at herself in the mirror, she tried to find the child in the Cove. She was less apparent on the outside than she was in. It was impossible not to have moods of disbelief in her luck. Moments came when she waited for the pinch that would nip her joy and return her to the narrow world of the Cove.

Dinner was gala, served on china and glass resting for a long time on top shelves. There were extra courses that made Mary Immaculate think she'd feel very full, but they came in small moulds making a fork seem like violation. Accompanying the food was sherry, and pale yellow wine, and port waiting on the sideboard.

Hannah was in the dining-room, and Mary Immaculate noticed that Lilas was made to pour the wine. Hannah was a tyrant! Knowing that the Salvation maid had signed the pledge to touch no wines or spirituous liquors, Hannah pushed her as close to them as she could.

Lilas poured wine with her mouth down at the corners and her top lip curled away from her teeth. She held the decanters like a saint cupping contamination. As the dinner progressed, her expression modified. None of the wine-bibbers would get to glory, but as yet neither of the men had fallen dead drunk at her feet! When the dinner was on the wane her face grew yearning and she circled the table gazing at David. Her expression seemed to say she wished he was saved.

Mary Immaculate watched and listened. Conversation flowed about people abroad, relations and places that they all seemed to know. She learned that David and Felice had been in the South of France, motoring on a coast they called the Corniche Road. How could a coast be a road? She thought of the granite indentations of her own shore and pondered. Felice was arriving during the first week in August, bringing Rufus. For a moment she held her breath. Would Rufus take the time she gave to Tim? Ensuing explanations made her smile. Venturing one small question, they turned in a body to tell her Rufus was a cat with a white shirt-front and socks, and on his back legs David gave him frilly Victorian drawers. She thought if David could mention drawers in front of his mother, she should be allowed to say guts.

In her black dress with sheer sleeves the mater looked animated. Her eyes had lost their dull look and she smiled a great deal. In spite of their absorption none of them forgot their new relative. The mater smiled at her, Philip leaned over and patted her shoulder, and at the end of the meal David looked at her with great interest.

"I'll have time for you tomorrow, darling, but when I come home I always wonder what makes me leave Mater. It takes quite a time to get used to her again. I've never been able to behave as badly as I'd like to, because she keeps cropping up."

"I know," said Mary Immaculate sympathetically. "Without saying anything she makes you want to be and do."

An appreciative laugh came from the brothers and a slight flush touched Lady Fitz Henry's cheeks.

"Mater," said David gravely, "have you ever had a finer compliment?"

"I think not," she admitted.

David broke other rules that she thought were set. She was not allowed to talk to Lilas at table, but he spoke quite frequently to Hannah. Once the old woman stood by his side laughing over some story of his childhood, and another time she almost cackled.

"Don't talk, Mr. David, I'll never know what makes you so untidy, with your mother so neat when her house was burning. Never will I forget her saying to the men carrying her stretcher, 'Be careful of the wallpaper, please.'"

The small jokes of the family! Those were the things she had wanted Hannah to tell her, but they were all withheld until David arrived. He broke many other rules. For two days the Place was in confusion adjusting him. He needed so many things. The wireless was antique and a modern one had to be installed; he had to hire a car for himself because Philip's was always in use; he had to have a perpetual supply of books and papers. He strewed as he went, and Hannah followed, evicting his possessions to his own quarters. Then he spent a whole day with his mother in the car, and Philip and she were left alone. It gave her the opportunity of seeing Tim.

At five in the afternoon he was sitting in the shaded corner of the privet hedge. Sinking down beside him she drew blades across her face while she told him all the Fitz Henry news. Tim sat with his arms round his grey-flannel knees with his wrists too far out of his blazer.

"Gretel," he said with gloom in his voice, "Mother knows about us."

"Oh," she said, nonplussed. "We're not quite alone any more."

"That's what I thought. She came to call me the last time for something and heard our voices. She went away, but she questioned me when I got home. Thank God she didn't tell Auntie Minnie."

"Would that be worse?"

"Much," he said almost viciously. "I don't like her. She laughs at the quartet and says it's just like the cats on the back fence. If she knew that we met nearly every day she'd put on her white gloves and call. That wouldn't do, would it?"

"No," she said. "I don't think so. Mater is—well, she couldn't laugh at the quartet."

"I know," he said moodily. "Aunt Minnie is awful. She howls over the sextette, too. Sometimes I wish she'd be like Kundry in *Parsifal*, condemned to eternal laughter, couldn't stop, had to go on—"

"Oh no!" she interrupted practically. "It would be such a lot of noise. What did your mother say, Tim?"

"She was decent," he said with careful justice. "She said she wondered why I seemed more contented lately. Didn't know I was discontented before, but she said I was."

He gave her his brooding smile from lids grown suddenly heavier.

"Then," he said musingly, "she gave me a little talk on how to behave to a young girl."

"People are queer, aren't they?" she said for him.

Next morning David was dressing near a window, inhaling his natal air. From the gravel path came a voice accompanied by the thud of a ball.

"Charlie Chaplin went to France
To teach the children how to dance,
And this is how he taught them:
Heel toe, over you go,
Salute the King,
Bow to the Queen..."

"What's this?" he questioned, leaning out. "The decadence of the folk-spirit?"

Mary Immaculate backed a few paces to see him more comfortably.

"David," she said, shaking her head, "everyone makes me folky? Am I folky?"

"It sounds so from what I hear. I made Phil sit up last night telling me about you, but he's so full of charts. On the twelve-thirty train the child was admitted, etc... Stupid fellow, isn't he?"

"Philip is..." she began defensively. Then she saw David sitting on the sill, with smiling lips under a savouring nose. "David, you're fooling," she told him with supreme equality. "Philip is like St. Joseph."

"Is he?" he said, roaring with laughter. "Personally I feel like a lily in the field. How do you feel?"

"Grand," she said expansively. "I nearly stepped from the window because I felt I could fly, and maybe if I was near I could try to walk on the water if it had that level look."

"Well, well," he said with great interest. "I'm glad you didn't come to this house before. We'd be in jail together. I feel I should say something about waxen wings but I won't. I always hated the moral."

"I don't listen," she said blandly. "I sign off when the interesting bit is over."

"M'mm," he said expressively. "There's a lot of things I've got to know, Mary? Phil gave me a case-history when I wanted—"

"What?" she asked warily, as he paused.

"To know how you felt," he said beguilingly. "Mary, you and I are going to have a day together. I'm going to the cottage to see the caretaker—"

"Oh!" she squealed. "I wish I could go but I can't—"

"Yes, you can," he said with a grin. "It's so near the holidays that another day can't possibly matter. Come in to breakfast and watch my high hand with dear Mater."

Opposition died in the mater's leniency to David.

As she went she wished Tim could pipe the children out of the Cove to see her high estate. It was a triumphal day. Sitting up with a regal back, David drove her through invisible arches while open-mouthed fisher-folk stood tranced on the side of the road. The grey sedan was a golden coach, and David's tailored suit robes of church purple.

In open country they passed through quiet farmland. Blue ponds were frequent, holding the strong colour of the sky. Cows grazed in fields or ambled on the roads. In massive maternity a hen escorted a brood of chicks. A pair of white ducks emerged from a ditch, making David brake quickly. Undisturbed they waddled away, intent on some aquatic pleasure. Self-forgetfulness took Mary Immaculate. Time-tables were routed, and hours that held no rhythm.

Wind was in the air. She could feel it between her fingers as she trailed a hand out of the window. Dabbling it up and down, she felt volume, giving a sense of immersion in dry water. Talking to David, she pondered on the difference between the brothers. If she could have expressed herself at that moment she would have said David was interested in how she felt and Philip was concerned with her conduct. In a further separation she made another deduction. David remembered days that were foolish and loitering and Philip was not so sure.

She could have driven miles looking at the country, but she had to share her interest with David. Knowing all her story, he said he knew nothing.

"Your adventure fascinates me, Mary. You must have a unity with nature or else it would have killed you. Did you people the trees with benign spirits to watch over you?"

"No," she said, frowning over his elaboration. "I didn't do anything grand. With the slice of bread under my feet I could let the Little People be company."

"Darling," he pleaded, "go back! Begin with the morning and tell me about the little rites you used to make. Phil hasn't my vulgar curiosity."

Nor your interest in things like that, she thought to herself.

For his sake she went back, recalling the wonder of that hot-cold day and presenting it to him with vivid memory.

"I know, Mary," he said sensitively, "our incredible silver thaws! They're very heady. Now tell me about your lovely superstitions."

David was very satisfactory, driving his car with a timeless rhythm. Very freely she described Josephine's rites for her family.

"Then," he said with a smile under his black moustache, "it's a moot point whether you were lost or held."

"Only here, not in the Cove. I'll be a story as long as the Cove."

"Immortality indeed," he drawled in his leisured voice. "But what I'm so curious about is how you felt and what you did. Four days is a lot of time to think and feel."

"There were lots of times I didn't think at all. I was never thirsty as I had snow to eat. Philip said I got light-headed, and imagined the Little People. They looked so pretty in the moonlight," she said retrospectively.

David's tone was a little dry.

"With all due respect to Philip, my sweet, even he must admit those conditions took time to develop. Come on, darling, empty your mind."

Waiting, he heard her voice, tentative at first, collecting impressions and experiences that had never found vent in words.

"At first when I knew I couldn't get home the sun was still shining and it didn't seem cold. I remembered Uncle Rich, and how sensible he was when he was held. I did what he did, turned my coat inside out and made the sign of the Cross, and walked on for a long time. But it didn't do any good, so I turned my coat back, because I thought if

I was going to be held I would like to be held right side out."

David laughed out loud. "Mary, I adore you."

"Then, David, I tried to remember sensible things about the poor man's compass. I knew the sun rose in the east and set in the west, and the junipers pointed to the east. That meant the junipers would be bending away from the sun at that time of the day. That should have been a help, but it wasn't much. I didn't seem to be able to remember where the sun rose and set in the Cove. I tried to put myself back in my bedroom and play it was morning on a sunny day, but it was worse than a sum you couldn't do. Sometimes, when Miss Good does an Algebra problem let x equal the unknown quantity, I think that x might have helped me. But I didn't know about x until I came to town. By that time it was getting dark and I felt cold. I walked to a clearing and found a drift raised up like a wave. It seemed to say stay. I knew Pop lay on spruce-boughs when he went to camp, so I broke off what I could. It was very hard, as the trees were all frozen. They were held, too. A few low down made enough to lie on. I sat down first and thought I'd eat the slice of bread. I hadn't eaten it before because Mom said to keep it until I was well out. It was on the way to my mouth when I thought of Molly Conway."

"Yes," he said, "Philip told me about her. The changeling who found you."

For a moment she paused, seeing poor Molly Conway. "Because of her, David, I stopped eating the bread. I trusted the Little People, but not that much. I was afraid I might lose my looks."

"It would have been a loss," he said, smiling at the road.

"So," she said with a long sacrificial sigh expressing her cold and hunger, "I put the slice of bread under my feet and lay down. Funny enough, I went straight to sleep. I'll never forget it when I woke up. The moon was above me all alone in the sky. There wasn't a star. It was white, awfully white everywhere, and the trees were like ghosts rapping together from a little wind. They sounded more like bones than boughs. It was a glass world, shining in the moonlight. It seemed to get into my head, and when I closed my eyes I saw moons like glass plates. I felt queer, so opened them and ate a bit of my roof. Then I *know* I saw the Little People, just as I like them, with shiny dresses and silver wings. They danced and danced without a sound and ran up to my feet and back, as long as I watched. It was like a game, and I remembered laughing out loud. Then I went to sleep again, and when I woke it was dull and heavy and all the silver was gone. It felt damp and grey and the sky looked like water. A few snowflakes came down and I thought Mother Holle was making her bed. You know, David, when it snows—"

"Yes, I know—Grimm!"

"I tried to get up, but I couldn't, because the backs of my rubbers were frozen to the ground and I didn't feel my hands at all. I took off my mitts and I saw my fingers were gone. I knew what to do and I dug them into the roof of my house, and by the middle of the morning they came back. How they tingled, David! It was much worse than the frostbite, so I let them go again. When I woke up I didn't know whether I had any feet or hands. After that it got mixed and I only knew when it was dark and light. Sometimes I'd be myself and think of Mom home washing dishes and then I'd be seeing the Little People hopping around me. When the snow fell in big flakes I thought it might cover me, but it fell so lightly that I scarcely felt it. I was sure I was the only person left in the world. Everybody had died, and though I felt queer I didn't feel sick. I thought I had to die, but it was easy and the silence was lovely. When I was free and running round I used to be sorry for the trees and flowers because they had to stay in the same place. But when I was part of the ground I felt part of it, as if I was just another plant or something that was dying to come up again in the spring. The wind used to sing me to sleep, and it was white and cold, and I felt like winter. David," she almost screamed, looking into his expressive face, "you've got a tear in your eye."

Without the smallest embarrassment he pulled at the handbrake, stopping by a clump of spruce trees, sheltering a round blue pond.

"Yes," he confessed. "I was always an emotional fool." He extracted a large handkerchief and wiped his glasses, and she thought his eyes looked naked without them.

"Mary," he told her in adult language, "people write learned books about the things you've said so simply. They exhaust themselves talking about microcosm in relation to macrocosm, which, in simpler form, is man in relation to the great whole—"

"Talk sense, David," she said in Benedict's manner.

He laughed, starting his car again.

"You remind me of cold dew, and then…"

There was silence, while she watched the country with irresponsible eyes. David recalled her again.

"I suppose there were many materialists who believed nothing but the bare outlines of your adventure."

She examined his face and then answered with great illumination, "I suppose you mean the people who said I was cracked."

"Probably," he said with a slight grimace, "though I hate slang from a dryad mouth."

The Fitz Henrys were exacting! Tim was the only human who thought she was right as she was. Driving through the country she occupied herself with the making of a man. Philip, David and Tim were shaken up in a bag to make a blend.

"Mary?"

"Yes," she said very politely.

"Have you told Philip how you felt in the woods?"

"Of course not," she said at once.

"Why?"

"He doesn't want to hear."

David gave her a very acute sidelong glance.

"What makes you say that?"

She hesitated.

"Tell David," he said beguilingly.

Instinct told her what she said would stay with him.

"Philip," she said quickly, "is only interested in Mary Fitz Henry."

"M'mm," he said, frowning. "No room for Mary Keilly?"

"None," she said lightly, as if it didn't matter.

"Do you mind?"

"No, of course not. Philip is—"

"I know, darling, like St. Joseph."

They both laughed together with sunny mutuality.

A wide curve brought them in view of the sea. The world fell away in a valley, full of alders and spruce, and a pair of waterfalls frothing as twins. There was enough beach for a whole shore. Descending, the road flattened and rose again to the height of a headland. Then David stopped beside a rustic fence with one row of dark trees. Peering through, she could see a long, low house.

"This, Mary, is my humble abode."

"It's grand for a cottage," she said, impressed.

"A few minor comforts, my dear. Out you get."

Through a rustic gate they went up a gravel path ending in a one-storyed garage concealed by a trellis. Morning glory climbed up, straining in the air like young question-marks. The house stood in a big square, sloping to a fence with a gate, opening on the headland. The sea seemed endless, widening away to dim land making a bay.

"Let's look at the sea first," he suggested, walking down the slope. The only garden had been suppressed to herbaceous borders growing at the base of the solid fences. Pale perennials seemed dimmed by a flaunt of peonies.

Mary Immaculate was running, sniffing and savouring.

"David, how gorgeous to smell the sea without fish. It gives you a chance to smell the earth, too. I love it. I killed one of Mater's plants just to get that wet smell."

The fact did not seem to depress him. He was smiling at the way her hair blew back from her face. Limping behind, he quoted to her back: "The divine earth sent forth new grass and dewy lotus, crocus and hyacinth!"

"David," she said reverently, "what lovely things you know!"

She brought up on her feet, frankly admiring his range. He went ahead, smiling at the sea.

"I was preparing for you all winter, Mary, by reading how much Greek and Roman poetry is identified with nature. You see, there *is* a unity. Come on," he invited, opening the gate.

With a wild young spurt she rushed through.

"Stop!" he almost roared.

She brought up on a brink. Poised on an overhanging bank she saw it fall steeply away. Steps broken by several platforms descended to the beach. Fastened to the fence was a bench built for long-gazing. David sat down, grabbing her with a long arm.

"You're a reckless little fool. You nearly went over."

"The sea couldn't drown me," she said omnipotently. "I was born on it."

"It couldn't wet you either, I suppose?"

Searching his face, she knew he was more amused than irritated. Her mind leaped ahead to her lunch. He would let her eat with supreme indifference to well-balanced food.

"David, you're lovely," she said from a full heart.

"Like St. Joseph, I suppose?"

"No," she said definitely. "St. Joseph is much more particular."

TEN

"SO YOUNG AND SO UNTENDER."

Her introductions were providential, weighted with cues lending hints of direction. She entered no one's life unobtrusively. Mild presentations and maidenly shrinkings did not belong to her. Her quality of youth could be piercing, blinding those of "gone by" with the light of "to come". Her step was impulsive, long and flowing from the hips as if to annihilate distance to many Meccas. Because she was Mary Immaculate of many identifications, her nose had begun to similize the Fitz Henry nostril. Her blood had been oxygenated at birth. She was born to breathe big.

Felice arrived at a time when she was unable to meet the boat. Signalled on Sunday morning, Mary Immaculate saw it enter the harbour, on her way to eleven o'clock Mass. There was an interminable sermon, the antithesis of the day.

Outside summer was in its prime. Inside, sunlight streamed through the stained-glass robes of saints and martyrs. Patches of blood-red, purple and blue coloured the congregation. Muffled through the panes came the sounds of the world. There seemed to be barks, shouts, swishes, and a sense of humanity urged hither and thither. Summer was fugitive, overfull of sea, sky and gourmand youth. As if oppressed with red blood, the priest preached of modesty, virtue, the brevity of bathing-suits and the audacity of shorts.

When the congregation was unleashed it surged in one leap from the thong of the Mass. Separating herself, Mary Immaculate ran under a stone arch bearing an exalted statue of St. John. When she arrived at the Place she found Felice and David had gone to the cottage.

Mary Immaculate could regret him as a delightful time-waster, an incessant talker and a frequent playmate, until he went with Philip on the train. He returned just as he left; pale, leisured and full of other conversation. He spoke of sportsmen he had met, flies he had not used, books he intended to read and silvery salmon he had not caught. Philip said nothing, but looked refreshed and well. Lightly bronzed, he unpacked a box of delicately smoked salmon and some fat trout lying in moss. Almost at once he put his holiday behind him in a quick change to the dark clothes of his profession.

Mary Immaculate's disappointment was mitigated by Philip's intention of motoring her to the cottage. It appeared Rufus had not travelled well and needed to be settled at once. Costing three pounds to transport, his appetite had failed and he had refused his first land meal.

Early afternoon found the mater immovable in a canopied chair on her lawn. The air was drowsy, insects idle and languid in their hum. Philip went without conscience. Feeling the measure of his mother's content, it bequeathed him his own. Further comfort in the disposal of his patients released him to the enjoyment of Mary Immaculate. Gay in a sprigged dress with a drawstring neck, she sat up with forward-gazing eyes. Lady Fitz Henry was training her to a control of her legs and arms, but she found it impossible to loll. Ease against cushions lessened the scope of vision. Rounding the curve descending to David's village, the sea appeared blue, green and lucent with copper paths. People bathed or stretched their bodies on smooth grey stones. She felt naked flesh must rise from the sea, stained with colour.

A dip to sea level, a rise to a headland brought them to David's cottage. Walking to the front facing the sea, they mounted five steps leading to a verandah. Ignoring the closed front door, Philip pulled a wire screen from floor-length windows.

"What's that?" asked Mary Immaculate, stiffening the long lines of her body. Fixed on the step of an exciting interior, she heard the hoarse squawk of some forest creature. Its shrill repeat took her mind off Dutch-blue walls, deep chairs with gay covers.

"Brute beast!" ejaculated David's disturbed voice.

An energetic stamp of a foot evicted a wild ginger streak. Almost unidentifiable in moving colour, it sped between Mary Immaculate's legs, hurled past Philip, leaving a deposit of hair on his trouser-legs.

"Good God!" said Philip, startled. "Rufus! His appetite has come back."

A light, tortured voice came from the hall.

"David, David darling, do something! I can't bear it! Oh, the poor wretched thing, what can I do? Look, look, David, it's all mangled and its wing is half off. Do something, I implore you, darling."

"Do, Felice, what can I do?" David's voice was full of distaste. Mary Immaculate could feel the unseen repulsion of his nostrils. Identifying the distress of a blackbird, she moved stealthily forward on feet seeming cushioned with animal pads. A backward fling of her hand commanded Philip not to tread on her heels. Magnetism claiming him, he followed on the tips of his toes. Easing through the door like a secret, she took a tortured situation from David and Felice. Either they had too much humanity or too little to forget themselves in action. Seeing it all, Mary Immaculate's eyes acquired animal glaze. There was a black-haired woman squatting in front of a corner, making ineffectual grabs at something replying in hoarse panic. David was leaning against a newel-post with his lips curled away from his teeth. He looked like Lilas pouring wine.

"God!" he said in bitter disgust.

Nervous hands had worried the bird out of a corner. As it hopped across a strip of carpet, it represented the cruelty of nature. Faculty of flight was gone in a wing dragging from a mangled back. Bare of feathers it was raw like slaughtered flesh. The agitation of its plight had entered small bowels emitting a series of watery droppings.

"Oh, poor thing, poor thing!" wailed Felice in a high, light voice.

"Shushhh—" breathed Mary Immaculate on long sibilance.

The bird had gone into another corner, swelling its chest with its bursting heart.

There was no thud in the way she fell on her knee, and her crawl was predacious, sinuous and slow with patience. Poising in immobility she crouched, gazing at the bird. Seeing the intense yellow of her eyes, David's shocked sensitiveness expected to see her grow tawny stripes. From interest and fascination they let her alone; Felice on her haunches, Philip filling the door and David rigid against the newel-post. The bird did not squawk or move. Whether in trust or mesmerism it awaited its fate. Hardly aware that her hand had moved, they saw it enclosing the bird. Falling back on her heels, she stroked the tiny head with the tip of one finger.

"Poor bird," she said pitifully, "you can't live like that. It's better to die."

"Yes, yes," agreed Felice, crawling forward on her knees. "David dear, you must knock it on the head."

"I will not," said David decisively.

"Philip will, then," she said, as if she knew he would accept the hard part.

"If you say so, Felice," he agreed, making a forward step.

Mary Immaculate met his eyes.

"It will hurt it more if you take it from my hand, Philip. I know what to do. Where's the kitchen?"

"There," said Felice, pointing to a closed door.

Mary Immaculate was through it while they were collecting themselves. Following, they saw a maid filling a bucket at a sink. The girl was square, fresh and a product of Mary Immaculate's own world. Understanding the impersonal earth, she moved quickly at the child's direction.

"There, miss," she said, stepping aside.

A decisive plunge took the bird into water. They did not see it again until she brought it up, bedraggled in feathers parting to show seams of white skin. On the palm of her hand it drooped with slacked neck.

"Is it quite dead?" she asked, holding it out to Philip.

"Quite dead," he said gravely.

Mary Immaculate had a strange capacity for changing servants into human beings. The maid walked to a stove and raised a damper.

"Fire is clean, miss," she said suggestively.

The child looked at the girl, seeing quiet eyes, and skin with the honey pallor of a Jersey cow.

"*I'm* a Catholic, and we don't cremate."

The maid smiled. "There's no churches in the forests, miss."

Mary Immaculate smiled back. "I ought to know that," she said, dropping the bird into the fire.

Startled elders saw the pair return to the sink, where the child washed her hands as the maid passed a towel.

"My dear," said Felice, returning to earth, "how are you? What an introduction! David wrote about you, but he hasn't described you at all. I'm delighted to see you at last."

"Hello!" she said, returning the towel and shaking hands. Looking at Felice, she tried to find an answer to David in his wife. In that capacity she was something of a shock. Balance suggested he should be complemented by a beautiful creature, tall like himself. She was short, meagre, with a long face. When women's brows were becoming increasingly conspicuous and napes were fully revealed, her head looked hot with a weight of hair. Eyes were green under black brows, and her smile was so wide that no teeth could fill it. In her quick graciousness she bared a generous expanse of gum. Hands were smooth and beautiful, and supple from the wrists. Clothes were well cut, depending on themselves for style.

"Come out of the kitchen, Mary," said David flippantly.

Felice slipped her arm through the child's, drawing her along. "Let them go, my dear. Come upstairs with me while I unpack. I'm in a disgraceful muddle. I've brought you a present—"

"Me?" said the child excitedly. "How gorgeous! What is it?"

"Wait and see. If you like it, we might use it. Let the men amuse themselves. We'll have time for them later."

Exuberantly Mary Immaculate mounted white stairs with grass-green carpet. In her cottage Felice had let herself go with colour as vivid as the shades of a summer world.

The brothers lounged through the large room, going out through the screen door. Rufus was sitting on the top step, gazing at the sea with round sinless eyes.

"Murderer!" growled David as he went down the steps. "What did you think of that bit of girlishness, Phil?"

"The doctor in me gave it full marks," he answered, seating himself in a canvas chair. Advancing his long legs he relaxed in the sun.

"Humph!" said David, doing the same thing. "But the *man* waited for her to hide her pretty head."

"I'm not so sure…"

"Well, I am," said David convincingly. "I'm shattered by that young thing doing something that would give me the creeps. When she was crawling across the floor I'm sure I saw jungle. I hope to God she won't change into a leopardess and eat you in your bed. You'd be useless with a—"

"Shut up!" said Philip vigorously. "It was a perfectly natural act of a child who's seen maimed creatures—"

"And I'm sure I saw whiskers, too," interrupted David, intent on his picture. "Knowing her, I hardly expected fear of a mouse, but I didn't anticipate anything quite so nerveless—"

"In her world she couldn't afford nerves. She's not a product of people who pay three guineas a time to discuss childish shocks—"

"The robbers," said David lazily. "Felice paid a hundred guineas to get cured of claustrophobia under trees. That's why I can't afford my own phobias. I'm sure I was born with one skin too little. I was excoriated in the fire of '92, or was it '46? Hannah will tell me. It left me with spiritual haemophilia. I'm a bleeder over life's agonies. It comes from a long line of spirits born to the purple—"

"You're a fool," said Philip amiably. "It comes from a line of time-wasters. That's a better diagnosis for your purple spirit—"

"You can go, Phil," said David, closing his eyes. "I'm unhappy because Mary is so brave and you're so sensible. You're excused to operate on any of God's creatures you find at large."

A long drowsy silence was shattered by the rush of Mary Immaculate's feet and the wild joy of her voice.

"Philip, David, look at me!"

The brothers sat up.

"Good gracious, darling," said David, blinking, "you're very bare and beautiful!"

"Yes, aren't I?" she agreed, strutting in front of them both.

There was something in the childish parade of her body that gave the men the consciousness that might have been hers. She was too tender with adolescence, easing childhood away. Felice had brought her a bathing-suit like a green sheath, with sandals, and a towelling-cape being twirled in the air. Her head was enclosed in a helmet outlining the neat skull, while legs and thighs shimmered with a white bloom.

"My back is bare, too," she said, craning her head over her shoulder to see the extent of her nudity. The brothers had the full benefit of the milky skin, narrow hips and tender curves showing barely perceptible womanhood. In her green-and-white, she suggested a flower springing from the earth.

Felice followed more decorously, wrapped in a cape. Her legs were frail and she stripped meagrely, but she had no consciousness. Being David's wife had removed all inferiority.

"We're going bathing, David. I'm so glad Rufus came back. I did think when I had him vetted he would stop eating the birds."

"Not exactly the same instinct, dear," smiled David, looking at the shimmer of Mary Immaculate's legs.

"Is it wise to go bathing, Felice, right off the ocean?" cautioned Philip. "Mary—"

"Why not, Phil? We had a good crossing and I feel very fit."

"Oh, don't stop us, Philip. I'm dying to feel the water. I'm sure it will blue me."

"Pagan," grinned David, rising from his chair. "Let's go to the look-out, Phil, and watch them, unless you'd like to go in yourself."

"I'm afraid I feel drowsy and the cold water will wake me up."

"The North Atlantic!" said David with a shiver. "Only these fat women can bear it. Run off, children! The old men will sit and watch Helen pass by."

"Who's she, David?" asked the child, running by his side.

"None of your business," he said with a charming smile.

"Rude, David," she grinned.

Outside on the bank David subsided on the seat against the fence. "Can you swim, Mary?"

"I expect so, David," she said, looking down on the bathers. "Come on, Felice."

Every step down the hazardous stairs was a joyous bound.

"Take care, Mary," commanded Philip.

The laugh that floated back went out to sea again like a bell of youth.

"Yes, Philip," she called with vocal co-operation.

His eyes watched her headlong descent until she gained the beach.

"I know how Faust felt," sighed David from his choice of idleness. "When I look at her I feel nothing can replace youth, living and loving, and being in tune with nature. She makes me feel jaded and conscious of my age. I doubt very much if she'll attract much physical love from men. She's too tall and white, and too much like cold dew. I can see her twenty, thirty, forty, still with that dryad look. It won't be sustained on virginity, either; it has a deeper quality, something from green fields and cold snows. Men will be conscious of smuts and luxuriate in an altar. Even if she had the fabric of a courtesan she'd find it hard to seduce. To a man it would be like defiling white samite. I—"

"Damn it all," exploded Philip, "you're talking of a child! It's, it's—"

"The simple truth," said David, unrepentant. "Other men will recognise the quality that compelled the first uncalculated action of your life. I've no manners, Phil! What do you feel about her?"

Protected from the sun by his glasses, David gazed searchingly at his brother. Like his mother, the pupil and iris of his eyes merged into one. Philip's eyes were wide and clear, and a more definite brown. They came back from the sea to endure his brother's scrutiny.

"If you must know, damn you," he said with concentrated sincerity, "I wish it was her eighteenth birthday today, and I'd make her marry me before she realised there was another man in the world."

"Now that," said David humorously, "is what I call an answer. No evasion—"

Philip's short laugh stopped him.

"What would be the good of evasion? You'd only ask me again."

"I think I would," David admitted, gazing at Philip with concern. "I love Mary myself, but she's more important when she affects you and Mater. Isn't it dangerous to indulge that one-minded way? Why not go out more and let yourself go? Now that you're established, you've more leisure. Some other interest might claim you. I see lots of flaming youth around."

"It can flame without me," said Philip decisively. "I happen to know what I want. Mater's comfort, the preservation of the Place and Mary! My leisure will go to her. This winter I'm going to flood the tennis-court and make a rink. I'll teach her to waltz—"

"Why not take her to the rinks?"

"Too many people and we'd be too far away from Mater. I think she knows how I feel, and in return no hand-picked companion could be better. If Mater is going to miss her, I won't send her to school in England."

"My dear Phil! Would you deny her normal advantages—"

"Normal advantages are here for her, Dave. I don't want her to go myself. She's so much to come home to; so happy and sweet-tempered, so full of conversation—"

"I know," said David quickly, realising the emptiness of his brother's emotional life. At thirty his knowledge of women was entirely clinical! Idealisation was dangerous allied to the uncertain returns from a beautiful unusual child. In inner disquietude David searched for the white helmet capping Philip's child. Felice was swimming away while Mary stood still, watching bathers enter and leave the sea. She seemed to turn more towards those who plunged forward in the icy blue. Suddenly she ran down the grey stones, throwing herself in the water with a luxury of immersion. The impetus of a long, springing motion took her far out on the shining sea.

"She can swim, then," said David absently. "My God, can she? Philip!"

His brother wheeled round to see white arms sawing the air in wild surprise.

"God, the little fool!" shouted Philip, leaping towards the steps. "I'm coming, Mary!" he yelled at the top of his voice.

"She's drowning!" screamed David to the beach, and answering calls came back with the sound of feet crashing over stones.

Herd anxiety ran like the throw of a chain.

"Yes," said David out loud, "the little fool! Can you swim? I expect so! We're the fools!"

Reaching one of the platforms of the crazy wooden steps, he realised the futility of another headlong descent. The sea showed no signs of Mary Immaculate. Sleekly it had closed over her, hiding its secret under an innocent level. Claiming its own, it was not permitted to hold. A strong body shot forward like a projectile, while sun made a glint on a Nordic head. Disappearing, it came up, followed by shoulders churning the water to a maelstrom. The co-operation of life saving was being upset by a wild struggle.

"God!" said David unhappily.

A brown arm made a curve in the air and spent its force against the bosom of the sea.

"God," said David again, "he's knocked her out!"

Peace came back to the water, disturbed only by a swimmer doing a job in a perfect way.

"He knows how," said David, addressing a company that was not there. Continuing his descent he saw his wife wringing her hands as she wavered towards her cape. His sensitiveness flinched to see the limp body of Mary Immaculate trailed at the side of a muscular young man. Within his depth he swung her across his chest, carrying her like some sacrificial offering. The downward droop of white arms and legs suggested beauty slain for some palliation.

Regardless of the fact of being fully dressed, Philip waded into the sea to take his child. Straddling like a colossus, the young man placed her across extended arms. As David trod painfully over the beach, the Nordic head and muscular body sent his mind to the clean modelling of Greek sculpture. The Hermes of Praxiteles was panting just a little as drops ran down his body like liquid diamonds.

"Sorry, sir, very sorry I had to knock her out, but I think she was surprised and couldn't realise I was saving her. She got me round the neck. I hated to do it, but it was the only way. I don't think she was in the water long enough to need artificial respiration, but she's certainly done in—"

"Thank you," muttered Philip, working his hand round to one of the child's wrists. "I'm a doctor, I—"

"It was beautifully done without the waste of a second," said David, more competent in the civilities following a rescue. "Cut along, Phil! I'll come up later."

"Yes, dear," said Felice, shivering in her cape. "We'll go! Get his card or something—"

A glance at the magnificent body rebuked the possibilities of his presenting a club address from a pair of blue shorts. He should have been given garlands or a laurel-wreath she thought vaguely, running after Philip's wet trouser-legs, speeding up the steps. A dangling white arm made a mute wave towards a rescuer still standing in the water. Blue eyes followed an ascent two things hastened. Philip's anxiety for his child and an intense desire to hide her from gaping spectators.

"Phil, take her to David's room. Mine is all luggage. What can I do? What do you want?"

"Her pulse is all right," he called back. "She's unconscious from the blow. Fetch my bag."

When Felice stepped under sloping walls a narrow bed had been stripped of glazed chintz with apple-blossoms patterned on white. Mary Immaculate's green bathing-suit was lying in a corner, while her prone body was wrapped in a fleecy blanket.

"Is she all right, Phil? It was an unfortunate present. I didn't know she couldn't swim."

"I didn't either," he said grimly, watching the effect of an aromatic capsule.

"I should have stayed by her—"

"Nonsense, Felice, I should have known she couldn't swim. Run and get dressed like a good girl and telephone Mater, in case she hears of this in an indirect way. Tell her everything is quite all right."

"Very well, dear, but you must change yourself. I'll put out some of David's things."

"It's too warm to take cold," he said indifferently.

"Will you leave her all night, Phil? I'll have a room prepared—"

"Impossible," he said instantly. "I have to get back and I wouldn't consider letting her stay without me. If she's not all right David can drive us and I'll hold her. Of all the most abandoned recklessness!"

As he spoke the child's eyelids fluttered, opened, while she stared round the room without focus. Glazed eyes came to rest on Philip, trying to blink him into sight.

"Take your time, Mary," he said in the fever-reducing voice she knew so well. "You'll be all right in a minute."

"Philip," she said restlessly as thought came flooding back, "I thought the sea was my friend, but it didn't hold me up like it did the others. I went down, down! Water in my nose and mouth! It hurt, terribly! I liked dying in the woods better. It was awful! I didn't feel brave…"

She shivered, and Philip became soothing and adequate.

"You were taken off your guard and you panicked. This time you were well and full of fight. Before, you were weak and depleted—"

He stopped as if he hated the subject himself. Then he gathered up the blanket-cocoon with an intensification of possession.

"It's over, thank God," he muttered.

Felice tiptoed to the door as if the occasion demanded muted feet.

"I'll get dressed and come back. Don't forget your wet feet, Phil."

Mary Immaculate flung back her head for bigger and better breath.

"I hated it," she said restlessly. "I came up and felt the sun hot on my face. I went down—I felt—I'll never know how I felt. It must be the difference in summer-dying—"

"Oh, stop, Mary! Don't dwell on it. You're safe now."

With an unreserved face and body she crowded against him. He was safety, sanctuary, and in the core of her shattered being she was awed at the miracle of natural breath.

"The men in the Cove who die that way? There were so many. It's not a pleasant death, Philip—"

"Why do you do such reckless things?" he said sternly.

She went still, feeling the hum of the natural day. It included his anger for her misdeeds.

"Are you very cross with me?" she asked with a desperate cling to his neck.

Her dependence ousted any mental attitude he might have. The bones were shaken out of him, and his voice became full and indulgent.

"No, I'm not cross. I know I was angry the day you went for that walk, but tell me why…?"

"I'm so mean," she sighed. "I've got to know what things are like. Today it looked so easy. People dropped into the sea and went forward in that lovely long way. I thought I could do it, too."

Surprise and humility over her incapacity made her press her wet head against his face. It seemed to remind him of her mortality.

"Go to sleep, Mary, and I'll hold you like I used to in hospital," he suggested tenderly.

"Can I learn to swim, Philip?"

"Won't you be frightened?"

"No," she said, shocked. "I couldn't bear to stay frightened of the sea."

"Yes, I'll see about it. Relax now and go to sleep."

"Felice said you must change your shoes, Philip."

A settling of herself precluded any such possibility taking place. She made of his chest and arms a pillow and bed. She closed her eyes pondering on the rude crash that could shatter the core of joy. So many high moments were a tightrope walk! Tim—What would happen to Tim and herself? Nothing, she thought cosily, we're too nice! Philip surrounded her. She gave a small contented wriggle, causing response from his arms. She seemed to be his patient again, under his control, body and soul. Nice, she thought, with gathering content.

Downstairs, Felice played a small cottage piano. Knowing that Mary Immaculate was asleep, her long fingers made soothing contact with a slumber-song. At one of the windows Rufus slept in an orange ball. David came through the screen-door, disposing his body in the deepest chair.

"Darling," said Felice, twirling round, "you look exhausted."

"Done in," he admitted with a humorous shrug; "it's the Mad Hatter's tea-party. I'm too old for such living. Do you think you could find me a drink? Pour it yourself, dear. I couldn't trust that Hebe who feeds our stove with dead birds. I'm beginning to question familiar things."

"Darling, what nonsense you talk," she said with palpable affection in her light voice. "Of course I'll get you a drink."

She left with the movements of a person who could walk through rooms without obtrusion. In a short time she was back with a dark-looking drink.

"Yes," he admitted, tasting, "you've been generous."

"We'll have tea as a chaser, darling," she said, sitting down beside him. "Who was the romantic rescuer?"

"I've been talking to him ever since, much to the chagrin of a young thing who was swimming with him dressed in lipstick."

"Spoilsport, David," she accused, drawing her slight legs under her body.

"Not this time, dear. He was lost already, gone in thrall to chivalry and Mary's legs. He was a charming boy," he said, smiling over the edge of his tumbler.

"But who was he, David? Anybody local? He had a very heroic look!"

"The Senior Service, dear, a naval officer on a sloop in town. I asked him up for a drink, but Miss Lipstick put her foot down. We made rendezvous for London; Naval and Military. I'm glad he didn't come up. If we presented him to Mary he might go to her disturbing little head. How is she and where's Phil? Doing his best bedside?"

"He is, on our bed, with the child cuddled in his arms, sound asleep. I peeped in, but he was getting on nicely without me."

David almost groaned. "What do you think of it, Felice?"

"I haven't had much time for thought. I was surprised to see Phil looking so youthful and well. He's been so staid..."

"There you are," said David disconsolately, "agreeing with me when I wanted you to say I was in my dotage. It's a case of belated adolescence! Just when Father died he would have been young and romantic over a child Mary's age. Now he's upstairs getting pins and needles in his arms, a definite indication of his state! Nobody but a boy could endure pins and needles and like it."

"Poor Phil," she said sympathetically, "he's an angel! Darling, you'll have to let it alone, hoping she'll grow up liking to sleep in his arms. I must admit I wasn't prepared for such dazzling good looks. She shimmers. Phil worships her, I can see that."

David groaned again. "But he doesn't know her a bit. He's too busy turning her into a mannerly little person, and she's not the type to be cloistered. I know he's going on the rocks, but what can I do? Here I am with a weight of worldly wisdom and quite powerless to show him sense—"

"Darling," she said with light decision, "the last quality Phil would acknowledge from you would be sense. In view of the fact that he's one of the hardest workers and you're one—"

"Of the lilies and languors," he said with a grin. "In that case, dear, I'll have another drink. Then play to me, will you, Felice, something andante, mostly diminuendo, for I assure you at this stage the wrong note will shatter the crystal vase?"

"You dear idiot," she said happily. "Here's the tea. I'll play to you after."

"A WHITE AND RUSTLING SAIL."

She was commanded to bed for a day, without books or amusements of any kind. Routine had been strict enough to make it another savour. Like a long-sailing ship she was content with a temporary anchor, while her mind recapitulated on many seas. In the manifestations of their concern she was amused. Philip inquired of her body as if it might break in two! Feeling the bound of her blood, she could smile to herself, but he seemed to expect her to feel some aftermath.

From her remote world the mater said very little. Rueful tolerance went into the shake of her head, but she uttered no reproaches.

Felice sent out a satin bedjacket by David, resulting in a rapture of appreciation. He stayed to lunch, and for a while the two tall brothers lingered in her room. From the glamour of the jacket she felt the mantle of some old regime. David lounged at the foot of her bed and in doing so violated another convention. Lady Fitz Henry did not tolerate wrinkled spreads. It was impossible for Philip to sit on a bed. He always stood as if a nurse must be behind him, placing a chair. Surprised to find no support, he would reach for one himself. It was not long before a drag at his watch made him depart with some urgency. "A good sleep, remember," he said from the door.

Smiling in agreement, she explained to David. "Philip has something special. I know by his walk. I expect it's a baby."

"My dear," he said startled, "does he discuss his cases with you?"

"He didn't at first," she admitted, "but I asked him questions and then he began to tell me things. I love hearing! Operations can be exciting."

"I don't think so," he disagreed. "I hate the vile body and its disgusting details."

For once she was very severe.

"It can't be disgusting, David, if it's natural."

"As you say, darling," he agreed in mock humility; "but I haven't got your natural philosophy. Just when I'm expecting the dryad I get a hard-headed young realist. What an unaccountable young thing you are! I thought you might let me anticipate your next form of expressionism. If you give me an inkling it will save wear and tear. Felice said I grew a grey hair."

The true black of his head denied the charge, but she accepted the possibility as an offering. Mocking her gently about her drowning, he stimulated her to wild curiosity about her rescuer.

"Could I see him?" she asked guilelessly.

"Certainly not! He's committed to guns and ships. As a family we're against hero-sons. They might take your mind off—"

"No," she denied at once. "But much wants much, doesn't it, David?"

"Single-minded people don't," he said as if he could follow her well.

"Do they have fun?"

"They're not looking for your kind of fun, Mary. Many people can't see beyond surface-sight, and they're apt to mistake certain intensifications…"

"I don't know what you mean, David. Philip wasn't cross," she said musingly.

"Is he such a martinet?" he asked casually.

"No," she said, shocked, "but when it's my fault I mind more. When I'm sure grown people are foolish I let them have their say and it's over quicker."

"Indeed!" he said. "Most comfortable."

For a brief flash he saw her from within, absorbed, inscrutable, pursuing her own way while giving the smile of acquiescence to all demands. His brown eyes held hers, and he recalled what he had noticed before, that she could smile with her lips while her eyes remained cold. Now they rested on his without shifting, as if she were conscious of his extra knowledge of her. The man in him shrugged in a baffled way. Her expression was too old, suggesting elements bearing investigation. Too tolerant to take her to task, he had no wish to add his voice to the many directing her. He was sure he had been fanciful when she gave a childish spring.

"He wasn't even cross when he saw Betty-Wetty and Mitchy-Bitchy."

David became tentative, venturing delicate inquiry.

"Just what, Mary...?"

"Two girls I hate in school, David. Betty Wilson and Mitchy Morris. Mater says I must not be combative or pert, so I have to be polite to them. But, as I go on feeling combative and pert, I inked their faces on my toenails. Then when I'm in the bath I make faces at them, and by the time I get to school I can be polite. I'm afraid the ink was very good because it remains in the seams of my toes, and when Philip saw my feet he was shocked, so I had to tell him. He didn't mind, but right away he got something out of his bag, ether or something, but though he took quite a long time..." Her voice seemed to suggest that Philip had enjoyed his task. "Though he took quite a *long* time, he didn't do away with them completely. Look..."

With impulsive unconcern she thrust her two feet out, placing them on David's knees. The delicate flesh was disturbing and he handled the offending toes gently.

"Yes," he said gravely. "I see some remains, but identification is difficult. What special annoyance has Mitchy-Bitchy—?"

"She wants to touch me. Mom would call her a great big staragon or do I mean stallion, David?"

"Staragon, I think, whatever it is," he said with cathedral gravity. "What's Betty-Wetty's trouble?"

"Oh, she's just spoiled," she said dismissingly. "But she calls me bay-noddy. I expect I am, but I'm still having voice during the holidays, so by the time I get back I think I'll be able to tell her she sounds *quite* American—"

"Oh, Mary, Mary," he said, shaking his head. "Dryad indeed! It's the most self-contained, calculating, wicked—"

"No, no, David!" she protested, making a forward spring into his arms. "Don't scold me, please. Let me say what I like to you. Some days—"

Breaking off, she sighed against his face with her arms round his neck. It had the effect of reducing his doubts to water. The privilege of beauty, he thought, with the double-barrelled attribute of personality. Perhaps Philip was to be the ideal influence in her life. In his single-minded possession she would have little opportunity of tantalising other men. It was impossible not to hold her affectionately.

"What did you promise Phil?" he asked gently.

"To sleep, David."

"Then," he said, putting her back on her pillow, "you can begin now. Felice sent her love and said to tell you she would be in on Wednesday for tea, and then you're all coming to the cottage for dinner. It's a public holiday, so Phil will have most of the day. In the meantime promise me not to jump off the roof of the house."

The very niceness of him made her kiss him with sunny appreciation. "David, you're lovely," she said in his ear, relishing the small jokes that make bonds between people.

"You're lovely, too," he laughed. "Now I'm going to tell Mater you're sound asleep."

Drowsing the afternoon away, she returned to twilight induced by the trees. It was shadowed, tranquil and full of rest. Through the screened window came sounds from the down-curve of the day. Flies tried to enter and a curtain tried to get out; branches touched the house, heavy with the weight of leaves. The blur of her content was shattered by Tim's whistle, holding a screech of command. What had come to Tim? The whistle came again with urgency increased. Quietude fled, ousted by curiosity. It was impossible to go out! It was impossible to stay in bed, with Tim blasting in her ear. Something must have gone wrong. Auntie Minnie had laughed too hard at the quartette? Torment came out of the whistle, making the mercury of her spirit rise to a high degree of fever. She had to go! *No*, she could *not* go! Incredible to hurt them when they were so kind! Lying down, she put her head under the clothes, trying to retreat to Fitz Henry

Place. The whistle blasted again, shrilling through attempted muffling. It seemed to assault the trees and shiver the veins of the leaves. Tim was disturbed past mind and manners. She would go, and commend herself to God.

She was out of bed, standing on a pile carpet of old-fashioned patterning. No sound came from the house save the languid swishes of rooms open to the air.

She would not commend herself to God! There were other departments with a greater understanding of sin.

"Mary Magdalen," she breathed, belting a blue robe round her waist, "Mary Magdalen, you were a sinner once, pray for me, pray for me!"

Bending towards felt slippers, she asked for intercession.

"Mary Magdalen, you couldn't let me hurt them when they're so good, but you'd have to go yourself if Tim whistled in your ear. Remember when you were a sinner and give them something to do away from the windows. Intercede for me, I beseech you, and don't let me be taken in adultery!"

Stepping on muted feet she went into the hall, standing a few feet away from the gallery. The mater was having tea and discussing with Hannah some details of the house. Thankfully she heard the mater say, "Don't disturb Miss Mary, Hannah, she's sleeping." So far so good she thought, laying her spirit at the feet of the sinner-saint. Gliding towards the rear of the hall she opened a door with exquisite caution. It led to a staircase running from the back porch to the attic. Down she went like a moving silence. From the underground kitchen Lilas was singing her doubts of this life.

> "There's no disappointment in Heaven,
> No weariness, sorrow or pain,
> No hearts that are bleeding and broken…"

"Stay there, Lilas," she breathed, "and you'll get what you want in Heaven. Mary Magdalen will arrange it."

With the face of a saint she stepped into the sun, running like a streak to the privet-hedge. Turning, she saw Tim crouched on the grass.

"Gretel," he cried, "you were drowned! You're hurt! You're in your dressing-gown."

Kneeling beside him, she clamped her hand over his mouth hoping his silence would be aid against detection. Through his half-open lips she could feel the jut of his two front teeth.

"Hush, Tim," she said to the inarticulate mumblings against her palm, "I can't stay a second. I'm in bed because I was drowned. Is that why you were rude with the whistle?"

Questioning him she denied him response. Above his muffled mouth his eyes smiled at his incapacity of speech. Impossible to use his strength against her when she knelt with one arm round his neck. Close to him she could see the curl of his hair and the way it was sun-bleached at the temples. Unlike the great girl in school she liked the smell of his hair. It was like earth on a warm day. Tim was a clean, dry boy, even though his arms came out of his sleeves. Free of anxiety about her he relaxed, nuzzling against her palm.

"No, Tim, you can't talk," she said severely. "You're bad for bringing me out. You know I've got to go, don't you?"

An energetic nod of his head convinced her, and she conceded him half his mouth.

"Gretel," he whispered in acknowledgement of her danger, "I'm sorry I made a row, but I was crazy to see you. Some of the fellows came in last night and told me about the accident. When they said it was you I tried not to show anything, but I saw Mother looking at me. When they went she said I could go out. It was decent of her! I climbed the fence and hid behind a tree, and I was there when you got back. The lame fellow was driving and the doctor carried you in. I nearly walked out and asked him how you were, but I was afraid I'd get you in wrong."

"Tim!" she ejaculated, awed with such devotion.

"I waited until I saw Lady Fitz Henry pulling down the blinds. When the lame one drove away I thought you must be O.K. or he wouldn't have gone."

"I was, Tim," she assured him, "only I had a headache and felt wuzzy when I stood up. Philip was lovely, but he fussed and made David drive us to town. Now I've got to go! I'm dreadfully afraid they'll find my bed empty."

One knee flexed to rise, he detained her with his arms round her waist.

"Gretel, I'll write you a letter tonight and wrap it round a present I bought for you after school."

"Tim!" she almost screamed, and then clamped her hand apprehensively over her own mouth. "Tim," she whispered, "I don't want you to spend your allowance on me. You know you're crazy to buy the records of Tristan."

For a second she rubbed her face against his hair.

"It was like a record of Tristan," he smiled with maddening mystery. "Listen to-night, when the doctor's car is parked I'll blow the tiniest whistle from here. Then you can let down a string—"

"Oh!" she said, thrilled to her very being.

"Will you be too sleepy to wait?" His tone held anxiety.

"I'll say I won't," she said fervently. "I've been asleep all afternoon."

"O.K., then! I'm so glad you're safe," he said, detaining her longer with the quality of his smile. Very lightly he touched the smooth line of her cheek. "Can I kiss you, Gretel?"

"Yes," she said instantly, putting her face against his. "'Bye, darling Tim, good-bye!"

"'Bye, Gretel!" he said, following her flight with his heavy-lidded smile.

Men's mouths were gentle she told herself, thinking of the two men and a boy who had kissed her since she came to town. Love was nice and kind-making, with a better feeling than prayers! Lovely, said her flesh, as she fell into an animal walk. Inside the back porch she heard Lilas still singing about Heaven. This time she was jubilant about houses without taxes or rent! It was not Mary Magdalen's department.

In bed, trying to emulate the peace of the day, she planned Acts of Mortification that would not be obtrusive to Philip. Visiting her as soon as he entered the house, his face showed a shade of annoyance as he felt her pulse.

"My dear," he said, shaking his head, "if you don't slow down a bit, you'll have to stay in bed tomorrow."

"I'm well," she said, looking at him with eyes like yellow lamps. Then he put his hand on her face, looking for fever. "I'm well, Philip. I could get up now and dance a couple of hornpipes."

"Well, you won't then," he said firmly, "you'll have a light meal and settle down early."

"Yes, Philip," she said very obediently.

The success of the afternoon made an augury for the night. The gods were benign, smiling at Tim and herself. In their interests the mater and Philip went to bed early, and, at eleven, she drew the clock into bed, for fear its ticking should trouble their rest.

The string? Fitz Henry Place was high!

Out of bed without a creak of betrayal, she culled the contents of a drawer. Possibilities were gathered and laid on a chair: two shoe-laces, three pieces of baby-ribbon, a bit of real string, a chiffon handkerchief to be tied corner-wise and a pair of stockings. Knotted together they made a string of many feet.

Infinite care went into the removal of the screen at the window, but even to her own ears she made no sound. Leaning out to the waist she nearly plunged her face in a mountain ash. A swing of her arm sent the string down to the ground. She had the world to herself, but not for long. A sound as soft as tuneful breath came from the top of the garden. Would he come from under the trees or down the gravel path? Would he remember that stones would crunch under his feet? When he stepped from the shadow of a trunk, she acclaimed him as a boy of sense. In their ears they could hear each other's laughter and the secret thrill of their blood. Neither thought that the present could have been tendered in the shade of the privet hedge. This tingling risk was the only way! High romance claimed them, and the soft stealth of the night. She saw light touch his stooping head, until he rose with a wave of his hand. The parcel was tied and the stage set for her. Hauling in hand over hand, she held her arms out so that the parcel would not thud against the side of the house. When it lay on the sill her arm was raised in exultant possession. Voicelessly she thanked him while he waved back from the tree. Then he faded against the trunk and she was inside with her treasure. When the screen was replaced she crept into bed and very softly opened her parcel.

"Oh," she breathed to the night, "oh, isn't it beautiful?"

She had uncovered an ivory ship, with a sail, a jib, a flag and a keel fitting snugly in a grooved black stand. White, with clean lines, it was a symbol of the sea-life that she knew. More than that it had white sails. White sails, white sails? Tim was always talking about white sails! It was her first letter from a boy. Feeling it should be contemplated, she opened it as quickly as possible.

Darling Gretel,

I love this ship and hope you will too, because it has a white sail. I saw it in a window and I've been afraid it would be gone before I could buy it for you. Remember the love-potion we drank when our hearts became fettered together. I am your vassal like the story in the Book of Operas, *and I want you to show a white sail for me always. I wish I could have been the fellow who saved you yesterday. That would have meant being your knight and your vassal. I looked at the life-saving badge I won this summer and wondered what good it was to me. I'm sure I could have brought you in without hitting you under the chin. I hate that fellow, and they say he's a naval swell. The sloop went out this afternoon and I'm glad. I must stop now. I hope old witchface didn't do any hocus-pocus on you. Tomorrow we must talk. I've got news. When I got home this afternoon Uncle was here for supper. He's taking me for a two weeks' trip on one of the coastal boats. He thinks it will be good for my geology. He knows a lot about glaciation and when the cliffs were laid down. The ways he talks makes me think the rocks are broody.*

Mary Immaculate giggled out loud and then put her head under the bedclothes.

I hate to go away because I'll miss you like anything, but I'll take my uke and I hear they have a piano on board.

I'm all ink,

With love from your vassal,
    TIM

Life was unbelievable in its promise. Gently touching the ship, the gift of her vassal, she saw it in the Place as a more poetic thing than it could be by the sea that had given her birth. What she would suffer if she had to return to the Cove! Her long walk from it was illustrated in a strange sequel to her accident.

On the Wednesday that David and Felice came to tea the family was lounging in chairs on the mater's lawn. Between them and the bulk of the house colour blazed from bells, cups and the discs of many flowers. In desultory conversation, continually animated by Mary Immaculate, and immobility challenged by her walks round the flower-beds, they saw Lilas approaching, followed by someone they did not know. The maid's mouth was down at the corners and her hair under her cap was as vivid as a nasturtium. Mary Immaculate had known for a long time that a tablespoonful of peroxide and half a lemon went into the water that washed it.

"Who can it be?" questioned Lady Fitz Henry. "It's unlike Lilas to let anyone in without telling me."

Mary Immaculate looked, and stood like a statue of incredulity.

"Mom!" she ejaculated.

An undefinable instinct brought the Fitz Henrys to their feet. Felice remained seated, becoming a receiver for their reactions. Detached, she saw Lady Fitz Henry smoothing a frown from her forehead. The fisherman's wife was invading her doorsteps! Philip was frowning over eyes that seemed to be searching for a paper denying maternal rights. David was merely curious and full of interest in a situation. They looked formidable in their similar front. Always on the side of the weak, she stood up to extend some alien comfort.

Over her shoulder Mary Immaculate looked back, exploring the possibilities of her mother's reception. Standing between her two families, she could not stir towards either.

Josephine advanced under their eyes, and nothing about her suggested ordeal. Her shoes were dusty, her nose shiny, but her walk suffused serenity. Days filled with work, and leisure given to prayer, gave her an equality beyond the standards of man. Frequently calling to mind the greatness of God and her own nothingness, she trusted the humility of others. She wore a brown knitted skirt, a cardigan coat over a wool-lace jumper. The newness of the suit was evinced in the startling whiteness of skin suddenly exposed against a red neck. Hair had been washed and frizzed by some agency and lay bunched under a toque of the same wool as her suit. Hands in cotton gloves clasped a cheap bag. Josephine had come to town! Molasses-brown eyes stared with frank interest, while full lips smiled away from teeth holding black-edged cavities.

Lilas left her with a down-curve of her mouth and an obvious air of having delivered something questionable.

Mother and daughter faced each other in a moment's silent regard.

"Mom," said Mary Immaculate, "how are you, Mom?" It was unmistakable that her nostrils held the Fitz Henry vibration. Scrubbed as she was, Josephine held a secret cling of dishwater and cooking, emanating from wool picked up at odd moments in a kitchen.

"Mom," she said again, "how is Pop and the boys?"

Newly acquired social sense asserted itself, but she made no attempt to tender the Fitz Henry greetings to Josephine. Neither did her mother gesture towards her daughter. Scrupulosity forbade that she should act like a mother, and the situation was too difficult for Mary Immaculate. All she could do was to smile in a wholehearted way. Her clothes and grooming had taken Josephine's breath away.

"My!" she breathed on a long exhale, "ain't you grand now, Mary Immaculate! Let me look at you! You've grown like a weed and no mistake! The like of it, in a real silk dress and not cut from a remnant I'll be bound!" She was fingering a bit of material between her gloved fingers. "Well, well," she admired in childish wonder, "and your hair! It's a dream and shows your grand pole!"

It was impossible not to smile with her. Lady Fitz Henry relaxed to cordiality and the frown disappeared from Philip's forehead. When Josephine raised the child's dress and examined her petticoat and knickers David laughed out loud. None of them hurried her or distracted attention from satisfaction in her child's clothes. When she was ready Mary Immaculate turned round.

"Mater," she said quietly, "this is Mom!"

There was no flaw in Lady Fitz Henry's greeting or easy presentation of her daughter-in-law and two sons. Josephine was so glad to see them that they found themselves smiling in reciprocal warmth. Soon she was seated in a straight canvas chair with the points of her unfilled gloves showing against her bag. Instantly she explained herself, looking at Philip.

"It was you, sir, who wrote me the kind letters when she was in hospital. I hope it's not against the paper to come today?"

"We're very glad to see you, Mrs. Keilly," interposed Lady Fitz Henry. Mary Immaculate stood between them like a hostage, and anxiety for the situation made her tall and taut.

Detached again, Felice debated with her S.P.C. mind. Over-sensitiveness made her feel the child's struggle with values. She seemed to be coping with the riddle of what constituted a lady. Without delusions of her state, her own mother shone with qualities reflecting good things. The mater was smooth and poised, with a gentle voice. The child looked from one to the other, standing midway between. Felice wanted to help, but she knew it was the child's own problem, and Josephine was sure of her purpose.

"I came unexpected, ma'am," she said, including them all with her eyes. "It was last Sunday after I washed up. I was tired and I lay down for a spell. I must have dropped off, for as clear as this day I saw my child in the sea. That wouldn't have troubled me much, but, level as it was, it went over her head. Then I knew something had happened and I had to come. In our world the sea mustn't go over the head! Her Pop said I was daft, but I had my own bit of money from the few eggs I sold and I didn't heed. I would have come the next day but I had a bit of knitting on hand."

It was plain that even in anxiety she must come to town in state.

The family exchanged glances, but Mary Immaculate smiled with a secret droop of her lids.

David rallied with the story. Sensing Josephine's romantic soul, he gave value to the accident of the past Sunday. Its colour and elaboration put it out of bounds of recognition, but Josephine's responses told them it held the core of her expectations.

"Drowned, sir, now didn't I know it?"

"Over her head and lying on the bottom! Glory be to God, to think of it now!"

"Couldn't swim, sir! That would be nothing to her if she minded to go. Blessed Joseph, 'tis you that's the Father and Guardian of Virgins! Mary Immaculate, aren't you ashamed now, giving them all that trouble?"

"Yes, Mom," she said blandly, while the family smiled together.

There was something spacious in David. Deciding to entertain Josephine, he disposed of the drowning and began to discuss the fishery as if baits, traps, trawls and hand-lines were a part of his life. His wife's hair came down lower on her brow. David was bound to get lost in a topic of which he had little knowledge. Philip rescued him twice, but when Josephine said, "I like him to go cross-handed, sir," his answer was merely agreeable, "Yes, indeed, Mrs. Keilly, it sounds much more interesting." Giving him a gentle look, suggesting silence, his mother put the conversation in the channels of intelligence. She was not the widow of a shipowner and fish-exporter without a knowledge of the seasons. She could talk to Josephine and place the bait in the right sequence and know when the trapping and trawling began and ended. It appeared that Benedict had been very successful with the trap-skiff and was looking forward to a good return from the hand-line.

"The autumn fish are better, Mrs. Keilly," said Philip encouragingly. Realising who knew her world, she gave David the smile of indulgence.

Wonder of her surroundings gradually distracted her, and she became absentminded in the quest of sights. "Ma'am," she sighed, "I wish I had the time for a few flowers, but it's as much as I can manage to raise a few vegetables."

"Would you like some flowers, Mrs. Keilly? Mary, run and fetch my scissors."

"Ma'am!" said Josephine, flushing with pleasure. "If I could have a bit of wet paper for the stalks?"

When Mary brought the scissors and paper Lady Fitz Henry went round the flower-beds, and the family could see the best blooms extravagantly gathered. Josephine watched the falling flowers and addressed her daughter.

"Mary Immaculate!"

The child knew the tone.

"Yes, Mom," she said distractingly, "how is Molly Conway?"

"The same! The like of her never changes."

"Do you ever give her a good feed, Mom?"

"That I do," said Josephine. "When I have a bit of a treat I send Ignatius down to get her. I knitted a few things, too! The poor thing was not much underneath."

"That was lovely, Mom."

"Mary Immaculate!"

"Yes, Mom, how are the boys?"

David smiled widely, listening to lightning evasion.

"Oh, I forgot," said Josephine, momentarily distracted, "Dalmatius is married."

"No, Mom!" said the child, startled. "Not Teresa Rawlins? Why, she's got consumption."

"Don't we know it," said Josephine acceptingly. "Your Pop says he won't get the winter out of her."

David choked, though Philip and Felice kept their smiles within bounds.

"Mary Immaculate," said Josephine with one-minded firmness.

"Yes, Mom," she answered, eying the Fitz Henrys in mute resignation.

"Do you go to Mass regular, and on Holy Days of Obligation?"

"Yes, Mom."

"Do you go to Confession and Holy Communion?"

"Yes, Mom."

"Do you remember the seven deadly sins and do none of them?"

"Yes, Mom," she said with her eyes instinctively gazing at the sky.

"Do you pray morning and evening?"

"Yes, Mom."

The family eyed their paragon doubtfully, but her face was too devotional to acknowledge the eyes of the world. A tiny smile lay in the corner of her mouth.

"Do you fast on the right days?"

"Mrs. Keilly, I—" interrupted Philip in a reasonable voice.

"Just a minute, sir," said Josephine firmly but respectfully.

"Do you fast, Mary Immaculate?"

"Yes, Mom," she said with gentle conviction.

"I should hope so," said Josephine, "with the good things you get to eat. Mind yourself, now, and remember the hopes of Heaven and the pains of Hell."

"Yes, Mom," she said agreeably.

Philip's frown was awful as he bent forward in his chair. Glaring at his child his mouth opened to speak. A definite kick from David restrained him and he transferred his frown to his brother. Imperturbably

David watched Josephine, delighting in her increasing bouquet.

"There, Mrs. Keilly," said Lady Fitz Henry, coming towards her with a cluster of colour. "The paper, Mary!"

"Oh," said Josephine, "aren't they beautiful now! 'Twill be grand to walk through the streets with them. I must be off, ma'am, and thankful I am that you didn't mind my coming."

"Can't we give you tea, Mrs. Keilly?"

It was obvious Josephine had no intention of breaking bread with them. She had been graciously received and she was graciously going. She had been three years in a kitchen like Lady Fitz Henry's.

"No, thank you, ma'am," she said, rising to her feet. "I came in at noon and I'm going out on the Shore train at six. Benedict will meet me with the skiff across the Bay."

The family stood up. "May I drive you to the station, Mrs. Keilly?" asked Philip. Had he been receptive Mary Immaculate's smile would have taken the frown from his mind.

Josephine laughed at the suggestion.

"Sure, sir, I wouldn't deny my eyes to run through the town that fast. 'Tis kindly meant but I'd like to walk. I like to see the bits of grass and the flowers, and the babies in pink and blue, and the shops with baskets of fruit. 'Tis a treat I'm going to give myself, so don't ask me to ride."

"Now we know," said David, touching Mary Immaculate's white cheek, "where this child gets her zest of living."

"Well, sir," agreed Josephine, "it's a grand world for them with eyes to see. I'll be thinking of you all and, if I might make so bold, I'll include you all in my prayers."

"We'll be richer for it," said the mater with real grace. "Mary and I will walk with you to the gate."

The child walked between them down the gravel path.

"What a natural woman!" said Felice, pushing back her hair. "What a gift of faith!"

"Isn't it wonderful?" agreed David, sitting down. "I'm worried about Dalmatius not getting the winter out of Teresa."

"You would, dear," reproved his wife; "you were positively vulgar the way you laughed. As for our remarks about the fishery...Wasn't

Mater marvellous? I had no idea she knew the country so well."

"She told a lie," said Philip as if he heard nothing else.

"Who, Mater?" asked David languidly.

"No, damn you!—Mary, and you know it. She doesn't do all of those things and you know she doesn't fast. She told a lie!"

"Obviously, my dear Phil, for your sake and reputation in her mother's eyes."

"Well, I'm damned—"

"Who refused to let Mary fast?"

"I did, for the sake of her body."

"Nonsense, she's as strong as a pony and, even if she weren't, in her mother's world her soul would come first."

"She lied," said Philip distastefully. "If she'd given me the opportunity I would have explained that medical knowledge requires growing children—"

"Don't be pompous, Phil! Use some imagination! It's mysticism Mary lied for, not sweet reason and science."

"I would have done the same," said Felice in a quick, decided voice. "It would be unfair to take away a vestige of faith."

They stopped suddenly when they saw the child and the mater within earshot. Mary walked straight into Philip's frown.

"You're cross," she said at once. The direct attack disconcerted him in view of the truth she seemed to represent.

"Yes," he admitted slowly. "I don't care for lies and I consider it most unnecessary."

"Mary understands her mother's life better than we do," said Lady Fitz Henry. "I like the truth, but I'm sure she had excellent reasons for lying."

Some of the strain of the visit went into the child's clasped hands. Looking from one to the other, she bit her lip. David extended a hand but pride made her stand on her own feet.

"If you don't see, Philip, it's no good my showing you. If Mom knew I didn't fast or observe the rules of the Church, it would make her sure there was something wrong with you. Nothing you could say from books would make Mom believe them. She'd go home miserable, thinking my soul was in danger. You can't believe that?"

"Yes, we can, Mary," said David and Felice together.

"Can you, Mater?" she questioned. "I'd never lie to you because you don't need lies to—"

"Hush, dear—"

"Your mother would have seen reason, Mary, and the importance of health."

The child looked at Philip and her glance held pity and childish scorn. "In religion like Mom's there's no directive thinking. Philip, could you dream and know that I was drowning just when I was?"

"No, I don't think so," he admitted.

"You don't dream, Philip," she said softly, "and you don't believe in the Little People! You couldn't be sure St. Anthony will find everything you lose. Mom does, as well as Heaven and Hell being places." Her lip was trembling and she was on the verge of tears.

"Mary dear," said the mater in a voice mitigating rising emotion, "will you please go and say we'll have tea now?"

The child turned without a word, seizing the privilege of time by herself.

"My son," said Lady Fitz Henry, "I think you're showing very little imagination. We promised to let her remain a Catholic. We must either let her be one completely or be satisfied with her conduct on occasions like these."

"I won't let her fast," said Philip as if he wanted it both ways.

"Then let her lie," said David easily. "Don't be a fool, Phil. The truth should always be handled sparingly. Where would you be if you told everyone the truth about their wretched insides?"

"Yes, where?" asked Felice like someone seizing on the perfect argument.

David smiled at his wife. "Felice dear, I hope I get the winter out of you."

His light touch restored balance. When the child returned she breathed normality.

As before, there was no compromise between herself and Philip. He was just the same to her, but sometimes she felt he had given her a black mark.

TWELVE

"HOME FROM THE NORTH."

Josephine's visit gave background to Mary Immaculate. She was no longer the atavism of fisherfolk or a frozen dryad of the snows. She was the begetting of flesh and blood.

Response came through individual mediums. Lady Fitz Henry charged herself with a monthly letter. David commanded Felice to send heads of wool. Felice sent some garments, sensing the pleasure in something ready-made. Philip had his own ideas of bestowal. Josephine's daughter was extravagantly photographed. Unselfconsciousness made her an excellent subject, though the results produced narcissism.

"Philip, I'm lovely," she said, hanging over her pictured face.

He recaptured the pictures, administering reproof to self love.

"They're for your mother, Mary, and I'm glad they flatter you."

For her mother! How could she get one for Tim? It would be a nice return for the white ship.

Tim was missed, but he lived in her thoughts. They had the ideal secret, something between two, and she knew he was no cause for Confession. He was the course where she flowed untrammelled. They could not avoid meeting outside, but he had determined their relations for those occasions. Walking between the mater and Philip she had seen him approaching with schoolboys. As separation lessened recognition retreated to their eyes. Barely by, she gave a backward glance. He was touching his cap with the same turn of his head. Instantly she smiled ahead, walking according to the mater's idea of deportment.

At the cottage an increasing knowledge of cliques made her treasure Tim as a classless boy. Perhaps he stayed in the garden because his mother and Auntie Minnie did not go to Government House. An orbit was uncomplicated, enclosing only themselves. From the people at the cottage she learned the standards of the town, the right English school, official position, big business and the dinner-list at Government House. Merely to attend the receptions and the garden parties was socially second-class. Schoolmates had bequeathed a wariness of women. They refused to see her for herself, and voices bade her remember the lowliness of her mother. Quick to scent patronage she could abandon it quickly. There was a special expression for those who did not matter, and a film for her eyes. Sensitive and insensitive, she became vulnerable only through people commanding respect. Those who did things received attention, and she hovered modestly in their circle. Talent was acknowledged and the grace of fine minds. Many women cause an instant detour; those who talked incessantly of bridge, bewailing the limitations of one playing-body. Frustrated, they seemed to gesture with shuffling hands. Neither did the too motherly woman attract. She hated the cluck of maternity smothering a child.

It was inevitable she should prefer men. They met her foursquare without staring beyond for the shadow of the cook.

If anything they gave her too much attention and often Philip took her away. He merely left her when she talked with older men, amused at the sea-knowledge of the child. Natural resources could be discussed intelligently when they did not encroach on her life.

The mater could not be induced to visit the cottage when other people were present. Occasionally she motored towards the fierce sunsets and watched the grey steal over the sea. The arrival of others caused a leisured exit, with Philip ready to take her home. In the

Place she received a few people for brief visits; some relatives of her husband, a sombre lawyer, the rector of her church and a bishop with an impressive hat. Seeing it in the hall, Mary Immaculate regarded it with awe. Even without Church-purple it was an exalted hat for heretics.

A thrill came in waving the family to dinner at Government House. They were going to dine with an Admiral. She could stay home like a Cinderella, revelling in her ashes. Eyes could recapture the wink of the mater's rings. Unexpected jewels had emerged from a case and different clothes were laid out by Hannah. Interest in the occasion made Mary Immaculate ingratiatingly friendly.

"Hannah, I didn't know she had things like that."

"And where would you see evening dress I'd like to know? Many a year she went out decked three and four times a week."

"Ermine," she said, smoothing the collar of a coat.

Hannah snatched it away.

"Don't touch; your hands are dirty!"

It was an extreme libel, but it was useless to protest.

David and Felice came to town to dress, and the child hung over the gallery watching the closed doors. Informality did not belong to such processes. They shut themselves up and emerged quite ready. The mater had only been seen in bed and fully clothed. Some instinct told her David would not be the same. He was not! At a certain moment his door was thrown invitingly open. The length of his legs, flat stomach and the black-and-white of his shirt and trousers brought instant admiration.

"Oh, David!—"

"Yes, I know, I'm lovely," he said, screwing up his face in the mirror.

She leaned against a tallboy watching every movement.

"Will it be very grand, David?"

"So, so; but we won't eat peas with our knives."

"Is the house grand?"

"Not any grander than the drawing-room downstairs."

"Why does Mater go to this and nowhere else? I heard a woman whisper it was snobbish to go to Government House and nowhere else."

"Did you, indeed? Mater was brought up in a tradition that considers an invitation like this a command. The Governor represents the King, and when the King says come, well, they come. Colonials have less traditional ideas."

"I'd like to go, David."

"I'm sure you would," he agreed dryly.

She was fingering something she suddenly identified.

"David," she shrilled, "you've got medals. Such little medals—"

"Yes, of course, I'm a hero. Those are miniatures for official occasions. I got them for wounds multiple, for returning without Arthur and John and for Father's premature death. Dearest possession and all that."

She shook her head in consideration.

"David, in polite places people don't get mad and bawl at each other. They get mad inside and it sounds worse."

"That's civilisation as far as it goes. A gentleman is not supposed to show his feelings. They beat it into you at school and then send you out with bayonets." He glanced derisively at the medals. "I'm against war and I don't care who knows it, and they're going to have it again, Mary, and all for nought."

"David," she said sympathetically, "your war was no good. You should have fought for the Church."

"Not on your life," he said in horror. "So that the other fellow could tell me where to kneel down? No, Mary, if it comes again you and I are going to the Cove to play with the Little People."

"If you don't mind, David," she pleaded, "I'd like to stay in the thick of it."

"God!" he shrugged with humour and horror. "Youth again, and more Arthurs and Johns. Laugh, Mary, or... No, you won't go mad," he said definitely. "You're too tough and you'll shake off the burden of personal sorrow, but be forewarned and forearmed. Have some special place to hide when—"

"Felice," she said like lightning, and then clamped her hand over her mouth for fear she had gone too far.

David frowned. "My dear Mary, I was just talking, and Felice will tell you it's the Greek chorus that goes with those medals. She's got one for being a Fany. I admit we did shiver together more than once." He settled into his coat. "Here, give me the damn things. I wanted to give them to the charwoman's little boy to play with, but Felice wouldn't let me."

Dressed, David was staring into a mirror as if he despised his reflection.

She made a step towards him, putting arms round his waist. Her voice was soothing and a shade motherly.

"David, I love you. You're so foolish! If Felice dies I'll marry you."

"Well," he said with a clearing face, "it's not exactly a prospect of undiluted bliss, but thanks just the same. It was a charming spontaneous offer, but I'm afraid you musn't build up any false hopes. I couldn't do without Felice. Perhaps Phil will oblige. He's so much younger and unspotted by shrapnel. If you don't marry one of us you'll have to live in another house, and we'll miss you a great deal."

"I wouldn't like that," she said, startled into giving him a possessive squeeze.

"No, I thought you wouldn't. Let's hope Phil will fall in line. He will if you're good to him. Make him laugh and make him play. He was quite a gay little chap until the war rolled over him. By and by he'll be able to stop this grind and go to Vienna, if there's any Europe left. He might take you along. It would be great fun to travel, wouldn't it—"

"Fun, it would be wonderful! I could see—"

"Yes, you could see a lot," he said impressively. "Keep it in mind, but ah—perhaps for the time being I wouldn't discuss it. Let it come about naturally...."

"Yes," she agreed with avid yellow eyes. "I'd like Europe very much. I'll be full of directive thinking."

David tilted her face until it was exposed to his view.

"Mary," he questioned, "are there sometimes you need spanking?"

"I don't think so," she said with limpid clearness. "I feel polite."

"Maybe," he said doubtfully. "I'm afraid you won't suffer much Karma if you look like that. I'll kiss you instead.... There! I know I'll find you out some day."

She slipped away, leaning against the tallboy.

"What will you find, David?" she asked with an empty face.

From a drawer he was extracting a white silk scarf. "Oh, just your original sin, your Achilles heel," he said vaguely.

"And when you find it, David, what will you do?"

For once he was uncomprehending. Her face was no longer empty. It was anxious and strained.

"Continue to love you like an indulgent fool, I suppose."

"Can I depend on that?" she asked, running to the hall at the sound of an opening door. Looking back, David was arrested again by her old expression.

"Mary!" called Philip. "Will you ring up Doctor—?"

"Coming, Philip."

David stood dangling the scarf. How odd of Philip to let her do his telephoning! More and more they were transferring the countless little services previously belonging to Hannah.

Tim was different when he returned. She saw it at once. His cheeks were red-brown, his brow peeling from sun and his hands suggested virility. Some granite of his country had gone into himself. Town-bred, he barely knew his environs for a radius of thirty miles. Consequently his coves and bays were as pastoral as places could be with their feet in the North Atlantic. That his town was in the same latitude as Paris gave it a moderation tempered by the Arctic Current. Newfoundlanders were accustomed to the world's ignorance about them, knowing how they were lumped together with Eskimos and husky-dogs. By sailing as far as Labrador, Tim had seen some of those things.

They met satisfactorily. Dwindling days forbade the mater the night air of her garden. Philip was at his surgery. Knowing Tim's ship had docked at five o'clock she was free to put on a coat and watch the light grown sombre over the plantains and dandelions. There was a sound of feet rustling through grass, shoes scraping against the fence, a retreat to the beech tree for a reconnoitre and he was down beside her. Hugging her in stronger arms, he even smelt different. She inhaled a tang of boats, ropes, tar and an essence of the sea. Eyes were wider open.

"Gretel, did you miss me? Kiss me and say you're glad I'm back—I thought of you everywhere. Your face came out of icebergs, whales and even dirty Eskimos. I hate dark people. Kiss me again.... I had a swell time."

He laughed out loud, showing his crooked teeth.

"Shushhh, Tim," she whispered; "Hannah is in and might be on the prowl. You look grand. What did you do?"

"Everything," he said largely. "First I felt a bit seedy. There were more smells than usual, but it's funny how you get used to them. Then, after we stopped at a few places, the town seemed very far away; all except you, Gretel, and you came with me. You must have seen everything, but I'll tell you, in case you didn't. When the wharves and lighthouses stopped we had to anchor at night, and if we wanted to go ashore we had to use the mail-boat. There were whales and flies and Eskimos and husky-dogs. But the icebergs, Gretel! Hundreds at a time! One day I stood at the rail without going to meals. I'll never forget them under the sun, and when the light went they looked like ghost-tombs. I thought I was sailing through a graveyard for Vikings, and I knew it was too big to be played on the piano. I thought of the biggest Beethoven—then I remembered Scott, Peary and Amundsen, and somehow they seemed the biggest of all."

"Tim," she gasped incredulously, "not greater than the *musician?*"

"Greater than anyone," he said with reckless repudiation of his gods. "They must be because they helped me to make up my mind to be an engineer. It seemed a fine thing up there. I've never really tried, because when I hear the names of the subjects I close up my mind. Now I'll give them a chance."

"Tim!" she ejaculated, acclaiming him with pride. Somewhere inside she shook her head. It was a mood. Tim was a poet, a dreamer, and he could never make mines and rocks his first loves. But she was not of the breed to daunt him.

"Yes," he went on as if bolstering his own decision, "it came over me all at once. I saw this country was more rock than art. If I lived in a different place—"

He stopped, staring out as if visualising countries with legacies of musicians. Instantly she stiffened his new resolution.

"If you're decided, Tim, it will please them. When your mind is made up you mustn't have two minds. David says it's important to live in harmony. Philip says conflict—"

"What's that?" he asked, startled by the sound of shuffling feet. Careful for her, he peered through chinks into the vegetable garden. "Gretel, witchface is picking some peas."

"Tim," she hissed, extracting a book from her pocket. "Go very quietly. I'm reading a very interesting book."

"Don't strain your eyes," he said with a smile in his voice. "See you tomorrow."

He faded into the trees with little sound.

Hannah could not possibly have seen, but she might have heard. There was no doubt about it, she was an extremely unpleasant old woman. The mater would never expect her to pick peas when it was almost dark.

Autumn coursed with red blood. A few leaves fluttered down, making a light scrape on the ground. As yet the wind only warned the trees of more vicious stripping. Neither was the earth ready to draw in its breath. Late flowers survived, flaunting with a last hot pulse of life. More intoxicating than nascent spring, Mary Immaculate felt restless from tooth to toenail. Beauty seemed to live in sound of a deep-toned knell. She walked to school in sunlight mixed with silver alloy. Midas fingers had ruffled the beech tree, suggesting a wish to sit on a branch and watch the gold drip away. What would the Fitz Henrys say when she and Tim were revealed in a fork?

David was as restless as herself, appearing continually and urging them towards the cottage. There the sea tossed with blue abandon, darting frothy tongues towards the colour on the land. The air held a screech of wild living.

"The flowers look indecent," said David on his own lawn. "Mary, why is autumn so headstrong?"

She was looking at spikes of hollyhock, over-topped by staring sunflowers. Stems were drowned in a wash of nasturtiums.

Her voice was dreaming, seeming to return from distance.

"Mom asked Pop that once, and he made a queer answer. Mostly Pop just grunted, but sometimes he said things."

"Husbands and grunts go together, Mary. What did Pop say on this occasion when he didn't grunt?"

"He said big beasts mate in the fall."

"Well!" said David, glad of Philip's absence. Perhaps a word to the mater would suggest a little talk about the papa and mamma flower and the flight of the bumble-bee. That, he supposed, was the process for gentle maidenhood. Recalling her background, he smothered a smile. Her white face must have been frequently turned to the hen and the dick, the ewe and the ram. It would be an insult to give her a book about pollen.

"Mary," he said with a rapid change of mood. "Felice is going to give you Rufus—"

"When?" she asked, looking round for instant possession.

"Not so fast, darling! You can't have him until we go, *but*—"

"But what, David? It sounds exciting."

"We're going to stay out until the first boat after Christmas. Will you like that?"

"Like it, David?" she said with satisfactory fervour. "I'd like you to stay forever."

Christmas was staged in a perfect winter dress. Snow was unsullied, tree-shadows were etched by the light of a full-sized moon, and a child in the house made a season. They found her unacquisitive but thrilled with gew-gaws and coloured lights. The family rose to the occasion and tripped cheerfully over decorations. All except Hannah! She had dismissed Christmas years ago and resented the bright shreds on her carpets.

Philip placed a tree on the mater's lawn and decorated it with lights from a wire in the house. Small bulbs cast vivid pools on the snow and the child never tired of dipping her hands in colour. To the family it was a resurgence of youth. On Christmas Eve they all went out of doors and stood round the tree. The high white solitude of the moon gave back a sense of cold peace. The child had been to see the

Crib and the night was full of meaning. Looking upward for the Star, the moon silvered a devotional face. She looked down! The sky held the infinite but the baubles shone on her hands. David, sensitive for nuances, saw the exultation leave her for the love of hot colour. She laughed with earth-bound defiance. As if her laugh had been a command some other person returned the perfect note. Clean and clear the "Adeste" came over the snow. With a smile on her lips Mary Immaculate opened her mouth and sang. Too subdued to make a large noise the family supplied a hum.

"My dear, how lyrical," said David, "and how talented is our Mary with her Latin! Let's find the accompanist and invite him to wassail."

Mary Immaculate was deaf, singing the second verse.

Lady Fitz Henry answered. "Some musical person lives quite near, David. I frequently hear whistles and mouth-organs. The instruments sound cheap but the tunes are perfect."

Philip's arm was round his child's neck. Her obvious joy fascinated him and he seemed to look at it as if it were tangible. From his height he could see the way her cheeks smoothed to her chin, the proud way her neck bore her head, and the stand refusing weight to the frozen ground.

"Happy, Mary?" he questioned.

"Bursting," she said wholeheartedly, and because she meant it so strongly she blazed the fact in his face.

She knew very well there was no sustained peak of perfection.

Hannah returned her present! Only tendered because the mater insisted on remembering the staff, she was most unsure of its reception. Wildest doubts did not encompass the ungracious return.

Hannah found her saying her prayers after an unbelievable day. She was addressing Heaven with her mind on earth when she heard the harsh voice.

"I don't take things where I don't feel right. 'Tis eating salt and betraying. Take them back."

She scrambled from her knees to receive a pair of black gloves. There was nothing to say. Hannah was gone! Always a reminder of the beach and a smell of offal! She knew the right words and symbols for

Hannah. Rancid, mildew, like mouldy sails! If you began to unfold her there would be dirty black spots, wet and a little sour. As an antidote she found the white ship and stood it in front of her eyes. Dear Tim with his talk of white sails! He was making a valiant effort, but it was useless to say he liked minerals and by-products. Sometimes after a long session of geology he came like an exile dragging his chains. His eyelids would be loaded and he sat pitch black. There were times when she had to work very hard to lighten his load, but he never left her without a restored laugh or a resurgence of purpose. Dear Tim, she thought. He should go to places like Dresden or Vienna, where there were opera-houses presenting his loves for little money. The land of the unborn children had made a mistake when they dropped Tim in Newfoundland.

Meanwhile there was the tennis-court in process of freezing. Philip and Felice could waltz and skate over ice like keels on a summer sea. She was determined to master the art in the shortest time, and sometimes when the afternoons made early night Tim could drop over the fence and skate by her side. Undismayed by the flaws of living, she tossed the black gloves in a drawer and wrapped the white ship preciously in a handkerchief.

THIRTEEN

"CHILDREN OF A LARGER GROWTH."

S he was seventeen and had not been to school in England. During the years the mater and Philip were often seen holding a prospectus. When she was too old for boarding-school, they sent for colleges and finishing-schools. From the fireside she was transported to many places. Returning, David and Felice raised their eyebrows and offered to take her themselves. Philip always looked vexed and said later.

They saw her development best. Every year a different girl met them at the wharf, causing a momentary intake of breath. David would stare and blink, reviewing her face. Change lay mostly in her body; mind and sense retaining the same childish zest. Neither could the mater ever modulate wild young laughter over sudden absurdities of every day. Something foolish in the street or Rufus remembering his kittenhood and springing at her heels as she went. Mental capacity increased, continually embracing new things. In her eighteenth year she could speak French moderately well and read it better. She was a zealous pianist because of Tim, though David said she had more temperament than technique. Performance suffered in comparison to Felice. Sports had been culled to perfect swimming, tennis and skating. Fleet-footed games attracted most, though she tried hard at golf for Philip's sake. With him it was a recent but accurate achievement. She found it distracting when vistas of sea appeared between hills, and woods were white with drifts of blossom. Some of her talents were not displayed. Doubt might have been expressed at the perfect timing of her tap-dancing or the wild grace of her hotcha.

She was tall with straight shoulders, narrow hips and small breasts set wide apart. Features gave harmony to one another, with the mouth growing a little fuller at the bow. There was a look of silver about her hair. With a natural wave at the top, the mater had conceded permanent ends, over-riding Philip, who wished her chained to nature's benefits. Voice had been trained and civilised, though it retained the peaks and variations of a fever-chart.

Companionship with Lady Fitz Henry had grown deep. Mother-and-daughter complex did not disturb them, and the relationship planted sturdy roots. The mater was nurtured like a bit of rare glass, and it was a challenge to keep her from walking upstairs too often. If anything her heart was better and more rested. The discovery that dizziness was caused by blood-pressure made Philip take her off protein meals, substituting vegetables and salads.

Lilas was married and another maid waited on them at table. The boy she hooked up to had been shamefully discarded when she was courted by a policeman. Much testifying and a stout heart in enduring second-rate kisses had brought rewards. Her husband was tall, broad-shouldered, with a plump face supported by a pink neck. From their first walking-out the end was inevitable. No male could resist such adoration. She made him feel godlike and a runner-up for Chief of Police. When he showed he meant marriage she could not believe her luck. A little blinded, she got glasses to see him better. Always avid for destiny, procreation pulsed in the whinny of her voice. Once convinced of the legal wonder of sleeping with him, she lost her instinct to testify. The policeman may or may not have dragged her down. She discarded the bonnet and poured his bottle of beer with a loving look. Periodically she appeared at the back door of the Place and babbled of conjugal felicity. Mary Immaculate was interested to hear she would not know she lived until she slept with a policeman. Then Lilas came again with young; proudly pushed in a perambulator. Philip offered to attend the confinements, but Lilas did not think it delicate, as she had passed him so many dishes.

The Place stood in perfect order, with the drawing-room re-decorated and its doors wide open. In spite of the invitation and enchantment of crystals they did no more than wink conspiringly as the family passed. Comfortable habitation was never earned and the iceberg mantelpiece was left to feel an affinity with winter. Sufficient to Philip that it stood like a museum-piece. After its restoration his next expenditure went into a modern room for his child. Sunshine-yellow lay on the walls, repeated in chair, bed and curtain draperies, patterned with orange flowers and autumn leaves. A limed-oak suite looked very tailored, with a miraculously flat bed. Mary Immaculate exulted in a kneehole dressing-table with a triple mirror. It was astonishing to see herself so many ways. Everyone approved but Hannah, and she went so far as to speak before them all.

"It's a fool of a room, Mr. Philip, all corners and flatness. In my young days beds were soft and chairs hard. Now it's the other way round. No Christian could grow up in a room like this."

Philip looked a little crushed. He thought the criticism was for him, but Mary Immaculate knew better.

Philip seemed to grow perpetually younger. His mouth curved more and his chin looked less flat. Strain had eased out of him. Neither did he work so hard or strive to answer every call. More selective, he waited for the right moment to go to Vienna. Three times he took short holidays in Canada and once he went to England with David and Felice. His departures left the girl with a curious feeling. As the gap of water widened between his ship and the wharf she felt defrauded. She wondered if she was getting spoiled like Betty Wilson. When Philip had a treat it seemed like a design for her special enjoyment. The many miles he travelled by himself were questioned when she remained to solace his mother. The trips made her oddly defiant. His quite definite absence bequeathed infinite hours to Tim.

Her slip into conventionality had earned her permission to walk abroad. Philip could see her go knowing she would not be the fleeing dryad. She no longer offered St. Anthony ten cents for the poor if he would find her lead pencil. She did not pray fervently when she saw a funeral.

It was easy and accidental for Tim to know the direction of her walks. There was enough wooded country to hide a million couples like themselves. Without arrangement he was frequently by the river where she had taken her first offending walk. They could talk, idle, dream and sometimes spit in the water. The rush and froth was a direct invitation, urging them to add more spots. Very particular about the performance of indoor music, Tim could produce a mouth-organ and play popular airs with gay abandon. There was a convenient bridge offering a nice surface for a bit of hotcha. Sometimes he would stop stone dead and be swamped by the mines of the world. He would lose his aptitude and feel crossed with the eternal veinings of the Andes. By-products confused him and he swore no metal lived by itself. Mary Immaculate tried to soothe him, but he would look past her face as if he was seeing the dark pits of the earth.

He had taken a three years pre-engineering course at a local college. Concentration from himself and push from his uncle had won him a pass, without distinction. During that time he talked vaguely of isometric and oblique projections and wallowed in space problems. He gloomed when he had to go to a survey-camp every summer, but came back with a temporary enthusiasm. Again she felt it was the effect of summer. and the sun on annoying space problems. But he achieved and stood ready for a start of professional subjects at a Canadian university.

Having outgrown her own school, choice lay between England or entrance into the same place as Tim. It was not the maidenly cloister to which she was accustomed, and for that reason it gained favour in her eyes. Her body yearned for the academic dress of cap and gown and the rubbing of shoulders at lectures and assemblies. Reluctantly Philip permitted her to start first year Arts. Examinations had been passed with distinction and there was no obstacle towards further learning. He gave her the choice of suspending school for a period, but her dismay was stupendous.

The college was a big bare structure with its back to open country. In winter, spindrift snow and wind whirled round, trying to shake its solidity. Then the students ran up frozen steps bent in a double. On wild days Tim made Mary Immaculate walk behind him with her face bent to his back. It was a gesture of gallantry accepted by his wish, but she would have preferred to walk by his side. Her face did not flinch from snow-slaps and the wild smack of the wind.

Philip, driving a protesting car, saw her walking with Tim. At least he saw her with a boy. At lunch she waited the immediate question.

"Who was your companion today, Mary? I was sorry I could not pick you up but I had a late call."

"I like to walk, Philip. It was one of the students who lives near here. Do you mind if I walk with them when they're coming my way?"

"Of course not," said the mater's deciding voice. "You must be part of your school; I'm afraid we've been selfish about companions of your own age."

That evening Philip read through a prospectus. But it was as if she had taken a hurdle and Tim had been normally claimed. He could continue to walk home with her. Easy of accomplishment, it was easier because Philip's hours did not coincide with hers. He thought Tim was an incident and not a habit.

It was late September, with a blue sky domed over gardens plump with bloom. A ship rested its sides against a wharf, waiting to take Tim away.

Mary Immaculate was watching the river flowing between granite rock. It looked busy, eddying through flats and hurling itself over falls in a headlong desire for the sea. Nothing weary about that river she thought. Behind her rose a grassy bank stuck with spruce and granite boulders. Some distance from the town the river held two steep paths of approach. Tim was coming up the one on her side. Lost in the spruce, he was seen again in sudden appearance at her feet.

Half-reclining, it was some time before he spoke. When he did his words came slowly while he plucked at blades of grass.

"Gretel, I sail tomorrow at twelve."

"Yes, Tim, I know. I read the shipping news at breakfast."

So familiar that he could be seen without acknowledgement, she examined him anew. He was someone important, who would not be seen for ten months or more. It gave him large significance. He was neatly dressed in grey flannel and a blue shirt with enough cuff for his wrists. The suit did not have the impeccable cut of the Place, but it was good enough for a boy.

Boy? He was in his twenty-first year and looked mature. Mines and by-products had aged his face. The height which made her tall for a girl made him only average for a man. It was right that their eyes should be on a level. She would have been irked if he looked over her head. His hair still curled over his deep head, with too much recession at the temples. Sun-bleach after summer and a survey-camp had edged his brow with baby fairness. In his suddenly short face his lips were parted and a trifle petulant, showing the two crooked teeth. Dentists had tried to straighten them, but they stayed hard and white in their little jut. His eyes were tired, heavier than usual, as if a lot of things anchored his lids. He looked dreamy, imaginative, brooding, although his skin held the look of outdoor activity and his hand the callus of field work. Her eyes accepted him for what he was.

"It will be next June before I see you again. Funny, what we talked of is here. I never expected it to arrive," she said.

"You never look ahead, Gretel."

"Because, Tim, tomorrow might not be as nice as today. Give me today and take tomorrow. Who said that?"

"Dunno, one of them I suppose."

She knew he felt pitch black with going. His voice held the heaviness of weighted things.

"Will you write, Gretel?" he asked, prepared for her instantaneous refusal.

"No, Tim dear, that would be arrangement, and they would ask a lot of questions at the Place."

"I could buy you a box at the post-office, and address them there. You could pick them up on mail-days."

"Oh no, Tim, I couldn't do that. That would be very deceitful."

"Have we been deceitful?"

It was the first question weighing their careless years. She was startled, hearing a voice of consequence.

"I don't feel deceitful, Tim. We were like Annabel Lee. I was a child and you were a child...."

"I'm beginning to wonder.... We've never met in a room outside of college. There must be rooms for you and me. It's all right about the letters. I knew you wouldn't write when I asked. I don't need them really. I don't lose you when I go away. I can talk to you as if you were there."

"And I to you, Tim."

"Perhaps I'll be able to get in an orchestra."

She shook a long admonitory finger.

"Tim, dear, you will remember that you're going to university to be a mining engineer. You've gone so far, so it's just as well to finish and take advantage of it. You're committed."

"O.K.," he said with more obedience than enthusiasm. Then he grinned, clearing his throat with hearty male assertion. His tone materialised his uncle. "Best years of your life, my boy. Opportunities such as I never enjoyed. Nurtured your father's estate to give you this chance. Make the most of your time, only young once. Try and pass with distinction—then work and a man's life—"

She laughed out loud. She had never heard his uncle talk, but Tim must do him very well. He presented such a bossy man.

"I don't think I'd like Uncle,"she mused.

"Like him?" said Tim emphatically. "He's a tyrant, a regular home-Hitler. Last night we had a family spread, last meal together and all that! It was awful. We had all the things Uncle liked, not what I liked. Then we went to the pictures. It was one of those weeping pictures that make you hate the lights when they come on. He heaved round like a porpoise and made Mother miserable. She's the sort who can't be happy unless the men are. Selfish brute! There was a deathbed scene and he rolled round in his chair as if the producer had invented death. When we got out—"

"I know, Tim," she interrupted. She cleared her throat in a big male way. "My boy, there's enough unhappiness in the world without taking it into our amusements. Give me Laurel and Hardy—"

Tim was quoting with her. Her knowledge of what Uncle would say made her so exact. Years of hearing about him had made her familiar with his loves and hates.

"Pity it wasn't slapstick, Tim. Then the evening would have been quite a success."

Tim laughed in sudden high humour. "How he loves it! A pie in the face—"

"And his best laugh goes to a kick in the seat," she said with happy inelegance. Uncle always uplifted them, though he was presented first in exasperation.

"Well, we all take our pleasures differently," she said bromidically. "He'd think we were mad unless we played Laurel and Hardy. He'd never understand Tristan. Think of all the pairs we've played!"

"I've just discovered that Romeo and Juliet are an opera, too."

"They were a pair of star-crossed lovers,"she said dreamily.

Tim stared into her face with intense blue eyes.

"Are we lovers, Gretel?"

"We're as we always were," she said a little uneasily.

"What is that?" he asked, looking away to the river.

"Children," she said at once, "having fun away from school."

"We're not children any more, Gretel, and soon we'll be the grown-ups looking back at other children who maybe will do as we did."

Now she inquired of him:

"What did we do, Tim?"

"I'm beginning to ask myself. Do other boys and girls do as we do?"

"I don't know any other boys."

"Your doctor isn't old," he said slowly.

"Isn't he?" she asked in surprise.

"Apparently not," he shrugged. "Auntie Minnie knows everything that happens in the town and the age of everyone. She says—"

"Never mind what Auntie Minnie says," she interrupted hastily.

"What are we going to do, Gretel?"

She stirred restlessly, looking ahead. The very core of the present she did not want to look at the future.

"Do, Tim, do? Don't be foolish! We'll do what we've always done. Keep to ourselves and remember we love Hansel and Gretel and hocus-pocus."

"And our witches' oven," he murmured. "We'll be foolish to other people."

"Have we been fools, Tim?" she whispered. "I've grown so used to Hannah calling me a fool that sometimes I feel, is it or am I?

Usually I don't hear Hannah, but the other day I was playing with Rufus. He was so wild that I laughed and laughed. Hannah came out of the dining-room and just looked at me. I couldn't go on playing any more. Then she said in an awful voice, 'The laughter of fools is like the crackling of thorns under a pot.' I felt queer, menaced, as if—"

"Old beast," he said, kicking a hole in the turf. "She knows about us. Why hasn't she split before?"

"I don't know," she answered wonderingly. "But I do know it's not for my sake. I've stopped worrying about it long ago."

"Do you ever worry, Gretel?"

"No," she said, feeling his moodiness. "I believe you'd like it better if I did."

He sat up and suddenly widened his eyes.

"Make-believe must come to an end."

She put her hands up as if to ward something off.

"No, no, you're queer today. Don't be any different. Remember you're going away tomorrow."

There was pleading in her voice, making him mutter his usual agreement.

"But when I come home we must talk and you mustn't put me off with your tin-whistle side—"

"Tim," she said appalled, "you're unfair. My tin-whistle side—"

"Yes, that's what I mean," he said, sticking to his guns. "The side they don't know at the Place, the side you can't take out with your doctor—"

"Tim, you're going away tomorrow. Let's remember today and perhaps yesterday. You seem so grown-up."

"Perhaps I am, Gretel. I'm three years older than you."

"We've almost been quarrelling."

"Yes, and I must go soon. I have Mother's car out on the road and she wants it. I wish I could drive you home."

"You can't, Tim, and I love the river bank. I'm going to pick some leaves."

She could pick autumn leaves, returning from his last good-bye! He was miserable, until his misery went at the sight of her face. He moved quickly, kneeling beside her. Eyes were heavy again and very wistful.

"It's good-bye," he said, putting his arms around her waist, and in return her arms went willingly round his neck.

"Timmy-Tim," she said softly. "I shall miss you."

One hand freed itself to touch his familiar face. A happier expression was traced under her fingers.

"Let me look at you, Gretel—I want to stack up for a long time. No girl ever had such a clean face and your voice is the voice of a garden at daybreak."

"Tim, we've caught the quoting habit. Say good-bye in your own words."

"I won't," he said softly. "Other people wrote it for me. They told me to streak your eyes until I came again."

Leaning back to look in his face, she shook her head.

"We shouldn't have read so much. We're just people out of books."

"No, we're not," he said decidedly. "Let me say what I want to say. Oh, Gretel..." he sighed against her hair. "I hate mining. If it were Arts I could bear it better. Sometimes I think I have no guts. If I had I would have stood up to Uncle and refused to be bossed around. I'm no good at firm stands."

"It's too late now. Perhaps it will be better when you graduate. Have you any money, Tim? Of your own, I mean."

"Not that I know of," he said with a shrug that she could feel against her body. "They didn't read me Father's will. Uncle is executor and he manages everything. Mother is treated as if she were a moron over money. When I want something Uncle doesn't there's no money, and everyone is being denied to put me through university. When he wants something for me there's plenty of money. Work that out.... Oh, Gretel! I'm always grousing to you and you're such an angel. This winter try and think of us..."

"I will, Tim," she said, surprised.

"Of course, Gretel, but try and think of us a little way ahead." He stopped a minute and then said vaguely, "Somehow I can't think of myself going down the mine. Never mind, nothing is right but you. Give me a million kisses and I'll go. Tonight I must pack. Why has a fellow got to have a new toothbrush every time he goes away? Gretel, please begin the kisses."

"Foolish Tim," she said sanely. "It would take such ages and they wouldn't be as nice as one. I'll kiss you—once—twice—that's good-bye—"

"And I'll kiss you once—twice—three times for good memory. Good-bye, dear Gretel. Stay here until I go, will you?"

"Tim," she whispered, "don't be unhappy. It will spoil everything. Please be happy before you go."

"O.K.," he said with a smile. "Gretel," he sighed instantly, "I wish you were coming, too. Lovely, lovely face, so clean—"

"I wash quite often."

"So do lots of people. It's not that. Good-bye, Gretel of the white sails." With a last touch of her lips and cheeks he was gone, running through the beech trees.

She sat on, gazing unseeingly at the river until its rowdiness became part of her head. Tim was dragging at her, running them both out of childhood. Now the covering over them was as light as leaves. How soon would the wind expose them? was the tiny question forming in her mind. She jerked her shoulders, throwing something off her back. Consequences she knew. Had she not been frostbitten and drowned? Those things had presented their bills with great speed.

She dropped her face in her hands and the river became rushing winds blasting her out of childhood. What was deceit?

She did not pick autumn leaves from the river bank. She had to run by them to drown the process of thought. There was the past ahead of her as she went into the future. The river was making a gigantic noise and she was running with it in a headlong drop to the sea. Going with the current was the only way she knew. Even so it did not stop the tiny peck in the core of her mind. It was the beginning of a ragged hole.

We are not children any more...

I was a child and he was a child...

Her tin-whistle side....

FOURTEEN

"DRAG ON, LONG NIGHT OF WINTER."

Life, holding the incalculable, ushered in the mater's death. Flesh became ignoble, betraying the fine spirit it housed. If their minds had portrayed her passing, thoughts would have been identical. Privacy would belong to her, peace and quiet breath. As it was she died in hospital, worried by clinical detail. It was a profanation of everything she represented and perhaps her greatest trial. Everything was wrong about it. Wind moaned with them and snow-swirls fretted at the windows. David and Felice were on the eve of sailing, and strapped luggage made the hall look migratory.

Ailing for a day, Lady Fitz Henry ailed in her own room. She said she was bilious, bidding them leave her alone. Even Philip was permitted no more than a finger on her pulse. He went unhappily, knowing it was an inadequate explanation for a woman of austere living. Hannah hovered round with every thought subdued to service.

Returning at four from her college, Mary Immaculate had to shake herself like a dog before she could get rid of winter. Mounting the stairs she heard a dreadful sound, clamping her feet to the floor. When it stopped she leaped ahead. David and Felice were waiting with blanched faces. He had the air of a stricken boy, incapable of decision.

"Mary," hissed Felice, "this has been going on for some time. Dare I call Philip?"

The girl nodded her head.

"Yes. I'll go in and tell her."

Inside, the bulk of the room was oppressive, full of snow-light. Hannah was holding a pan while Lady Fitz Henry's body bent double in agony. When the paroxysm was over the old woman retreated with the pan. The girl was appalled. There was fatality about it, a strong elemental smell. The starkness of the Cove came rushing back, with its straight talk of mortality. Repulsion surged for a moment until it was subdued before the need of a beloved body. It was she who made the mater fresh again and smoothed the bedclothes.

"Thank you, dear," whispered Lady Fitz Henry. Her face was grey, with pinched nostrils. As she looked, the girl saw the invisible bulk of a coffin. For herself she glimpsed the fall of a curtain before the act was over. With a great effort she spoke through stiff lips.

"Mater dear, you're ill. We've sent for Philip. It's unfair not to let him help you."

"Very well," came the remote answer.

Uncertain and unhappy the girl knelt by the bed, holding Lady Fitz Henry's hand. Very soon stillness was replaced by a long rigour rippling down the bed.

"Hannah," she entreated as the old woman returned. "Please get hot-water bottles. She's awfully cold."

For the first time in her life Hannah took an order from the interloper.

Felice entered the room and it was her last privacy with her mater.

At five the avenue was packed with cars, lopsided in the snow. Storm-coated men shook themselves, stamping snow from their feet. Big linen handkerchiefs mopped professional faces. Philip was like a ghost but, as Mary Immaculate thought irreverently, he looked as calm as God. He was the doctor now before the son, and as usual doing the hard things. Directing, consulting, guiding from room to room, he permitted one opinion at a time. He told his family in one fleeting visit he had suspected her state in the morning.

The others sat in the mater's sitting-room lacing their fingers together until David began to walk. Mary Immaculate got up and looked out of the window. Some of the doctors were going, with a terrific protest of engines and wild whirring of tires. Wheels spun until chains got a grip, letting them jolt away.

At six there was an ambulance at the door, making the most fiendish fuss of all. Machinery was afflicted by the storm. Big and black it snorted for Lady Fitz Henry. Strange men entered with a stretcher and stood outside her door. A white-clad nurse unwrapped herself and went inside. Philip superintended everything with an economy of noise. Eventually he entered the sitting-room, muffled in an overcoat, and with the legs of his trousers tucked inside Arctic gaiters. In respect to his efficiency they kept in the background.

"Philip, can I do anything?" whispered Mary Immaculate, slipping her hand in his arm.

"No, my dear," he said steadily. "They'll operate as soon as possible. One of the doctors has gone ahead to make the arrangements. I'm going in the ambulance with her. Fortunately the plough has been over the roads and it will be fairly easy. I'll telephone as soon as it's over."

"Will we go?" asked David, deferring to Philip.

"I think not," he said. "We must be as quiet as possible. It's appalling for her. All that crowd. Yet what can I do?"

He looked stricken. As a son he knew he was doing all the things his mother hated. As doctor he was making a desperate effort to preserve her life.

"It's obstruction," he explained briefly. "No hope without imme-diate operation. Doubt if her heart—nothing left—Oh God I…"

For a second his control was shattered.

"Don't, Philip," whispered Mary. "You're better off. We've got to wait. Aren't you lucky you can help most?"

She was the genius for saying the right thing to the family. He turned with a straightened back.

"Can we see her go, Philip?"

"No, darling," he said, putting on his gloves. "They gave her a needle and she's drowsy. Don't you think if she saw your faces—she might think—the Place and all that…" he said incoherently.

David got up.

"I'm going in to kiss her, and no one can stop me."

"Very well, Dave."

They watched him limp away, waiting until he returned. Quite unconscious of them he sat in a chair and cried.

"She's going to die," he said desolately.

"Shushhhh, David," said Felice firmly. "This is no time to give way. We must cancel our sailings at once."

"I'll telephone, Mary," Philip said, looking into her steady face.

"I'll sit by it, Philip."

She felt any token of affection would disturb him so she stood very still. "I'll pray, Philip," she said, instinctively beseeching her altars.

Philip left, shutting the door. They were left with sounds, the fall of heavy feet, the thud of weight, the scrape of a something against the wall. This time the mater did not ask her carriers to be careful of the wallpaper. As Hannah had accompanied her on the previous descent she accompanied her now. When the last door was shut and the ambulance had started with a dreadful belch, they could hear Hannah's sniffling ascent. Without ceremony she burst in, sitting down with a thud.

"She's gone," she quavered in old despair. Her face was a riverbed for tears, running criss-cross, diverted by wrinkles. In a little time she looked sodden; as if crying with her whole body she damped her clothes. They did not have the heart to disturb her, and Mary Immaculate knew there was no comfort to bridge the years of dislike. Felice became practical.

"Hannah, I expect Lady Fitz Henry will want some things packed for the hospital. Find a suit-case and put in all her toilet articles, night-dresses, bedjackets and whatever you think necessary."

Occupation was a challenge. Hannah rose, sniffing her way out. "All right, Mrs. Dave, all right."

"And, David dear," said Felice with a soothing firmness, "you must ring for a taxi. In spite of Philip you're the eldest son, and it's grossly unfair to keep you away."

Mary Immaculate became defensive.

"It's for his own sake, Felice."

A brief glance acknowledged the fact but she answered quickly. "That's just the point. Phil must not be left alone, David."

Her decisive voice shattered her husband's indrawn state.

"What did you say?" he asked as if he had missed an important direction.

"Come, dear," she urged, "you must have some dinner first."

He stood up obediently. "Yes, dinner," he muttered. "Like France, bully-beef when your brothers—funny, isn't it?"

"No," she said normally. "It's natural."

The girl was left alone, leaning against a window squared in dim light. The wind spoke of violence, but she knew its voices were impersonal. The soul must stand four-square to them or it would cower in fear. She went back to those cold dying days in the woods, remembering that nature was not hostile if one went with it. Unnecessary to wonder if the mater would be staunch. She was not the structure to be licked off like flotsam. If the storm screeched with her passing, it would carry her to a lee-tide. The girl shivered suddenly. "God," she prayed from some savage memory of the Cove, "spare her the death-rattle."

She went into the hall and sat by the telephone.

It seemed days later. She was praying to a wild tumult of wind when the telephone shattered her ear. She shook like a disturbed animal and dragged at the receiver.

Philip spoke as if he had prepared a lesson. He might be reporting to an unknown family.

"The operation was entirely successful, very quick with as little surgical shock as possible. I'm sorry to say she nearly failed on the table. We thought we would have to discontinue, but we stimulated and she rallied, so we went on. Now it's a question of vitality, fight, which…"

His voice cracked, giving the first oust to the doctor.

"Yes, Philip," she said, subduing any solicitude. "Have you had any dinner?"

"I'm going to get a bite now and, Mary—"

"Yes, Philip?"

"I'm staying at the hospital all night. Dave is going home. Go to bed like sensible people and I promise to call you if—if…"

"You want us to go to bed as if nothing had happened?" she asked with incredulity in her voice.

His voice sounded impatient, but she knew if she saw him it would be because he was showing strain.

"What good will it do to sit up? Every possible thing is provided for. Go to bed like a good girl."

"All right," she agreed obediently. "Philip—"

"Yes, Mary dear. Don't think me unsympathetic, but one must be ordinary in case of—"

"Yes, yes," she agreed. "Philip," she ventured nervously, "has she asked for Holy Communion?"

For a moment there was silence like a wall of blackness.

"Will you hang on, Mary—I'll—"

After a long wait she heard a rattle of the receiver and his voice again.

"I spoke to the nurses who prepared her. They said before they touched her she received Communion and seemed very content. Does that satisfy you?"

"Yes," she whispered. "Thank you, Philip. Good night. Try and get a little sleep."

"Good night. Thank you for not making a fuss."

Surprisingly she slept, lulled by the wind and the driving snow. In the morning she struggled back to a world that held a weight. Not until her brain had assured her of her body did she remember the dread of the house. There had been no call in the night. The mater had survived the first test! One leap took her to the window.

"Dear God!" she said like a prayer. "What a day! What a day to die!"

A thickness of sky pressed down on the earth. Because the trees were bare she could see other houses. Dormers wore cowls, round windows were hooded and icicles hung short, long, thick and thin. Dementia spun in the ground drift, whirling like the madness of ghosts. From the distant sea a fog-horn bleated above the wind.

It was the first day she had ever wakened in the Place without the mater. She shivered, glad to turn inwards to the warmth of hot water.

At breakfast they talked with muted voices, strung for the first call from Philip. Felice seemed to give Lady Fitz Henry anxious but second thought. Her concern was for David and her job of holding him up. He was very quiet with his ready words reduced to automatic courtesies. Behind his glasses his eyes looked swollen and red.

"That fog-horn," shuddered Felice, giving way to some gloom. "It takes me back to the war and Mournful Mary announcing an air-raid; I can see myself flying to a dug-out. Mary, did you sleep? You look very white."

"I'm always white, Felice."

"Different white," she said decidedly.

"Valley lilies, whiter still than Leda's love," quoted David as if part of his mind went on by itself.

Mary Immaculate thought of Tim! He would have to be thinking of her in that hour.

"God!"

They all leaped at the sound of the telephone, but Mary got there first.

"Yes," she said with a pounding heart.

Philip's words came like conversational doom.

"Mary, I must tell you she's sinking. The comeback is definitely not there. It's a matter of a few hours..."

The blood was leaving her head, running out through scuppers in her feet. She had never fainted in her life and this was no time for innovation.

"Yes, we will come," she whispered steadily, bending her head almost to the floor with the mouthpiece under her lips.

"Yes, you must all come. Call a taxi at once."

It was one of those incredible days leaving a carbon copy on the mind. The storm tried to hold them with vindictive delays. The distance from the taxi to the hospital door seemed the core of a cold maelstrom. Fur pointed to tails in a few seconds. They stood round in outdoor clothes with the misery of wet cats. Finding a waiting-room, they waited for Philip, seeing the trundle past of stretchers and carts with prone bodies going to unknown miseries. Then Philip came with a drawn black-and-white look, escorting them without a word. There was a long, shocked halt by a narrow bed with no greeting from its suffering occupant. Then they were evicted for some treatment. Cruelty lay in the stimulation holding her back from death. Why torture her? was the unspoken question in every unprofessional mind. They went to and fro while grapnel-hooks went into time. Once there was inclusive recognition from the mater's eyes and the sound of her voice.

"My son, must this go on?"

They knew what she meant; the salines and sips. Philip was suspended in torture between his role of doctor and son. Glad enough to leave her in peace, he had to fight to the last for the preservation of life. It was a supreme courtesy when she seemed to divine it.

"Let them continue," she said, closing her eyes.

They left again, biting their lips. Back once more they knew they would wait until the end. Twilight had come to the endless day, and a cessation in the storm, but unrest had come inside to Lady Fitz Henry. She stirred and wandered whispering the incoherencies of departing minds. Once she told Mary Immaculate to shut the door as she went and to stand up straight. The girl won control on her knees, her lips moving in a silent entreaty for peace at the last. Philip stood like a rock and the nurse made a motionless outline at one side of the bed. David sat with his head down and Felice beside him. It seemed the only room in the whole institution. No other sounds were heard but the mutter of the woman who had always kept her thoughts to herself. Deep relief breathed in the room when the voice became mute and the body slacked in a straight line. Mary Immaculate rose from her knees. Nobody stopped her when she leaned over the still face. Death was not frightening her, concerned as she was in following it as far as she could. Putting her hand on the brow, she nearly jerked it away. This, she thought, must be the death-dews. The shock over, she let her fingers make a contact with incipient death. Some communion was established. After a long time, the girl heard the ghost of a whisper.

"Mary."

"I'm here, Mater dear, smoothing your hair."

What was said the others could not hear. Their eyes saw some agreement from the fair head while their ears heard the soothing corroboration of her voice. "Yes, Mater, whatever you say."

For a fleeting second Lady Fitz Henry unclosed dull eyes and the others crept close to her bed.

"My sons," she whispered. Then, as if she had overlooked something, she struggled towards, "Felice—"

Dropping back, two of them cried, but too softly to intrude on her passing. Philip stood unchanged, a tower of a man, while the girl let her hand continue towards its cold tryst. They did not know whether it was seconds or minutes, when they heard a small snort and saw the sag of a jaw. In a split second the girl's hand held it up.

"Philip!" she cried in agony.

With equal quickness his hand replaced her own, speaking over his mother's dead face.

"Go home, Mary, all of you."

"No, Philip, we'll wait for you."

What had they done? When all arrangements were completed Philip had to give his mother to other hands. There was nothing left but to return and receive her. They shivered with depressed vitality and gained the warmth of the hall. There stood Hannah like a figure of woe.

"How is she?" she asked in a grating voice.

Philip ran his hand over his forehead.

"I thought you'd rather hear from us than on the telephone. She died an hour ago."

There was a fateful silence as they all leaned against things, too exhausted for further battering. Every word of Hannah's was a flay to their nerves.

"Do you mean to say, Mr. Philip and Mr. David, that you let my mistress go to her Maker without the help of my hands? Her whom I've served for fifty years. Have you done that to me?"

They had! Philip did not seem to have any imagination left to realize his great fault.

"She was unconscious, Hannah, and you never go out in the winter. Death is impersonal, you know."

"Mr. David, did you think of me?"

"No," he said, reduced to automatic honesty. "It was all so sudden—"

"*She* was there," said Hannah, pointing to Felice, "and *she* was there," she accused, making a projectile of a finger at Mary Immaculate.

"Of course," said Philip sharply. "Hannah, please don't make a scene. We're very tired. I'm sorry you feel wronged, but you must admit there was little time for thought. A mere day and a half's illness and then this...."

"Mr. Philip is right, Hannah. It's a time to help and not to blame. We're all sorry for you, but she had no room for any of us at the last. It would have been a worry—"

"I was never—"

"And," interrupted Felice firmly, "there's work to be done. She'll be returning in a couple of hours and the room must be prepared. Shall I ask the maids and let you go to bed?"

"Let me do it, Felice," whispered, Mary Immaculate, clutching at activity.

"*You will not*," said Hannah in harsh refusal. "I'll do the work in this house. Then I'll know I was at least her servant."

Turning from them, she shuffled towards the drawing-room doors. The dazzle of the great chandelier hurt their eyes. Before they had the energy to move, Hannah was pushing back furniture against the walls. She worked as if she knew funeral preparations.

"Come," said Felice, slipping her hand in David's arm. "We'll be sensible and sit by the fire and talk about her naturally. She's only been half here since..."

"Yes," muttered Philip. "Felice, do you think we did all we could?"

"What human hands could, Philip," she said in a quick, comforting voice.

Felice must have shaped up to death before, thought the girl. She seemed so adequate with all her nerves beaten down. For herself, she was in awe to the fact of death; that strange dropping of the screen on replying lips and eyes. Now that the ugliness was over, it seemed a majestic enchantment. It was her first intimate experience of it, something she had to travel on with. A bit of herself was going to the other side. It puzzled her that she had no inclination to tears. David's facile acceptance of emotions let him weep, also Felice. Philip was full of control and black shadows, though he looked as if the tears were running down inside the taut line of his jaw.

"Let's go," said Felice, urging them out of immobility.

They moved down the hall with a united front, dropping their things as they went. In the mater's sitting-room, the fire was bright and the curtains drawn.

"I'm sorry about Hannah," said Philip exhaustedly. "It was one of the things we didn't do...."

Generous, he was using the plural. He had done it all and was searching his mind for deficiencies of service. Mary Immaculate could not bear it. Privately she thought Hannah had never been any more to the mater than a capable servant of long standing.

"Philip," she said, "it was not one of the things that would have helped. Hannah would have cried and sniffed, and that would have been disturbing...."

"Yes," said David irrelevantly, "she only saved a pillow from the fire."

A bit of himself had come back to his voice. He was talking, rather than criticising Hannah, although he continued appraisingly:

"Age hasn't sweetened her. I believe she minded our poverty more than Mater. What will we do with her now? She'll be one-winged without her. I fancy she's gone sour. Felice dear," he said to his wife, "let's all have a drink. We're becalmed in great heaviness."

It was his way of playing up.

"Of course, darling. I'll fetch it myself. The maids are busy. Can't Mary have a drink, Philip?"

"Yes, if she wants it."

"I don't," she said. "I don't need what I've never had."

David reached for her hand.

"Darling," he said very sincerely, "you were so sustaining, rubbing her dear head and holding up her chin. Wasn't she, Phil?"

"Yes," he said briefly.

"But, David," she asked in wonder, "what difference can death make between two people who love each other. I somehow can't see—perhaps I'm foolish—I'm new..."

"Can't see what, Mary," they both asked together.

"I can't see the separation. Don't they live on in you—us— because it's we who will carry them round."

David blew his nose very loudly, struggling to control ready tears. Philip got up to open the door for Felice. As he rose he bent over the girl, kissing her hair.

"Mary, would it be intruding to ask what Mater said to you? Was it for you or for all of us?"

She looked up very steadily. "It was for me, Philip."

Later, the scrunch of snow and the loaded tramp of feet was hard to bear, carrying in its sounds the very sight of the mater's return. It was Hannah who had her moment then, and, in reparation, the family stood back, letting her feel authority.

When the house had settled back to its own creaks and moans they went in a body to look. The light was very strong, and the iceberg mantelpiece, with its reflecting mirror, invited them for a long walk. Mary Immaculate dropped on her knees and prayed. When she rose she looked with personal eyes. The whiteness and cold majesty nearly threw up a barrier, but the tough quality of her mind put death in its proper proportion. Quite naturally she stooped down and looked in the mater's face. How the nose lived on in its chiselled perfection. As if to reassure the mater of their presence she drew her hand lightly down the cold cheek. Its ice startled her, but there was no recoil in her hand.

"Dear, *dear* Mater," she whispered, with an intensified wish to penetrate her silence.

David collapsed on a chair, giving way to unaffected tears. Felice stood over him, silently stroking his hair.

Philip stood with his nose as chiselled as his mother's. He looked as if he might join her if restoration did not come. Health seemed to be cracking in the tight strain of his face. Stepping to his side, the girl slipped her arm through his.

"Philip, you're very tired. You've been up all night. Listen, Philip, I know what she was like as a mother, but she's remembering what you were like as a son. It's natural to cry...."

His face was in her hair, and his body shook with grief and exhaustion. She guided him to the settee she had sat on when he told her the mater had a weak heart. Kneeling on it with one leg, she knew the experience of holding a man's body in her arms while he cried. When he started he did it rather terrifyingly, with long gasps coming from the depths. They were not David's facile tears, but hard tears of repression.

With her eyes on Lady Fitz Henry's dead face, the girl's mind stirred in shocked reflection. Where was she in all this? The mater had used her last few breaths to tell her to do as Philip said. That meant the end of Tim, and to say so was to betray like Judas. What had she started in the garden? Hocus-pocus, childish enchantment. Tim was as bound up in her as he was in his music, and to do without both would be to whirl him to some dark pit of futility. Philip was in her arms, crying exhausted tears and giving her a feeling of his taut, long body. Felice had her arms round David, and the expression on her face said that she was grieved but happy. At that moment David had all her motherhood. Felice was suggesting that they all go to bed with hot drinks. David stood up as if in obedience to direction, looking red-eyed at his mother's face. Felice slipped her arm in his, and they had a moment of still contemplation. Now, thought the girl, Felice will take him to bed and put her arms round him and help him to go to sleep. Tonight she could help Philip like that, smooth his head and let him drop into sleep, empty of thought. But the mater was dead, and she had lost direction. When she got lost again, there would be no calm black-and-white woman to come and see her, reducing the foolishness in her. Bereavement became intensified, running down her body in long dread. Instantly Philip forgot himself.

"Mary, you're cold and you haven't cried, yourself." He looked up in her face with his black hair tumbled on his forehead. "You shouldn't ask me to do what you don't do yourself."

A light hand tidied his hair.

"I would cry if I could, Philip, right out loud at the top of my voice."

"You sound exhausted, my dear. Let's all say good night and go to bed. If Mater were here she'd insist on——"

"Common sense," supplied the girl. "She thought that was the most important of all."

Felice seemed to collect them in a solid little bunch.

"Tomorrow the house won't be our own. Let's make this our last look."

In dead silence they looked down at the calm face as white as the satin around it. Then Philip drew up a panel.

"I hope the snow stops," he said in a relaxed voice.

"God, such a winter funeral!" said David rebelliously.

"But it's so fresh and clean," said Mary Immaculate. "The sun will get in the grave before her."

Her hand in Philip's arm, she knew he would sleep like someone felled.

They left the lights full on and closed the doors.

So different from the girl's childish memory of death. Then people sat up all night in the room with the body. Always they ate, and a wake was one of the occasions of the Cove. The smell of oranges round the mater? Appalled at the different ways of living, she shivered to bed, where she stared wide-eyed into darkness.

FIFTEEN

"DESTINY WILL FIND A WAY."

David and Felice were receiving condolence calls while Mary helped Philip list letters, wreaths and cables.

Already Philip looked better. His face had dropped the mask of strain and the smudges round his eyes. His health was resilient. A man of controlled appetites, it was never abused. Not for him the large drink when he was exhausted. David could stay himself that way, but it was a point of honour with Philip never to attend a case smelling of spirits.

In the midst of her occupation the girl became conscious of his long brooding over a letter. Continuing apparently absorbed, she saw nothing in front of her.

"Mary, read that," he said, passing the letter. "That last bit..."

She was mute with surprise that Philip should be portentous over the written word. She read: "Applaud us when we run, console us when we fall, cheer us when we recover, but let us press on—in God's name, let us press on."

She was used to direct speech from Philip. What was he trying to say? Above all, his eyes were searching the effect of the significant sentence.

"I can't imagine not pressing on," she ventured tentatively.

The ease of mutual work was over. She could merely suspend her pencil and wait.

"Mater was the right person for you,"he said as if delighted with the survey of his eyes.

Chop and change, she thought. But she was sure if he stared deep enough he would see Tim sitting in the middle of her forehead. She could trust her face only so long, and Philip was regarding her with a long, rolling boil of eyes that would not break.

She stirred, sitting up. "Yes, Mater was wonderful, everything—"

"I expect she knew you best," he said in some bafflement. "I wonder if you're what I think you are?"

"I believe you'd like me better if I was like that," she said vaguely.

"I couldn't like you better, Mary."

The reply was indirect. Were both her men finding flaws in her? She was somehow unsatisfying to them both. Since Tim's going she had reluctantly blazed a trail towards self-analysis. Hitherto the preoccupation in herself had gone into an intense cram of living, and, when the day was spent, she had pulled the pillow low under her neck and dropped to extinction. Now she knew Philip had stopped being a son. It was as if he had prayed and fasted long enough. The Place was his with his mother's income. In addition, he was solidly established and might become formidable in his security. Impossible to imagine him a prey to indecision. Having put his nose to the grindstone, he was in sight of his deserts. He was no happy Jack, she thought. But Tim had worked, too, knowing the joyless grind of application without ambition. Had he not tried to make her face up to an adult life? She had the sensation of running by the river bank, away from the question in his heavy-lidded eyes. Where could she run now, from Philip? Between the leather chairs, the library table and round and round in a circle? Was she part of Philip's inheritance? Was she different from other girls, with some changeling qualities? Many of her contemporaries seemed sure of love, past thought and action that did not include some boy. They appeared to live with little incidents they intensified in their imaginations. They would pine and roll their eyes and long for a sight of the boy. Then, if they saw him unexpectedly, they would blush to the roots of their hair and run away.

Such conduct confounded her. If she were in that ecstatic state she would be delighted to see the boy, and enjoy him without blushes and palpitations. What were men and women to each other to make them act in that demented way? Would all the joys of every day be lessened if she married Philip or Tim? A vivid picture of the mater commending her to Philip made her jitter with responsibility. Cold as it was in the new-fallen snow, she wanted to go out and walk away doubts in the evening air. But Philip was talking. More chop and change! There were housekeeping plans, Hannah in temporary charge, with Felice keeping the accounts.

"It will be lovely to have them for the winter," she said, grabbing at a safe conversational straw.

"You won't go back to college until after Christmas, Mary?"

"No."

"Do you want to go then?" he asked, inviting denial.

"Yes," she said faintly but firmly. If she gave way an inch the water would be over her head. For the first time in her life she felt utterly inadequate. She was slipping, and there were no footholds. Fortunately he did not notice, sitting with the light making a black shine on his hair.

"Mary," he said, putting the tips of his fingers together.

A diagnosis, she thought to herself, "Yes?" she questioned faintly, laying her pencil on a table.

Then he noticed her strangeness effecting the stifling of his words. "My dear, what is it? You look different. Is there anything wrong? That is beyond dear Mater."

Supposing she said yes, wildly. Would he console her? He would not, she thought definitely. In the emotional softness from his mother's death he might not be angry, but he would insist on a line of conduct that shut Tim out forever. He would have to press on without her. What a betrayal that would be, reducing her to a stark Judas outline. She was the bolster for his mining, the liberation for his mind, and the note left behind from his frustrated music. Facility of speech was gone, but some answer was needed in view of Philip's vigilant eyes. How brown they were, and what black lashes he had! How differently she was seeing him since his mother's death. He was a good-looking man with his winged, high-tempered nose. At this moment the nostrils were calm, so she was safe from his emotions.

"There's nothing, Philip. It's just—just…"

"Of course," he said soothingly. "It's been a great strain for you. You shaped up magnificently, Mary. That last scene touched me beyond words."

Instead of being grateful she was irritated. Smooth nerves were being sandpapered. Her own dilemma made her want to blast him out of his security.

"But, Philip," she said quite crossly. "I loved her. There's nothing wonderful—"

"It was wonderful to me, Mary."

She had been irritable, and he did not mind. Instead he got up and sat on the arm of her chair, holding her shoulders, with his chin on the top of her head. Because she had grown up with his touch she leaned against him, remembering the sanctuary he had been before.

"My dear, do you know that Mater has left you nearly all her personal possessions? All her jewellery except a few pieces for Felice."

"What, Philip?" she gasped, leaning back to search his face.

"Yes, my dear. It shows how she felt about you. Some of her things are very good, but the settings are old-fashioned. Some day we'll have them reset."

We, we, we! Her conflict flew into her eyes, making a naked display to Philip.

"My dear Mary," he said firmly. "I feel sure you're upset in some way. Tell me, what is it?"

To conceal her face she rested against his chest.

"I'm just confused, Philip. This and that and so many rings for my fingers," she said childishly. It was sufficient to make him laugh.

"You feel all right, then?"

"Have I ever been ill?"

"Not since you drowned yourself. Your health is a delight to a doctor. When I see you I often think disease is an offence against living."

Did he love her because she could exist without mixtures that must be shaken three times a day?

"My dear," he said, cupping one cheek. She could feel hunger in his hands, not knowing how she identified it. Had she not been jolted out of childhood the day Tim went away? No matter how much she pursued her heedless youth, it receded before a widening horizon. Yet she did not know how to contain her new attributes of growth. This time she did the wrong thing by closing her eyes, permitting Philip to kiss her with lips having no relation to the kisses of the past. Very honestly she admitted there was nothing in her disliking the kiss.

"My dear," he said softly, "I don't want you to feel bereft because Mater is gone. Let me try to make up for her loss. I love you, Mary. I always have, since you appeared as a frozen little waif, and I always will."

"I love you too, Philip,"she said helplessly.

Did she not speak the vital truth? Did she not love him? Were not the associations of everyday, things that brought good returns? Loyalty, gratitude and remembrance of the mater's bequest did not have to be summoned consciously to her mind. But there was September last? Then Tim had been sighing against her hair, demanding a million kisses? The way of her present life was apart from her wild-stepping youth. Tin-whistle side? She wished Tim had not expressed it in those terms. It reduced them to an Endymion world that could not find habitation in rooms. Was she a bad girl, liking many people and loving none? Again Philip was talking over her head, suggesting future plans. There would be England, London with David and Felice, then across the continent and a long stay in Vienna. She would like to go by herself, untrammelled by responsibility, gypsy-wild and free to look. The thought of a companionless flight made her jump to her feet.

"Let's go upstairs, Philip. I think the people have gone. I heard the door shut."

Again he was patient. "As you say, my dear. Felice will attend to those letters."

The absence of admonition and direction said he was raising her from the status of a child. It was more intensified when he took her arm, complaining she was too thin.

"You must take a tonic," he suggested gently.

"I will not,"she said with definite decision. The fact that he only smiled in return made the refusal significant. He had become the suppliant instead of the mentor.

Even though the mater was dead, and she had the weight of a problem, she found she could speed upstairs. Was she not Josephine's daughter, leaving everything to the will of God? Philip was ten steps below, Tim was at university in Canada. Fate would decide.

There were so many letters, one more was not noticed.

Dearest Gretel,

I dared write when Mother told me about Lady Fitz Henry. I knew there would be letters, and this might wander in. We've always had enormous luck with each other. We may not be star-crossed lovers after all, and all this winter I've been frightened about you and me. But I did not intend to talk about ourselves. I was shocked and unhappy when Mother wrote all the details. Of course, Auntie Minnie had the news about the hospital and how wintry it was. I can't get her face out of my mind, having seen her so often from the beech tree. I'm sure she was a grand person because she made you so lovely. Now that I'm away I can see you better. What a day that was for me when I piped you up in the tree! Now anything that hurts you hurts me dreadfully. It has been and always will be. I know about death, dear Gretel, and the letters that come in full of little verses. I wish I was there to make you feel how near I am in this.

Things will be different now! I wish I could talk about us, but that will have to wait, and I know you want it that way.

Can I go on now and talk of something else? I can't stop when the opportunity has come to write you one letter. One thing about this made me want to cry like a baby. Mother offered to let me come home for Christmas! She said she had saved some money and it was ample to take me home and back. I was desperately tempted to take it, but it was too much. The fact that she saved it says she feels Uncle's domination over money. If he knew she had it he'd pester her until she invested it in some bond. They always seem to promise things in fifty years. I'd like one good bust in the present, before my fingers stiffen on the keys. Just one loaf round Europe and then I can take it. That is with you beside me.

I could go on writing forever about life here. Needless to say I have gravitated to a musical crowd, and it helps the professional subjects. Everybody talks a lot. Mostly I just sit and listen. What amazes me is the way some fellows have their minds made up. Their way seems cemented, and they simply can't get worked up over music, art or literature. It's a crowd to hold one's tongue with. I can see them as uncles born to plague a fellow like me. Then there are the playboys and the smart Alecs who like the thing out of bounds. They have a drunken way of enjoying themselves. The girls all have coxcombs and curls, and nails like the blood of bullocks. I have only to think of you to want nothing from them. Nobody could love you more than I do, dear Gretel, or remember every bit about you. It makes a fellow reel in terror that it might not go on. Darling, look at the white ship and think of your vassal.

TIM

The letter hurt her. She could see him so plainly, with his eyes rich with his feelings. She who liked a good pace found the way too fast. Towards herself Philip and Tim seemed so concentrated. She applauded the latter for his self-denial, consoled him for his unselfishness towards his mother; but she knew it was useless to expect him to press on without her. His mother must love him in some dumb way. Her tentative steps to ease his uncongenial career had been evinced several times. The girl wanted to look at his mother with recognition. She knew her by sight as well as the redoubtable Auntie Minnie. The former was inclined to be square and slow-moving, with a pasty face and Tim's heavy-lidded eyes. She walked past the gates of the Place with uninquisitive eyes. Her clothes were always neat but not smart. Auntie Minnie's were neither. She was inclined to accessories as decorated as a dessert with a cherry and a strip of angelica. Her marcel wave was knife-edged, as if a hairdresser had been challenged to make it everlasting. Always going out with her work, she walked with a bag. Her legs in motion held a hop, while her brown eyes darted inquisitively around. Tim said she read the morning paper from cover to cover, and knew the names of all the incoming and outgoing passengers. Briefly, Auntie Minnie was a nosy parker!

The letter stored in her mind, Mary Immaculate sailed on with her chin up, causing David to remark to his wife:

"Mary's chin has a tilt. I wonder what it means. What is she defiant about?"

"You see too much," said his wife. "Perhaps some student at the college has been making love to her, and she's slapped his face."

David was shocked.

"Do you think she has followers?" he asked naively.

"Fool!" said his wife. "You and Philip never see Mary as an ordinary girl. I doubt if she has much opportunity though. I find she takes no part in anything but the academic life. I hear around she's a brilliant student, but never mixes..."

"Why?" said David.

"You'd better ask Philip, Dave dear. He didn't want her to attend the college at all."

"Well, we'll see it out this winter," said David with a little shiver. "I don't relish the thought of the eternal snows, even for Mary."

The girl was to look back on that winter as a harmonious season. There were four of them, and it was a perfect number for most things. Study became a cram, so as not to interfere with pleasure. They played bridge, went to cinemas, skated, read, enjoyed infinite music and saw whatever there was to see. David occasionally asserted himself, and he definitely refused to put crepe on the doorknob for his mother. After a few deep frowns, Philip went his way. He began to play and enjoy playing, making no attempt to order Mary Immaculate around. She was rock-bound in the ways of the mater, and showed no desire to spill over. Wise enough to bide his time, his conservatism refused to speak of love to a girl who was still going to school. Occasionally the air palpitated with something, quickly eased by David and Felice. If the girl herself saw signs of widening circles, she was adept in evasion. Instead of going with the tide, that winter resembled a comfortable rest on a lee shore.

Episodes made her ponder. An evening skating alone with Philip on the flooded tennis-court. It was a night of rare beauty, white in austerity. The moon was alone in the sky, casting a blue light on the ice. The stars were niggards, withdrawn from the flaunt of the moon. About six or seven stars, thought the girl, skimming over the ice in Philip's arms.

Skating, they achieved perfect harmony, she having grown to a height that made her a faultless partner. To her it was the very ecstasy of motion, a rhythm, intoxicating to the body. She was just under his chin, with yellow eyes fixed on the moon. It looked insolent with aloofness, alone in cold beauty. She would like to be free and take that wide survey.

Philip was keeping the time unmarred, by a careful avoidance of a ridge in the ice, but when he could he stared at her face. She was bareheaded, wearing a brown flared skirt and a leather coat, zipping to the throat. When the music stopped he did not release her, letting the gramophone needle scrape on. She gave a long sigh, standing easily in his arms.

"Nice, Philip!"

"Perfection, my dear, and what a night!"

"Philip, I wish I was the moon up in the sky. Think of seeing everything going on."

"I haven't that much curiosity, Mary. Come back from the moon. I'm uncomfortable with infinity."

She laughed, still staring up. Then she knew he was stirred by the sight of her face. In the cold clear night he kissed her rather slowly, surprising her with the feel of warm lips in frosty air. Hot-cold she thought instantly, remembering the morning she had licked the snow in the valley. Philip gave her a gentle shake.

"Come back, Mary. You're so often an enigma. Dave seems to meet you. I believe you would have been much happier if he had adopted you," Philip's voice needed reassurance. Instantly she came to loyal defence.

"David happens to have done a lot of interesting things. He's had time, you haven't. When you have money you can pick and choose."

"I'd still be a doctor, Mary, if I had his money. I couldn't be idle. All I know is having a job and doing it and returning to something that's really my own."

"Nothing is really your own, Philip."

"I think it is, Mary," he said, tightening his arms on his possession. "It's the ordained way of living. A job, a roof, a wife, children..."

"But you don't own children, Philip. Their bodies are just about," she said vaguely. Dare she joke about a bone of contention? "And," she ventured softly, "they are not all full of directive thinking."

To her intense relief he laughed, giving her another shake. "You've always had your tongue in your cheek about that, Mary. Even as a small girl when I wanted to slap you."

"Why didn't you, Philip?" she asked with narrowed eyes.

"Because, my dear, even when you made me mad I loved you. Sometimes I think I started you on the wrong foot, Mary. You know why, don't you?"

"Yes, I think so," she said blandly. "Because I was full of fantasy."

"More than that," he said gravely. "Some of the doctors went as far as to say you were—"

"Dippy, Philip?" she asked, laughing on a high young note with her head back under his face. He could see the moon making gleams on her white, rounded teeth. "Hannah always said I was cracked."

"Well, thank God," he said, laughing with her. "I was right and they were not. They said it was impossible to lie out for three days if you were normal."

Mary Immaculate's eyes narrowed again. "I'm sure they're all very wise, Philip, but could they know what effect it should have?"

"I don't yet," he said with a frown. "You've forgotten it, haven't you, Mary?"

It was a foolish question. The first twelve years of a life are the sharpest in memory.

"I've forgotten nothing, Philip. Let's skate again. It's a lovely night."

Frowning a little, he slid towards the gramophone. He was a man in sight of Mecca, and did not know what to concede to other gods.

They waltzed without a word, disharmony withdrawing from their bodies. Silently in the porch they took off their boots and skates. Before him she ran upstairs to David in her stockinged feet.

"Darling," he said, reaching out a welcoming hand, "you must be frozen. Where's Phil?"

"On my heels," she said lightly. "We had a divine skate under the moon. All the witches and cats have been frightened away, and the hocus-pocus doesn't know what to do with itself. It can't even wander in the shadows, because there aren't any shadows."

Entering, Philip heard her talking with her tongue in her cheek. David looked from one to the other, shaking his head.

"Mary, you sound naughty! I must forgive you because you look like gardenias on ice. Come and sit by the fire."

"Thanks, I'm going to bed," she said lightly. "I go to school, you know."

When Philip had opened the door for her he went himself, without a word.

"M'mmm," said David expressively. "Was that cold air they brought in?"

"I'm afraid so."

"She looked just as readable as the sphinx. I know that mood. Felice, has she ever told you what Mater—"

"My dear Dave, if she hasn't told you she'll tell no one."

"Where is she going? I think Phil should give her some time away before he ties her down. If she doesn't love him sheer loyalty will make her accept him."

"Isn't it better to let her ease into marriage than go where he might lose her? If we take her home with us, very soon she'll be dining and dancing, and rushing from this to that..."

"And men will be trying to kiss her in the backs of cars, and making love to her when they're one over the eight."

"I wouldn't worry about that. She can be as cold as ice. She's much more likely to see the world as a place than as people."

"Will Phil be a lover, Felice?" said David, turning off the radio and settling for conversation. "He's very celibate."

"You married young, dear, somewhat instinctively—and you're his brother."

"Well, well, well, three holes in the ground! We won't go into that. I was in! France! Somewhere in France there's a lily! We didn't have the luck to meet one—"

"Fool!" said his wife, undisturbed. "Don't you think love like Phil's is bound to get returns, and, after all, dear, he's a doctor."

"That's a help," said her husband with a grin.

She was skating alone in the glow of the western sky when she saw Hannah looking from a second-storey window. Because the shrubbery was bare she could be seen very plainly. Rufus was sitting on the ledge, baking in the rich orange of the sun. For a second the girl feared for the cat, Hannah looked so like an old witch. Suitably she should have had him hung on the tail of her shift while she danced in the centre of fire. The sun suggested the picture. But Hannah was not dancing. She was silent, fixed and stealthy, as if she might be crouched over a tripod, brooding on an oracle. When it was revealed she would whirl into words. Curtailing a backward three, the girl sat in the shade of the hedge. She did not like the fixity of Hannah. Since Lady Fitz Henry's death she had stopped grumbling and goading her, but that had been better than rancid silence. When her work was done she crouched over the fire, working her old hands. Felice found her very difficult. She refused to take orders, and frequently meals appeared that had not been planned. She was sullen to everyone except David, and she found it impossible to maintain a grudge against him. In more than the others, she rambled to him about the past, perpetually reliving his childhood days. He was kind and sympathetic and, in pity for her loneliness, let her bore him very often. Her lost mistress had stipulated that she should be maintained for the remainder of her life or, if Philip wished, to be kept in comfort at some agreeable home.

Several times she took her bewilderment to the cemetery, gazing at the mater's grave. She lay with many others, under a granite monument surrounded by an iron railing. All the Fitz Henrys were recorded, as well as the two who had died in France. The girl's throat felt tight when she saw the brevity of Arthur and John. The snow would have to melt before the mater's name could be cut. A winter cemetery was very lonely. Marble and snow swept coldly together. One white angel fascinated the girl. She was perched up aloft with body-length wings and a marble dress, bloused at the waist. Holding a basket of flowers, she bent with one bloom in an extended hand. The girl was inclined to wait until the angel dropped the flower. Occasionally she picked flowers from the conservatory and let them make bright stains in the snow. Once she stuck a geranium in the angel's hand, and when she went back it was frozen, making a blood-spot against marble flesh. Strangely enough she knew Philip had been to the cemetery, too, because he noticed the angel.

"Mary," he said, "you've been to the cemetery recently."

"How do you know?"

"Because of the angel near Mater."

"Do you like that angel, Philip?"

"Not much," he admitted.

"Neither do I," she said. "But I gave it a real flower for a change. Please don't put an angel over me when I die, Philip."

"I won't," he assured her gravely. "I hope you'll be in the same plot with us."

She was startled beyond measure. His plans included her resting-place with the Fitz Henrys—Mary, beloved wife of...If she lived long enough the fisherman's daughter would begin to feel dynastic. "And madly play with my forefather's joints." Was she in such a plight that she should be clubbed with some great kinsman's bone? To keep her mouth straight she said hastily.

"I often go there after school. This time I wanted to decide my graduation dress."

"Anything you like," he said, always generous towards her needs.

It was then he told her something she had not known.

"Mary, that money the American cabled when the Press—"

"Yes," she said, surprised.

"It's quite intact. I merely paid your hospital bills, and the interest has brought it back to the original sum."

"Philip," she said excitedly, "I can go to a bigger university and finish my Arts."

"I was afraid of that," he said quietly. The minute the words were said she could have bitten out her tongue. Without a word of gratitude she had seized on a venture only possible through his generosity.

She walked to his chair, sitting on its leather arm. His very quietness brought him infinite returns. She put her arms around his neck in palliation for selfishness. "Philip, what a beast I am! Instead of thinking of your goodness to me I just plan to spend the money. I think I've been spoiled with too much. I wasn't used to it, and it went to my head. Please, please forgive me—"

"Mary dear, I don't want gratitude. When we took you, money fell in line. I took the risk of your walking out someday, but I felt the money was yours and I should preserve it for you...."

She placed her cheek against his hair, rocking a little in contrition. "What do you want me to do, Philip?"

In a second he pulled her down across his knees. "Don't you know, Mary?"

He smelt familiar, always a little antiseptic.

"Don't you know, Mary?" he repeated.

"Don't tell me," she said quickly. "I've—I've got a lot to do."

"As you say," he said, turning up her face and looking at her in fresh wonder. "Mary, do you know you'd be more human to me if I saw you one day with a pimple."

Nothing could have reassured her more or dissipated the high tension. She laughed until she could have cried. "Philip," she said against his face, "if you like I'll eat chocolates every meal and ice-cream between. That might be a help."

"No, you won't," he said, laughing himself. "I shouldn't kiss you, Mary, when you're at school."

"But, Philip, what would make you stop kissing me?"

At that moment there seemed nothing.

"AND STOOD ALOOF FROM OTHER MINDS."

"If I were a flower I'd refuse to bloom," said David, frowning at the mud-spattered tulips.

"Oh, but they're beautiful, David! Not quite unspotted from the world. They want a west wind—"

"Darling, gardens are worse than people. They always want something they haven't got. Dirty little things," he said, addressing the tulips and shivering in the wind. In spite of the sun it blew with the flick of a cat-o'-nine-tails. His face was pallid from indoor heat, and his hands held a blue tinge. Mary Immaculate was walking round the flower-beds in a green knitted suit. There was no shrinking in her flesh or bleak look on her skin. She walked with a young insolence, showing the line of her shapely legs.

"House-cat," she said pityingly. "I suppose, dear David, if we have a frost to-night you won't come to see me graduate."

"Yes, I will," he said nobly. "I have an intense curiosity to see you get your diploma. What do you want for a graduation present? Don't be shy. Tell me what you want, even unto half of my kingdom."

She sat down on the grass edge of a flower-bed, while he towered above her.

"You'd better tell me, my dear. The wind is east, and it might freeze the genial current of my soul."

"I don't want anything, David. I have everything material."

"Gracious," he said lightly, "you must be growing up, suffering the birth-pangs of frustration. To wish for the intangible is a sure sign."

"I've always wished for the intangible," she said reprovingly. "I think I'm a Glaucus girl. I ate grass and changed into a—"

"Sea-nymph, I think. Remember, Glaucus was smothered in a cask of honey. It must have been a sticky end. I can't give you the worship of fishermen or boatmen, but I can give you the present. Speak up, girl! You're too old for a doll."

"Funny," she said, smiling at the spattered flowers. "I never had a doll."

"The girl who never had a doll! It sounds odd! My first memory of you seems to rule them out. You looked so tall, and disdainful of dolls. It would have taken some daring to present one. What can I give you that's not a doll?"

"Thank you, David," she said gravely. "What I want you can't give me." Her tone was resigned, as if her wishes were out of reach.

"My dear," he said, bending her head back to see her face. "What do you want? I insist on knowing."

"Nothing I can have," she said with resignation. "I want to finish my Arts. The college has lots of affiliations with England and Canada, and I could get a third year status wherever I went. I'd rather go to England. I want the Old World more than the New. Then I'd like to ramble over Europe and perhaps Asia, certainly Egypt, and see everything I've read about."

"Small programme," he said dryly. "Couldn't you be content with third year Arts ?"

"I thought I'd tell you the lot, David, as a bit is just as impossible as the whole."

"Nonsense," he said decisively. "What's stopping you? You can certainly have the university."

"David," she challenged, "can I?"

"Certainly," he said in the same tone. "If Philip won't send you, I will."

"You can't send me without his consent. He has control of me until I'm too old for it. And it isn't for lack of money." She told him about the fund for her education.

"Heavens!" he said in surprise. "Fancy Phil saving all that! If he's not the canny Scot! He must be better off than I know."

"Yes, but he spent his own money on me. For that reason I can't ask him to let me go with my own money."

"Well," he said consideringly, "we'll see. Why don't you fight for it, Mary, if you want it very badly?"

She shrugged under his eyes.

"How can you fight against things that are planned? I've always done what I was told, that is more or less," she said, clutching at scrupulosity. "It's easier to conform as much as you can. Besides, I promised Mater."

David shook his head, forbearing to question her closely.

"Mary, sometimes you're a regular diehard Catholic. I suppose you come by it honestly."

"I expect so, David. Mater took my gypsy away. You can't be foot-loose when you're tied to hot and cold water, and indoor plumbing."

"Mary, you kill me," he said, laughing out loud. "You have the merit of being the most unexpected woman I know. I could go round the world with you, and love every step of the way."

"I'd love it, too," she said agreeably. "We'd have fun."

"We would, indeed," he responded with enthusiasm. "A gallivant-ing time while I showed you all the places that have given me pleasure. We must go to warm places first, where I can forget this east wind. I suggest Italy; Rome and Florence, and some Tuscan towns. We'll go next May, when the air is soft and scented. You'll love the vines, Mary, the chestnuts and the clumps of blossom so magnificently blossom...Think of it! No, we won't think of it—" he said abruptly. Her face was uptilted, glowing, and her eyes lucent with sun. It was the face of a girl who would pull up her roots and travel with the zest of the vagabond. David looked at the solid structure of the Place and frowned.

"Go in, my dear, and wash your face for your graduation."

Mary Immaculate looked at him with narrowed eyes.

"You're mean, David," she said softly. "You show me the world and then order me in to wash my face."

She walked out of his sight with a dignified back.

"Damn," he said out loud, kicking the muddy flowers. One broke off and listed against another. It had a mute, fainting look, with its trumpet humbled to the earth. "Damn," he said again, stooping to pick it up. To satisfy himself he returned to the house, dropping the flower in a vase. At least, he thought, I'll see that she gets her Arts.

The family was impressed with her graduation. There had been an element of tolerance in their attitude towards the limitations of her college. So little had been said of her work that they realized her reticence when they saw her mounted behind the President, the faculty, the governors and an eminent personage laced in gold braid. They knew she had recently passed through an examination week, but she had sailed through it as a normal routine. Later she had casually remarked the winning of distinction in five out of six subjects. Even then they had not quite realised the high standard required. When they saw only four of her class graduating in Arts, and only two with distinction, they murmured amongst themselves and stared at their student with appraising eyes. From her elevation her scrutiny was as cool as a drift of snowflakes. Others looked harassed, the men pulling at their collars in dread of the ordeal of getting down from the tier and across the platform without mishap. They seemed conscious of the size of their feet. The girls looked fresh but unpowdered. Inside it was very warm, and congestion and excitement caused a nervous exudation of oil. Their charge was conspicuous by the dry look of her fine-pored nose. As the President stood and the students sat, the girl went into immobility. There the mater's training and own balanced body helped. It was impossible to detect one restless movement. To them she looked curiously unfamiliar in her cap and gown, which austere garb gave her face inscrutability, extending to hands lightly clasped in her lap.

"Felice," whispered David, during an adjusting lull, "it's a long time since I've seen anything like this. I wish you'd hold my hand. They look so raw and so young and so full of ideals. It's worse than a wedding. Do you know Mary like this?"

"No," she whispered back, "and I'm feeling conscience-stricken. I was talking to her while she dressed, and she said she missed Mater terribly. She was the only one who followed her studies and knew the subjects she was taking. What have we done for her this winter?"

"Nothing," he said with a frown, "except patronise her."

It was not long before the men looked extremely conscience-stricken themselves. As some grave girls filed down for their diplomas, a figure appeared from the wings, presenting bouquets of flowers. All were not favoured, and some maidens retreated unadorned. Felice leaned towards Philip. "Did you arrange anything, Phil?"

"No," he said with his brow worried into pleats. He pulled at his watch as if he could rush for flowers at this late moment.

"It's too late now," said Felice with a shrug. "We ought to be ashamed of ourselves. She looks lonely as it is."

There *was* an aura of loneliness about her, emanating to them all. Perhaps it was because her nose did not oil and conform, or because she did not pluck nervously at her gown or keep patting the curls at the back of her neck.

"Here she comes," whispered Felice.

Mary Immaculate was treading delicately down towards the President and the gold braided-donor. They saw her accept her diploma, bow and receive a smile from eyes seeming gracious to her beauty. As she retreated to the ascending aisle a hand passed her a sheaf of white carnations. She received them without surprise, holding them like a baby across her arms. The family breathed audible relief, mixed with other emotions.

"Somebody had more thought than we had," said Felice to Philip. He looked extremely perturbed, whether with himself or the interloper it was impossible to say. Further incident made deeper pleats in his brow. The girl was just seating herself when a hissing voice demanded behind them, "Who's that lovely girl?"

"That's Mary Fitz Henry, awful young snob! My own Mary says none of the students know her. She just comes and goes, and the boys are terrified of her. By right of her work she should be secretary of the S.R.C., but she doesn't mix. The Fitz Henrys have made her a prig. She hasn't attended any of the graduating affairs. Make you sick! Yesterday there was a picnic, and a dance last night. She might be giving the valedictory only—"

"Shushhhhh," hissed another voice. Perhaps the fond relations had been feasting their eyes on their sons and daughters, impervious to the row of Fitz Henrys. Recognition must have come, wafting a feeling of suddenly red faces. Intermittent whispers went on with a lowered sibilance. The first questioner pressed on. She appeared to be the type who would press for information, regardless of place. The family shamelessly lent an ear to fugitive comment. While Philip looked haughty and annoyed he had every appearance of listening.

"Look, there's my own Mary. Sweet, isn't she? It's a new dress, though it seems a waste under her gown. No, she didn't pass with distinction, but at least she's a human being and not afraid to dance with any of the students...." The whispers dropped, then became revivified. "Crazy about her...on his way home from a Canadian university...just scraped through last year...only good at the cultural subjects...popular in a queer way, romantic-looking...hipped on music. They had a year together. He went to everything, but never looked at another girl...would play for them until his hands dropped off, but no one could vamp him off the piano-stool...I wouldn't be surprised...stuck up...There's the valedictory...."

Through the men's valedictory the Fltz Henrys examined their hands with varying expressions. Not until long-shadowed events had taken place did they sort the whispers, placing them in their proper significance. When a gentle, gracious girl was delivering the valedictory they all felt Mary Immaculate had been defrauded. Through interminable speeches there was ample time for reflection. The seats were cramped, and David's and Philip's legs were long. During much advice to youth, and frequent references to *provehito in altum*, David grew a little plaintive.

"Are the elders giving themselves a treat?"

"Of course," she whispered.

"Why are the men so verbose?"

"Probably mute in their homes," hissed his wife. "We'd better have a celebration for Mary after, to make up for the flowers."

"There's nowhere to take her, darling. It will be closing time."

Felice gave her husband a look of mute tolerance.

"The celebration is for Mary," she said dryly; "non-alcoholic. You can have a pineapple-soda and look as if you liked it."

"Must I, Phil?" he asked, leaning over to his brother.

"We could have it at home," he answered conservatively.

"Not as nice as going out," whispered Felice. "We'll go to a place with booths and ice-cream and pop. She's young enough to enjoy it."

Time was getting on.

"My God," said David with desperation, "if another person tells them to plunge into the deep I'll follow with pleasure. My knee is like a hot coal."

"It's just a closing," said his wife soothingly. "There, somebody is creeping to the piano. It must mean God save the King! Gracious, no, a glee!..."

"God," groaned her husband. But he listened attentively to glees grave and gay.

"Very nice! Why isn't she in it? She has a nice voice."

"Be quiet, David," she ordered, seeing Philip shuffling his legs.

At last they claimed her, released to cool night air. They found her at the main entrance in a loose white coat, with her arms laden with cap, gown, flowers and diploma. Philip relieved her of all impedimenta except the flowers.

"You looked charming, my dear."

She laughed, walking beside him down a flight of stone steps.

"I wasn't there to look, Philip. I was there to get a diploma."

Inside the car it took some time to get away. When they were out of the grounds he asked at once, "Who sent the flowers, Mary? I'm sorry they had to be from someone else, but I didn't seem to realise—"

"That I was graduating as far as I can go, and passed with distinction? It really is a college, you know, with an exacting standard."

Was she piqued? Not by her voice, which remained cool without the smallest edge.

"Darling," said David from the back seat, "*I've* been beating my breast ever since I saw you mounted aloft. You looked positively donnish. It would be wicked, positively wicked not to foster that expression. When you graduate from some famous university, we'll come in a body, won't we, Phil—"

"Who sent the flowers?" he asked, braking for a stop sign.

Half-turned to the back, they could see her face illumined by a street light.

"There was no card, nothing to say," she said innocently. "Somebody must love me."

"But you must have some idea, Mary," persisted Philip.

Felice rescued her, brushing curiosity aside.

"Probably some classmate too shy to divulge his name or hers, maybe! My dear, it was quite an occasion. We all enjoyed it very much, and the speeches were particularly good."

"Very," said Philip enthusiastically. "So good of them to give us so much of their time. We were left in no doubt of your motto."

"No," she said blandly. "It's a good one to throw us out with."

She was different, emanating a flavour of college life. They felt outside, aware of having patronised something deeply significant.

"Mary," questioned Felice, "we'd like to do something, but it's too late for anything exciting. Would you like a drink or a sundae or something?"

The offer was tentative, making her husband endorse it with deferential persuasion.

"We feel we should strew roses and laurel, Mary, but limitations, hour..."

Her reply was satisfactory, dispelling some gathering fears.

"Well, David, I'd like a sundae with strawberries, marshmallows and whipped cream; the nuts spoil it."

"Do they?" he said with great interest. "I once read the diary of a flapper's stomach, and it was full of superstructures just like that. Do you think after a graduation—"

"Maybe I'll eat two," she said, sitting closer to Philip.

"You can have a dozen if you want them," he said somewhat fatuously.

"Is Mary a prig ?" questioned Philip anxiously.

Back in the Place the door had closed on her slender back.

"Aren't we all ?" questioned his brother flippantly. "Felice dear, give me another drink. My palate is polluted with phosphate."

"Felice?" questioned Philip, ignoring his needs. "Did you hear those comments behind us? Such effrontery—"

"Oh, I don't know," she said with a smile. "I thought that was the best part of the show. Unrehearsed things always are. Snobbish and priggish! Poor Mary, it's quite a lot."

"Well, my dear," drawled David, "she's brilliant and beautiful! Two unforgivable sins! They might have been overlooked if she'd mixed well. Apparently she's been a poor little half-breed, something objectionable to her classmates—"

"I think she knows she's unpopular," said Felice, "but it doesn't seem to bother her."

"Pity," said David, watching the bubbles in his glass. "She should bother. She needs to rub shoulders with her own age and to raise merry hell with the half-love of calf-love. Do you realise, Phil, that she's never had a friend of her own age? You're young enough, but you're old to her."

"Too much perfection is always a suspicion to classmates," said Felice pleasantly. "She'd be much more attractive if she could be finished off properly. None of this family ever considered education complete until three or four years had been spent abroad. Of course—"

"Of course what?" snapped Philip.

"Actually, she's not a Fitz Henry."

"She is," said Philip defiantly. "Hasn't she had the best education the town could offer?"

"Of course, Phil," said David agreeably, "but you could hardly call this the cultural world. Have it your own way. If you want her to be a half-baked little prig...?"

"And so charming-looking, too; but a girl can't expect appearance to compensate for drawbacks."

David and Felice seemed to be in collusion. Between them they painted a girl nobody could possibly love, honour or cherish. She was lightly discussed, weighed in the balance and found wanting, but they went on until Philip positively squirmed.

"I think she's quite perfect," he said in strong defence of his idol; "but if you two find her so objectionable she'd better go across in

September for a while."

"Perhaps the completion of her Arts," said David idly.

"That's what I meant," he answered as if he had planned it himself. "I'll go to Vienna."

He got up with determination, as if he had to catch a train to a new venture. "Good night," he said briefly, "I have to operate early in the morning."

"Felice," said David, settling deeper in his chair, "I feel like a dog. It was positively painful to lambaste her like that, but I promised her a B.A. Poor darling, there was something about her tonight that made her look solitary. Who did send the flowers, Felice? I noticed you kept Phil from badgering her. I carefully examined the male element, but I couldn't light on one face I could connect with that virginal bouquet..."

"Maybe a girl—collar and tie—in thrall to her looks."

"Gracious, Felice," said her husband, "this is not the Isle of Lesbos."

"It bloweth where it listeth," she said vaguely. "Have a drink, darling, and come to bed."

"Just a spot, dear, the phosphate seems to linger."

SEVENTEEN

"DRUNKEN, BUT NOT WITH WINE."

F rom the moment she woke up everything seemed dedicated to boundless delight. That it would crescendo, making a descent into bitter darkness was something she could not know. She did not have Josephine's faculty of seeing the event travelling along. The morning sun fell on her face, drawing all snow from her skin. Through the open window air breathed delicately, seeping through fresh, nascent leaves. A bed of lily of the valley sent up intoxicating fragrance, causing a vibration of the family nostril.

Tim's boat must be arriving! Royal weather for her vassal's return!

Why was everything so easy? Had she evoked the vigilance of Mary Magdalen too often? David and Felice had disappeared to the cottage for a few days by themselves. They had gone casually, with no attitude as to the suitability of the girl's residence with an eligible bachelor not of her blood. Hannah seemed an adequate sop to the conventions. More subtly they knew the girl had been demoted. Since Philip's capitulation to third year Arts, Mary Immaculate was again the cherished child of the house, and she followed him gladly for fear of causing significant action. Something would happen to show her the way. Philip had been impressed by her cap and gown and, while acknowledging capacity for academic life, it did not go hand in hand with emotional advance.

Summer had come with a blast. A most dramatic country, days were assaults or calms. Nothing was done by halves. Meadows were lush squares, with a light powder of bloom: feathery juniper made the evergreens look tired; roads ran through banks of Rhodera, and veils of blossom drifted uphill. Only a savage country could make such a turn-about and blaze with fugitive splendour. Mary Immaculate got up, feeling a flower-burst ecstasy spinning in her head. Tim was coming home, and Philip was choosing that day to act as consultant for another doctor. In lucid arrangement, the girl heard him on the telephone, calling up hospitals and private cases, freeing himself for a seventy-mile drive up one of the shores.

She was at breakfast first, sure that the wine-coloured carpet had grown richer overnight. Philip ran down, greeting her with a pat as he went to his place. Felice not being there, the girl had to pour; but Hannah had arranged that she should not sit at the head of the table, by placing the tea-service at the side.

Even Philip looked vitalised and content with his prospects. There was abandon in the way he dug his spoon into his grapefruit.

"Mary, I'm going out of town as consultant."

"All day?" she asked with interest.

"All day, my dear. And," he said, quite gaily for him, "if there's nothing too urgent, we're going to put in a couple of hours' fishing before we return. There's a marvellous pond with some fine native trout."

"Nice," she said enthusiastically. "Is it the same way as the cottage?"

"Yes, but I won't stop." Some thought made him suspend his spoon. "Would you like to go out for the day? I could pick you up on the way back."

"No, I don't think so," she said, as if pondering. "I'll potter in the conservatory. It's red-hot in there and I love it. Don't worry about me. I haven't had a whole day to myself for years. It will be fun."

"Nasty little thing," he said with a friendly smile at her. "You're never lonely, least of all for me."

"Well," she said in the same tone, "are you lonely for me when you're seeing people's insides?"

"Not the same thing at all! However, we won't discuss that. Not now."

"Not now, when the wind calls," she quoted lightly. Nothing could have pleased her more than a day of not now. The minutes impelling her to Tim were enough for a one-day clock.

"No recklessness,"he admonished, caught by some quality in her voice. "You haven't been reckless for a long time. Ah, there's the paper. Do you want it, my dear? I haven't the time."

"Yes," she said, taking it from the maid and scanning the pages indifferently. It was unfortunate that people were doing violent things when Tim was coming home! As Philip went he leaned over her chair, tilting her face.

"Sure you won't mind being alone?" Impossible not to know he liked looking at her face.

"No, I won't mind a bit," she said truthfully.

His arm made a circle round her head as he kissed her.

"Be good, Mary," he said, kissing her again with delicate pressure.

Plodding through the hall with his fishing-tackle, Hannah had seen. When the old woman had watched him run upstairs she gave the girl a sour look.

"Nice to run two of them, isn't it ? In my time we called your sort a hussy."

Mary Immaculate was shocked. What a vulgar word! Opening the paper she said casually, "Mr. Philip will be out all day, Hannah. I'd like a hot lunch." The day suggested cool salads and iced jellies. In asking for a hot meal she was sure of a cold.

"Would you, indeed?" said Hannah sarcastically. "And who's going to cook over a hot stove for you? The maids can have a rest."

The girl had not heard. Searching the paper she saw that Tim's ship must be in. Moreover, there was a note in the personal column—"Mr. Timothy Vincent, who has been a student at a Canadian university for the past year", etc. etc. Her blood gave a little bound as her mind followed him from the waterfront to his home. Would he be different? It was tragic that he should have missed her graduation, but his flowers were still fresh. That had been a difficult moment! Liberated as a bird, she jumped up to see Philip go. The lush day made him kiss her again, as if he had not done so at breakfast.

Creatures of weather, she thought, remembering her own mother. Even Philip could be affected. He was foot-loose for a day, ready to ride away with the triple feel of her mouth. It was the first time since her graduation he had been so forthcoming. Now within a space of twenty minutes he had kissed her three times. He must be in love, she laughed to herself, as he drove towards the gate. High overhead came the song of a white-throated sparrow. Someone had interpreted the notes with such accuracy, "Good-luck, friend-fisherman, fisherman, fisherman!" The sweet, reiterant notes thrilled after him, bidding him be careless and gay.

The morning slipped away with her sunny potter, bringing her to a lonely meal of cold ham with a clovey edge, and a cool green salad. Hannah seemed to be interested in her cooking, scowling as the girl ate with undeniable relish.

"Thank you, Hannah, for giving me such a delicious lunch," she said blandly.

"You said hot, didn't you?"

"Did I, Hannah?" she asked gaily. "I meant cold. You must have made a mistake."

"Not me," said the old woman cryptically. "Will your high and mightiness be home for your tea?"

"I'm taking a walk, Hannah, and maybe I'll go for a swim."

"And where to, I'd like to know? Mr. Philip won't like you to go swimming with anybody in a pool."

"The sea is wide," she said, waving her hand. "I feel like walking a hundred miles. A cove, a bay, a river! I'm sure to find a spot. Here in this little Bay—"

She ran upstairs before the old woman could say more. In her own room she examined her clothes and put on a yellow dress that swung gaily as she walked. Then she packed a rubber bag with bathing-things and ran out of the house. The trees arched above her as she walked down the avenue, but no bird bade her good-bye. It was a lazy time of the day when most things droned and drowsed. She felt fateful. The town could not hold Tim on his first day home without some gorgeous meeting. Why else had everything been so well arranged? Whenever before had she been all alone? Her steps slowed like a person prolonging anticipation. Emerging from the trees to the glare of the road, she blinked and paused, watching dust swirl from passing cars. Almost in front of her eyes Tim came driving, very spruce and smart, in brand new clothes of an urbane cut. The brakes of his mother's car were terribly assaulted as he came to rest by her side.

"Gretel," he whispered.

She saw that his lips were trembling as his hands reached towards her. What she lacked in girlish quiver she made up in radiance.

"Timmy-Tim," she exulted, "I knew it. I felt it would happen when I came down the avenue. How lovely to see you! I didn't know how much I missed you until you're back again."

Her head was in the window very close to his face. Accustomed to being secret they forgot the road. One hand caressed her face as he kissed her, quickly, without thought of her danger. As soon as he had touched her his lips stopped trembling and he could speak in his own voice. To her it sounded more poised and a little deeper.

"Gretel darling, I got in this morning. After all the business mother lent me the car, and I've been driving up and down in the hope that I'd see you walk out. I never dreamed you'd come alone. Gosh, it's great to see you. If only, if only...?"

"If only what, Tim?" she asked breathlessly.

"If only you could jump in the car and come for a drive?"

Mary Immaculate flung up her head and her curls danced on her neck. "The gods planned it, Tim, not you and me! I'm all alone and I will."

In a second he was out of the car, opening the door for her. They were fleetly back again, sitting staring at each other, searching for difference.

"Tim," she said frankly, "you're better-looking. You're wearing a new suit. You look—you look lovely," she said with high disloyalty to David.

Tim regarded his pinstripe sleeves with some satisfaction.

"I blew myself, Gretel, and I saved at Christmas. Is it really nice?" he said, pulling his tie nonchalantly.

She laughed out loud. "Tim, you're delighted with yourself and you know it. I didn't know how tired I was of people with straight teeth."

"Now I know I'm home," he said with a grin. "I haven't heard about my teeth since I left. Now that I've got you, what'll we do? Let's go into the country and find a quiet spot, and you'll tell me all you've said and all you've done. Darling Gretel," he said, suddenly abashed, "I was so glad to see you, that I forgot about her."

"Never mind, Tim," she said quickly, "your letter was lovely, and today she must be all smiles, like us. Let's be foolish today and leave all the news till tomorrow. I haven't been foolish since you went. I've worked and worked, and been sad for dear Mater, and, Tim, I got distinction in five subjects, and, oh, Timmy-Tim, your flowers were lovely, and they're still fresh in my room. I missed you at the college, and I must tell you this—after graduation they thought I might really be a student, and I'm going to England for third year Arts."

Tim's face changed to a radiant smile, and she saw all of his eyes.

"That's news, indeed, Gretel. I wish I'd known it before. I've been eaten up all winter, wondering, worrying about that last day by the river."

"Why, Tim?" she asked quickly, and then regretted her question.

"Because, Gretel, when you put me off, about us, I thought I might come back and find you doing something else. I don't want to be a boy any more—"

"Not even today, Tim?" she said beguilingly. "Not even to run off and be just ourselves?"

"Just ourselves, Gretel," he said, breathing hard, "not just our make-believe? I've been thinking hard all winter." Then he smiled a little. "I bet they said the same thing to you at graduation, the usual stuff about launching your own ship and grappling with your problems."

"They did, Tim, real *provehito in altum* stuff."

"Launch into the deep, Gretel! It's a clarion call for us, telling us to get out of the garden and face up before people."

"Tim," she said with wide eyes, "you're not faithless to Gretel and Isolde?"

He smiled in a much older way than she remembered. Travel abroad must be ageing!

"Not faithless, ever, to one bit of you and me, Gretel, but I'd like to add to it, plunge into ordinary life with you."

"Tim,"—she smiled with eyes that had to be met—"just for today can't we really be *provehito in altum*, meaning, can't we go for a swim, out in the country, and do things we've never done before? Timmy-Tim—I must go on with my Arts—and..."

"O.K., Gretel," he said with his usual agreement. "I'll give you today because it's more than I dared dream of, and I'd hate to waste a second. I must get my bathing-things."

She was out of the car before he could even open the door.

"I'll walk up the road. Get your things and pick me up. Pity to take off the new suit, Tim."

With a laugh of high delight she sped up the road, and the proud slope of her legs was a challenge towards speedy pursual. When he caught her up she had walked half a mile. Easing by, he opened the door and she was beside him before he had really halted.

"Now we're off," he said with a laugh as infectious as her own. She rolled down the window, and a soft summer breeze became intensified by shattering speed.

"Tim!" she gasped.

He seemed impervious to rules or regulations. His eyes were no longer sleepy, and if he could spare a glance from the road it was for her and not for the beauty of the countryside. She did all the talking, letting him take her where he willed. They ran out of the town by a coast road high above wide blue sea. Useless to tell him to look at the great clumps of Rhodora. When they had mounted to a dizzy precipice they shot into a grove of spruce trees. The ground on either side was tawny, pungent with fallen needles. Tim turned into a grassy lane and they were lost from the sight of the road. He dragged on the brake, and they sat in sudden suspension. The slight tremble had come back to his lips.

"Gretel, I must kiss you. All this long time I've thought of you, and kept you in front of my eyes. Millions of times I saw your face between me and my book. Gretel, tell me you're glad I'm back?"

Tim had grown up. His arms were experienced through a burning devotion. His lips were gentle through reverence for her youth. When he kissed her his eyes were closed; hers were open, seeing the blue sky and the high points of the trees. Against her mouth she felt the jut of his two crooked teeth. When she felt her own eyes droop with some impalpable rival to the summer day she sat up in trepidation.

"Tim," she appealed, "we came to swim." He sat back, still holding her shoulders.

"Gretel, you're not half as happy to see me as I am to see you."

He looked puzzled, as if some of his joy had been quenched. He might have just come away from a swamping bout of geology. It was impossible not to make her usual return. She leaned forward, stroking his face. "Tim, I'm bursting because you're here, and we're free and it's such a lovely day."

His face suggested the answer was unsatisfactory, but she opened the door with decision.

"I'll race you down to the head if you're not afraid of your new suit."

The way was beset by stumps and boulders. Sometimes they were in his way and sometimes in hers. The odds made them arrive on an open headland at the same time. Instinctively they brought up together, arm in arm. The blue sea belonged to them if they could get down to it. He knew how to do it. Turning to the right, he plunged into a grove of spruce. It was her native heath, although Tim was the vassal, holding branches from her face. Crashing through the smothering green, feet trod on needles, squeezing out a richer fragrance from the ground. There was a rush of water in their ears. Emerging breathless on a river, they saw it splash against rock, tear through flats, hurl over a long drop and widen with estuarine ease to the surge of the sea. So much water called for immediate immersion.

"Tim, I'm going to undress. Turn your back and find your own dressing-room."

Dallying did not have any place in her mind. In less than a minute a spruce tree held a few frail garments, and long white legs plunged into a royal-blue bathing-suit. When he emerged she was poised on a rock with nerve-destroying balance. Tim did not plunge with the same confidence. The sight of her milky body accomplished his last enslavement. He appeared to dismiss the aching beauty of the day, and find nothing to admire but herself. He was a boy sorely tried by his own emotions. She dragged him out of them, as she had done many times before.

"Tim," she screamed, "let's stay in the river, unless we let the waterfall wash us down to the sea. It's not very far—it might be fun—people have gone over Niagara in a tub."

"Don't be foolish, Gretel," he said more sanely. Her leap to another rock brought her into the current, and there he joined her. Wearing her own flesh without consciousness, she expected him to wear his. Only a childhood's friendship could give forth such naive candour. "Tim, you're a nice white boy," she said approvingly. "The same height as me, and I'm glad you've got no whiskers on your chest." It was impossible not to lose some of his emotional surge. The sun on his back suggested he should be pagan and not personal.

A river is an endless source of enchantment. The body can soak in black pools, loll on grey rocks, be floated on a current and impelled towards danger. They found a submerged ledge under a gradient, leaning back, while the water flowed over their shoulders in a foaming cape. From their necks to their knees they were part of the river, with their chins on its bubbling bosom. From a distant meadow came the sound of a cow-bell, and a white-throated sparrow made its fisherman's call. Mary Immaculate flung an arm into the air in wild salute.

"Good-luck, friend-fisherman, fisherman, fisherman," she intoned again and again.

"Yes, it's just like that," said Tim with his head cocked in the air. "I'd like to play this—the rush of the river, its flats and falls, that cow-bell and how I feel myself. If I knew exactly how you feel, I'd play your part first. Once I thought I knew how you felt, but now I don't know."

"I'll feel as you feel, Tim," she said happily. "Only make me a little more treble. First violin and second violin, they play the same part. I wish I could play the violin, Tim, and then we could do some Brahms sonatas for violin and piano. I'm crazy about Brahms."

He looked at her almost in awe.

"You must be liking them, Gretel, because I willed you to, this winter. I'm crazy about them myself."

"Tim, you've been directing me from long distance," she said, holding out her arm for drops to shine like diamonds. Tim sat forward, half sideways, taking a shoulder from his watery cape. He made a reach for her arm, playing on it with his lips as if it might be a flute.

"Your skin is so cool and smooth, Gretel! I think I love touch," he said with a little pucker of his brows. "Love can't be just great crashing chords. It must be the whole gamut of scales and harmonies."

"That's what I think, Tim; something with a long taste. It would be dreadful to come to the bottom of the glass too soon. I love watching David drink golden lager from a big tankard. He has a glass one, and it takes a bottle and a half. It seems to go on for ever."

Tim hardly heard. He was staring at her arm as if treading on the tail of a thought. Looking out to sea, one white-sailed boat gleamed against the far horizon.

"Gretel; my dream!" he said thoughtfully. "This must be it. Last night it was quiet coming in, and I went to sleep very quickly. I dreamt right away. I was running as hard as I could, dragging you by the hand. For once in your life you were behind me and I was ahead. We seemed to be racing for dear life, away from loud noises and people and something I couldn't see. Then we got into the open, and we were by the sea. I ran and ran, and there was a ship with a white sail, just setting out. You ran with me until I got to the rail, and an arm reached out and gave me one great tug and pulled me on board."

"Didn't I go, too, Tim?" she asked carelessly.

"No, I seemed to be sorry about that, but just as I turned back to get you I heard lovely music, and I looked up the deck. Then I woke up. Some fellows were having a binge and were talking in the alleyway. I wonder what I would have seen if I hadn't waked up."

Mary Immaculate shook her head. "I don't often dream, Tim. Mom does, though, and always waits for things to happen. She didn't dream the night before I went into the woods, but that must be where I fooled her. Good thing, too, or she would have kept me home, and I would never have come to town. Things must be arranged, Tim. It's foolish to think otherwise."

"I expect so, Gretel, but I'm not going to wait."

"Let's swim in the sea now, Tim. My back is cold."

The way was hazardous, but her white flesh dipped amongst granite rock. They descended by the land, sanity forbidding Mary Immaculate to use the waterfall as a plank. She raced to the sea, plunging into its blue. Warmth lay only in its colour. It was freezing cold, as if it had just dissolved its icebergs. They shivered until exercise raced their blood.

"Now, Timmy-Tim,"she said, throwing an arm round his neck. "I'm drowning! Life-save me!"

She gave a realistic exhibition of drowning, making him grab her by the arm. As if to make it difficult for him, she caught him in a stranglehold.

"This is what I did before,"she gasped. "Will you knock me out?"

"No," he said, swimming with his legs. Her white helmet bobbed near his face, and he put his arms round her body, hugging her strongly under water.

"Mermaid's kiss,"he grinned, giving her a very wet salute with his mouth. The sun yellowed her eyes to clear topaz.

"Save me, Tim," she said dramatically, floating sensuously on the water.

Lax and languorous, she let him hold her head out of water and swim towards land, with her body trailing beside him. With her head tucked in the crook of his arm, she recited softly:

"And the judge bade them strip, and ship them, and bind,
Bosom to bosom to drown and die…"

Tim gave her a deep, wakening glance. For a moment his eyes went naked. Because she knew little poetry that he did not know, he muttered through his teeth, "You're not fair, Gretel. Remember, the white girl winced and whitened, but he caught fire—and they died, drowned together."

"Sorry, Timmy-Tim," she said contritely."It's unpleasant, drowning, no matter how poetical." Turning into his neck she kissed his shoulder.

"Tim, let's dress, and go and find something to eat. I'd like a chocolate bar, an ice-cream cone and a package of gum. Have you got any money ?"

"Tons," he said, laughing out loud and shipping some sea in his mouth. "Gretel, I know now why you're not a musician. You never could rest to perfect one bar."

They had reached the shore, relaxing on hot stones, with their legs in the water. She was reproachful.

"Tim, and I've tried to play all the things you liked."

That there could be any fault in her seemed an appalling heresy, in sight of her body lying so near. All at once he pressed his head in her shoulder, nuzzling against her neck.

"Gretel," he sighed. "I love you, love you, love you, and I wish we could go down with locked hands and feet."

"Timmy-Tim," she said, patting him with a wet hand, "it's Heaven today. Let's dress and get something to eat."

The glitter had gone out of the sky, and the day was easing to night. The sea breathed on the land, wetting the air to a fog. Caplin weather, thought the fisherman's daughter; bait for the cod! She could visualise little coves and bays and fishermen casting-nets.

She tramped round the flower-beds with no diminution of restlessness. The electric afternoon had forked her veins with lightning. Tim was different, more of an individual, and several times he had taken the reins out of her hands. Returning to her lonely meal and Hannah's sour comments, she had circumvented conversation by propping a book in front of her. Reading *Les Noyades* again, it seemed disturbing, full of possession by death. Why was literature so full of death, with lovers embracing it in exultation? It seemed a morbid union, when the world was round like a rich girdle. Tim would be melancholy if he were left to himself. With her, his notes soared in alt. Impossible to remember the afternoon in tranquillity. Tang of sea-water made it hot-cold, with the feel of her head clasped by Tim's arms. There was the blue heat of his eyes, and his wet sea-kiss. The whole afternoon returned a sense of touch. Heaviness of winter, grief for the mater, the burden of study had slipped away, catapulting her to communion with Tim. His mouth on her arm, her shoulder and his strong under-water embrace held new elements. They seemed like the edge of some felicity, towards which she was being impelled.

Sweet hard kisses are strong like wine! Having read for intoxicating words, they now seemed promises of delicate delight. What more? There must be a whole lot more, like an ease into the current, and the forward rush over the waterfall. Yet Tim had bade her be sane when she suggested foolhardiness.

Hannah was inside the privet hedge plodding about, examining green vegetable shoots. Hooked up in black, she looked as crude and changeling as Molly Conway. She had been there a long time, so long that the girl wished her rheumatism would send her inside to nurture her joints. The garden was not Hannah's care, except that everything seemed her self-appointed burden since Lady Fitz Henry's death. She had no life of her own when her work was done, except to moil at grudges. Often she muttered to herself in some muddy communion.

There was an undeniable swish of feet and a scrape against the wall. The girl brought up on her feet, and underneath the stalky part of the hedge, she saw the old woman's dress become limp with listening. In her hand she trailed a long twisted root. The girl's imagination seemed fearfully acute. Had it shrieked like a mandrake when it came from the earth?

Silence came down like a fall of black flakes. Nothing stirred as Tim played a waiting game. If Philip were fishing he would certainly stay for the perfect hour when flies flew low on the water! The girl continued her walk, round and round, and round again. The air increased in dampness, threatening the bones of age, but it was almost dark before Hannah left the vegetables.

"Why don't you come in out of the damp? There's the evening paper? Not as interested in it as you were this morning, I'm thinking."

What was the use of answering? Hannah passed like a bent black sail. The girl sped up the garden, as Tim dropped from the fence.

"God, Gretel," he said, brushing some rind from his hands. "I thought she'd never go. What's old witchface up to?"

She was so careless and confident in her long sustained luck. Lightly callous, Hannah was dismissed.

"She's dippy, Tim. I never take any notice. Were you late for your supper?"

"Let's sit on the bank, Gretel." He took her arm, drawing her down beside him. The seriousness of his voice dismissed eating and drinking.

"Gretel, listen to me."

"Yes, Tim," she said, surprised.

"I mean," he explained, "listen to me without any interruption. I have some funny news, and I've had a terrific row with Uncle, and walked off with Mother's car. I was steaming away when I remembered you said the doctor had gone for the whole day, and I came on the chance of seeing you. You couldn't come for another drive, could you? It's easier to talk when we're going."

"No, Tim," she said briefly, obeying his first injunction.

"Very well, then." The light was good enough to see him looking ahead at the grass. "After supper Uncle came round to have one of his advisory chats with me, checking up on how much benefit I had received, etc., etc. I think I behaved very well, at least I hope I was civil, although you can never tell when you feel inside that your voice has an edge. Then he informed me, as if I didn't know, that I'd be twenty-one in a couple of months! I was expecting a lecture, when he took the wind out of my sails by telling me that Father had provided a clause in his will to the effect that I could have a long trip when I was twenty-one—"

"Tim!" she ejaculated.

"And," he said impressively, "it seems a lot of money to me. I was thrilled, and a whole row of countries passed in front of my eyes—*when*..."

"Yes?" she asked urgently.

"When he fished an itinerary out of his pocket, with ships and places all marked in red dots, which was mainly a trip to South America, to see mines! He had arranged it all! I didn't have to do a thing but follow red marks."

His voice was weighted with bitter scorn.

"I saw red! It was Father's present to me. I Goddamned something awful. Then I stood up and said I'd take the trip as soon as I was twenty-one, but I'd go to Europe and do just what I liked. Mother was frightened to death, and Auntie Minnie, the old nosy parker, spoke up and said all the things that made me want to blast her as a by-product. Then I barged out of the house and shot off, but I had lots of time to cool while I was waiting for old witchface to go in. From where I was I could see you walking round the flowerbeds. Instantly I got it—" He stopped dead, leaning towards her. "Don't you want to know what I planned?"

"You told me not to say anything, Tim."

He laughed and put his arms round her, whispering in her ear.

"Gretel, you're coming with me. We'll get married the morning of my birthday, and honeymoon in the wide world."

"And afterwards?" she questioned fearfully, she who never thought of afterwards.

"I'll get a job," said Tim confidently. "It's got to be. If you want to be open about it, you must take me in to your men and say: 'This is Tim. He's my vassal, and we're going to be married.' That's all. It's so easy."

Motionless against him, she lay seething with perplexity. It had come, the deciding day! Tim was talking into her hair, waxing with enthusiasm over his definite plans. She felt herself catching trains, boarding ships, heard the sound of foreign tongues, saw London and smelt Paris in spring. Opera-houses and picture-galleries were tossed on the tennis-court.

"You want it, Gretel, don't you? Think, this afternoon I was aching to make you say you'd marry me. But I had nothing to offer, except a long wait. Now this...you must love me a little; and once this afternoon, in the water, I felt I had you. We must be lucky— we've always had luck."

"Luck when we're alone," she said woefully. "There are some things, Tim, that are lovely to yourself, but when other people handle them they seem so different. It's like the happiness of children. You're soaked with content and you come home and find you've torn your dress or wet your feet, and it all gets dimmed. Talk to me, Tim, and let me think. I don't know where I am...."

"But it's such a stroke of luck."

"Luck, Tim ?" And strangely and unnaturally she burst into tears, giving her frightened vassal the greatest shock of his life.

Perhaps her disbelief in her gods made them suddenly retreat at that moment. Filing past the house they must have paused at a window, earthbound with interest. Philip was in the library, talking to Hannah. She was passing him a tray, which he placed on a table, loading it with large fat trout from a basket. Perhaps in answer to some question the old woman's lips moved, and Philip stood stock still with a trout in his hand. Suddenly he flung it down where it slithered to rest beside its brethren. Hannah sat and folded her hands, talking, talking, words without end. Philip seemed choking, until he went to a window and flung it wide. His voice rushed out, shivering the nerves of the night. Leaves shrank back in the trees, cringing from bitter amazement.

"You're out of your mind, Hannah I I don't believe a word of it. Bring Miss Mary in and ·she'll explain. She's been alone all day, and found some way of enjoying herself."

The old woman's voice was implacable in persuasion.

"You can try and fool yourself, Mr. Philip. But every word I've said is the truth. She's made a fool of you all, and most of all of you. Now what's to be done with her, stealing off as she does, and hugging and kissing and loving? To my mind she's not as good as she might be, and they're young, with hot blood. If there's any trouble they'll say it's you, and there's never a person will call you in, with that disgrace on your name. 'Twas a bitter day when you took the like of her—"

"Stop," he said like a bite. "She'll speak for herself. Bring her in."

Hannah got up with stiff alacrity, leaving the master of the Place holding on to a chair like a stifling man.

She had stage-managed well. At the back porch she did something to a switch, cackling to herself in dirty delight.

At the end of the garden Tim and Mary Immaculate were suddenly illumined in cold white light. Dazed in each other's arms, they blinked quickly. Instantly the girl knew. There was a wire from the house for skating in winter. Hannah had replaced the bulbs. Tim and she were stripped of their secrecy.

"We're for it, Gretel," said Tim instantly. He stood up, dragging her to her feet. Adjusting her hair, she said quickly:

"Tim, do I look as if I'd been crying ?"

"No, Gretel!" He took her by the shoulders, as if pressed for time. "This is the end of this! Kiss me once, for what's gone."

The same height as himself the girl went into his arms, meeting lips on a level with her own.

"Tim," she said, "you can go, and let me face it alone."

He laughed in scorn.

"It's what I want. Gretel, keep your chin up. The last thing we can be is Jakin and Lew—I'll pipe you across the garden."

At that moment Hannah turned the corner of the hedge. Her voice held harsh unction, like one who had scored with good effect.

"You're to come in and see Mr. Philip."

The girl flashed by like a blade of scorn. Tim followed more slowly, pulling at the sleeves of his pinstripe suit. Then he sprinted after her, following through the back door.

"This way, Tim,"she said, reaching for his hand.

Inside the library they stood motionless. They did not have to blink with a guilty return from night. Hannah had helped by her illumination. They were a tableau in an old mellow room, with an anachronism of fresh trout. The girl identified a Rainbow and a German Brown.

They stood bravely, more than a little defiant with the tossing heads of youth. Tim's lips trembled sensitively as if his responsibility was greater, but he took refuge in the typical male squirm inside his collar. The girl looked overwhelmingly innocent, giving her eyes instantly to Philip, and for a while she simmered in a gaze like live coals. Withdrawing his eyes he glared at the boy. There was a long search over Tim, a rude investigation of eyes lost to manners. He looked as if he were searching for other counts on which to condemn her. Tim took it well, and his own sleepy eyes gave back some appraisement. Unequal height was compensated by the exact level of his shoulder with the girl's. Philip's head was down, lowered to their level to see them as he thought they were. What he saw did not reassure him. Yet there was no humility or shame. What they saw did not help them. Savagery induced a defensive armour, an extenuation of themselves, making them belittle their own deceits. Had they been summoned to a detached judgment their lives might have been aired in convention, and returned to await a seasoned decision. Detachment was in tatters, jolted from a mind seeing a degraded altar. Philip's exacting virtue made him blind and pitiless, and neither his mother nor David were there to temper him.

It was so short and so sharp when speech came; a rain of words without sense. The girl spoke first. She was ready to stand up to consequences, but not to scorch in the heat of prolonged silence.

"You wanted me, Philip?" she said, and her voice was cool and then faint, as she tried to endure his eyes. "This is Tim Vincent," was all she could say.

"Why did you bring him in? You've kept him to yourself for a long time. Did you want to exhibit your lover?"

"No, sir," called Tim.

"Shut up," ordered Philip with concentrated insult. A flush ran up Tim's fair cheeks, and his sleepy eyes opened wide.

"I will *not* shut up," he said, making a step forward. "*I'm* Tim Vincent, and I live in the little house next door."

"I don't know you. Apparently Mary does, only too well."

The words held a subtle insult, making Tim flush deeper red.

"You're all wrong, sir. I'm in love with Gretel—"

"Her name is Mary," barked Philip. "And I thought she was too young—had to go to school again—God, this deceit, this rottenness...!"

He loomed over Tim like a menace, and because he was so tall he looked dangerous. Mary Immaculate threw an arm between them in a silent plea for separation. Both men pushed it down. They were primitive, glaring at each other with flaming eyes. Tim stammered a little.

"You're m-making a mistake."

"Philip, I'll tell you," said the girl. "Stop being so angry and listen to us. We're friends, Tim and I, we've been friends for a long time. We started by playing pairs, all the lovers in the world—and now—"

"Now you're lovers," said Philip viciously. "An advance, indeed!"

The girl stamped her foot at his jeering tone.

"There's nothing to be ashamed of in love, Philip. It's natural—"

"Gretel, let me talk," said Tim, laying his hand on her shoulder. The gesture infuriated Philip.

"Damn you," he said, "have the decency to own up when she admits it herself." His eyes ran over the girl, standing like a white vestal.

"Bah," he said from some frustration defying coherency. "Get out, get out, the both of you, or I'll not be responsible for my hands."

"I'm not afraid of your hands, Philip," she said, now in high temper herself. "You're crazy, as you always are when you're mad. When you're like that I don't want to explain. I *will* go, until you come to your senses."

"You'll go and you'll stay." His voice was a merciless expulsion, freezing the heat in her veins. Wheeling on her feet, she faced him again.

"Do you mean," she asked in a flat voice of incredulity, "that you're sending me away ?"

"That's what I mean," he barked; "and take your lover with you."

Tim threw out his arm. "It's all wrong." Staring from Gretel to Philip, he went mute, losing all inclination towards explanation. He looked like a person seeing solution.

"Come, Gretel," he commanded, "I know what to do."

"Yes," she said, "I'll go. Look after Rufus, will you, Philip? It's all I own in this house."

The childish speech bombed some words from Philip's lips.

"Damn you," he exploded. "You need not remind me you own my mother's things."

Without a word she took Tim's arm, going out through the hall, past the big drawing-room, and into the summer night. As they went down the steps Hannah crept after them, locking the door. Then her hands clasped each other as she sidled towards the stairs, with eyes shifting away from the library. She might have disposed of her enemies, but she did not want to see. She scuttled upstairs, afraid to look out or back at her master.

She was driving again with her hair streaming behind her. Tim was going much too fast, giving the illusion of a ship cutting through black water. To retain a contact he let his hand rest on her knee. He needed it for the wheel, but protest had run out of her. She was flat, drained, both scuttled and scuttling, going ignominiously away with a boy who looked like a stranger. His head was back, and his face made a white oval in the darkness. His mouth was a little open, not quite smiling, but drawn back from his teeth. He looked more faunish than usual, and in some way recklessly triumphant. The expression was not one that she knew. This was the strangest event of all. As the mater's daughter she felt violated, a creature of bad taste, prostituting convention. She had brought it on herself, she had betrayed her adoption. This consequence was full of mental and spiritual wounds. Other consequences had fallen on her body, showing results which hospital could speedily restore. This afternoon, this early evening, she thought she must have Tim, regardless of loyalties. Now she knew neither him nor herself. Useless to protest. There was no way out! Her philosophy would have to suffice. Go with it, when it was as stupendous as this.

She sat up adjusting her coat. Then she saw they were rushing past David's cottage. Her hand crept to the door to jump out. Fear did not restrain her. It was the mental picture of herself, appearing a little soiled and bedraggled. No, she would never crawl. Tim and she would set out. Philip, the mater, the Place? The rooted loyalties of five years? It did not bear thinking of. She was the proven fool, the lightweight, the dog with the bone who had dropped it for its shadow. Substance was drowning. Knowing what drowning was like, she thought no physical sensation could equal this black sink of the mind. Mental suffering was new. She sat in the car with Tim, silent and writhing with savage regret.

They turned off the main road with a hideous screech of tires. There was a lane and a little square house, lying in lilac bushes.

"Now," said Tim.

Giving him her hand, she let him draw her towards a green door with an iron knocker.

EIGHTEEN

"TOO LATE TO CAST ANCHOR
WHEN THE SHIP'S ON THE ROCKS."

At David's cottage the sounds of the day were reduced to an evening hush. Dew lay on the grass, and the garden was cool from the mist of the sea. Far down on the beach, little waves spent themselves like swishing sighs. From the highway came the mechanical din of the world. Cars screamed by, carrying the shrillness of youth. It needed tempered spirits to savour the modulation of the evening. David and Felice had been part of it until Philip rushed in with his story.

Striding up and down, he talked for a long time, flicking ash from a cigarette before it had time to gather. His nose was like a prow, cutting tempestuously through shadows. Watching him, Felice felt he was inhaling the darkness. David and she were paralysed, each in a pool of light. Her hands had dropped from the piano, while her husband sat with his fingers between a book, with his legs far out in the room. As his brother barely avoided them, he sat up with sudden energy.

"Do you mean to say," he asked with weighted words, "that you turned her out like a heavy Victorian? Never darken my doors again sort of thing! No conduct could justify such an action. Think of the Place."

Felice heard her husband sting his brother on two counts. It had the effect of making him flick his cigarette harder.

"God Almighty!" he said, "don't I know it? I was beside myself. It was so sudden, such an incredible jolt. For a moment I could have murdered her. I'd built up so much. Even now I think it's a filthy dream, until I remember the boy. The one I suppose who sent her the flowers. If he hadn't gone I would have been in the courts for assault." He gave a short laugh, ending in a staccato bark. "As for her, she stood there looking so God-damn clean. The things that go on in a man's house without his knowledge! The awful things Hannah suggested! Things a man could not think himself. To do that to me—to Mater—to you and when I told her to go she went like a young queen! That unashamed walk! God—God!..."

Collapsing in a chair, he dropped his head in his hands. David regarded him impersonally, withdrawn to stupefaction. His mind reviewed Philip's story, threw it away, recalled it again, until he jerked protestingly.

"There must be some mistake," he insisted. "It's fantastic."

The word was unfortunate. Philip leaped up, striding towards the mantelpiece.

"Fantastic," he clipped, gesturing with a long hand, "hasn't she always been fantastic?"

Then they argued backwards and forwards over the incredible, David supplying vindications, and Philip recalling her crimes. True, thought Felice dryly, but those are far cries from a lover at seventeen. She had lied to her mother! Philip was arguing David to a cohesion of thought, driving him to shocked acceptance. In cold reason Mary Immaculate seemed convicted. Confronted by the illicit taint in their home, modernity dropped from them. Dismayed at her husband, Felice saw him assume the ancestral aura of a man thwarted in the control of women. True, he was deeply shocked, and Philip was being most impressive because of the outrage to his own idealisation. At the very word lover, bitter jealousy had accepted the worst imputation. A growing irritation in Felice questioned whether David should not have more balance. Both were sure she should trail chastity like a banner. Both were now blind to judgment. They were smirching her themselves, jerking her from her pedestal, and distorting her reckless escapades. She hated them both, despised them

with her mind. With an effort she dismissed them, calling the girl to
her own tribunal.

Two widely divergent girls appeared, difficult to dovetail. Mary
running to the woods, striking the harebells to make the fairies leap
out. Mary nearly losing her life through her own foolishness, Mary
lying to her mother because it was the most comfortable way out.
Then there was Mary, the most docile of girls, waiting on the mater
hand and foot, never needing to be jogged to perform the most
exacting routine. That girl was always good-tempered, laughing and
gay, making life tolerable in a sombre winter at the Place. Funda-
mentally she was as sound as a good nut. It seemed an insult to their
mother and Josephine to doubt her. The men were looking at her
through a film of jealousy, the leaning side of love.

Felice was on the side of the weak. This time she felt she was on the
side of the wronged. Her voice startled them like the vindication of
womanhood.

"I'm ashamed of you both. I don't believe a tenth of that story.
I'm not condoning her, but I think you're both blinded by common
male jealousy. Snap out of it, and use your brains."

"My dear," said David, sitting bolt upright.

"She admitted it herself," Philip almost snarled.

"Admitted what?"

"That she and the boy were lovers and had known each other for
a long time."

The shock to his brain was apparent. His speech was unconsciously
sexual.

He went on in a brooding tone.

"He called her Gretel, as if he owned her."

"Heavens!" said Felice despairingly. "Did you ever read your fairy-
tales, Philip? Hansel and Gretel! It's just what you might have
expected from her. Have you ever for one second realised the welter
of folklore she was brought up in, and have you ever considered the
effect her adventure might have had on her mind? Considering her
life, she's a miracle of sanity."

Both men were momentarily speechless. They were not accustomed to Felice in accusation.

"Hansel and Gretel?" muttered her husband. "Brother and sister!"

"And," continued Felice truly inspired, "it seems that Hannah has supplied the witches' oven. The things that can go on in a man's house! You don't know, do you, Philip, that Hannah has been baiting her for years? Something came up one day and I made her tell me. She said it was too little to bother about, and please not to mention it to the family. Further, Hannah is getting in her dotage and has a grudge against us all because Mater died without her." Felice could not stop there. The theme seemed to have taken hold of her imagination. "If Mary has been foolish and secret, and gone off on many occasions with that boy, I'd look for sensible reasons. I've been psycho-analysed myself, even though it's a process that produces scorn from some minds." Her green eyes flashed at Philip, defying him to repudiate psychic derangements of the mind. "She absorbed secrecy from childhood; may have a neurosis about it, arising out of those three days in the forests."

"Nonsense, Felice," said Philip, returning to a professional outlook. "She's the healthiest girl I've ever seen. I've never seen the slightest need of a neurologist."

"She probably needed one tonight," said Felice cruelly. "And what did you do, Philip? From your own confession you swallowed Hannah's story, glaring at Mary as if she were contamination. Am I right?"

The picture was too true.

Philip sat, growing icy cold. His wild anger was dying, giving way to reason.

"God, what have I done?" he said heavily.

"Have a drink?" suggested David anxiously, but his brother turned on him with venom. "Damn you, no! I must go and find her."

"Yes, you must," said Felice decisively. "I can't bear to think of Mary, really reckless. At this moment you might have driven her to anything. She's very young, impulsive, and too attractive to be suddenly at the mercy—"

"Stop," said Philip frantically. "You need not rub it in."

David had lost his faculty of words. His wife was more severe than he had ever known her. He looked at her, and, if his fine features could assume such an expression, he appeared a trifle sheepish.

"I must go," said Philip, getting up.

He was not to go. At that moment there was a sound of feet, running with great urgency, rushing up the steps leading to the screened french windows. A body fell against them, while hands fumbled with frenzied inaptitude.

"David, Felice! David, Felice!"

"God Almighty!" said David, starting up. "Phil, get into the sun-parlour. She may bolt if she sees you here."·

To the left they had added a sun-porch, dim with wicker furniture. Had not the girl fallen foul of the doors, she would have been in the room before David had pushed Philip out of sight.

"We don't know anything," hissed his wife. "Let her talk."

Now the girl was inside, as if she had attained sanctuary, leaning back with arms outstretched against the curtains.

"Mary dear," said Felice with normal surprise, "what's the matter?"

"Felice," she gulped. "David..."

"There, my dear," he said at her other side. "Something has happened. Take it easy. You're shivering."

"Yes," she said with chattering teeth, "it's happened, it's happened. I knew it would. I knew I couldn't stop it as soon as Tim showed me we were growing up. All I could do was to wait, and now, and now—poor Tim, he's left with my tin-whistle side. Oh, David; oh, David! Felice, help me! He's gone tearing up the Shore, driving much too fast, but I couldn't help it."

Words poured out in supreme agitation. Felice grabbed her hand, pulling her away from the wall.

"Mary dear, David and I are here to listen to everything you've got to say."

She looked at them as if she saw them for the first time.

"Of course, David and Felice," she said. "I thought of you both and began to run. We were near here, and I just came."

"Come, my dear, and sit down," said Felice firmly. Perhaps the girl divined the recent betrayal of David. It was to Felice she turned, permitting herself to be placed in a chair with its back to the glass porch. She settled as if reaction had claimed her and she needed support.

In silence David and Felice seated themselves opposite, scarcely daring to breathe. Behind, they could see Philip, merely as a dark blur in the sun-parlour. They did not hurry her, as she went inward for elucidation. Her first words rocked them unspeakably.

"Philip turned me out of the Place, and I'm married."

"What!" said one voice.

"God!" groaned two, but so perfect was the timing that it might have been one.

"My dear," said Felice recovering. "Begin at the beginning. We're very glad you came to us, aren't we, David?"

"Mary must know that," said David gravely. "She knows I have no attitudes."

Does she, indeed? thought his undeniably devoted wife. She should have seen you walk over to the Pharisees a few minutes ago. Out loud she said loyally:

"It's quite true, Mary. David and I will help you if you tell us. Would you like a glass of sherry?"

"No, thank you," she answered. "Tim ordered beer. I saw him through the window. He didn't drink at the university because he was so happy, waiting to come home to me. As soon as things went wrong, he drank."

The eyes of husband and wife met, and David's shifted uneasily. It was as if the girl had discovered a male weakness, and wondered over it out loud. She looked at them and blinked. "I'm being foolish, talking backwards. I'll begin at the right place." Laying her hands along the arms of the chair they stayed supine through her whole tale. They heard her in dead silence, and it seemed as if certain explanations were projectiles, for directed places.

"A long time ago there was a boy who piped me up in the beech tree. It was after Philip was so mad because I went off and picked cuckoo-flowers. I knew I'd have to go again. It was lovely at the Place, but there were so many altering everything about me that I felt crazy sometimes to be as free as I was in the Cove. There, I always played alone. Perhaps that's why I grew to like having things belonging to myself. I used to play and not know where time went. At the Place it was sliced up into little bits. When I was with Tim I forgot the time-table. We had such fun, telling each other the things we never mentioned to anybody else."

She frowned with the burden of her tale, and the strain of long clarification; then went on to present a lucid picture of Tim's life. It was impossible not to see his mother as a woman afraid of decision undirected by a man, Auntie Minnie as a busybody and Uncle as a genial bully. Tim's music and his uncle's slapstick made two lines that could never meet.

"Because of that I became his music. Almost at once he called me Gretel, because I had been lost in the woods and he said angels had walked down the cloud-stairs to save me. Then the Hansel and Gretel opera seemed to fit in. It was full of the hocus-pocus that we loved, and Hannah was such a perfect old witch. We knew she spied, and every day I expected Mater to call me in and say whether I could go on with Tim, but it never happened. Hannah never tattled, and I'm sure it wasn't for my sake, because she hated me always. Every time we speak of her Tim wants to play the Crust Waltz."

Felice watched her husband when she told of their identification with romantic pairs, some of the avenues David having opened himself. He was shading his face when she came to the presentation of the ship.

"He was my vassal," she said softly, "and he gave me a white ship. I think Tim always was afraid of black sails. We went on, and I didn't feel coddled any more, or have to depend on the girls for friends. At five I was peeling potatoes and turnips, and I knew if those twelve-year-old town girls took a knife they'd cut their hands off. It's a wonder the wind didn't blow them away. They were always whispering and asking this and that, and one day, just for fun, I told them I had seen a cow have a calf, and they were as shocked as if it was my fault a cow calved that way. They," said Mary Immaculate with added clearness, "made me sick."

There was no room for laughter, reasons being obvious that had compelled her to more full-flavoured companionship. Then the points of honourable conduct were presented for their judgment.

"Except for today when Tim came home—today was marvellous," she whispered. "Except for that, I only saw Tim three times outside my free time."

"Mary," said Felice suddenly, "is Tim the boy who sent you the flowers, who went to a Canadian university, and who all the town knows is crazy about you, but us?"

The girl opened her eyes in surprise.

"I expect so, Felice," she said, answering part of the question. "We always walked home together. Philip saw me once, and I told him it was one of the students. Philip can get so mad that I was always glad he didn't see us again. He was so mad tonight, so ugly. He believed things that were silly. But now Philip seems like the things I have lost, the regularity of meals, the order and being part of a house."

For a few seconds she went incoherent, talking of bits and pieces that could not be put together.

"Mary," said Felice, determined to be sane at all costs. "You're getting away from the subject. Begin at the time when Tim began to change, and you felt he wasn't a boy any more."

"Yes," she said, as if glad of a lead. "Last September when he was leaving. I knew he wanted to talk about us, but I was frightened and kept putting him off. He showed me that I never looked ahead, and when he made me say what we were to each other I said we were children. He wasn't satisfied, and I knew it. Perhaps I wasn't, too, but I don't know. I was nearly crazy all winter, especially when Mater died. Then I knew that Philip loved me like a grown up person."

Felice made a gesture. Her eyes asked her husband if the girl should be permitted to go on. David held her eyes, denying interruption.

"I know I'm very fond of Philip. It would be impossible not to be, when he's so good to me."

"Philip would not be satisfied with gratitude, dear," said David gravely.

For the first time the girl stirred restlessly.

"David," she said helplessly, "I don't know about love. I liked it when Philip put his arms round me, but I liked it when you did, too. Tim always put his arms round me since the day we met. I like that awfully, too! Today for the first time there seemed a difference in arms—it was exciting and yet I kept putting Tim off—I don't know about love." She spoke with more energy "It seems that I can't know, like the girls in college who go dippy about one boy, and cry their eyes out when he sees another girl home or something." She fell back in the chair in a slump. "What does it matter, anyway, I'm married to Tim."

David was growing frantic with the slow elucidation of the tale. He opened his mouth several times to urge her to a quicker speech, but there was a lost quality about her, forbidding coercion. He left it to Felice, who was showing infinite patience.

"When did you marry him, dear ?"

"Tonight, of course, Felice, when Philip turned me out, but I don't feel married, so I ran away."

"Can't you explain, Mary? Help us understand. You've known Tim for years, you love being with him, you found him exciting this afternoon, and yet you ran away?"

"Felice, I ran away because I had to, but I think there were a lot of reasons. I was to blame myself. You need not tell me. Nobody need, but, bad as I've been, I don't think I deserved what Philip did. Then Tim did something wrong, so it seems we're all alike."

"What did Tim do, Mary ?" asked David with grave concern.

"I didn't realise until after I was married what sort of things Hannah had told Philip. When I talked about lovers, I forgot the people like Mary Magdalen. I was thinking of the games we had played, and Philip wouldn't listen to explanation. Then, I got mad myself, and I didn't care if I ran to the ends of the earth. But," she said impressively, "that's where Tim let me down. He knew what Philip meant, and he opened his mouth really to convince him, when he remembered that he was coming into some money on his twenty-first birthday, and it was his chance to take me with him. He waited until we were married to tell me what he had done."

"Young cad," said David involuntarily.

Mary Immaculate looked him straight in the eye.

"David," she said with a twist of her mouth, "'speak of *me* as I am, nothing extenuate'." David's eyes dropped, hearing the special voice and words she had always reserved for him. "And," she continued gently, "please don't call Tim a cad."

"Where did you get married ?" asked Felice, sliding over the intangible.

"We left the Place and he drove very fast. He said to leave it all to him. He knew what to do. There was nothing else. We would drive out to some minister in the country and get married. Then go to a road-house and back to his mother. I felt so flat, flatter than I thought anybody could ever feel, and just very bad taste. Worse than that, Tim looked like a stranger, a boy I'd never seen before. He was excited, the wind blew through his hair, and he was smiling all over his face. The night was so dark and we passed everything on the road. He seemed to know where to go. We stopped at a house in a lane and went in. It was just a little village house, and the minister had on his bedroom slippers. He refused to marry us, but Tim seemed to know what to say. He told me afterwards that often students made runaway marriages, and the way to make the minister marry was to say that you'd go off and sleep together if he didn't. At last he consented, and we went into a small room with a table with a plush cloth. He called in two other people, and Tim and I just stood up while he read something very ordinary from a book. Tim used his father's signet ring."

As the signet ring was not on her finger, neither questioned where it was. Then the Catholic spoke in wondering scorn.

"Marriage! One of the Sacraments! How could anyone call that marriage? There were no vestments, no altar, no candles and no Latin. The minister did not even wear a black coat, and right behind his head was the picture of a fat child, walking down some stairs. Then we signed something and came away. Neither Tim nor I looked at each other, and we were both shivering. It felt cold. Tim said the road-house was quite near. On the way he had to tell me what Philip thought. It didn't seem to make much difference. It only made me feel flatter. When we got to the house Tim ordered some supper, and neither of us could think of anything to eat, and then we both said ham and eggs, as it seemed the only food we could remember. Then he looked at me and said: 'Gretel, this is the first time we've been in a room together, except for school.' I think he was going to kiss me when he saw a piano. He looked so excited, and took my hand and dragged me over. I had to sit down while he played and played and played. I think for a while he was really and truly happy. He quite forgot we were married, because it was the first time he had been able to play the piano to me. His hands looked so firm and at home on the keys that I knew he should have been allowed to study music, even though he starved for a few years. He played bits of a dozen things, but

I can't remember one note of what he played. I only heard sound, not music. Oh, I was so flat so—flat—as if I had no knees or elbows...."
She slacked in the chair, going as supine as her hands. David did the same thing, as if he must show some sympathy. She commenced to whisper.

"I began to see the room. There was a hooked mat of the Union Jack over the back of a chair. I suppose it was there, because you couldn't step on the flag. You could only lean your back against it. What made me run away was the cushion..."

For the first time in her life Felice wondered if the girl had a cast in her eyes, she withdrew to such an inward stare.

"A cushion, Mary?" she said briskly enough to bring her back.

"Yes, a cushion! It was red satin with a lot of butterflies herringboned to the top. They went this way and that way, and looked as if a needle had sewed them as they flew. While Tim was playing I felt like the butterflies, more held than I had ever been in my life. I was paralysed and couldn't move. I had to go then, and I couldn't go. I was as cloven to the chair as the angel in the cemetery who had been holding the marble flower for thirty-nine years. I was no more married to Tim than I was to anyone else, and I had to get out before he brought me home to his mother and his Auntie Minnie. I fancied I saw the butterflies move, and I jumped so quickly that Tim jumped too. I said, 'Tim, I can't stay. You must let me go, to think. I'll go to David and Felice and tell them all about it.' Then I knew he had remembered we were married. He looked at me and his eyes went so heavy when he said, 'Gretel, so it is your tin-whistle side that I have!' Nobody ever felt so awful, so dreadful! I tried to tell him it was too sudden, that I was jolted out of the Place and I must think, but he just sat on the piano-stool with his hands hanging between his knees. I shook him and implored him to remember the fun we'd shared together, and if we'd been deceitful we'd both been the same way. I tried not to blame him for not telling Philip that he was ridiculous to think we'd done anything shameful, but he blamed himself and called himself names for a long time. Felice," she said with bewildered bitterness, "we were two people who did not know each other at all. We couldn't meet anywhere."

"Yes, I understand, Mary, very well indeed. It is often like that. It will come right again when things are normal."

"Normal, Felice? Perhaps he'll come back in the old way, but it will take a long time to wash out tonight. He blamed me for making him go on with his mining, said he couldn't go on if I let him down—then he got gentle, and talked very softly, and put his arms round me, but I felt dead, dead. Then, then...Oh God, God!—it was so funny—oh God!..." She began to laugh with a dreadful undercurrent of tears, and her body shaking on the edge of hysteria.

"Hush, Mary," said Felice firmly, "that's not like you to give way. Here, my dear, take my handkerchief." But no tears had fallen. They had merely gone into wild laughter.

"Felice, Felice," she said, dropping her head, "at that moment the maid came in to say the ham and eggs were ready."

Felice looked at her husband. Life's anti-climaxes! He had nothing to say. He had gone into the girl's story.

"Tim got rid of the maid somehow, and he stood leaning against the door. For a moment I thought he was going to use force to keep me. But I said, 'Tim, please, let me go,' and without a word he moved away from the door, and said, 'O.K., Gretel,' as he always said. Then I could have cried out loud. For the first time I wanted to stay, and make him see how awful we were, starting on one of the Sacraments with just a man blessing us in his bedroom slippers, and with the picture of a fat child for an altar. To me that could never be marriage, even if I hadn't been thrown into it. Then I remembered Mater and Philip—and I thought I was going foolish—but I left! I just looked back at Tim, and he smiled in the old way—'O.K., Gretel,' he said again. 'I know it's black sails for me!' I ran out wishing I could cry and cry, but I'm not used to that...."

Now David was letting a tear fall on the leg of his trousers. Felice met his eyes. Whatever the girl might feel, her marriage to the boy was irrevocable, for life. It was a country without divorce! Then his eyes brightened. She knew he saw annulment. Mary's voice was getting dreary.

"As I ran out I saw the ham and eggs on a table. The fat had grown cold. When I was outside I ran down the road, but the headlights of a car were coming, so I hid behind a spruce tree. From where I stood

I could see into the window. Tim was there, standing where I had left him. Then he went to the piano and played like a maniac with the loud pedal down. The girl came in, and he said something, and she came back with a tray and three bottles. He opened them and drank all three. Then he paid and rushed out of the house, past the tree, and down to where his car was parked. I never heard such a noise as the way he started, with everything grinding. Then I ran myself—"

Felice had been listening. She was the only one in the room whose outward ears could function during the girl's incredible story. She had heard the clang of the gate and a distant scrunch, increasing to a loud tramp of feet. There was no care in the feet. They came with violation of this family secret. Were late visitors going to crash in? So many casual people thought a country house was an agreeable end to a long loafing evening. This must be a large party. No, everything about this approach was unrestrained, high, shrill and full of herd excitement. The sound rolled to the steps, clattered to the balcony and paused, before a loud assault of rings and knocks. Every sound was full of resentment for locks and keys. It held confusion and urgency, demanding the right of instant entrance.

The maids were in bed.

Mary Immaculate had come to a dead stop, with her ears caught at last.

"Darling," said Felice softly, "go to the door."

The words coiled over to David, making him rise to his feet. Arriving at the noise, he must have opened the door suddenly, the increase in volume was so great. It had a tumbril quality, rattling with the crescendo of a mob. It was difficult to sort words, until they heard one voice beat down others by sheer shrillness of sound.

"...hell to pay, sir. Would Doctor Fitz Henry be here? Someone said they saw his car on the road. Shocking accident half a mile up. Fellow coming back to town; sloven without lights in the middle of the road. The driver went into the ditch to save going through it, but he side-swiped—the horse is dead—"

"Well, my dear fellow, my brother is not a horse doctor, and I'm afraid you must get someone else." David's voice was like a cool douche on excitement. It had its effect in lowering the suppliant voice.

"Sorry, sir. I mean to say, there's two men dying or dead. The driver of the sloven was crushed, and the young fellow is stuck full of glass—"

Young fellow! The awful casualness of David's voice.

"Too bad! Perhaps I can get the doctor if it is urgent. Would it be anyone we know?"

The name was creeping along the hall.

"Well, sir, the man on the sloven is a farmer up the Shore. The young fellow was…" A dozen mouths said it, with a triumph of knowledge.

"Vincent! Name of Vincent! Tim Vincent! Young fellow home from university! Son of a widow! Nephew of…"

As Philip stepped out of the sun-porch, Mary Immaculate leaped to her feet like the spring of a fountain.

"Jesus of Nazareth!" she said like a wild prayer. "You, Philip—"

Hands sawed the air, trying to clutch at something that might hold her. Legs crumpled, and she sprawled in long spent lines over a green chair. David was in the room, with half the invasion at his back.

"Just a moment," he said coolly, closing the door in its face. "Phil, you heard, are you going?"

Philip stood looking from the door shut on the mob to the death-like girl in the chair. She was related intimately to the mob.

"I'll look after this, Philip," said Felice, giving him a shove. "I can cope with a faint. David, go with him."

NINETEEN

"DESPERATE PILOT."

A s David pushed Philip towards a car parked behind the trellis, he thought: This is worse than France. At least that was organized. He had to admire his brother. Temper and unreason seemed to be confined to his personal life. Even before the significant issue of this emergency, self had retreated. As he started his car and saw the crowd, his voice was a whip to impediment.

"Stand back, all of you! Do you want another accident? Open the gate, somebody."

The command made the crowd surge ahead. As the headlights picked it up, David saw men and women flatten themselves against the darkness while Philip roared by. There was no time for comment over Mary Immaculate's startling revelations, and what the outcome would be neither dared conjecture. Safety lay in concentrating on their outward way. It seemed as if none of the joy-riders had gone home. This macabre finish to a summer evening was being witnessed by countless eyes. Better than a fire, people were running helter-skelter to see. Headlights were witless beams, picking up summer colour— the gleam of a girl's hair, or the splash of her painted mouth. At a congested spot some cars had been slanted to illumine the core of excitement. The outcome of the boy and girl's long secret lay in merciless exposure. A car was crumpled in the ditch, bonnet down, with its back wheels reared in tortured surprise. A pony and cart were horribly fused, looking as if the latter had been urged into shaggy haunches.

"Stay here, Dave, and turn if you can. Pass my bag."

A crowd is as sensitive as a single unit. The doctor's arrival stirred every head in his direction. He moved in the fullest limelight.

"Stand back! Stand back! Stand back, I tell you!"

A baffled roar from some official throat was barely heeded. The crowd moved reluctantly. The curtain was up and the doctor was there to speak the pieces. Philip moved forward, taller than most men, with the light accentuating his white face and black hair. David heard his voice quite distinctly, the professional voice falling idly on fever.

"If I'm to work, kindly give me room. Has anyone telephoned for an ambulance?"

"Yes, sir," answered a policeman. "It's on the way. There you are, sir. We've made a circle."

David was able to see. Two figures lay on the road. One had been straightened and lay supine. First aid must have been rendered at once, as the figure had been eased on a sheet, ready for lifting. The sheet was full of dark stains. Near its white edge lay a slighter body, crumpled in a mute heap. First aid seemed to have been supplied there. There was a tourniquet on one wrist, and a thick pad tied above one knee. Philip bent from one to the other, straightening in momentary indecision.

God, thought David sensitively, has he got to decide which one to save? That's a nice problem in his state. If he lives, the boy will have to face a trial for manslaughter. The beer that he drank! The road-house will give evidence, and if the marriage comes out they'll say he was crazed. What publicity! I must get busy on that—find the editor—Phil has made up his mind—the boy! What else could he do?

He saw his brother kneel to the crumpled figure, and turn it over with experienced hands. From the arm turned to the ground came a high jet of blood, with the light giving full value to rich arterial red. Ichor blood, thought David, with a sick feeling in the pit of his stomach. For a moment he lowered his head, and when he looked again he saw the deft adjustment of another tourniquet. The boy must have recognized his doctor. Agitation had gone into limbs making a defiant effort to rise. Philip seemed to be adequate. As he leaned towards the boy David saw the difference in the two heads. The very dark and the very fair! Whatever was said effected a return to mute weakness. Philip stood up, walking determinedly towards his brother. The crowd craned to hear, but he leaned inside the car.

"Turn, for God's sake! We can take the boy in. There's nothing to do with the other case until the ambulance comes. Hopeless, I'm afraid. Crushed at the thigh and terrific shock. The boy is urgent. Severed an artery, and he's lost a lot of blood. Get going, Dave."

David had his own idea of leadership. Leaning out of the window he made a cool announcement. "I'm going to turn. This is the doctor's car, and he's taking one of the cases in. Every man for himself."

Even in the confusion there was a good-humoured laugh. Ready to be distracted, the crowd turned the car almost by hand. Tim was carried to the open door. Stepping inside, Philip received his head and shoulders, propping them sideways, and arranging his legs across the seat. Then he sat on the edge, supporting the body of Mary Immaculate's husband.

"Get going, Dave. The police are making the hospital arrangements. Go as fast as you can."

It was difficult, but at last they were isolated, leaving the mess of cars behind to wait for the removal of the other case. For a while there was no sound until the uneasy silence was broken by a young bitter laugh exploding over sobbing breath.

"God, the Fitz Henrys! What a joke! One of those ironical stories the French write."

The personal equation had been scuppered from Philip. His voice was at its most fever-reducing pitch.

"Take it easy, Vincent. You can choose your doctor as soon as you get to town. I'll pass you right over. Just at present try to conserve your strength."

There was a conceding sigh and a reply drained of rebellion.

"No, patch me up if you can. She says you're swell."

"Very well," said Philip tersely.

More black silence writhing with raw emotions.

"Am I done in, sir?" He was showing the deference of youth to an older man, although his voice held defiance.

"Not if you show sense, Vincent. You're using yourself up."

"It doesn't matter any more," said Tim with another sobbing breath. "God!" he continued restlessly as if tortured with one thought, "that it should be you, after tonight! Her doctor—"

"And, my dear chap," said Philip soothingly, "you're her husband. Isn't that worth living for?"

David's feet nearly jittered on the pedals. The reserves that people can pull up! The angel and devil in man! Out of this mess Philip was being the perfect doctor, soothing, encouraging and pointing the way to a future. "You're her husband, Vincent," he said again, as if he might have forgotten it. "We know about it, and we'll help all we can. Don't worry."

Tim's weak voice was despairing.

"She doesn't think so, sir! Tin-whistle side, that's what it was." He seemed to slump, then gather his forces for a final effort. "Sorry I was a cad, not to speak up when I saw what old witchface meant. Witches' disenchantment—no, no, she can't do that to Gretel and me—"

"No, she can't," said Philip firmly. "Vincent, nothing can undo what I did tonight. Help me to repair it by saving your own body."

It was an appeal to intelligence rather than emotion. The boy went very silent, thinking perhaps over Philip's Gethsemane. With the egotism of youth he needed to be shown other sorrows than his own. David seemed to follow him, even through a resurgence of defiance.

"Damn you, sir," he exploded, "why should I apologize when you thought such things? If you can't see she's as clean as God, why should I tell you?"

"Why, indeed?" said Philip with weary bitterness.

"You never knew her," accused the boy, determined to spend himself for his idol. "Gretel never threw her sex in a fellow's face. She's not a bitchy girl. You took her, and stuck her up like your own damn family. Who are you, anyway?"

Philip's voice was very patient and courteous.

"Just people who make mistakes."

Apparently it was an effective reply. Tim gave a bitter, heartbroken sob. "Sure, mistakes! We don't know what we're doing. Did anyone telephone my mother?"

"Yes, they did. She'll be at the hospital."

The boy was beyond thought of his own state. The gigantic muddle of the evening had shattered his last reserve. He cried hard young tears. "Poor Mother! In her own way she's been swell. Now I'm giving her this. God, I should care, but can only think of the mess I've made for Gretel. I don't care who knows it. She's all I care about because she is my life."

"Vincent," said Philip with slow emphasis, "you're doing everything to kill yourself. Mary will be there for you when you get well. Now can't you trust us and relax?"

The lights of the town were in sight, cool in their shine on dark roads. Windows blinked as if opening eyes under black lids. The town slept, oblivious of violence. Only the trees and grass shivered with the emotions of the night.

The boy was either resting or unconscious. Once, looking back for a brief second, David saw his brother holding him. The fair head had slumped towards the black one. Philip had blood-spatters on his cuffs, and a dried smear on his forehead.

On through the sleeping town towards the dimmed bulk of a building, and up a dark avenue. Tim spoke once more, mumbling from thought jerking him back from coma. "Did I kill anything, sir? Couldn't live and kill—"

"A man injured like yourself, Vincent. The sloven had no lights. You couldn't be to blame. We'll do our utmost, and let you know how he is. Don't worry, there's a good fellow."

Tim had given himself up. Philip had him to work on, regardless of issues. He was as mute and white as death when they carried him in. Watching the shattered retreat, David went back through the years, seeing prone bodies and the ghosts of his own brothers.

David had a long vigil. Telephoning Felice, she reported Mary Immaculate brushing her faint aside and prowling round like a tormented creature. He told all he knew, saying he would ring again when Tim had been stitched and ligatured. Hesitating on telling them to be ready to come to town, he hung up. Why anticipate Tim's black sails? What would be worse? Tim taking his opportunity to die or facing a trial for manslaughter? His culpability was bound to come out. Supposing the girl had to be a witness of his wild flight up the Shore? What notoriety! It was unbelievable, unthinkable, so many consequences from a single night! No, thought David, that was not the start, it was the result of a child's romantic secret. In that raw drive David had divined the fabric of Tim. His voice was charming, and in health he must have a dreamy, unusual face. Above all he was Mary's contemporary, the boon companion of her youth. And now they had been hounded out of their gentle places. Lines tripped across David's mind as he walked gloomily up and down.

> Oh, why in all a world of sweet
> Bird-song and dew and light and heat
> Comes this malignity of death ...

Was the boy predestined? In telling of his life the girl had portrayed him born with music, rendered frustrate. He had spirit, and had spent himself in tearing down Philip's ivory tower. Tin-whistle side? There, he was wounded, being too young to understand a virginal flight from gun-shot marriage.

A long wait brought long thought, until David's vision was compelled to objective survey. He saw the other case brought in, a prostrate mass on a stretcher, with doctors and nurses swarming round. One brief glance at an underprivileged face made David resigned to the man's passing. There was no stamina where stamina would be needed. Conviction for manslaughter was certain, with a boy driving a car under the influence of three bottles of beer. Then he saw people who were undeniably the relations so graphically described by the girl. The mother was identified by her likeness to the boy. She walked down the corridor in passive calm, emotion hidden under her eyelids. By right of her maternity she disappeared to more intimate contact with her son, while the others waited. These must be Uncle and Auntie Minnie.

Uncle was large, dominant, with convex eyes. His stomach was the same shape, neatly buttoned into a summer overcoat. He would have been inspiring as a policeman. David could imagine the stomach shaking with laughter over slapstick comedy, and the eyes dozing through all the things Tim liked to see and hear. Auntie Minnie carried her bag. Evidently the type who never wasted a moment! Even as she waited in the corridor, she sank to a seat, knitting some coloured wool. It was impossible not to notice her stabbing eyes. It was the restless gaze of a woman resenting closed doors, and people entering where she was denied. When her eyes found David, she half rose from her chair. Without conscious discourtesy he became rapt before a picture of some starched nurses. Even when his right flank was exposed he decided it was beyond his capacity to cope with Auntie Minnie tonight. He was relieved beyond words when they passed down the corridor, with the obvious intention of being nearer the scene of operations. Alone for an unconscionable time, he must have dozed in a chair, when he awoke suddenly to see Philip standing above him. The ghastly whiteness of his brother's face foreshadowed the worst.

"Phil, for God's sake, he's not…?"

"No, not yet, but he's going to, and he had a chance. God, some people should not be allowed to have children!—I'd like to start a school for parents, and be the first pupil myself. I thought Mary was showing the usual rebellion to authority when she described that boy's life. Now I've seen for myself…."

Philip sat down, supporting his head in his hands. He seemed to rock with the misery he contained. Independent of emotion went bitter anger, the mortification of a doctor frustrated in a vital conflict.

"Phil, what happened? For God's sake tell me."

His brother looked up. "We got on very well. He was quiet and co-operative and I managed to soothe him down—"

"You were splendid, Phil—"

"After being the complete fool! We'll skip that for the time being. There was enough shock to be worrying, but he's a clean boy with resilience. His nerves are too keyed, but I thought he would get on. Then, before I could stop it, that galumphing uncle burst in, and at the very sound of his voice the boy faded. I asked him to go, and what did he do before he went?"

"Can I guess, Phil? I saw the type. He told the boy the man's case was hopeless—"

"That's just what he did," said Philip without surprise. "The mother tried to stop him.... Then he said not to worry—he would bear the expenses of the trial, get the best lawyer—"

"God, it's not credible!"

"The pulse died,"said Philip savagely. "We've stimulated as much as we dare—but I'm sure he's going out. When he rallied a little his mother asked if he wouldn't like to see Mary. He looked at me, and I promised to get her. I can't go, Dave—"

"I'll go at once," said David, rising to his feet. "I'll telephone first and tell Felice to drive my car. Then I'll meet them half-way."

"Do you think she can take it, Dave?" asked his brother, as anxious for his patient as for the girl.

"Positive," said David reassuringly. "She's tough. Look how she was with Mater."

"Rather different, isn't it?" suggested his brother bitterly.

"Yes, it is," agreed David; "but I think we can leave it to her. She'll know what to say and do. Is the other case hopeless?"

"Quite," said Philip briefly. "Weak lungs, an impossible case for anaesthetic."

To go and see Tim die, Mary Immaculate got her second wind. She achieved an inspired naturalness that gave him a baby's death. No one who saw her enter doubted her capacity. They had always been alone. Now it was the same as if they were in the beech tree, the shade of the privet hedge, or lolling on the river bank. When he saw her, his face became tormented, and weak tears oozed from his eyes.

"Don't want to die, Gretel—sickening to be always sorry for myself."

"Timmy-Tim, you never were," she said, bending over him, and wiping the tears away. "I've come to be with you, to tell you I only ran away because I was frightened, but not of you, Tim.... Tell me, please tell Gretel, that it's not tin-whistle side you remember."

"No," he whispered, "Hansel and Gretel."

"Then it's O.K., Tim," she said, kissing his lips.

"O.K., Gretel."

In front of their eyes she lay down on the bed beside him, easing her arm under his shoulders. Lying on her side, there was ample room on the narrow bed. When he turned into her shoulder it was apparent he was used to her touch.

"I feel queer, Gretel," he sighed. "It's queer, dying—"

She made no attempt to deceive him, as she talked into his hair.

"Timmy-Tim, I was like it once when I was dying in the woods. I know just how you feel. Don't hold yourself back. When it gets floaty go with it and don't be afraid. It won't hurt you. Don't even think. I'm here beside you. Remember the rose-bush and the vine that intertwined! Remember how you made me be the vine, and how we drank the love-potion and our hearts became fettered together. Think of white sails, and setting out in our little ship. And the music, Tim, gorgeous, heavenly music, the swelling kind that makes your scalp shrink on your head. If you leave me, Tim, I'll never hear a note without thinking of you—"

"Must leave, Gretel—so tired—we've had an awful lot of one day."

"Yes, Timmy-Tim, we've had an awful lot of one day, and this morning we were just as we used to be...."

It was too much for Philip. For once in his life he failed to be the doctor. He turned his face to a wall, neglecting his patient. It was impossible to get out of the sound of her voice. Felice could have howled like an anguished dog. The beauty of their isolation, and their selfishness. Tim's mother was in the room and she did not get a glance or a word. Life was crowding Tim, and his last breath was dedicated to the secret that he loved. The mother sat with her head down, silent and motionless. She looked as if she might be as unobtrusive in his death as she had been in his life. Effects were not bothering Mary Immaculate, and at last she had come to a place where she had to give all of herself. The bed seemed to be in a circle which the others could not enter. When he asked her to talk to him until...she began a whispering monologue lasting through infinite minutes. To her, effort seemed negligible, and her whispers were freighted with associations, making bridges of fluency. When she began comforting him about the man he had so shockingly injured and who must surely be dead by now, Felice marvelled at the picture she drew of him, from the few facts contributed by David.

"Timmy-Tim, the poor fellow had weak lungs, and it was only a matter of time before he'd die after a dreadful long illness." She drew up a dread picture of consumption, making it something a man would exchange for the most violent death. Perhaps she had seen many people, hollow-cheeked, sitting in doorways, and spitting blood in a rag.

"It's a dreadful disease, Tim. The Cove was full of it, just wasting and wasting, spitting up blood, and such a cough! Nobody would want to die like that. Now if the man dies he'll go quick and clean. And if he has weak lungs and was alone on the sloven I don't suppose he's married, but, if he is, we'll see. I expect he was very tired, driving his pony and cart to town day after day, and not having enough energy to put a light on his shafts. He'll be at rest. Don't worry about that, Tim. And you won't have to be a mining engineer. I knew, when I saw you playing tonight, you should have had a chance. Your hands were so smooth and firm. Your music was lovely, Tim, and those things will be there, independent of us. Now it won't be any different, I'll carry you round, like I do Mater, and I hope, dear Tim, it won't be so good and grand where you're going, that you'll forget me and our hocus-pocus."

He had gone too far for vocal reply. Only the top of his brow was visible, leaning in ghastly whiteness against her lips. A bare stir of his head made his last repudiation of her fear. Her voice got deeper, like the notes of a tone-poem.

"I was a child, and she was a child! Remember, and the wind that came out of the clouds chilling Annabel Lee. There's nearly always a bit of cold in the wind, Timmy-Tim, but days come when it's all west. We had such fun, Tim, and we didn't seem to mind the storms—"

Who would tell her she could stop talking? Philip was incapable. There was no nurse. Perhaps that was why Philip had stayed himself, all the time, in a subconscious effort to lessen the publicity that must surely surround them. Only four of them attended this death-bed, with David outside the door. Would Felice ask Philip if Tim were dead? He looked like a child asleep, with no sound of breath. The girl would go on until she was released. She was like a voice now in a dream.

"Remember spring by the river bank, Tim; the pear-blossoms, and the purple Rhodora. They're just over now, and the cherry-blossom fell last week. How many times did we see them by the river, and how vulgar we were when we used to spit in the water. Anything is fun, Tim, when two people do it like you and me. I could never have done all those lessons at the Place, or remembered my hair and teeth, if you hadn't come. I would have been in awful trouble...."

Tim's mother rose to her feet and stared at her son. She looked a beaten type of woman, with an acquiescent expression. Now her lips smiled in a twisted, heartbroken way. It was apparent she had no resentment for the two figures on the bed. She moved heavily, putting her hand on the girl's shoulder.

"Say good night to him, my dear."

Mary Immaculate raised herself on one elbow, looking down at Tim. "Is he dead?" she asked wonderingly. "He doesn't look very different. Why is he so pale?" Looking up at the woman, she gave her identification. "You're Tim's mother." She looked back at her son, seeming to sense what she had done. "Forgive us," she whispered; "we've been very selfish to you."

Felice thought the answer the most despairing a mother could make. "My dear, I couldn't comfort him when he was a little boy. I never knew what he wanted. I can only thank you. Some day..."

Her face broke, and she sobbed in a distorting way. Still lying on the bed, the girl looked back at Tim. "There's lots to cry about, Timmy-Tim. Your foolishness and my foolishness, that brought all this." She put her lips against his face for a last whisper. "I'm going now. Your dream, Tim, meant leaving me!"

She got off the bed, and Tim's mother blotted out the sight of his face.

"Come, my dear," said Felice, wiping her nose very noisily, "we'll go back to the cottage. It's nearly dawn, and the air will be fresh."

"Yes, the cottage," she agreed, letting Felice take her arm. It was without intent that she ignored Philip, standing like a statue against the wall. Capacity was gone. The first intimate death is steadying, the second is overwhelming when it is violent and personal with long consequences. Besides, the girl was sloughing off a skin something like a cap and bells she had worn too long. The skin held all the trappings of her make-believe, and the changeling heart she had brought from the Cove. She had been jolted to bed-rock reality, and she was utterly dazed. The tough fibre of her body permitted her to walk firmly. Outside the door David met them. Words died on his lips when he saw her face. His news was received with dumb indifference. The other case had died on the operating table. He made one remark :

"I'll stay with Philip for a while." He kissed the girl, letting her go with his wife. Felice drove through air bleak with dawn. The water was metallic, tarnished with brown spots running from the shore. Sky and sea met in a blurred line. Sea-fog writhed inland, touching the land with a ghostly kiss.

The girl did not speak. When they entered the cottage Felice found evidence of her husband's thought. The maids were up, the fire was in, and hot-water bottles were in the beds. Creature comforts did their best. It was useless to persuade the girl to eat. She sat stunned, with glazed, tearless eyes. Felice undressed her, slipping one of her own nightdresses over her head. It fell midway to the girl's legs. Under the clothes she lay in a long line, staring ahead. Mary Immaculate was not the type to cling or invite the spontaneous caress. One hesitated before proffering the arms of comfort. Felice bit her lips, wondering what to do. Already she had won the girl's confidence when they had waited after her faint. Sitting down on the bed, she decided to attack.

"Mary, I've just thought of something. You and I are going to England for a few months. You can do what you like, find yourself without rules and routine. Can you pick yourself up and do it?"

The girl shivered a little. "Felice," she said, as if she had not heard, "I'm beginning to see. I thought I could do as I liked, I believe I enjoyed the risk of knowing Hannah might get me into trouble at any moment. I never feared Mater. She was so understanding, and I was always ready to tell her everything. Tim and I have never had a shameful thought."

"Of course not, Mary. That was easy to see. My dear, you were ideal to him tonight...."

"No, no," she said, irritated as she had been when Philip said she was adequate with the Mater. "That sounds silly, Felice. Tonight I was Tim. I know him so well, and ever since we were children we could put our arms round each other at any time. I knew how to talk to him. I'll never lose him. It's what I've done to others—I feel like Judas—ever since last September. I've been waiting, like somebody on a see-saw, waiting for something to weight a side."

"You don't hate Philip?" asked Felice tentatively.

"No," she said, shaking her head. "It's just how I would have expected him to act. Before Tim died—Felice—Felice—we had such fun—"

She turned her face into the pillow, shivering hard. Felice bit her lip, hoping the girl would cry. She did not, looking back with a hard, set jaw. "Felice, did you say you would take me away?"

"Yes, my dear. David will stay with Philip, and we'll go and have a lovely trip together. If you'll promise me you won't shut me out of anything? Mary, what you need is complete confidence in someone—"

"I had in Tim."

"But, darling," said Felice earnestly, "it was in a place where you did not have the right to place it. Don't you see that?"

"Yes," she said with chattering teeth, "I've never been a human being. Felice, take me where I can be ordinary, where I'm not always playing up to something. I want to be some thing by myself. I think I'm deceitful. God, God!—I could cry and cry and cry..."

"Why don't you, Mary?"

The girl regarded the black-haired woman with the compassionate smile showing her gums.

"Felice," she said, closing her eyes, "help me not to be a fool any more? I've been like somebody in a story-book, and now Tim is dead."

Suddenly she flung herself into Felice's thin arms, shivering like a person walking in spiritual zero. Holding her, Felice felt a body as fresh as spring. The girl was clearly at the end of her tether.

"Mary," she said, "you're going to take a sedative for me, and go to sleep, will you?"

"Yes," she said.

Obediently she washed down two little pills, with her teeth chattering against the glass. Felice covered her up, sitting down by the bed. Several times the yellow eyes opened and shut, as if to rest on some security. Then they closed, and the long body slacked to the limpness of extreme exhaustion. Felice did not move until she saw

David in the room. A hand warned him away, and they tip-toed to the living-room. Fire still burned, and Felice added a birch-log. David crouched over it, shivering himself. For a long time husband and wife talked in the daylight increasing behind the curtains.

"I'm not surprised now, Felice, when I know it. Often I saw her like a sleek little cat, looking as if she had an extra supply of cream she could put her tongue into at any time. Why was she the perfect child to Mater and Phil? Because she had the perfect escape. They were the fools to think she could exist without youth."

"How is Phil?"

"Asleep, I hope. Actually I bullied him, if you can imagine it. We went back to the Place, and I told Hannah to keep out of sight. At present Phil has forgotten her. We've travelled so far from the starting-point. Then he raved, blasphemed against himself and acted like an hysterical girl, calling himself a murderer, a double-murderer, that he'd been strict with Mary because he was afraid of the diagnosis saying she was abnormal."

"She's not, David, only the product of two ways of living. I think from now on she'll be ordinary. It seems to be her one desire." Telling her husband of her suggestion to take the girl away, she was surprised at his answer.

"I was going to suggest it myself. I'll stay for a few months and try to get Philip to live here and drive to town in the mornings. We've both got a job. But, Felice, will you go and see the boy's mother? She nearly broke my heart."

"I will, Dave, I will. I could have howled when she just sat. Dave," she asked softly.

"What, my dear?"

"What do you think of Mary and Tim?"

David looked into the fire burning a little dead at that hour in the morning. His face had the grey tinge of depletion.

"Did you hear her?" pressed his wife.

"Every word," said her husband. "Does anybody ever know anyone else, Felice? I thought I knew Mary, but I realized she was beyond me when she was talking. Do you know what broke me? When she spoke of spitting in the water. The companionship that can run the whole gamut and be vulgar together. Two stages of life can produce that. Something in childhood when the flesh does not call, and adult attainment when the flesh is beyond. I gather the boy was getting dissatisfied, and attempting to wake her up. That he did not stampede her is all to his credit. Did you notice how true to form she ran? The Pagan side. When Mater died she worried about Holy Communion and prayed at her bed. She did not say a word of orthodoxy tonight. Phil says he died easier than he ever remembers a case, other than a baby. It's better so, Felice. Try to picture a sensitive boy being hounded by lawyers looking for convictions, and Mary, herself, having to give evidence. It may be cowardly, but I'm glad it's like this. Thank God Mater is not here."

"It would never have happened if she had been here, Dave dear."

"No, you're right, and we should never have left them together. Phil only commands himself as a doctor. As a lover he shows all the resentments, makes all the wrong answers, and that shows his inexperience. I really booted him tonight, and then made him take one of his own damn potions and go to bed. For the first time I came down hard on the elder brother side, and bossed the existence out of him. I had it in mind to suggest sending Mary to England at once. Take her, and let her be free as air. She was the independent breed, and Phil turned her into a cherished little darling, chaperoned every minute of the day."

"She says she feels like Judas, about what she's done to others."

"All the better," shrugged David. "It will keep her in sight of Phil. If she marries someone else he'll have to take it. I'm going to insist on Vienna. He can afford it at any moment, but I'll give you a few months in England first. I wish to God he'd go sleeping round with a few other women to make him more earthbound…. He's as young as herself on some counts—"

"I think she's very old," said Felice thoughtfully. "Dave, if she's able to go with it, as she told the boy, she'll save herself many stiff necks looking backwards."

David looked at his wife.

"Yes, Felice. We've never seen Mary. She comes of people who have lived generations in a predatory fight with nature. People who sail schooners to Labrador, and take the hazard of the seasons. She's as tough as a young Eskimo. They can watch the Northern Lights guiding their dead, and wake up and shoot their caribou. Poetry and predacity!"

"Poor Tim," murmured Felice.

"Poor young devil! He had spirit, and he used some of his last breath to tell Philip what he thought of him.... Well, they had enchantment, and that's something, my dear...." David sat on, staring in the fire, quoting gloomily to himself: "Music, moody food, for us that trade in love!" Before his wife could speak he went on, "Do you think she'll wear sackcloth, and walk softly for her Tim?"

"I think she'll be as good as gold, and I'm keeping her here, Dave, where she can talk herself out."

David smiled at his wife, knowing her faith in the liberation of psychic poison.

"Hannah is a problem!"

"But not tonight, dear,"said Felice firmly. "Order flowers for Tim, something from us and something tremendous from Mary. It will please the mother. Auntie Minnie will probably broadcast everything, but we can't help that."

"No, we can't help that. Let's go to bed, and don't worry, Felice, if you wake up and find Mary walking over the hills. It's her way, and she'll come back. Quite definitely do not encourage the university. It's another cloister...."

"I won't," said Felice "I'll give her—people!"

TWENTY

"CHANGE, THE STRONGEST SON OF LIFE."

In the empty silence of the place, she was sorting the accumulation of five years. The trees shut out the sun, but the pale limed oak gave back gleams of sunshine-yellow. Already the room looked neglected. Hannah had not included it in her routine.

The melancholy of her task and the association of objects depressed her mind in the channels of the past. The mater seemed to be there, giving her this and that. She ached for the modulated direction that was gone, and the something shattered from life. The white ship stood where her eyes could see it. Tim was in her heart, but he was not in the garden where she could see his face. Before she left she was going to climb the beech tree and sit in the bowl of green leaves. The tacks would be there where he hung things up, and the shelf where he rested his books. Tim's note was in everything, and now she knew it held a timbre never quite joyous, like one who drooped in the shadow of black sails.

Black sails! Shocked to sudden stillness, she knew her privacy had been invaded even before she smelt mildew. The room had grown stuffy, without wind or air.

"I suppose being the young, you blame the old?"

From a bottom drawer of the kneehole dressing-table, she looked up. Hannah was dreadful to see, with a hag-ridden face and harsh voice. Hands held on to each other, as if to still their own jitters. The pad of the pompadour was out, coarse with sheep's wool, but her voice continued, implacable in judgment:

"Nothing to say, I suppose, for all the years of deceit? Now that the reaping has come you haven't done a thing! All you can do is to sit there with your white face that's nothing but a lie to what you are."

Mary Immaculate swayed to her feet with a brevity of motion. She needed to stand to face Hannah, and look down on something that must be evicted at once.

"Haven't I known about you since the first day you stopped your practice? And I waited, so that my dead mistress wouldn't know the thing she took into her house."

Mary Immaculate looked at the white ship, willing herself to silence. Like Kundry, bound to laughter, Hannah seemed bound to speech.

"What I did, I did for the best, so that my foolish young men should know the truth. 'Twas better for Mr. Philip to know your lightness—"

"Stop!" said the girl like a jet of anger. "Get out of my room. You and I have nothing to say to each other. There are some things that always go apart, like winds. West and east, and north and south. Some mix and blow together, but nobody ever heard of an east-west wind, or a north-south wind."

"Nor I, myself," said the implacable old voice. "And I'm not taken in by your talk. Mr. David is lost to sense! Haven't I heard the two of them talking, since he turned you out? Identification with nature, indeed! So it is, but not nature as they see it."

The girl was trembling, from tooth to toenail. Unaccustomed to violence she did not know how to contain it. She felt pregnant with something she had to eject at the old woman. When she was almost exhausted with struggle, she heard a cool voice in the centre of her head, "Don't mind old witchface, Gretel, don't mind." Serenity rippled down her body from Tim, like a cruciform in her heart. In a light faraway voice she spoke to Hannah:

"Tim died, you know, Hannah, because of your evil thoughts; but boys like Tim don't die. They live on in the people who love them. I'll always be rich with Tim. Just then he told me not to mind you, and

I don't any more. He spoke to me, but you couldn't hear, because you've never put your ear to the ground. It's a long time since you were young, but perhaps you remember Hansel and Gretel, and the old witch with her hocus-pocus? You tried to disenchant Tim and me, but we're not disenchanted. Somewhere, this minute, Tim must be playing the Crust Waltz." She held up her hand with a compelling gesture, "Listen, Hannah, you must be able to hear it!"

The old woman was shaken. As the light voice continued it returned to the puckishness of childhood. Hannah was too closely allied with make-believe to let her be liberated too soon.

"Do you know, Hannah," she whispered, "what happened to the old witch when she had taken the children? She got baked in her own oven—and the children came back! Yes, Hannah, the children came back, and the oven blew wide open, and there was the witch, baked to a great ginger-bread."

A sudden thought turned her voice to bitter ice, cruel in implication.

"Humperdinck must have been a Catholic, Hannah, when he made the oven for the old hag, and the oven in real life is Hell—Hell—"

"Stop!" said Hannah, putting up her hands, as if the girl was making a physical assault. "Don't curse me. I'm old—"

"Yes, but we were young, Hannah," she whispered with sudden dreariness. Shivering had come back, crumpling the sword-blade straightness of her body. With the need for support she dropped on the bed.

"Please go," she asked dismissingly.

In the sight of outward capitulation, the old woman mustered to a last retort.

"It's you who's going," she said scornfully, "and the Place will come back to its own. As for me, I've got a right here as long as I live—"

"By my wish and discretion," said a deadly quiet voice.

Philip stood in the doorway, and the change in him made the girl fix wide eyes on his face. Outwardly composed, he was stark as an etching.

"Philip, you look very ill," she said spontaneously.

"Why shouldn't he look ill?" asked Hannah with harsh accusation. "Who's fault is that?"

"Get out, Hannah, get out! Didn't I tell you, order you, not to disturb Miss Mary's packing?"

"You did, Mr. Philip," was the defiant answer, "but it would be strange if I heeded a child whom I raised from its first breath of life. My orders came from her, and glad I am that she's not here—"

"Stop!" said Philip, like the crack of a whip. "I know now you didn't dare speak of Miss Mary while Mater was alive. You know enough about us to realize she would have seen the truth instantly. You also knew you could poison my mind, knowing how I would act."

His laugh was a bitter bark.

"Yes, Mr. Philip," agreed the old woman, almost complacently. "You could always be depended on to lose your temper. You were a jealous boy—"

"Oh, stop, Hannah!" said the girl, seeing the goaded line of Philip's jaw.

"Get out," he said quietly, advancing until she circled backwards and out the door.

"Yes, I'll go," she said, holding up her hands in front of her face. "My fingers have worked to the bone for you, and now you turn on my grey hairs—"

A vehement bang of the door shut out the rest. Philip was inside with Mary Immaculate, while a dead boy stood between them.

"I'm sorry about Hannah," was all that he said.

She straightened, bracing herself for what was to come. It was not necessary to stand to face Philip. He was afraid of her, tormented by self-blame, looking nailed against the door, in black-and-white.

"It's all right," she said quietly. "She's never been any different, only just then it mattered terribly."

"Yes," he said inadequately. "Mary, why didn't you tell us about Hannah?"

The question sounded unreasonable, in view of her greater silence. She answered as best she could.

"Everything was so wonderful when I came. Wouldn't it have been churlish to complain about a woman you had known all your lives?" She continued more slowly: "You wonder, Philip, how I could have seen Tim so often without your knowledge? I also wonder how you failed to notice Hannah's hate of me?"

His answer made a baffled protest against the past.

"I thought we were guarding you so well. Did Mater know about Hannah?"

She shook her head. "No, we were always friendly in front of her. She was devoted to Mater. You have to admit that. Philip—"

"Yes," he answered unhappily.

"Thank you for what you said to Hannah about Mater understanding—"

"Don't, don't, my dear," he entreated in a wrung voice. "Mary, that boy, that boy…"

In his effort for control he seemed to hit his head against the door. She grabbed her lower lip to stop its trembling. Her eyes felt as heavy as Tim's, but as yet she had not shed a single tear. Her unyouthful control made him fling himself across the room.

"Mary," he asked with the candour of desperation, "what have I done to you? I who wanted to guard you and give you the best. God," he ejaculated, dropping on his knees and wrapping his arms round her waist, "it's torture, you and that boy, and the thought of Mater shaking her dear head at me." His black head moving on her lap, worried the silk of her summer dress. Over him she felt old, with the burden of women's effect on men. She learned that their needs were important, and she did her best to meet them. There was no protest in her body, towards his desperate grip round her waist.

"Philip, you musn't agonize over Tim. We killed him between us. His Uncle for forcing him to mining, Hannah for insulting his decency, I for leaving him when I should have stayed, and he, poor Tim, helped, too, by not speaking up and saying we weren't lovers as Hannah meant."

"That is also my responsibility, Mary. Tim can't be blamed for that—"

"It's also Tim's," she said firmly. "He knew it, himself, didn't he?"

"Yes, but it doesn't help me, Mary. I can't live with the thought of his murder."

"No," she protested wildly. "Tim isn't murdered! That's a sin crying to high Heaven for vengeance. Don't, don't—oh, Philip, it's all mixed up. Even the dark night was in it, and the sloven without a light. David laughs at my acceptance of some tenets of the Church, but if we didn't accept, we'd go crazy wondering. I have to be like that, and when Mater died you talked about pressing on. Remember, 'Console us when we fall, cheer us when we recover'. You must, you must! Felice has been to see Tim's mother, and she's awfully resigned. She goes to his grave and feels she's got him, like she had when he was a baby. It's all queer and muddled, but all you can do for me, Philip, is to let me go with Felice. I must—I don't need to go to Tim's grave to be with him. He's part of me."

"Mary, I could manage to go on and let you go, if I could get back your trust, and feel that you would come to me as a friend. David has been showing me myself in a most inhuman light, but now—"

"Philip," she interrupted, "the first week I was at the Place, Mater said something to me that I've always remembered: 'It's disgraceful to stumble against the same stone twice.' Couldn't we try…"

Her tone was desperate, exhausted. He sat up on the bed beside her, with sudden decision.

"Mary," he said, pulling a letter from his pocket, "your own mother knew about it. Dave has written to her."

She gave a sudden dry sob. "Mom and Tim could dream, when I knew nothing. I'm no good, Philip."

"Hush," he said, soothingly, "read her letter."

Dear Sir,

I know my child has been lying out again without a roof. The only time I didn't know about her was the day she ran off. This time I saw her flying by the sea, while a wave tried to break over her head. It was snowing, and the flakes were black. As they touched her dress she kept trying to brush them off. Then there was people talking and shouting and blood-spots falling on the water. I've dreamt about her since, sir, and she's always washing herself as if she was dirty. I'm anxious, and too sick to come and see for myself. My legs are swelled something awful. Put your finger in them and there's a dent that don't come out …

Josephine's kitchen replaced the luxurious bedroom.

"Philip," she asked irrelevantly, "is Mom going to die? What would legs like that mean?"

"It sounds like oedema, Mary, swollen tissue from other conditions."

"Is it serious?"

"It can be, but your mother will never give up. If I sent for her to come in for treatment, she would refuse."

"I know," said the girl, seeing the multiple tasks of Josephine's lot. The Fitz Henrys had improved it, but daily drudgery still went on.

"There's bound to be a third death," she said fatefully.

Philip opened his mouth and then closed it at once. So strong is habit that he was about to reprove her for superstition. The girl saw it at once, and something of a smile came into her eyes.

"We'll always be ourselves, Philip. We are as God made us."

"And often a great deal worse," said David cheerily from the door. He had entered without their knowledge, seeming restored to joy by the sight of them sitting side by side on a bed. Even if they had been different, David would have seen no awkwardness in the situation. There did not seem to be any emotions he could not cope with.

"Well," he said, "you've read your mother's letter, Mary?" He tilted the girl's chin and examined her face. "Darling, I'm always playing the woman with my eyes just to put you to shame. You look as if a good old-fashioned cry would do you good."

"I cried once, David," she said gravely, "and Tim was frightened to death."

The eyes of the brothers met. The speech was small, but significant. It was the first time since Tim's death that she had mentioned him naturally.

"Your boat goes tomorrow afternoon, Mary. Are you packed? Come and have a drink, Phil, and let her get on with it."

The understanding of David. He had cleared Philip out, leaving her free to go to the mater's bedroom, and out to the garden to say good-bye.

While the ship was sorting visitors and passengers they stayed in their cabin. Philip blocked the door to any who might have entered to wish them God-speed. Felice was sailing without intimation to any of her friends.

In a dark redingote coat over a print dress Mary Immaculate looked very tall. A hat revealed all of her hair, but shaded her eyes. Disposed on the two small beds lay all the creature comforts the mind could enumerate. Overhead and from the alleyway came sounds of feet, and voices keyed to a pitch of farewell. Setting out would have been stupendous without the weight of reason. Sitting on one of the beds, David talked on, maintaining an easy tempo, as if they might be going away for the week-end. Philip leaned against the door in black silence.

"All visitors ashore! All visitors ashore!"

A monotonous voice reiterated the one sentence all down the alleyway. The girl laced her fingers together, drawing in her breath.

"Well, darling," said David, taking her in his arms. "It's just *au revoir*. You do the sights, and when I come I'll introduce you to the fleshpots."

Without a word she put her arms round him, giving him little appreciative pats on his back. Then David turned to his wife, very thoughtfully turning his back on her farewell to Philip. He came forward, very set, letting her make the first move. Mary Immaculate had made the discovery that supreme naturalness came when the mind was terribly occupied with big adventures. She put an arm round his shoulder, raising her face. "It's good-bye for a while, Philip."

Incapable of speech, he crushed her in arms, going frantic with imminent loss. She pressed her face against his, whispering, "Thank you for letting me go." Then he relaxed, holding her lightly. He seemed to forget himself and speak naturally.

"Mary, if you could remember what I asked, that you'll come to me, with anything and everything? Believe me, dear, Mater's little motto…"

She gave him a pat, with something maternal in it.

"Don't worry, Philip. It's the good things I remember. Please, Philip, don't leave Rufus to Hannah. See that he gets his liver."

David and Felice laughed out loud. It was so relieving to think of Rufus.

"I'll ring the butcher myself," David said with a grin. "Come, Phil, let's go."

Laying his hand lightly on his brother's arm, he drew him out. They were left alone with the sounds of a ship. Without a word Felice started to sort the packages on the beds, while the girl leaned her head against the port-hole, seeing the arms of the harbour, parted at the wrists to form an entrance to the sea. She was going to England! She, Mary Keilly, who had become Mary Fitz Henry, and Mary Vincent for about six hours.

"Felice," she asked, without turning round, "am I a widow?"

Over an open suit-case Felice looked startled. She had discovered that the best medium to the girl's confidence was the straightest answer.

"Technically, I suppose so, Mary, but, personally, I don't think you can be a widow without being a wife. Your passport is made out for Mary Fitz Henry, and your identification signature for the bank. You were not thinking of calling yourself Vincent, I hope, dear. David took a great deal of trouble to keep that secret. It was better so."

"Yes, yes, of course, Felice. I was just wondering what I really was. I'd rather know at this end, and start new. Then I'm not a widow! I wish I had been Tim's wife, Felice. Now I can see him so much better, and I know he was gentle when he might have been rough."

"Believe me, dear," said Felice gently, "it would have made your loss a great deal more."

"Yes, I expect so," she said thoughtfully.

"You've been lucky, Mary," said Felice reassuringly. "You've had young love, full of idealism. Don't worry about Phil. Dave will be splendid. He's lazy, but he gets terrific spurts of energy, and just now he's decided to take Phil in hand. That will include the gradual disposal of Hannah. Phil will fall in line, and if I know my husband they'll be very busy. When I'm not there Dave surrounds himself with people, including glamorous girls. Perhaps Phil will fall hard for one, you know, reaction."

"Oh," said Mary Immaculate, appalled.

"Why 'oh', Mary ?" asked Felice idly.

The girl looked quite desolate, drooping in her beautiful lines.

"Then, Felice," she said in utter tragedy, "I won't belong anywhere."

In that cry Felice saw how stability had taken its roots. It was Lady Fitz Henry's daughter speaking. Unprepared to add another drop of bewilderment to the girl's cup, Felice walked over, putting an arm round her waist.

"Mary, it's eyes front just at present, and you must take what comes. Remember, you're free. Go around and see what you really value. Just remember, my dear, the condition I made when I left David. Give me your confidence."

"Yes, you left David for me," said the girl. For a moment her eyes were very yellow and a little cold. Felice remembered that David had said she smiled often with her lips and not her eyes. Now she smiled with warmth flooding her eyes and mouth.

"Felice, I do want to talk to you. You and David—it would be difficult to imagine what it would have been like without you. You've been like Mater since that night. I will be good! Is that all right, Felice?"

The girl looked really anxious, as open as the sea towards which they were sailing. Felice squeezed her shoulder.

"Quite enough. Now we'll unpack and go up on deck."

TWENTY-ONE

"INTERCHANGE OF LETTERS A CHIEF LINK."

Felice to David:

David darling,

The fourth day out and the first clear day. I am not sailing as well as usual, due, I think, to our recent upsets. Mary is comfortable and promises to be a neat traveller. Her emotional state is unobtrusive, but she spends hours watching the sea with Indian stillness. I let her alone and am ready to talk when she comes back. There is the usual inert game of bridge, deck-games and too much time. So far she has participated in nothing, but seems to have attracted the unearned devotion of five tweedy young men. They are in mixed stages of scholarship from English universities, and appear to be taking a round trip to see the raw red side of the world. Very patronising about what they call America. Mary seems to confuse them, as their ideas of Newfoundland comprise pictures of Eskimo women. In St.John's they were surprised that they were not met with komatics and husky-dogs. Disappointing, no doubt, but we managed to produce an iceberg as we left the coast, and they were appeased.

They are personable enough, but no particular value to conversation. They are also extremely piqued by the way Mary treats them, but continue to be there for her to stumble over. Should she drop anything there is mass prostration like a football scrum. Having failed to attract, they weep on my

shoulder at intervals, and I compensate by playing popular melodies. *Soppy music and dry Martinis reduce them to sentimentality, and they confide in me that she is beautiful, but definitely without sex-appeal. That they might lack it themselves, naturally, is a question that would never arise. I think women are her greatest need at the present moment.*

Mater was marvellous, but too rarefied, and she has missed the rough-and-tumble of boys and girls. It's a strange mind, a mixture of profundity and utter childishness. If it's any comfort to Phil, I'd say she had definite roots in the Place, and feels keenly the loss of its background. This terrible shock has had a steadying effect, and I should say she is living below her stature for fear she may do something wrong. What she might have been, if she had continued her dual role, is hard to visualise. She may have failed to realise her own size and ridden roughshod over things, through sheer intrigue of living.

I shall cable from Liverpool and London as you suggest. I know the relatives will be stunned to see me at this time of year, but I am not daunted by the prospect of a summer in town. It has the savour of novelty, and I feel the edge of all that Newfoundland wind. Many times lately I wanted to push down the hills to get a wider view. I expect we are all depleted with our high emotional estate. How I keep thinking of that boy, Dave dear. That mother of his! She was difficult to talk to, with an old-world passivity; but from the shape of their faces I should say Tim and his mother have some foreign blood. However, it's too late to sort them out now. From what Mary tells me she and Tim compared notes on everything. It would be interesting to know how much Tim knew of us.

Give Phil my love and tell him how comfortable we are. Having a suite has been a help, as we can be comfortably alone. He is very generous, and it is a pleasant prospect to be able to take her round in a munificent way.

For yourself, my dear, I can only say I am one winged without you.

Always,

    FELICE

David from Mary Immaculate :

Dear, dear David,

Felice says you might like a letter from me, and to hear how I feel on the sea. Isn't it strange that though I was born on it, I've never really been on it? It fascinates me, and I seem to be in the centre of that poem by Swinburne. He must have loved the sea, when he called it a green-girdled mother. When we go up and down it's so like 'rise with thy rising, with thee subside'. I sometimes think Tim is in it, as he wanted to go down that last day like Les Noyades. It's unreal, all of it, and I wonder if I have to wake up and find Mater at the top of the table, and me on my way to school. Perhaps when we get to Liverpool I'll feel more substantial. I seem to eat a lot, but it doesn't give me much mooring.

Felice is so comfortable to be with, and I don't have to think about how she will feel when I ask her anything. I feel awful for having taken her away from you, because I know, dear David, you must be a lot to leave. It is foolish to try and tell you how I felt the day I left. Philip looked so miserable that I was more than ever convinced of my faults. Yet, dear David, if I cried for the rest of my life I couldn't undo it, could I? and I can't help being interested in the sea, and the fact that I will soon be in England. I find lots of people have had awful things happen to them, and yet they look ordinary outside.

Our bedroom steward went to sea when he was twenty-two, after his wife had died having a baby, and the man who waits on us at table has a stomach ulcer, and he has to look at food he can't eat. I like hearing their stories, as they sound more interesting than a lot of boys in tweed jackets who look like quintuplets. They're foolish! They think nothing goes on in Newfoundland but salmon and caribou. They've asked me to do things in London, but I have refused. They talk about tradespeople, so I feel, dear David, if they knew I was a fisherman's daughter they couldn't bear it. It's better not to take any chances, than have them discover my low birth later. At first, anyway, I'd rather see a lot of things alone.

David dear, does Philip want me to write to him? Please thank him for everything, and the lovely way we're travelling.

Lovingly,
        MARY

Felice to David :

David darling,

Even I am excited at being in town again. Mary is in a thrall and does nothing but look. We are in a hotel at Marble Arch, overlooking the Park, which looks so tailored after the sharp-pointed beauty of Newfoundland. We have been here a day and I am writing before I go to bed. We have communicating-rooms, which suits us both, as I find she has a terrific sense of privacy. We docked at a very grim hour, and I was conscious of the depressing atmosphere. I wanted it to be at its best for her, but it was filthy with that dreadful screech of the gulls. It always seems to be their Christmas dinner at the Hornby Docks. Mary was appalled at the dirty water. However, we did not linger, but got through the customs with the help of the five young men. They appeared again at Lime Street, which always makes the fresh impression of being the world's most dismal station. I wonder whether a Grand Central would suit the English temperament, or would they feel they were embarking from the Halls of Belshazzar. I can't help thinking, in contrast to America we prefer discomfort.

I thought we might remain here for a while, as the view is so open, but I gave her the choice of doing what she liked. We were settled soon after lunch and she went out instantly by herself. When she returned, I found she had walked, walked, mark you, to Hyde Park Corner, through Piccadilly, Haymarket, Trafalgar Square, Northumberland Avenue and the Embankment. I'm thankful to say at that point she took a taxi and came home, with, Dave dear, a tentative request that we stay a week in several hotels so that she can learn London from several points. Our next place is Piccadilly, and then Northumberland Avenue. That's as far as she got in one afternoon, but if we continue the weekly exodus, you will doubtless be hearing from me at Amen Corner. It may be interesting, though I intended hiring a piano for myself. However, it is a small sacrifice as I expect I shall be busy.

Mary gathered in a bus map, a Ward Lock Guide Book which she is studying most diligently. I find she has a vicarious knowledge of London, and it is interesting to be told that Marble Arch was once intended to be the portal of Buckingham Palace, but was too narrow to admit the State Coach. We live and learn! We had dinner and sat and watched the people. She wore her graduation dress, which made me decide instantly to equip her suitably for the evening. It is ridiculous not to put her in long dresses. With her height and figure she could be dressed off the rack, but I am tempted to take her to my woman, and give her a free hand. It might compensate for having dressed me for years, without distinction. If Mary shows a disposition for a few good things, I shall do that. In the meantime she has decided to spend tomorrow in the National Gallery, and for the evening we are going to hear a concert which includes a Brahms and Haydn Symphony. With London wide-open, I thought the choice rather pathetic, but I suppose it is her own idea of loyalty.

This afternoon, while she was out, I rang up a few people. I also long-distanced the family, who wanted me to come down to the country, but I won't do that at present. I am like Mary, in thrall to Town. Kitty is at Regent's Park, and has had Ann's girl up from Devon since April. After her surprise was over, she launched into a tirade against youth in general, and declared herself at her wits' end with Maxine, and was thinking of sending her home. Said she was as wild as a goat, and has a young man with a car that she knows is not paid for, and they go motoring all day Sunday, so far and so wide that she is sure they go round the county twice. Kitty was amusing when I told her I was also in loco to youth, and implored me to bring Mary along at once, as she was sure a good, steady girl would tone Maxine down. I made no promises, as a little detecting might be wise first. I will feel safer thinking of her in the galleries and crypts, rather than night clubs. She is further planning a daily French lesson at a Berlitz school. Withal, my dear, I find her a vivid companion and full of such interest that I feel young again.

Very anxious to hear from you. Mails seem to take so long. Thank you, darling, for the cables and the flowers. Love to Phil and all to yourself.

FELICE

Interval of three weeks.

Mary Immaculate to David :

David,

I am nearly crazy with London. There doesn't seem enough of me to go round. It is the most marvellous place in the whole world, because it seems to have everything. Right out of the heart of it you can go into the parks, and it is another world. The birds by the Round Pond and in St. James' Park make me think of the groves at home, only England is so smooth. How funny it would be if it rained granite boulders, and they made gouges in the grass. English gardens are so mannerly. We are now staying in Northumberland Avenue, and will move soon to another hotel in Kensington, near the Albert Memorial, which seems a lot of memorial for one man. I like moving around and going back to the same places from different points. Then the little churches are something by themselves. I started at those way down in the City, beginning with St. Bartholomew's and St. Sepulchre's. When I go into one and sit long enough I get exactly the same kind of feeling I had in the forests. It's funny to feel suddenly like that when I've just eaten a gorgeous pastry with sleek brown icing and cream that makes a rich squirt.

Then there's a place in Jermyn Street with little flames under silver dishes, and expensive-looking people. There are so many strange-looking people in London, and I can't imagine why some of them look as they do. Women dress like men, and men look like girls, but Felice explains everything I ask. One morning I got up at five and went to Westminster to see the sky-line, and a very nice policeman thought I was out too early and wanted to look after me. When I told him why I came out, he said he'd never noticed the sky-line before, but now that I pointed it out it looked very pretty. Sometimes I feel quite bad form when I am ready to burst with excitement, but I try and look too wilted for words.

Last week Felice took me to a beautiful house in Regent's Park, where I met her niece, Maxine. After a while I liked her awfully, but I didn't think I would at first, because she finds everything lousy, or too devastating, and what isn't like that is completely shattering. I can't find anything lousy, nor am I shattered. After she had asked if I didn't find it too backwatering to come from Newfoundland, she said she must do something about it, as I looked all right on the outside. I've been going places with her ever since. She took me to a cocktail· party in Queensborough Terrace. An awfully nice man saw I wasn't drinking and he taught me how to refuse cocktails gracefully. There are several ways—I can be studying voice—or I can be in training and need my wind. It was great fun, and he was soothing and fatherly, and asked me to lunch. Another man asked me to dine at the Berkeley, but when he told me I had the most beautiful legs in London I refused at once. I know Mater would think it most peculiar if I dined with a man who spoke of my legs. But he said it in such a beautiful voice that I concluded an Englishman's insults sounded like compliments.

Then something delightful happened. I saw a man staring at me, until Maxine brought him up and said he couldn't drink a mouthful unless I'd close my eyes. I might have been shattered myself, except that he was very good-looking in that rather basted way the Navy has. When he asked me to close my eyes I did, because he seemed so much in earnest, and he said at once, 'You were a tall white child on a beach one Sunday afternoon, who got drowned and did not have the manners to open her eyes and thank her rescuer.' And, dear David, it was the Lieutenant-Commander who saved me, only he wasn't a Commander then, and you know him yourself. I was so excited, and when he asked me to go dancing I accepted at once. I've seen him several times as he's on leave and does not have to join his ship for quite a while. He is delightful to me, and says he must take me places if only to compensate for hitting me six years ago.

I've worn my new dresses every evening, and Felice says I must have another. My clothes are exciting! I have a town suit, two lovely prints with hats to match and a dinner and evening dress. I feel rather naked, but the woman said I must not be dressed lamb-fashion, only, dear David, she said jeune fille. It appears I am a sophisticated type, and I could mannequin tall slender models at any time, which is comforting to know, in case I have to work for my living. Maxine likes my clothes, and it takes a lot to satisfy her. Privately, I like going out alone with the Lieutenant-Commander better than with Maxine and her crowd. I think they must be what the Americans call hotcha, but everything is fun, and I am glad to have the opportunity of going out in the evenings. Felice is an angel, and lets me do what I like as long as I tell her. Often she comes with me to see pictures, porcelains and bronzes. I like selected exhibitions best. They are choice and few, and do not confuse me.

There is tons more to say, but not enough time to write it. Thank you for your lovely letters, and the hint to write to Philip on my own. Perhaps you had better not let him read this, as you know, dear David, he might be mad about the man who spoke of my legs.

Your own,
MARY

Mary Immaculate to Philip :

Dear Philip,

I have started many letters to you, but when they got on paper they looked strange and stilted, so I tore them up. Felice says to be myself and not try and write for effect. I expect she means you know my worst, so it's all right to say anything. That should be a help, but it isn't. I can't help thinking that I should not be indulged with this lovely time, and that it would be more suitable if I were praying on cold stones. I have tried to be penitential, and deny myself things, and one day I went into the Brompton Oratory and knelt down in one of the darkest side-chapels, but I found my mind very distracted with the mosaics and decided it was foolish to pretend, so I went out and had *tea and three French pastries. The best I can do is give some pennies to the beggars. I prefer the ones with dogs, though Felice says a lot of them are bogus. I am not very proud of myself for not breaking my heart or making a brine-pit of my tears. It is not that I could ever forget and lose Mater and Tim. Mater is marvellous about telling me what is good and bad, and Tim goes with me. I hope I don't misbehave much, but London is exciting, marvellous and bursting with things to do. I would like to go on and on, and see the world. I have met a lot of Mater's family, and they seem like her, only older and yellower.*

We are wondering when you will arrive, and hope you will not have to wait until November. Felice is busy house-hunting and can get one in Chelsea for six months, beginning October. It is nice, with a roomful of window and grand piano. I think Felice will take it.

I hate to explain myself over here. People seem so sure of what should be. Their opinions are polite, but seem to be set in cast-iron. How awful if I had to explain the skiff to the Lieutenant-Commander. Maxine occasionally drops out a word about me, but, if it suits her, she says I was born on an iceberg when my mother was being driven to the hospital by a reindeer. Nobody listens, but they accept the iceberg. People can be trying, and English people are ignorant about the Colonies.

Philip, thank you for everything, and all the money. I'm afraid I've bought expensive things. I have definitely decided not to go to University. I am sad and glad together, and I send my love.

> MARY

Cable from Philip to Mary Immaculate :

Thank you for letter stop do not bother about the Brompton Oratory stop I want you to be happy stop London in November stop love to Felice and yourself write again. Love.—PHILIP

Cable from Mary Immaculate to Philip

I will, Philip.—MARY

TWENTY-TWO

"...A GREAT STREAM OF PEOPLE THERE WAS
HURRYING TO AND FRO."

I n London five months, she was
awakened one morning by the
plop announcing a gas-fire. English fires were little, she thought,
visualising the gigantic fires at the Place. Hearing the snap of curtains,
she came closer to her surroundings. Would this be another portentous day? Felice had hired three servants and a house in Chelsea, and
the scene was set for Philip and David.

Philip! His name kept making two terse syllables in her mind.
What now? she wondered. Felice was in Liverpool meeting the boat,
and before another day had passed they would be together again. The
Place was resting, waiting for the tread of a new generation, with a
gardener living in the basement to temper its desertion. Hannah was
in a home, muttering through the last lap of her life, and Rufus had
disloyally capitulated to the gardener.

Her nose vibrated, feeling peevish with London air. November
staged a dingy substitute for the high winters she knew, but it was not
daunting. London was in her bones, and she could sop up its murk as
well as its sun. Five months of intensive living had been like a various
finishing-school. The levelling and impersonal education of a great
city had steadied her. Liberty had been an intoxication, but it
had stayed mainly in her feet. She could pillage the faceted heart of

England and chatter about it to Felice. Her record was good, and she had not lost her way in town vagabondage.

Stretching luxuriously, she approved the quilted-chintz look of the room. Other people's things! David and Felice found them satisfying. That they could be foot-loose and content with various mansions would confound Philip. He would be the man of property, liking his forefather's clutter.

She hoped Maxine would go before the family reunion. Definitely she did not want an outsider when Philip and David arrived. To determine the possibilities of Maxine's departure she turned over to study her in the other bed. Her eyes fastened on a closed olive face fumbling towards consciousness with pucker and strain. Maxine looked tormented, on the threshold of a morning ushering in her devils. Maxine had devils, and she housed them in a big way. Particularly of late she had indulged the rough edge of her tongue. Why did she like Maxine? Because of her brittle no-nonsense attitudes or because she could reveal a world Felice did not inhabit ? In her casual way she had been kind. Having been gathered up as an initiate, Mary Immaculate had set out to find her feet in Maxine's world. Often they contended like two strong personalities refusing to concede an inch. Then their differences were punished by Maxine's insolent departure, while Mary Immaculate did something else, sure of Maxine's return. The latter used few words to condemn, but when she did, American, Colonial, Provincial, came forth as biting accusations.

Mary Immaculate could laugh and understand Maxine a little better. After five months she knew any outworn London welcome was better than a return to her Devonshire home. Further, any distraction was acceptable provided the other fellow financed it. In appearance she was an enhanced, elongated edition of Felice, with a spurning walk and a figure that was an asset to slender models. Occasionally she took part-time jobs as a mannequin, and from her Mary Immaculate could consider the possibilities of exploiting her own face and figure. She learned from the same source that love and marriage could be casual, entered into unadvisedly, unsoberly and more as a convenience than as a remedy against sin. Despising the men of that world, she thought Maxine's qualities were more offensive when they were entirely male. By this time she knew homage could be claimed for herself by just sitting and looking. All of Maxine's friends capitulated to good exteriors. They were not people to know about Josephine and Tim.

"Your breakfast, miss," said a maid presenting a tray.

"Shall I bring Miss Maxine's?"

"Certainly," said a voice speaking decisively for itself.

Maxine left her bed at once, as if consciousness impelled her to instant motion. Belting a gown round her waist, she began to prowl up and down the space at the foot of the beds. As she walked she smoked, and when her breakfast came she drank without eating. Picking up a letter from her tray, she crumpled it in her hand with scant regard for its contents. Absorbed, Mary Immaculate studied a letter of her own. Watching her balefully, something about her inspired Maxine's devils. "You'll soon know it by heart," she mocked. "Lieutenant-Commander, I suppose."

"Yes?" murmured the girl. "Malta! He's asked me to marry him again."

Maxine walked as if the information was offensive.

"Of course! Marriage is an old English custom. Naturally the Services would remember it first."

Mary Immaculate stared over the letter. "What's the matter?" she asked mildly. "You drink at night and you're cross in the mornings."

Maxine gestured impatiently. "Any word of the boat?"

"No, but they're sure to be here this evening."

"Aren't you dining?"

"Yes, with Mater's brother, Major—"

"Extraordinary girl! What a waste of an evening. He'll take you to his Club...!"

"What's wrong with that?"

Maxine's shrug indicated the hopelessness of explanation.

"What's Philip like?" she demanded.

"Younger, slighter than David, better eyes and lashes, very active!"

"Is he rich?" asked Maxine, as if an important fact had been admitted.

"No, certainly not. Just well-off."

"It takes money to cross oceans and stay away for six months."

"M'mm, but he's not poor. He's worked hard and saved."

"Going to marry him?"

Mary Immaculate gave her a still look. It did not do to answer Maxine's personal questions. She took everything apart and it was never the same thing again. Without replying she got out of bed, picking up a gown on her way to the bathroom. When she returned, trailing bath-essence, she was surprised to see Maxine reclining on the bed and flicking cigarette-ash recklessly on the carpet. Instinctively the girl thought how the mater would despise such slovenliness! A sidelong glance told her Maxine was not resting. Momentarily still, she seemed merely leashed by will-power. It was not the easiest thing to dress under critical, baleful eyes, but she went on, reassured by her fresh reflection. Something about it seemed to wake Maxine's devils. From utter stillness she exploded into motion and comment.

"God, get out of my sight!" she commanded. "You look so clean. I hate the sight of your face."

"Sorry," mocked Mary Immaculate equably, "I'm so sorry, but if you don't like me you know what to do. I happen to be the hostes… *Maxine?*' she questioned on another note. Her voice trailed away, stifled by something she could not comprehend. Then she saw with the eyes of her hard-won experience. Maxine's face was desperate, hunted, even as she stood superbly in defiance.

"Maxine, tell me," she whispered. "There's something wrong."

She knew Maxine for an ultra girl. Now she became galvanic with drama. Flinging her dressing-gown on the bed, she drew herself up to her spurning height.

"Do I look natural ?" she demanded.

"Yes," faltered the girl.

Maxine ripped off her nightdress with a crackle of electric sparks. "Now look!"

Mary Immaculate stared, seeing nothing but slim olive nudity, very reminding of the bronze girls she had found years ago in David's room. Then a thought hit her, wilting the support of her legs. Instinctively she dropped on the bed, whirling towards the incredible.

"So you see?" said Maxine desperately.

"No, no, I don't see! I just think. You're insane—"

"I'm pregnant," she said in a knife-cutting voice.

Like a projectile the words hit the two terse syllables beating in her mind. Philip! She could see them drop dead from this large assault. Swiftly and selfishly she wanted to rush Maxine out, hide her away with all other irregularity. When she had the courage to look she was swamped by a memory of being outcast from the Place. Tim and herself had once been the children of disgrace. Philip's cruelty, the cruelty of men to women simmered in her mind.

"Put on your gown," she commanded, "and close the door."

Sitting on either bed with knees touching they faced each other with some mutuality. Maxine looked drained, as if her confession had sent her devils in retreat.

"What are you going to do, Maxine ?" she asked, evoking a programme that seemed prepared.

"I have an address! I found that part very simple. The difficulty was to get the money to go with it. It must be in notes, paid before the operation. I hear there are two methods. One, you go in the morning and stay—"

"Don't tell me," commanded Mary Immaculate sternly.

"Very well, if you're so particular," agreed Maxine with a twisted mouth. As if glad of an invitation to stark outline she went on: "There's nothing for you to do but get me sixty pounds for an abortion."

The request was too staggering for comment. Mary Immaculate stuttered until she took a firm grip on protest and speech.

"You're out of your mind," she accused. "I will not!"

For a second the two glared at each other until Mary Immaculate softened. This time the battle was not even. "Couldn't you marry him?" she suggested gently, unprepared for the volley of scorn spat in her face.

"Bah! I might have known you'd say that! What, go crawling hat in hand, asking a man to marry you? I'd take the river first, and that's not a gesture. I'll marry in pride or not at all. Men are worms enough, but if you give them the whip hand—"

"I don't know men like that," protested the girl proudly. Then she went on with hardy resistance. "Doesn't he know?"

"No, and I'm not going to tell him. It would be a waste of time. Besides, I wouldn't marry him. I couldn't!"

"But if you could—"

"Oh, don't be a fool," ordered Maxine. She got up, beginning to walk again, with tormented steps. "There are hundreds of bed-worthy men you could never marry. Of course, if he had money I'd borrow it," she explained casually, "but he hasn't a penny, and you've got lots."

"I have not! If you'd asked me months ago when I first came over—"

"I didn't want it then," interrupted Maxine impatiently.

"But why have you come to me ? You've got lots of friends."

"Friends! Yes, dozens, hundreds, when I've got something to give them," agreed Maxine wildly. "There's only Aunt Felice, and that means—"

"No, no," protested the girl, with her mind on Felice waiting so happily for David.

"With those two men it's dead easy for you."

"You're crazy, Maxine! Even the most generous men don't give sixty pounds to a minor without knowing why."

Maxine clasped her hand until the knuckles showed white. "I must have it, I must have it," she entreated like a desperate litany. "Mary, this agony of mind, it's a torture! I don't feel any different, but I went into a Public Library and read whole chapters on the symptoms of pregnancy. Then I knew it was true. Every second I wait for it to make a visible appearance for everyone to see." She put her hands over her eyes as if to shut out a sight. "God, the way you can feel! The other night some vulgar brute asked that definition about optimism, you know, pregnant flapper rubbing vanishing cream on her tummy. Someone laughed and I wanted to scream. I know, I feel it, some wretched girl did that out of desperation."

"Yes, yes," said Mary Immaculate sensitively.

"Oh," continued Maxine with hard liberation, "you think you know it all, and you can snap your fingers at the old taboos. You can, so confidently when you're on the right side of convention. But once the cut has come it's as separating as the guillotine. Your head and your body part, but you don't die. You feel yourself outside your tradition, and your family looking at you as filth. When I think of them, being so ordinary—"

"Yes, yes, ordinary! It's so wise to be ordinary," agreed Mary Immaculate with a long shiver.

Silently both girls rocked a little, suffering acutely for the burden and responsibility of woman. There was a long silence until Mary Immaculate spoke sharply, ejecting spontaneous thought.

"Maxine," she accused, "what you plan is murder!"

Maxine whirled round like a fury. "There you go again—"

"With my provincial mind, I suppose," agreed the girl sternly. "I know better. It's better to marry and go with nature than go against it."

"Rubbish! It's absurd! Murder for something that's barely started?"

"It's life," said Mary Immaculate inflexibly.

"Oh, shut up!" ordered Maxine rudely and desperately. There was more hard silence broken by the sounds of the house and Maxine's nervous breath. With indrawn eyes Mary Immaculate looked at the carpet, thinking hard.

"Maxine," she asked slowly, "isn't it a terrible thing to ask a qualified doctor to perform an abortion? Isn't the very word insulting?"

Maxine shrugged. She was so frantic for the medical outrage that she could not consider professional ethics.

"Perhaps," she said grudgingly; "but addresses are legion." Staring hopefully at the younger girl, she tried persuasion. "Mary, there's nothing to say when the consequences come—"

"I know, I know," muttered the girl.

"How do you know?" said Maxine sharply.

"Never mind, odd things have happened to me," was all the information she would concede. "I can understand how awful you feel."

"If it's any encouragement to you I'll tell you, when I come out of this there won't be enough bishops in England to bless my marriage-bed."

"Let me think, Maxine, let me think."

She went to the window, flinging it up, admitting the acrid air. Her head went down in her hands, and she tried to think in what freshness

London had to offer. Behind her Maxine coughed spontaneously, but she did not heed. She felt herself being propelled along, assailed with the fatality of a natural lead. Would this bit of irregularity be the final bit of the jigsaw completing her, or would it show her up as the bit that could never fit? Nothing in her was shocked that Maxine was pregnant. From earliest years she had heard strong talk of procreation. Everything in her was shocked that Maxine planned an abortion. To ask Philip to finance it would be an outrage! On every count he would be rocked unspeakably. There was her own youth he held so preciously, the sordidness of the request and the conflict with his professional integrity. Yet what man could visualise the special agony of a woman outside convention? By the very nature of things it was impossible. Philip had insulted *her* girlhood chastity and made her feel like an abomination. Tim was dead! Poignantly, vividly, she relived their pitiless expulsion from the Place. Coldly she entertained a thin streak of cruelty running like steel through her veins. Some new attribute in herself demanded recognition, and she saw it as the capacity to hurt someone deeply important.

"I'll get the money," she said with hard decision.

Maxine gasped, collapsing on the bed. For a moment the younger girl saw her impersonally, wondering if Maxine was capable of tears. She hated tears herself. Maxine did not cry. In a second she had flung up a head, proud as Lucifer even in shame. Surprisingly she turned to the breakfast-tray, beginning to eat like a starving person. The spontaneous natural reaction affected Mary Immaculate strongly.

"What will we do today, Maxine?" she asked gently.

"Will you spend it with me?" asked Maxine almost gratefully.

"Yes, anything you say."

"Thanks, I'll take myself off before they come. I couldn't bear a doctor's eyes. Make it right with Aunt Felice, will you?"

"Yes."

"We'll meet for lunch tomorrow, but today let's go tearing round, will you?"

"All right," agreed Mary Immaculate, returning to the dressing-table. In that way she and Maxine were similar.

They had the same high-powered capacity for storming the event.

It was ten-thirty when the maid opened the door of the Chelsea house.

"Are they here ?" she asked, slipping off her cloak.

"Yes, miss, in the studio-room."

As the maid retreated she leaned against an ornate chest in the hall, wondering why no one rushed out to welcome her. They did not appear to know of her return. It was a padded house with stealthy carpets. From a closed door came voices apparently all talking together. Three inside, one outside! Would she be finally outside after tonight? Above the Italian chest a mirror showed her how she would appear to the men. She was wearing a soft green dress floating like a lace fog, and the fair crests of her hair gave her face a terribly clean look. As she studied herself her hand made a contact with something on the chest, and she saw it was the mater's locked jewel-case. Philip had brought it over! Some day we'll have them reset! Courage dripped out of her in the instinct to accept the easiest way. Philip would be so glad to see her that they could continue light-footed together.

Maxine might take an overdose or plunge into the river! Hard, courageous people did hard, desperate things. It would be the soft, clinging girl who would sob and grovel at people's feet.

"Timmy-Tim," she prayed, "pipe me across the hall!"

As if she had seeped through the door to their consciousness, it was flung open and they faced her in a solid bunch. Felice was in travelling-clothes, with a radiant face under untidy black hair.

"Mary," she expostulated, "what are you doing? I've been waiting to show you off. Come in at once."

"I think I was nervous," she said childishly, seeing the two tall men standing in tableau with greetings snatched from their lips. Unable to advance, their eyes looked like arrested wonder. Inconsequentially she thought they were held!

"You nervous?" mocked David, advancing and propelling Philip along with him. "I'm nervous, Phil is overcome! We feel like country cousins."

"Mary," ejaculated Philip as if he couldn't help it, "I can't bear it if you grow any better-looking."

He made no attempt to touch her, and too familiarly she saw the disturbance of his nostrils. She should have smelt anaesthetic, but it seemed to have been blown away by the winds of the North Atlantic. The feeling of belonging swept over her. These men were her own, making her walk between them holding an arm of each.

"Oh!" she said happily. "Oh!..."

"We're lovely," said David, and they all roared together.

"Oh!" she said again, and not knowing who to kiss first she brought their faces against her own. Following her lead they kissed her cheeks with great naturalness.

"Darling, it took your 'ohs' to make me feel comfortable," said David.

"Come in, come in," commanded Felice. "Dave, Phil, what do you think of her? Have I done well? Do you like her hair? Do you like her dress? I take all the credit. I feel she's my glamour-girl."

The generosity of Felice who could exult in another woman's looks! She acted as the girl's showman until they were reminded of the day Josephine had come to call.

"My, my," grinned David, "Mary Immaculate, ain't you grand now! Let me see your grand pole?"

She surprised a look between the brothers, but just then she could do nothing but bask in appreciation. Philip looked well, restored, with eyes that told her he was more fascinated with her womanhood than he had been with her childhood.

Felice asked for Maxine, carelessly shrugging with happy exasperation when she heard of her sudden departure. An unsatisfactory relative was dismissed by them all. They were so happy to be alone.

Maxine really receded! Mary Immaculate could live the happy hour and forget the bad moment, tripping along. Praise was so sweet, and to them she was so newly adult. She found she could claim the conversation and make the men listen with interest and homage. She drew in her breath, trying to cram the delights of five months into one rippling report. Even as she talked she was conscious of the smooth feeling of equality. The child was ousted by the woman, and if she chose she could use the full battery of privileged womanhood to gain her own ends. As she talked something in her said she would not use the effect of herself on Philip. She would not wangle, she would not be soft and womanly, she would not stir him with her physical self. There was only one way for her now. She must leap in, go under, become submerged or swim on. Under light, happy inconsequential chatter she had the feeling of running by the river, waiting for someone to tell Philip about Tim and herself. This time he would be bombed with an abortion.

Felice and David had gone after a light warning that they were spending the next day together and she must make do with Philip.

It was just as she had imagined. Philip was regarding his surroundings without approval.

"I couldn't live in a furnished house," he said decisively.

"It's a nice house," she said in automatic defence.

Constraint was invading the room. Fellowship had retreated with David's welding effect.

Philip was least influenced, walking from object to object, picking up this and that with no intimacy in his hands. During that general hour she had been impressed by his attitude, though she might have known he would let no grass grow under his feet. His programme loomed ahead, alarming with energy. Immediate interest in London was to be subservient to a side she had not explored—hospitals, clinics, unique operations and men of his own calibre. She had forgotten the volume of his days. No man could be defenceless who had such a definite purpose. He was firmer than she was, capable of being blasted tonight and rising tomorrow to study the eye, ear, nose and throat. Cat-and-mouse attitude with him was gone. Even as she searched for the doting lover she was frantic with her intention of insulting the doctor. David had done a lot for him during their time alone, making him more casual and easy in everything.

Then she knew he had lost all interest in other people's possessions. She got up, feeling she must be on her feet when the scene was on. She remembered her first morning at school when her back had needed the trunk of a tree: Now there was only a wall.

"Well," he said quietly in a balanced tone, easing towards the weighting of issues.

"Well," she said, herself, feeling if he looked long enough she would not need to speak at all. Further examination of her face changed his tone at once: "Mary, I've seen that expression before. What's the matter?"

"Philip?"

"Yes," he said, becoming taut and anxious at once. Her tone did it, she knew, but for weal or woe she was on her way.

"Philip, have I any money left?"

"Yes," he said guardedly.

"Then may I have sixty pounds?" she asked without preamble.

"Sixty pounds," he said slowly like a man who knew the value of money.

"Yes, just sixty pounds," she said, belittling the amount.

"Without explanation?" he asked, probing her for the possibilities of expenditure.

Now she wondered if she would like to have it that way. "Yes, if it's possible," she said slowly. "Philip, do you remember telling me to come to you at any time?"

"So you've come," he pondered indecisively. "Mary, would you tell Dave or Felice why you want the money?"

"No, no, not them," she said in a betraying tone.

"Why not them?" he said at once.

Afraid of directing his thoughts she said nothing, letting him stare on as if he would wrench Maxine from behind her brow. Then, dismissing her outward self, he turned away, seating himself at a desk while his hands automatically played with a long green pen. Every line of him reported a will to avoid domination, and a wish to meet her half-way, but something in the rat-tat of the pen expressed irritation for any further mystery. Then, as if his mind was made up, he extracted a cheque-book from his pocket.

"You can cash this at Waterloo Place," was all that he said.

Beginning to write he stopped dead, questioning her with strained casualness. "I presume this is for lessons or education of some kind. I would not consider advancing it for other purposes. Have I your word?"

"No, you have not," she said definitely.

"Then it must be my money," he said, beginning to rat-tat the pen again.

"No, no," she protested genuinely, "you've spent so much on me."

"That or nothing," he said inexorably, "unless you can present a good reason for the spending of sixty pounds."

A glance over his shoulder made him rise in spite of himself.

"Mary," he said, taking her hand, "come away from the wall and sit down." Drawing her to a lounge, he stood over her, retaining her hand.

"My money or your confidence," he said gently but implacably.

It would be a waste of time to beat herself against that tone. It would be equally futile to accept his money and preserve a mystery. He would torture himself, thinking of every closed book. From the beginning had she not planned to bomb him? she asked herself with ruthless honesty. She sat up, squaring her shoulders.

"Philip," she said, without elaboration, "I want sixty pounds for an abortion."

It was a split-second of doubt, but it was enough. He collapsed on the couch like somebody felled, dragging her with his fall. Literally she bore the full weight of his body across her knees. On the hand that lay on her lap she could feel the ooze of his sweat, damping the lace of her dress. Wildy she knew she might have taken a gun and wounded him with less pain. Her own stupidity appalled her. So sure of her chastity she had not contemplated he might think it was her abortion.

"Philip," she almost screamed, "it's not me! What have I done? It's not me, I tell you! How can you be so blind? It couldn't be me!"

"No, no," he muttered.

She shook him until his body seemed less of a dead weight. Then her hands strained at his shoulders, dragging him up, seeing the change a few seconds can stamp on a face.

"No, no," he said in a dazed regard of her face, "it couldn't be you when you look like that?"

Then she went into extreme quietude, feeling the antagonism that can well up between a man and a woman. Even his obvious shock and confusion did not soften her.

"Philip," she said proudly, "twice I've shocked you terribly, and twice you've insulted my chastity."

She had done what she had not intended to do. Through the medium of herself she had turned the tables on him completely, making him cringe to outraged purity and trust.

"It was only for a second," he muttered in extenuation, dabbing his brow with his handkerchief. They sat in long silence, and she let him think his own thoughts.

"I begin to see," he said slowly, "you've been going round a lot. The money is for—"

"No!" Her hand over his mouth made a quick stifling of names. "Don't guess," she commanded, but he removed her hand, speaking with professional coldness and distance.

"I presume your friend knows the risks, the possibility of infection…"

"Yes, yes, but don't tell me, Philip; I don't want to know any more. It's not our affair."

The possessive pronoun did something to galvanise him into action. With a businesslike air he removed himself to the desk, probing her with hard brown eyes in a grey-white face.

"Mary, didn't you know exactly the effect that request would have on me?"

"Yes, Philip."

"Didn't you know what I might think—"

"No, Philip, I couldn't think of that in connection with myself," she said proudly. "I just thought of it as a thing."

"I'm glad of that." He picked up the pen again, but he did not write. "Didn't you also do this definitely with some thought of punishment for me?"

She met his eyes, feeling a strong will towards self-revelation.

"I think I did, Philip. When it happened I remembered all over again, and I saw there was some suffering beyond a man's understanding. You were coming, and it seemed a lead. Since Tim's death I've sorted a lot of my feelings, and I know his dying was not as wounding as my eviction from the Place. Perhaps I've held the thought of revenge in my heart. I don't know, but it came over me again, the awful agony of being outcast—the feeling of walking down the steps…"

"I see," he said in a tormented voice, "in some ways it was a settling of accounts? Mary, will Vincent always come between us?"

She stared at him with infinite candour. "Philip, Tim lives in me like the memory of the loveliest childhood. If that stands between me and anything, it must stand."

His eyes lowered to the cheque-book and he wrote on it, at once, as if he could say no more.

"There, it's on my account. Say no more about it."

"Thank you very much," she said, feeling it was the end of an infinite day. "I wouldn't be surprised if it's not paid back, Philip."

He shrugged, as if other payments were more considerable. "I'm going to bed," he said briefly; "are you going?"

He had sent her to bed so often! How odd it was to adjust herself to her new status with him. He walked to the door as if she could do just what she liked.

"Good night, Philip," she said faintly.

Before going through he turned, facing her once again. "Mary, I've got something to tell you. Perhaps I should prepare you..."

"No, tell me right out," she said with an unaccountable feeling.

"Your mother is dead," he said as if glad to be spared long words.

"Mom!" she breathed. "Mom dead!"

Stock-still she retreated from London in long backward thought. Literally she could smell the Cove, see the ravine, and Josephine going round and about in perpetual rugged work.

"Poor Mom," she mused out loud. "Oh, Philip, how I hope, how I pray that she won't be disappointed. There must be saints, there must be angels, it wouldn't be fair—oh, there must be..."

She looked at him as if he must produce her mother's requirements of Heaven. He smiled gravely, like a deeply reassured man. "I sent flowers from you, Mary."

"Oh, thank you, Philip. She was such a good woman."

"As good as they're made, my dear, and you're her daughter."

What did he mean? He was distant, wounded, with a darkly shadowed face, but he had stepped back to see that she went upstairs before him.

"Philip," she said like a hostess, "I have an appointment for lunch. Will you have tea with me tomorrow?"

"Mary, you know I never take tea."

"Very well," she said, sweeping out with a Lady Fitz Henry back.

"But," he said to the back of her head, "if you mean, will I be in when you return, I will."

"Four-thirty," she murmured, and, dropping her dignity, she ran quickly upstairs.

Nothing is ever as it is pictured before the event. Mary Immaculate wanted to laugh. It looked as if she had done all the agonising. Maxine met her with the laconic contribution that it was a lousy day. She might be frantic inside her smart coat, but she sat at a table looking at other people as if they were less than the dust. Maxine received the notes, slipping them into her bag as if they were trivial, Woolworthian, of no conequence whatever. But Maxine invited her to lunch with sudden spaciousness, paying for it as if she had enough money for a dozen abortions. Then there was another picture of Maxine coughing in Piccadilly Circus from suddenly acrid air. In that position her slim-fitting coat seemed taut over tension and rack.

"Thanks," she said finally in a congested voice. "Any trouble?"

"Not at all," said Mary Immaculate, shutting her lips on explanations. She wanted to get away before Maxine convinced her abortions were as ordinary as cups of tea. "Let me know if you're all right."

"Thanks, good-bye, Mary."

"Good-bye, Maxine, really, good-bye."

"You mean—"

"Yes, I'm going places," she said decisively. "Good luck."

Maxine turned towards Lower Regent Street and Mary Immaculate sped through Piccadilly. She walked as if rid of an incubus. Something else had threatened her and she had survived. Her steps grew lighter as her spirits rose in the tarnished day. November had a dark-brown taste, but she sailed on, unconscious of pollution. She would walk to Sloane Street, to King's Road, and time herself to be in just after Philip. Why her spirits continued to surge she did not know. Philip was as distant as the pole star, her mother was dead, Maxine was having an abortion, the day was as dirty as a maulkin, and by all accounts she should be an abject girl.

Then she saw a cat trying to cross a London road. Such a feat was as full of hazard as the way to Mount Everest. Mary Immaculate stopped, watching many tentative attempts and scuttling retreats. It seemed as if the cat could never get past the traffic-peril alone. Stripping off her gloves, she advanced to the pavement's edge, holding out a coaxing hand.

"I'll help you over, puss," she said soothingly.

It was a town-cat, huddling under her arm like a mass of suspicion. As she reached an island it dug five fierce claws in her hand. As she reached the other side of the road it writhed away, leaving a spacious scratch on the back of her hand.

It was a very thorough cat, she thought, watching blood-spots ease out from the scratch. It would take a London cat to suspect her, she who had beguiled wood-creatures for twelve years of her life! Instead of being daunted she laughed out loud, until she saw people seeing her as suspiciously as the cat. She retreated to a window to look out at the world. Words rose up to describe it in her mind.

> ...great stream of people
> There was hurrying to and fro,
> Numerous as gnats upon the evening gleam...

A streak of lightning comprehension seemed to illumine the whole of living. Brief as lightning it passed, leaving her with a feeling of the largest flash. She sensed unity, making her see London for the first time with balanced eyes. If she stayed here long enough she would begin to feel pinched. This need be no more, this could be much less, than the Cove. There people stood foursquare to natural peril. Here people cowered under man's unnatural threats. Everyone said some day London would be destroyed from the air. It was a turning away from the natural earth. It was what she meant when she had accused Maxine of murder. Go with it or jar the hum of the earth. Her bit of earth was the Place! Everywhere life was going on with large invitation. Other men could show her other earth.... Instinctively she turned her back on all the men who had offered her any homage. She was intimately connected with Tim, her handful of people and, above all, to Philip! It mattered terribly how she behaved towards them. In that flash of unity she was sure Tim's death was the moment for his rebirth. God, she prayed enthusiastically, be kind, and let him be born on a piano-stool. Tim had bequeathed her a white ship, but she knew she must sail with much ballast.

Her spirits soared higher and higher, and she knew in that moment of revelation she was one of those whose first love would always be life. But her fantasy about it was transmuted. She would walk carefully without the deviation of witless experiment. Her way was cemented. Who had said that?

Tim, when he spoke of the boys who seemed sure of their way. She must know where she stood and how. She was used to a routine and she wanted some of it back.

She could hardly wait for the opening of the Chelsea door. "Is Doctor Fitz Henry back yet, Marion?"

"Yes, miss, ten minutes ago. Mrs. Fitz Henry telephoned to say they would not be home for dinner. Would you and—"

"Yes, yes," she agreed hastily, "we'll be home for dinner, I feel sure. Take my things upstairs, please."

She surrendered her hat and coat, and patting her hair in front of the mirror she saw the terrible scratch on her hand. It made her whirl round and make a headlong entrance into the studio-room. Philip was staring out, seeing a square of grim November garden.

"Philip," she called to his unhappy back.

"Mary," he answered, wheeling round in a startled way.

"Philip," she said, advancing towards him with an out-stretched hand, "do you remember saying I'd be more human to you if you saw me with a pimple? Look, a London cat has scratched me."

"Mary," he said, utterly confused, "I've been worrying…."

He took her hand, seeing the scratch, and it was significant that he did not suggest iodine at once. "It has scratched you," he murmured, "but you look—"

He stopped in a baffled way, and then went on to speak with great simplicity:

"Mary, you confuse me utterly. I've been useless all day, thinking of you mixed up in that sordid affair, and you come back so fresh and unaffected. When I think you're near me you're furthest away. When I feel you've quite gone you sweep back like a happy child."

"I'm not complicated to myself, Philip, only to you."

He shook his head, giving her the fascinated regard she could always command from his eyes. "I'll never know you, Mary, never really know you."

"Philip," she said, like an adult speaking to a younger generation, "I was thinking today we'll never see a fraction of the earth. No matter where we travel there'll be places out of reach. People are like that, but why should we try to know them all? Isn't it enough to be near, give what we can—?"

"Mary!"

His hand went out, fastening on her shoulder, seeking her very bones, and she felt it without any shrinking of her flesh.

"What are you saying, Mary?"

"Philip, do you love me ?"

He gave a short hard laugh. "Love you, Mary? You've been like a long thirst. I've worked and tried to stamp you out, and let Dave have his way with my leisure, but every other girl…Well, what is there to say about things like that? I just love you beyond myself. I get tired and drab, and I see you and hear your voice, and I feel refreshed. It's been like that in some ways since the first day in hospital. I simply can't help it."

"Why should you help it, Philip?" she asked with beautiful directness.

"Mary," he said, gripping her shoulder desperately, "don't say what you don't mean. You know what I'm like, and all the discipline in the world can't change a man completely. I won't have anything from you unless you're sure. For the sake of my work I must ask you not to trifle with me. Once you give way and let me…I couldn't go back," he said restively, "I wouldn't have the strength after that terrible regret…"

"Philip, the past is so dead and still so alive. Now we both know Tim. I'm quite sure. I'll marry you, and go with you anywhere, any day."

He still seemed to doubt her, standing like a man who had repressed himself too long to give way too fast. She had to go the whole way and step into his arms. Over her head he seemed to expel repression from his handsome nose. Then his arms and his hands came to life. But he held her like a man unsure of happiness. She put her arms round him to reassure him, knowing her first job would be to teach him to recognise joy.

"Philip," she said persuasively, "it's so easy for me to be happy, but I'm much happier now."

"Mary, my dear," he said with lips venturing on her flesh as if he had never touched her before. "Mary, I feel so hungry for you."

She lifted her face and felt her mouth swamped but not stifled. He was sweeping on as a lover, and nothing in her held back. She felt adult and not girlish, understanding from deep primal roots the normality of natural appetites. Moreover, she could identify his deep-toned tenderness and his great protection of herself. Before she closed her eyes she saw the unbelievable softening of his face. Then she whirled back to the Cove to tell Josephine she was minding what they said! She whirled to the Place to tell the mater she was doing as Philip said. She stood pat in her own flesh, playing a tune with Tim. She rested in Philip's arms, feeling a man's ecstasy round and about her. She felt her veins rippling with life, and the wingspread of her spirit craving infinite future.

M argaret Duley was born in 1894 in St. John's, Newfoundland, and died in 1968. Her four novels—*The Eyes of the Gull* (1936), *Cold Pastoral* (1939), *Highway to Valour* (1941), and *Novelty on Earth* (1943)—were published internationally and praised by contemporary critics. Her place in Canadian literature was recognized in 1981 with a National Historic Plaque, mounted on the exterior of the Queen Elizabeth II Library of Memorial University.